K

Mary Roberts Rinehart

Contents

CHAPTER I 7
CHAPTER II 20
CHAPTER III 26
CHAPTER IV 35
CHAPTER V 45
CHAPTER VI 52
CHAPTER VII 61
CHAPTER VIII 67
CHAPTER IX 72
CHAPTER X 79
CHAPTER XI 85
CHAPTER XII 91
CHAPTER XIII 101
CHAPTER XIV 114
CHAPTER XV 125
CHAPTER XVI 134
CHAPTER XVII 140
CHAPTER XVIII 152
CHAPTER XIX 160
CHAPTER XX 168
CHAPTER XXI 180
CHAPTER XXII 190
CHAPTER XXIII 200
CHAPTER XXIV 206
CHAPTER XXV 212
CHAPTER XXVI 223
CHAPTER XXVII 236
CHAPTER XXVIII 244
CHAPTER XXIX 255
CHAPTER XXX 262

K

by

Mary Roberts Rinehart

CHAPTER I

The Street stretched away north and south in two lines of ancient houses that seemed to meet in the distance. The man found it infinitely inviting. It had the well-worn look of an old coat, shabby but comfortable. The thought of coming there to live pleased him. Surely here would be peace--long evenings in which to read, quiet nights in which to sleep and forget. It was an impression of home, really, that it gave. The man did not know that, or care particularly. He had been wandering about a long time--not in years, for he was less than thirty. But it seemed a very long time.

At the little house no one had seemed to think about references. He could have given one or two, of a sort. He had gone to considerable trouble to get them; and now, not to have them asked for--

There was a house across and a little way down the Street, with a card in the window that said: "Meals, twenty-five cents." Evidently the midday meal was over; men who looked like clerks and small shopkeepers were hurrying away. The Nottingham curtains were pinned back, and just inside the window a throaty barytone was singing:

"Home is the hunter, home from the hill:
And the sailor, home from sea."

Across the Street, the man smiled grimly--Home!

For perhaps an hour Joe Drummond had been wandering up and down the

Street. His straw hat was set on the back of his head, for the evening was warm; his slender shoulders, squared and resolute at eight, by nine had taken on a disconsolate droop. Under a street lamp he consulted his watch, but even without that he knew what the hour was. Prayer meeting at the corner church was over; boys of his own age were ranging themselves along the curb, waiting for the girl of the moment. When she came, a youth would appear miraculously beside her, and the world-old pairing off would have taken place.

The Street emptied. The boy wiped the warm band of his hat and slapped it on his head again. She was always treating him like this--keeping him hanging about, and then coming out, perfectly calm and certain that he would still be waiting. By George, he'd fool her, for once: he'd go away, and let her worry. She WOULD worry. She hated to hurt anyone. Ah!

Across the Street, under an old ailanthus tree, was the house he watched, a small brick, with shallow wooden steps and--curious architecture of Middle West sixties--a wooden cellar door beside the steps.

In some curious way it preserved an air of distinction among its more pretentious neighbors, much as a very old lady may now and then lend tone to a smart gathering. On either side of it, the taller houses had an appearance of protection rather than of patronage. It was a matter of self-respect, perhaps. No windows on the Street were so spotlessly curtained, no doormat so accurately placed, no "yard" in the rear so tidy with morning-glory vines over the whitewashed fence.

The June moon had risen, sending broken shafts of white light through the ailanthus to the house door. When the girl came at last, she stepped out into a world of soft lights and wavering shadows, fragrant with tree blossoms not yet overpowering, hushed of its daylight sounds of playing children and moving traffic.

The house had been warm. Her brown hair lay moist on her forehead, her thin white dress was turned in at the throat. She stood on the steps, the door closed behind her, and threw out her arms in a swift gesture to the cool air. The moonlight clothed her as with a garment. From across the Street the boy watched her with adoring, humble eyes. All his courage was for those hours when he was not with her.

"Hello, Joe."

"Hello, Sidney."

He crossed over, emerging out of the shadows into her enveloping radiance. His ardent young eyes worshiped her as he stood on the pavement.

"I'm late. I was taking out bastings for mother."

"Oh, that's all right."

Sidney sat down on the doorstep, and the boy dropped at her feet.

"I thought of going to prayer meeting, but mother was tired. Was Christine there?"

"Yes; Palmer Howe took her home."

He was at his ease now. He had discarded his hat, and lay back on his elbows, ostensibly to look at the moon. Actually his brown eyes rested on the face of the girl above him. He was very happy. "He's crazy about Chris. She's good-looking, but she's not my sort."

"Pray, what IS your sort?"

"You."

She laughed softly. "You're a goose, Joe!"

She settled herself more comfortably on the doorstep and drew along breath.

"How tired I am! Oh--I haven't told you. We've taken a roomer!"

"A what?"

"A roomer." She was half apologetic. The Street did not approve of roomers. "It will help with the rent. It's my doing, really. Mother is scandalized."

"A woman?"

"A man."

"What sort of man?"

"How do I know? He is coming tonight. I'll tell you in a week."

Joe was sitting bolt upright now, a little white.

"Is he young?"

"He's a good bit older than you, but that's not saying he's old."

Joe was twenty-one, and sensitive of his youth.

"He'll be crazy about you in two days."

She broke into delighted laughter.

"I'll not fall in love with him--you can be certain of that. He is tall and very solemn. His hair is quite gray over his ears."

Joe cheered.

"What's his name?"

"K. Le Moyne."

"K.?"

"That's what he said."

Interest in the roomer died away. The boy fell into the ecstasy of content that always came with Sidney's presence. His inarticulate young soul was swelling with thoughts that he did not know how to put into words. It was easy enough to plan conversations with Sidney when he was away from her. But, at her feet, with her soft skirts touching him as she moved, her eager face turned to him, he was miserably speechless.

Unexpectedly, Sidney yawned. He was outraged.

"If you're sleepy--"

"Don't be silly. I love having you. I sat up late last night, reading. I wonder what you think of this: one of the characters in the book I was reading says that every man who--who cares for a woman leaves his mark on her! I suppose she tries to become what he thinks she is, for the time anyhow, and is never just her old self again."

She said "cares for" instead of "loves." It is one of the traditions of youth to avoid the direct issue in life's greatest game. Perhaps "love" is left to the fervent vocabulary of the lover. Certainly, as if treading on dangerous ground, Sidney avoided it.

"Every man! How many men are supposed to care for a woman, anyhow?"

"Well, there's the boy who--likes her when they're both young."

A bit of innocent mischief this, but Joe straightened.

"Then they both outgrow that foolishness. After that there are usually two rivals, and she marries one of them--that's three. And--"

"Why do they always outgrow that foolishness?" His voice was unsteady.

"Oh, I don't know. One's ideas change. Anyhow, I'm only telling you what the book said."

"It's a silly book."

"I don't believe it's true," she confessed. "When I got started I just read on. I was curious."

More eager than curious, had she only known. She was fairly vibrant with the zest of living. Sitting on the steps of the little brick house, her busy mind was carrying her on to where, beyond the Street, with its dingy lamps and blossoming ailanthus, lay the world that was some day to lie to her hand. Not ambition called her, but life.

The boy was different. Where her future lay visualized before her, heroic deeds, great ambitions, wide charity, he planned years with her, selfish, contented years. As different as smug, satisfied summer from visionary, palpitating spring, he was for her--but she was for all the world.

By shifting his position his lips came close to her bare young arm. It tempted him.

"Don't read that nonsense," he said, his eyes on the arm. "And--I'll never outgrow my foolishness about you, Sidney."

Then, because he could not help it, he bent over and kissed her arm.

She was just eighteen, and Joe's devotion was very pleasant. She thrilled to the touch of his lips on her flesh; but she drew her arm away.

"Please--I don't like that sort of thing."

"Why not?" His voice was husky.

"It isn't right. Besides, the neighbors are always looking out the windows."

The drop from her high standard of right and wrong to the neighbors' curiosity appealed suddenly to her sense of humor. She threw back her head and laughed. He joined her, after an uncomfortable moment. But he was very much in earnest. He sat, bent forward, turning his new straw hat in his hands.

"I guess you know how I feel. Some of the fellows have crushes on girls and get over them. I'm not like that. Since the first day I saw you I've never looked at another girl. Books can say what they like: there are people like that, and I'm one of them."

There was a touch of dogged pathos in his voice. He was that sort, and Sidney knew it. Fidelity and tenderness--those would be hers if she married him. He would always be there when she wanted him, looking at her with loving eyes, a trifle wistful sometimes because of his lack of those very qualities he so admired in her--her wit, her resourcefulness, her humor. But he would be there, not strong, perhaps, but always loyal.

"I thought, perhaps," said Joe, growing red and white, and talking to the hat, "that some day, when we're older, you--you might be willing to marry me, Sid. I'd be awfully good to you."

It hurt her to say no. Indeed, she could not bring herself to say it. In all her short life she had never willfully inflicted a wound. And because she was young, and did not realize that there is a short cruelty, like the surgeon's, that is mercy in the end, she temporized.

"There is such a lot of time before we need think of such things! Can't we just go on the way we are?"

"I'm not very happy the way we are."

"Why, Joe!"

"Well, I'm not"--doggedly. "You're pretty and attractive. When I see a fellow staring at you, and I'd like to smash his face for him, I haven't the right."

"And a precious good thing for you that you haven't!" cried Sidney, rather shocked.

There was silence for a moment between them. Sidney, to tell the truth, was obsessed by a vision of Joe, young and hot-eyed, being haled to the police station by virtue of his betrothal responsibilities. The boy was vacillating between relief at having spoken and a heaviness of spirit that came from Sidney's lack of enthusiastic response.

"Well, what do you think about it?"

"If you are asking me to give you permission to waylay and assault every man who dares to look at me--"

"I guess this is all a joke to you."

She leaned over and put a tender hand on his arm.

"I don't want to hurt you; but, Joe, I don't want to be engaged yet. I don't want to think about marrying. There's such a lot to do in the world first. There's such a lot to see and be."

"Where?" he demanded bitterly. "Here on this Street? Do you want more time to pull bastings for your mother? Or to slave for your Aunt Harriet? Or to run up and down stairs, carrying towels to roomers? Marry me and let me take care of you."

Once again her dangerous sense of humor threatened her. He looked so boyish, sitting there with the moonlight on his bright hair, so inadequate to carry out his magnificent offer. Two or three of the star blossoms from the tree had fallen all his head. She lifted them carefully away.

"Let me take care of myself for a while. I've never lived my own life. You know what I mean. I'm not unhappy; but I want to do something. And some day I shall,--not anything big; I know. I can't do that,--but something useful. Then, after years and years, if you still want me, I'll come back to you."

"How soon?"

"How can I know that now? But it will be a long time."

He drew a long breath and got up. All the joy had gone out of the summer night for him, poor lad. He glanced down the Street, where Palmer Howe had gone home happily with Sidney's friend Christine. Palmer would always know how he stood with Christine. She would never talk about doing things, or being things. Either she would marry Palmer or she would not. But Sidney was not like that. A fellow did not even caress her easily. When he had only kissed her arm--He trembled a little at the memory.

"I shall always want you," he said. "Only--you will never come back."

It had not occurred to either of them that this coming back, so tragically considered, was dependent on an entirely problematical going away. Nothing, that early summer night, seemed more unlikely than that Sidney would ever be free to live her own life. The Street, stretching away to the north and to the south in two lines of houses that seemed to meet in the distance, hemmed her in. She had been born in the little brick house, and, as she was of it, so it was of her. Her hands had smoothed and painted the pine floors; her hands had put up the twine on which the morning-glories in the yard covered the fences; had, indeed, with what agonies of slacking lime and adding blueing, whitewashed the fence itself!

"She's capable," Aunt Harriet had grumblingly admitted, watching from her sewing-machine Sidney's strong young arms at this humble spring task.

"She's wonderful!" her mother had said, as she bent over her hand work. She was not strong enough to run the sewing-machine.

So Joe Drummond stood on the pavement and saw his dream of taking Sidney in his arms fade into an indefinite futurity.

"I'm not going to give you up," he said doggedly. "When you come back, I'll be waiting."

The shock being over, and things only postponed, he dramatized his grief a trifle, thrust his hands savagely into his pockets, and scowled down the Street. In the line of his vision, his quick eye caught a tiny moving shadow, lost it, found it again.

"Great Scott! There goes Reginald!" he cried, and ran after the shadow. "Watch for the McKees' cat!"

Sidney was running by that time; they were gaining. Their quarry, a four-inch chipmunk, hesitated, gave a protesting squeak, and was caught in Sidney's hand.

"You wretch!" she cried. "You miserable little beast--with cats everywhere, and not a nut for miles!"

"That reminds me,"--Joe put a hand into his pocket,--"I brought some chestnuts for him, and forgot them. Here."

Reginald's escape had rather knocked the tragedy out of the evening. True, Sidney would not marry him for years, but she had practically promised to sometime. And when one is twenty-one, and it is a summer night, and life stretches eternities ahead, what are a few years more or less?

Sidney was holding the tiny squirrel in warm, protecting hands. She smiled up at the boy.

"Good-night, Joe."

"Good-night. I say, Sidney, it's more than half an engagement. Won't you kiss me good-night?"

She hesitated, flushed and palpitating. Kisses were rare in the staid little household to which she belonged.

"I--I think not."

"Please! I'm not very happy, and it will be something to remember."

Perhaps, after all, Sidney's first kiss would have gone without her heart,--which was a thing she had determined would never happen,--gone out of sheer pity. But a tall figure loomed out of the shadows and approached with quick strides.

"The roomer!" cried Sidney, and backed away.

"Damn the roomer!"

Poor Joe, with the summer evening quite spoiled, with no caress to remember, and with a potential rival who possessed both the years and the inches he lacked, coming up the Street!

The roomer advanced steadily. When he reached the doorstep, Sidney was demurely seated and quite alone. The roomer, who had walked fast, stopped and took off his hat. He looked very warm. He carried a suitcase, which was as it should be. The men of the Street always carried their own luggage, except the younger Wilson across the way. His tastes were known to be luxurious.

"Hot, isn't it?" Sidney inquired, after a formal greeting. She indicated the place on the step just vacated by Joe. "You'd better cool off out here. The house is like an oven. I think I should have warned you of that before you took the room. These little houses with low roofs are fearfully hot."

The new roomer hesitated. The steps were very low, and he was tall. Besides, he did not care to establish any relations with the people in the house. Long evenings in which to read, quiet nights in which to sleep and forget--these were the things he had come for.

But Sidney had moved over and was smiling up at him. He folded up awkwardly on the low step. He seemed much too big for the house. Sidney had a panicky thought of the little room upstairs.

"I don't mind heat. I--I suppose I don't think about it," said the roomer, rather surprised at himself.

Reginald, having finished his chestnut, squeaked for another. The roomer started.

"Just Reginald--my ground-squirrel." Sidney was skinning a nut with her strong white teeth. "That's another thing I should have told you. I'm afraid you'll be sorry you took the room."

The roomer smiled in the shadow.

"I'm beginning to think that YOU are sorry."

She was all anxiety to reassure him:--

"It's because of Reginald. He lives under my--under your bureau. He's really not troublesome; but he's building a nest under the bureau, and if you don't know about him, it's rather unsettling to see a paper pattern from the sewing-room, or a piece of cloth, moving across the floor."

Mr. Le Moyne thought it might be very interesting. "Although, if there's nest-building going on, isn't it--er--possible that Reginald is a lady ground-squirrel?"

Sidney was rather distressed, and, seeing this, he hastened to add that, for all he knew, all ground-squirrels built nests, regardless of sex. As a matter of fact, it developed that he knew nothing whatever of ground-squirrels. Sidney was relieved. She chatted gayly of the tiny creature--of his rescue in the woods from a crowd of little boys, of his restoration to health and spirits, and of her expectation, when he was quite strong, of taking him to the woods and freeing him.

Le Moyne, listening attentively, began to be interested. His quick mind had grasped the fact that it was the girl's bedroom he had taken. Other things he had gathered that afternoon from the humming sewing-machine, from Sidney's businesslike way of renting the little room, from the glimpse of a woman in a sunny window, bent over a needle. Genteel poverty was what it meant, and more--the constant drain of disheartened, middle-aged women on the youth and courage of the girl beside him.

K. Le Moyne, who was living his own tragedy those days, what with poverty and other things, sat on the doorstep while Sidney talked, and swore a quiet oath to be no further weight on the girl's buoyant spirit. And, since determining on a virtue is halfway to gaining it, his voice lost its perfunctory note. He had no intention of letting the Street encroach on him. He had built up a wall between himself and the rest of the world, and he would not scale it. But he held no grudge against it. Let others get what they could out of living.

Sidney, suddenly practical, broke in on his thoughts:--

"Where are you going to get your meals?"

"I hadn't thought about it. I can stop in somewhere on my way downtown. I work in the gas office--I don't believe I told you. It's rather haphazard--not the gas office, but the eating. However, it's convenient."

"It's very bad for you," said Sidney, with decision. "It leads to slovenly habits, such as going without when you're in a hurry, and that sort of thing. The only thing is to have some one expecting you at a certain time."

"It sounds like marriage." He was lazily amused.

"It sounds like Mrs. McKee's boarding-house at the corner. Twenty-one meals for five dollars, and a ticket to punch. Tillie, the dining-room girl, punches for every meal you get. If you miss any meals, your ticket is good until it is punched. But Mrs. McKee doesn't like it if you miss."

"Mrs. McKee for me," said Le Moyne. "I daresay, if I know that-- er--Tillie is waiting with the punch, I'll be fairly regular to my meals."

It was growing late. The Street, which mistrusted night air, even on a hot summer evening, was closing its windows. Reginald, having eaten his fill, had cuddled in the warm hollow of Sidney's lap, and slept. By shifting his position, the man was able to see the girl's face. Very lovely it was, he thought. Very pure, almost radiant--and young. From the middle age of his almost thirty years, she was a child. There had been a boy in the shadows when he came up the Street. Of course there would be a boy--a nice, clear-eyed chap--

Sidney was looking at the moon. With that dreamer's part of her that she had inherited from her dead and gone father, she was quietly worshiping the night. But her busy brain was working, too,--the practical brain that she had got from her mother's side.

"What about your washing?" she inquired unexpectedly.

K. Le Moyne, who had built a wall between himself and the world, had already married her to the youth of the shadows, and was feeling an odd sense of loss.

"Washing?"

"I suppose you've been sending things to the laundry, and--what do you do about your stockings?"

"Buy cheap ones and throw 'em away when they're worn out." There seemed to be no reserve with this surprising young person.

"And buttons?"

"Use safety-pins. When they're closed one can button over them as well as--"

"I think," said Sidney, "that it is quite time some one took a little care of you. If you will give Katie, our maid, twenty-five cents a week, she'll do your washing and not tear your things to ribbons. And I'll mend them."

Sheer stupefaction was K. Le Moyne's. After a moment:--

"You're really rather wonderful, Miss Page. Here am I, lodged, fed, washed, ironed, and mended for seven dollars and seventy-five cents a week!"

"I hope," said Sidney severely, "that you'll put what you save in the bank."

He was still somewhat dazed when he went up the narrow staircase to his swept and garnished room. Never, in all of a life that had been active, --until recently,--had he been so conscious of friendliness and kindly interest. He expanded under it. Some of the tired lines left his face. Under the gas chandelier, he straightened and threw out his arms. Then he reached down into his coat pocket and drew out a wide-awake and suspicious Reginald.

"Good-night, Reggie!" he said. "Good-night, old top!" He hardly recognized his own voice. It was quite cheerful, although the little room was hot, and although, when he stood, he had a perilous feeling that the ceiling was close above. He deposited Reginald carefully on the floor in front of the bureau, and the squirrel, after eyeing him, retreated to its nest.

It was late when K. Le Moyne retired to bed. Wrapped in a paper and securely tied for the morning's disposal, was considerable masculine underclothing, ragged and buttonless. Not for worlds would he have had Sidney discover his threadbare inner condition. "New underwear for yours tomorrow, K. Le Moyne," he said to himself, as he unknotted his cravat. "New underwear, and something besides K. for a first name."

He pondered over that for a time, taking off his shoes slowly and thinking hard. "Kenneth, King, Kerr--" None of them appealed to him. And, after all, what did it matter? The old heaviness came over him.

He dropped a shoe, and Reginald, who had gained enough courage to emerge and sit upright on the fender, fell over backward.

Sidney did not sleep much that night. She lay awake, gazing into the scented darkness, her arms under her head. Love had come into her life at last. A man--only Joe, of course, but it was not the boy himself, but what he stood for, that thrilled her had asked her to be his wife.

In her little back room, with the sweetness of the tree blossoms stealing through the open window, Sidney faced the great mystery of life and love, and flung out warm young arms. Joe would be thinking of her now, as she thought of him. Or would he have gone to sleep, secure in her half promise? Did he really love her?

The desire to be loved! There was coming to Sidney a time when love would mean, not receiving, but giving--the divine fire instead of the pale flame of youth. At last she slept.

A night breeze came through the windows and spread coolness through the little house. The ailanthus tree waved in the moonlight and sent sprawling shadows over the wall of K. Le Moyne's bedroom. In the yard the leaves of the morning-glory vines quivered as if under the touch of a friendly hand.

K

K. Le Moyne slept diagonally in his bed, being very long. In sleep the lines were smoothed out of his face. He looked like a tired, overgrown boy. And while he slept the ground-squirrel ravaged the pockets of his shabby coat.

CHAPTER II

SIDNEY could not remember when her Aunt Harriet had not sat at the table. It was one of her earliest disillusionments to learn that Aunt Harriet lived with them, not because she wished to, but because Sidney's father had borrowed her small patrimony and she was "boarding it out." Eighteen years she had "boarded it out." Sidney had been born and grown to girlhood; the dreamer father had gone to his grave, with valuable patents lost for lack of money to renew them--gone with his faith in himself destroyed, but with his faith in the world undiminished: for he left his wife and daughter without a dollar of life insurance.

Harriet Kennedy had voiced her own view of the matter, the after the funeral, to one of the neighbors:--

"He left no insurance. Why should he bother? He left me."

To the little widow, her sister, she had been no less bitter, and more explicit.

"It looks to me, Anna," she said, "as if by borrowing everything I had George had bought me, body and soul, for the rest of my natural life. I'll stay now until Sidney is able to take hold. Then I'm going to live my own life. It will be a little late, but the Kennedys live a long time."

The day of Harriet's leaving had seemed far away to Anna Page. Sidney was still her baby, a pretty, rather leggy girl, in her first year at the High School, prone to saunter home with three or four knickerbockered boys in her train, reading "The Duchess" stealthily, and begging for longer dresses. She had given up her dolls, but she still made clothes for them out of scraps from Harriet's sewing-room. In the parlance of the Street, Harriet "sewed"--and sewed well.

She had taken Anna into business with her, but the burden of the partnership had always been on Harriet. To give her credit, she had not complained. She was past forty by that time, and her youth had slipped by in that back room with its dingy wallpaper covered with paper patterns.

On the day after the arrival of the roomer, Harriet Kennedy came down to breakfast a little late. Katie, the general housework girl, had tied a small white apron over her generous gingham one, and was serving breakfast. From the kitchen came the dump of an iron, and cheerful singing. Sidney was ironing napkins. Mrs. Page, who had taken advantage of Harriet's tardiness to read the obituary column in the morning paper, dropped it.

But Harriet did not sit down. It was her custom to jerk her chair out and drop into it, as if she grudged every hour spent on food. Sidney, not hearing the jerk, paused with her iron in air.

"Sidney."

"Yes, Aunt Harriet."

"Will you come in, please?"

Katie took the iron from her.

"You go. She's all dressed up, and she doesn't want any coffee."

So Sidney went in. It was to her that Harriet made her speech:--

"Sidney, when your father died, I promised to look after both you and your mother until you were able to take care of yourself. That was five years ago. Of course, even before that I had helped to support you."

"If you would only have your coffee, Harriet!"

Mrs. Page sat with her hand on the handle of the old silver-plated coffee-pot. Harriet ignored her.

"You are a young woman now. You have health and energy, and you have youth, which I haven't. I'm past forty. In the next twenty years, at the outside, I've got not only to support myself, but to save something to keep me after that, if I live. I'll probably live to be ninety. I don't want to live forever, but I've always played in hard luck."

Sidney returned her gaze steadily.

"I see. Well, Aunt Harriet, you're quite right. You've been a saint to us, but if you want to go away--"

"Harriet!" wailed Mrs. Page, "you're not thinking--"

"Please, mother."

Harriet's eyes softened as she looked at the girl

"We can manage," said Sidney quietly. "We'll miss you, but it's time we learned to depend on ourselves."

After that, in a torrent, came Harriet's declaration of independence. And, mixed in with its pathetic jumble of recriminations, hostility to her sister's dead husband, and resentment for her lost years, came poor Harriet's hopes and ambitions, the tragic plea of a woman who must substitute for the optimism and energy of youth the grim determination of middle age.

"I can do good work," she finished. "I'm full of ideas, if I could get a chance to work them out. But there's no chance here. There isn't a woman on the Street who knows real clothes when she sees them. They don't even know how to wear their corsets. They send me bundles of hideous stuff, with needles and shields and imitation silk for lining, and when I turn out something worth while out of the mess they think the dress is queer!"

Mrs. Page could not get back of Harriet's revolt to its cause. To her, Harriet was not an artist pleading for her art; she was a sister and a bread-winner deserting her trust.

"I'm sure," she said stiffly, "we paid you back every cent we borrowed. If you stayed here after George died, it was because you offered to."

Her chin worked. She fumbled for the handkerchief at her belt. But Sidney went around the table and flung a young arm over her aunt's shoulders.

"Why didn't you say all that a year ago? We've been selfish, but we're not as bad as you think. And if any one in this world is entitled to success you are. Of course we'll manage."

Harriet's iron repression almost gave way. She covered her emotion with details:--

"Mrs. Lorenz is going to let me make Christine some things, and if they're all right I may make her trousseau."

"Trousseau--for Christine!"

"She's not engaged, but her mother says it's only a matter of a short time. I'm going to take two rooms in the business part of town, and put a couch in the back-room to sleep on."

Sidney's mind flew to Christine and her bright future, to a trousseau bought with the Lorenz money, to Christine settled down, a married woman, with Palmer Howe. She came back with an effort. Harriet had two triangular red spots in her sallow cheeks.

"I can get a few good models--that's the only way to start. And if you care to do hand work for me, Anna, I'll send it to you, and pay you the regular rates. There isn't the call for it there used to be, but just a touch gives dash."

All of Mrs. Page's grievances had worked their way to the surface. Sidney and Harriet had made her world, such as it was, and her world was in revolt. She flung out her hands.

"I suppose I must do something. With you leaving, and Sidney renting her room and sleeping on a folding-bed in the sewing-room, everything seems upside down. I never thought I should live to see strange men running in and out of this house and carrying latch-keys."

This in reference to Le Moyne, whose tall figure had made a hurried exit some time before.

Nothing could have symbolized Harriet's revolt more thoroughly than her going upstairs after a hurried breakfast, and putting on her hat and coat. She had heard of rooms, she said, and there was nothing urgent in the work-room. Her eyes were brighter already as she went out. Sidney, kissing her in the hall and wishing her luck, realized suddenly what a burden she and her mother must have been for the last few years. She threw her head up proudly. They would never be a burden again--never, as long as she had strength and health!

By evening Mrs. Page had worked herself into a state bordering on hysteria. Harriet was out most of the day. She came in at three o'clock, and Katie gave her a cup of tea. At the news of her sister's condition, she merely shrugged her shoulders.

"She'll not die, Katie," she said calmly. "But see that Miss Sidney eats something, and if she is worried tell her I said to get Dr. Ed."

Very significant of Harriet's altered outlook was this casual summoning of the Street's family doctor. She was already dealing in larger figures. A sort of recklessness had come over her since the morning. Already she was learning that peace of mind is essential to successful endeavor. Somewhere Harriet had read a quotation from a Persian poet; she could not remember it, but its sense had stayed with her: "What though we spill a few grains of corn, or drops of oil from the cruse? These be the price of peace."

So Harriet, having spilled oil from her cruse in the shape of Dr. Ed, departed blithely. The recklessness of pure adventure was in her blood. She had taken rooms at a rental that she determinedly put out of her mind, and she was on her way to buy furniture. No pirate, fitting out a ship for the highways of the sea, ever experienced more guilty and delightful excitement.

The afternoon dragged away. Dr. Ed was out "on a case" and might not be in until evening. Sidney sat in the darkened room and waved a fan over her mother's rigid form.

At half after five, Johnny Rosenfeld from the alley, who worked for a florist after school, brought a box of roses to Sidney, and departed grinning impishly. He knew Joe, had seen him in the store. Soon the alley knew that Sidney had received a dozen Killarney roses at three dollars and a half, and was probably engaged to Joe Drummond.

"Dr. Ed," said Sidney, as he followed her down the stairs, "can you spare the time to talk to me a little while?"

Perhaps the elder Wilson had a quick vision of the crowded office waiting across the Street; but his reply was prompt:

"Any amount of time."

Sidney led the way into the small parlor, where Joe's roses, refused by the petulant invalid upstairs, bloomed alone.

"First of all," said Sidney, "did you mean what you said upstairs?"

Dr. Ed thought quickly.

"Of course; but what?"

"You said I was a born nurse."

The Street was very fond of Dr. Ed. It did not always approve of him. It said--which was perfectly true--that he had sacrificed himself to his brother's career: that, for the sake of that brilliant young surgeon, Dr. Ed had done without wife and children; that to send him abroad he had saved and skimped; that he still went shabby and drove the old buggy, while Max drove about in an automobile coupe. Sidney, not at all of the stuff martyrs are made of, sat in the scented parlor and, remembering all this, was ashamed of her rebellion.

"I'm going into a hospital," said Sidney.

Dr. Ed waited. He liked to have all the symptoms before he made a diagnosis or ventured an opinion. So Sidney, trying to be cheerful, and quite unconscious of the anxiety in her voice, told her story.

"It's fearfully hard work, of course," he commented, when she had finished.

"So is anything worth while. Look at the way you work!"

Dr. Ed rose and wandered around the room.

"You're too young."

"I'll get older."

"I don't think I like the idea," he said at last. "It's splendid work for an older woman. But it's life, child--life in the raw. As we get along in years we lose our illusions--some of them, not all, thank God. But for you, at your age, to be brought face to face with things as they are, and not as we want them to be--it seems such an unnecessary sacrifice."

"Don't you think," said Sidney bravely, "that you are a poor person to talk of sacrifice? Haven't you always, all your life--"

Dr. Ed colored to the roots of his straw-colored hair.

"Certainly not," he said almost irritably. "Max had genius; I had--ability. That's different. One real success is better than two halves. Not"--he smiled down at her--"not that I minimize my usefulness. Somebody has to do the hack-work, and, if I do say it myself, I'm a pretty good hack."

"Very well," said Sidney. "Then I shall be a hack, too. Of course, I had thought of other things,--my father wanted me to go to college,--but I'm strong and willing. And one thing I must make up my mind to, Dr. Ed; I shall have to support my mother."

Harriet passed the door on her way in to a belated supper. The man in the parlor had a momentary glimpse of her slender, sagging shoulders, her thin face, her undisguised middle age.

"Yes," he said, when she was out of hearing. "It's hard, but I dare say it's right enough, too. Your aunt ought to have her chance. Only--I wish it didn't have to be."

Sidney, left alone, stood in the little parlor beside the roses. She touched them tenderly, absently. Life, which the day before had called her with the beckoning finger of dreams, now reached out grim insistent hands. Life--in the raw.

CHAPTER III

K. Le Moyne had wakened early that first morning in his new quarters. When he sat up and yawned, it was to see his worn cravat disappearing with vigorous tugs under the bureau. He rescued it, gently but firmly.

"You and I, Reginald," he apostrophized the bureau, "will have to come to an understanding. What I leave on the floor you may have, but what blows down is not to be touched."

Because he was young and very strong, he wakened to a certain lightness of spirit. The morning sun had always called him to a new day, and the sun was shining. But he grew depressed as he prepared for the office. He told himself savagely, as he put on his shabby clothing, that, having sought for peace and now found it, he was an ass for resenting it. The trouble was, of course, that he came of fighting stock: soldiers and explorers, even a gentleman adventurer or two, had been his forefather. He loathed peace with a deadly loathing.

Having given up everything else, K. Le Moyne had also given up the love of woman. That, of course, is figurative. He had been too busy for women; and now he was too idle. A small part of his brain added figures in the office of a gas company daily, for the sum of two dollars and fifty cents per eight-hour working day. But the real K. Le Moyne that had dreamed dreams, had nothing to do with the figures, but sat somewhere in his head and mocked him as he worked at his task.

"Time's going by, and here you are!" mocked the real person--who was, of course, not K. Le Moyne at all. "You're the hell of a lot of use, aren't you? Two and two are four and three are seven--take off the discount. That's right. It's a man's work, isn't it?"

"Somebody's got to do this sort of thing," protested the small part of his brain that earned the two-fifty per working day. "And it's a great anaesthetic. He can't think when he's doing it. There's something practical about figures, and--rational."

He dressed quickly, ascertaining that he had enough money to buy a five-dollar ticket at Mrs. McKee's; and, having given up the love of woman with other things, he was careful not to look about for Sidney on his way.

He breakfasted at Mrs. McKee's, and was initiated into the mystery of the ticket punch. The food was rather good, certainly plentiful; and even his squeamish morning appetite could find no fault with the self-respecting tidiness of the place. Tillie proved to be neat and austere. He fancied it would not be pleasant to be very late for one's meals--in fact, Sidney had hinted as much. Some of the "mealers"--the Street's name for them--ventured on various small familiarities of speech with Tillie. K. Le Moyne himself was scrupulously polite, but reserved. He was determined not to let the Street encroach on his wretchedness. Because he had come to live there was no reason why it should adopt him. But he was very polite. When the deaf-and-dumb book agent wrote something on a pencil pad and pushed it toward him, he replied in kind.

"We are very glad to welcome you to the McKee family," was what was written on the pad.

"Very happy, indeed, to be with you," wrote back Le Moyne--and realized with a sort of shock that he meant it.

The kindly greeting had touched him. The greeting and the breakfast cheered him; also, he had evidently made some headway with Tillie.

"Don't you want a toothpick?" she asked, as he went out.

In K.'s previous walk of life there had been no toothpicks; or, if there were any, they were kept, along with the family scandals, in a closet. But nearly a year of buffeting about had taught him many things. He took one, and placed it nonchalantly in his waistcoat pocket, as he had seen the others do.

Tillie, her rush hour over, wandered back into the kitchen and poured herself a cup of coffee. Mrs. McKee was reweighing the meat order.

"Kind of a nice fellow," Tillie said, cup to lips--"the new man."

"Week or meal?"

"Week. He'd be handsome if he wasn't so grouchy-looking. Lit up some when Mr. Wagner sent him one of his love letters. Rooms over at the Pages'."

Mrs. McKee drew a long breath and entered the lam stew in a book.

"When I think of Anna Page taking a roomer, it just about knocks me over, Tillie. And where they'll put him, in that little house--he looked thin, what I saw of him. Seven pounds and a quarter." This last referred, not to K. Le Moyne, of course, but to the lamb stew.

"Thin as a fiddle-string."

"Just keep an eye on him, that he gets enough." Then, rather ashamed of her unbusinesslike methods: "A thin mealer's a poor advertisement. Do you suppose this is the dog meat or the soup scraps?"

Tillie was a niece of Mrs. Rosenfeld. In such manner was most of the Street and its environs connected; in such wise did its small gossip start at one end and pursue its course down one side and up the other.

"Sidney Page is engaged to Joe Drummond," announced Tillie. "He sent her a lot of pink roses yesterday."

There was no malice in her flat statement, no envy. Sidney and she, living in the world of the Street, occupied different spheres. But the very lifelessness in her voice told how remotely such things touched her, and thus was tragic. "Mealers" came and went--small clerks, petty tradesmen, husbands living alone in darkened houses during the summer hegira of wives. Various and catholic was Tillie's male acquaintance, but compounded of good fellowship only. Once, years before, romance had paraded itself before her in the garb of a traveling nurseryman--had walked by and not come back.

"And Miss Harriet's going into business for herself. She's taken rooms downtown; she's going to be Madame Something or other."

Now, at last, was Mrs. McKee's attention caught riveted.

"For the love of mercy! At her age! It's downright selfish. If she raises her prices she can't make my new foulard."

Tillie sat at the table, her faded blue eyes fixed on the back yard, where her aunt, Mrs. Rosenfeld, was hanging out the week's wash of table linen.

"I don't know as it's so selfish," she reflected. "We've only got one life. I guess a body's got the right to live it."

Mrs. McKee eyed her suspiciously, but Tillie's face showed no emotion.

"You don't ever hear of Schwitter, do you?"

"No; I guess she's still living."

Schwitter, the nurseryman, had proved to have a wife in an insane asylum. That was why Tillie's romance had only paraded itself before her and had gone by.

"You got out of that lucky."

Tillie rose and tied a gingham apron over her white one.

"I guess so. Only sometimes--"

"I don't know as it would have been so wrong. He ain't young, and I ain't. And we're not getting any younger. He had nice manners; he'd have been good to me."

Mrs. McKee's voice failed her. For a moment she gasped like a fish. Then:

"And him a married man!"

"Well, I'm not going to do it," Tillie soothed her. "I get to thinking about it sometimes; that's all. This new fellow made me think of him. He's got the same nice way about him."

Aye, the new man had made her think of him, and June, and the lovers who lounged along the Street in the moonlit avenues toward the park and love; even Sidney's pink roses. Change was in the very air of the Street that June morning. It was in Tillie, making a last clutch at youth, and finding, in this pale flare of dying passion, courage to remember what she had schooled herself to forget; in Harriet asserting her right to live her life; in Sidney, planning with eager eyes a life of service which did not include Joe; in K. Le Moyne, who had built up a wall between himself and the world, and was seeing it demolished by a deaf-and-dumb book agent whose weapon was a pencil pad!

And yet, for a week nothing happened: Joe came in the evenings and sat on the steps with Sidney, his honest heart, in his eyes. She could not bring herself at first to tell him about the hospital. She put it off from day to day. Anna, no longer sulky, accepted wit the childlike faith Sidney's statement that "they'd get along; she had a splendid scheme," and took to helping Harriet in her preparations for leaving. Tillie, afraid of her rebellious spirit, went to prayer meeting. And K. Le Moyne, finding his little room hot in the evenings and not wishing to intrude on the two on the doorstep, took to reading his paper in the park, and after twilight to long, rapid walks out into the country. The walks satisfied the craving of his active body for exercise, and tired him so he could sleep. On one such occasion he met Mr. Wagner, and they carried on an animated conversation until it was too dark to see the pad. Even then, it developed that Wagner could write in the dark; and he secured the last word in a long argument by doing this and striking a match for K. to read by.

When K. was sure that the boy had gone, he would turn back toward the Street. Some of the heaviness of his spirit always left him at sight of the little house. Its kindly atmosphere seemed to reach out and envelop him. Within was order and quiet, the fresh-down bed, the tidiness of his ordered garments. There was even affection--Reginald, waiting on the fender for his supper, and regarding him with wary and bright-eyed friendliness.

Life, that had seemed so simple, had grown very complicated for Sidney. There was her mother to break the news to, and Joe. Harriet would approve, she felt; but these others! To assure Anna that she must manage alone for three years, in order to be happy and comfortable afterward--that was hard enough to tell Joe she was planning a future without him, to destroy the light in his blue eyes--that hurt.

After all, Sidney told K. first. One Friday evening, coming home late, as usual, he found her on the doorstep, and Joe gone. She moved over hospitably. The moon had waxed and waned, and the Street was dark. Even the ailanthus blossoms had ceased their snow-like dropping. The colored man who drove Dr. Ed in the old buggy on his daily rounds had brought out the hose and sprinkled the street. Within this zone of freshness, of wet asphalt and dripping gutters, Sidney sat, cool and silent.

"Please sit down. It is cool now. My idea of luxury is to have the Street sprinkled on a hot night."

K. disposed of his long legs on the steps. He was trying to fit his own ideas of luxury to a garden hose and a city street.

"I'm afraid you're working too hard."

"I? I do a minimum of labor for a minimum of wage.

"But you work at night, don't you?"

K. was natively honest. He hesitated. Then:

"No, Miss Page."

"But You go out every evening!" Suddenly the truth burst on her.

"Oh, dear!" she said. "I do believe--why, how silly of you!"

K. was most uncomfortable.

"Really, I like it," he protested. "I hang over a desk all day, and in the evening I want to walk. I ramble around the park and see lovers on benches--it's rather thrilling. They sit on the same benches evening after evening. I know a lot of them by sight, and if they're not there I wonder if they have quarreled, or if they have finally got married and ended the romance. You can see how exciting it is."

Quite suddenly Sidney laughed.

"How very nice you are!" she said--"and how absurd! Why should their getting married end the romance? And don't you know that, if you insist on walking the streets and parks at night because Joe Drummond is here, I shall have to tell him not to come?"

This did not follow, to K.'s mind. They had rather a heated argument over it, and became much better acquainted.

"If I were engaged to him," Sidney ended, her cheeks very pink, "I--I might understand. But, as I am not--"

"Ah!" said K., a trifle unsteadily. "So you are not?"

Only a week--and love was one of the things she had had to give up, with others. Not, of course, that he was in love with Sidney then. But he had been desperately lonely, and, for all her practical clearheadedness, she was softly and appealingly feminine. By way of keeping his head, he talked suddenly and earnestly of Mrs. McKee, and food, and Tillie, and of Mr. Wagner and the pencil pad.

"It's like a game," he said. "We disagree on everything, especially Mexico. If you ever tried to spell those Mexican names--"

"Why did you think I was engaged?" she insisted.

Now, in K.'s walk of life--that walk of life where there are no toothpicks, and no one would have believed that twenty-one meals could have been secured for five dollars with a ticket punch thrown in--young girls did not receive the attention of one young man to the exclusion of others unless they were engaged. But he could hardly say that.

"Oh, I don't know. Those things get in the air. I am quite certain, for instance, that Reginald suspects it."

"It's Johnny Rosenfeld," said Sidney, with decision. "It's horrible, the way things get about. Because Joe sent me a box of roses--As a matter of fact, I'm not engaged, or going to be, Mr. Le Moyne. I'm going into a hospital to be a nurse."

Le Moyne said nothing. For just a moment he closed his eyes. A man is in a rather a bad way when, every time he closes his eyes, he sees the same thing, especially if it is rather terrible. When it gets to a point where he lies awake at night and reads, for fear of closing them--

"You're too young, aren't you?"

"Dr. Ed--one of the Wilsons across the Street--is going to help me about that. His brother Max is a big surgeon there. I expect you've heard of him. We're very proud of him in the Street."

Lucky for K. Le Moyne that the moon no longer shone on the low gray doorstep, that Sidney's mind had traveled far away to shining floors and rows of white beds. "Life--in the raw," Dr. Ed had said that other afternoon. Closer to her than the hospital was life in the raw that night.

So, even here, on this quiet street in this distant city, there was to be no peace. Max Wilson just across the way! It--it was ironic. Was there no place where a man could lose himself? He would have to move on again, of course.

But that, it seemed, was just what he could not do. For:

"I want to ask you to do something, and I hope you'll be quite frank," said Sidney.

"Anything that I can do--"

"It's this. If you are comfortable, and--and like the room and all that, I wish you'd stay." She hurried on: "If I could feel that mother had a dependable person like you in the house, it would all be easier."

Dependable! That stung.

"But--forgive my asking; I'm really interested--can your mother manage? You'll get practically no money during your training."

"I've thought of that. A friend of mine, Christine Lorenz, is going to be married. Her people are wealthy, but she'll have nothing but what Palmer makes. She'd like to have the parlor and the sitting room behind. They wouldn't interfere with you at all," she added hastily. "Christine's father would build a little balcony at the side for them, a sort of porch, and they'd sit there in the evenings."

Behind Sidney's carefully practical tone the man read appeal. Never before had he realized how narrow the girl's world had been. The Street, with but one dimension, bounded it! In her perplexity, she was appealing to him who was practically a stranger.

And he knew then that he must do the thing she asked. He, who had fled so long, could roam no more. Here on the Street, with its menace just across, he must live, that she might work. In his world, men had worked that women might live in certain places, certain ways. This girl was going out to earn her living, and he would stay to make it possible. But no hint of all this was in his voice.

"I shall stay, of course," he said gravely. "I--this is the nearest thing to home that I've known for a long time. I want you to know that."

So they moved their puppets about, Anna and Harriet, Christine and her husband-to-be, Dr. Ed, even Tillie and the Rosenfelds; shifted and placed them, and, planning, obeyed inevitable law.

"Christine shall come, then," said Sidney forsooth, "and we will throw out a balcony."

So they planned, calmly ignorant that poor Christine's story and Tillie's and Johnny Rosenfeld's and all the others' were already written among the things that are, and the things that shall be hereafter.

"You are very good to me," said Sidney.

When she rose, K. Le Moyne sprang to his feet.

Anna had noticed that he always rose when she entered his room,--with fresh towels on Katie's day out, for instance,--and she liked him for it. Years ago, the men she had known had shown this courtesy to their women; but the Street regarded such things as affectation.

"I wonder if you would do me another favor? I'm afraid you'll take to avoiding me, if I keep on."

"I don't think you need fear that."

"This stupid story about Joe Drummond--I'm not saying I'll never marry him, but I'm certainly not engaged. Now and then, when you are taking your evening walks, if you would ask me to walk with you--"

K. looked rather dazed.

"I can't imagine anything pleasanter; but I wish you'd explain just how--"

Sidney smiled at him. As he stood on the lowest step, their eyes were almost level.

"If I walk with you, they'll know I'm not engaged to Joe," she said, with engaging directness.

The house was quiet. He waited in the lower hall until she had reached the top of the staircase. For some curious reason, in the time to come, that was the way Sidney always remembered K. Le Moyne--standing in the little hall, one hand upstretched to shut off the gas overhead, and his eyes on hers above.

"Good-night," said K. Le Moyne. And all the things he had put out of his life were in his voice.

CHAPTER IV

ON the morning after Sidney had invited K. Le Moyne to take her to walk, Max Wilson came down to breakfast rather late. Dr. Ed had breakfasted an hour before, and had already attended, with much profanity on the part of the patient, to a boil on the back of Mr. Rosenfeld's neck.

"Better change your laundry," cheerfully advised Dr. Ed, cutting a strip of adhesive plaster. "Your neck's irritated from your white collars."

Rosenfeld eyed him suspiciously, but, possessing a sense of humor also, he grinned.

"It ain't my everyday things that bother me," he replied. "It's my blankety-blank dress suit. But if a man wants to be tony--"

"Tony" was not of the Street, but of its environs. Harriet was "tony" because she walked with her elbows in and her head up. Dr. Max was "tony" because he breakfasted late, and had a man come once a week and take away his clothes to be pressed. He was "tony," too, because he had brought back from Europe narrow-shouldered English-cut clothes, when the Street was still padding its shoulders. Even K. would have been classed with these others, for the stick that he carried on his walks, for the fact that his shabby gray coat was as unmistakably foreign in cut as Dr. Max's, had the neighborhood so much as known him by sight. But K., so far, had remained in humble obscurity, and, outside of Mrs. McKee's, was known only as the Pages' roomer.

Mr. Rosenfeld buttoned up the blue flannel shirt which, with a pair of Dr. Ed's cast-off trousers, was his only wear; and fished in his pocket.

"How much, Doc?"

"Two dollars," said Dr. Ed briskly.

"Holy cats! For one jab of a knife! My old woman works a day and a half for two dollars."

"I guess it's worth two dollars to you to be able to sleep on your back." He was imperturbably straightening his small glass table. He knew Rosenfeld. "If you don't like my price, I'll lend you the knife the next time, and you can let your wife attend to you."

Rosenfeld drew out a silver dollar, and followed it reluctantly with a limp and dejected dollar bill.

"There are times," he said, "when, if you'd put me and the missus and a knife in the same room, you wouldn't have much left but the knife."

Dr. Ed waited until he had made his stiff-necked exit. Then he took the two dollars, and, putting the money into an envelope, indorsed it in his illegible hand. He heard his brother's step on the stairs, and Dr. Ed made haste to put away the last vestiges of his little operation.

Ed's lapses from surgical cleanliness were a sore trial to the younger man, fresh from the clinics of Europe. In his downtown office, to which he would presently make his leisurely progress, he wore a white coat, and sterilized things of which Dr. Ed did not even know the names.

So, as he came down the stairs, Dr. Ed, who had wiped his tiny knife with a bit of cotton,--he hated sterilizing it; it spoiled the edge,--thrust it hastily into his pocket. He had cut boils without boiling anything for a good many years, and no trouble. But he was wise with the wisdom of the serpent and the general practitioner, and there was no use raising a discussion.

Max's morning mood was always a cheerful one. Now and then the way of the transgressor is disgustingly pleasant. Max, who sat up until all hours of the night, drinking beer or whiskey-and-soda, and playing bridge, wakened to a clean tongue and a tendency to have a cigarette between shoes, so to speak. Ed, whose wildest dissipation had perhaps been to bring into the world one of the neighborhood's babies, wakened customarily to the dark hour of his day, when he dubbed himself failure and loathed the Street with a deadly loathing.

So now Max brought his handsome self down the staircase and paused at the office door.

"At it, already," he said. "Or have you been to bed?"

"It's after nine," protested Ed mildly. "If I don't start early, I never get through."

Max yawned.

"Better come with me," he said. "If things go on as they've been doing, I'll have to have an assistant. I'd rather have you than anybody, of course." He put his lithe surgeon's hand on his brother's shoulder. "Where would I be if it hadn't been for you? All the fellows know what you've done."

In spite of himself, Ed winced. It was one thing to work hard that there might be one success instead of two half successes. It was a different thing to advertise one's mediocrity to the world. His sphere of the Street and the neighborhood was his own. To give it all up and become his younger brother's assistant--even if it meant, as it would, better hours and more money--would be to submerge his identity. He could not bring himself to it.

"I guess I'll stay where I am," he said. "They know me around here, and I know them. By the way, will you leave this envelope at Mrs. McKee's? Maggie Rosenfeld is ironing there to-day. It's for her."

Max took the envelope absently.

"You'll go on here to the end of your days, working for a pittance," he objected. "Inside of ten years there'll be no general practitioners; then where will you be?"

"I'll manage somehow," said his brother placidly. "I guess there will always be a few that can pay my prices better than what you specialists ask."

Max laughed with genuine amusement.

"I dare say, if this is the way you let them pay your prices."

He held out the envelope, and the older man colored.

Very proud of Dr. Max was his brother, unselfishly proud, of his skill, of his handsome person, of his easy good manners; very humble, too, of his own knowledge and experience. If he ever suspected any lack of finer fiber in Max, he put the thought away. Probably he was too rigid himself. Max was young, a hard worker. He had a right to play hard.

He prepared his black bag for the day's calls--stethoscope, thermometer, eyecup, bandages, case of small vials, a lump of absorbent cotton in a not over-fresh towel; in the bottom, a heterogeneous collection of instruments, a roll of adhesive plaster, a bottle or two of sugar-milk tablets for the children, a dog collar that had belonged to a dead collie, and had put in the bag in some curious fashion and there remained.

He prepared the bag a little nervously, while Max ate. He felt that modern methods and the best usage might not have approved of the bag. On his way out he paused at the dining-room door.

"Are you going to the hospital?"

"Operating at four--wish you could come in."

"I'm afraid not, Max. I've promised Sidney Page to speak about her to you. She wants to enter the training-school."

"Too young," said Max briefly. "Why, she can't be over sixteen."

"She's eighteen."

"Well, even eighteen. Do you think any girl of that age is responsible enough to have life and death put in her hands? Besides, although I haven't noticed her lately, she used to be a pretty little thing. There is no use filling up the wards with a lot of ornaments; it keeps the internes all stewed up."

"Since when," asked Dr. Ed mildly, "have you found good looks in a girl a handicap?"

In the end they compromised. Max would see Sidney at his office. It would be better than having her run across the Street--would put things on the right footing. For, if he did have her admitted, she would have to learn at once that he was no longer "Dr. Max"; that, as a matter of fact, he was now staff, and entitled to much dignity, to speech without contradiction or argument, to clean towels, and a deferential interne at his elbow.

Having given his promise, Max promptly forgot about it. The Street did not interest him. Christine and Sidney had been children when he went to Vienna, and since his return he had hardly noticed them. Society, always kind to single men of good appearance and easy good manners, had taken him up. He wore dinner or evening clothes five nights out of seven, and was supposed by his conservative old neighbors to be going the pace. The rumor had been fed by Mrs. Rosenfeld, who, starting out for her day's washing at six o'clock one morning, had found Dr. Max's car, lamps lighted, and engine going, drawn up before the house door, with its owner asleep at the wheel. The story traveled the length of the Street that day.

"Him," said Mrs. Rosenfeld, who was occasionally flowery, "sittin' up as straight as this washboard, and his silk hat shinin' in the sun; but exceptin' the car, which was workin' hard and gettin' nowhere, the whole outfit in the arms of Morpheus."

Mrs. Lorenz, whose day it was to have Mrs. Rosenfeld, and who was unfamiliar with mythology, gasped at the last word.

"Mercy!" she said. "Do you mean to say he's got that awful drug habit!"

Down the clean steps went Dr. Max that morning, a big man, almost as tall as K. Le Moyne, eager of life, strong and a bit reckless, not fine, perhaps, but not evil. He had the same zest of living as Sidney, but with this difference--the girl stood ready to give herself to life: he knew that life would come to him. All-dominating male was Dr. Max, that morning, as he drew on his gloves before stepping into his car. It was after nine o'clock. K. Le Moyne had been an hour at his desk. The McKee napkins lay ironed in orderly piles.

Nevertheless, Dr. Max was suffering under a sense of defeat as he rode downtown. The night before, he had proposed to a girl and had been rejected. He was not in love with the girl,--she would have been a suitable wife, and a surgeon ought to be married; it gives people confidence,--but his pride was hurt. He recalled the exact words of the rejection.

"You're too good-looking, Max," she had said, "and that's the truth. Now that operations are as popular as fancy dancing, and much less bother, half the women I know are crazy about their surgeons. I'm too fond of my peace of mind."

"But, good Heavens! haven't you any confidence in me?" he had demanded.

"None whatever, Max dear." She had looked at him with level, understanding eyes.

He put the disagreeable recollection out of his mind as he parked his car and made his way to his office. Here would be people who believed in him, from the middle-aged nurse in her prim uniform to the row of patients sitting stiffly around the walls of the waiting-room. Dr. Max, pausing in the hall outside the door of his private office, drew a long breath. This was the real thing--work and plenty of it, a chance to show the other men what he could do, a battle to win! No humanitarian was he, but a fighter: each day he came to his office with the same battle lust.

The office nurse had her back to him. When she turned, he faced an agreeable surprise. Instead of Miss Simpson, he faced a young and attractive girl, faintly familiar.

"We tried to get you by telephone," she explained. "I am from the hospital. Miss Simpson's father died this morning, and she knew you would have to have some one. I was just starting for my vacation, so they sent me."

"Rather a poor substitute for a vacation," he commented.

She was a very pretty girl. He had seen her before in the hospital, but he had never really noticed how attractive she was. Rather stunning she was, he thought. The combination of yellow hair and dark eyes was unusual. He remembered, just in time, to express regret at Miss Simpson's bereavement.

"I am Miss Harrison," explained the substitute, and held out his long white coat. The ceremony, purely perfunctory with Miss Simpson on duty, proved interesting, Miss Harrison, in spite of her high heels, being small and the young surgeon tall. When he was finally in the coat, she was rather flushed and palpitating.

"But I KNEW your name, of course," lied Dr. Max. "And--I'm sorry about the vacation."

After that came work. Miss Harrison was nimble and alert, but the surgeon worked quickly and with few words, was impatient when she could not find the things he called for, even broke into restrained profanity now and then. She went a little pale over her mistakes, but preserved her dignity and her wits. Now and then he found her dark eyes fixed on him, with something inscrutable but pleasing in their depths. The situation was: rather piquant. Consciously he was thinking only of what he was doing. Subconsciously his busy ego was finding solace after last night's rebuff.

Once, during the cleaning up between cases, he dropped to a personality. He was drying his hands, while she placed freshly sterilized instruments on a glass table.

"You are almost a foreign type, Miss Harrison. Last year, in a London ballet, I saw a blonde Spanish girl who looked like you."

"My mother was a Spaniard." She did not look up.

Where Miss Simpson was in the habit of clumping through the morning in flat, heavy shoes, Miss Harrison's small heels beat a busy tattoo on the tiled floor. With the rustling of her starched dress, the sound was essentially feminine, almost insistent. When he had time to notice it, it amused him that he did not find it annoying.

Once, as she passed him a bistoury, he deliberately placed his fine hand over her fingers and smiled into her eyes. It was play for him; it lightened the day's work.

Sidney was in the waiting-room. There had been no tedium in the morning's waiting. Like all imaginative people, she had the gift of dramatizing herself. She was seeing herself in white from head to foot, like this efficient young woman who came now and then to the waiting-room door; she was healing the sick and closing tired eyes; she was even imagining herself proposed to by an aged widower with grown children and quantities of money, one of her patients.

She sat very demurely in the waiting-room with a magazine in her lap, and told her aged patient that she admired and respected him, but that she had given herself to the suffering poor.

"Everything in the world that you want," begged the elderly gentleman. "You should see the world, child, and I will see it again through your eyes. To Paris first for clothes and the opera, and then--"

"But I do not love you," Sidney replied, mentally but steadily. "In all the world I love only one man. He is--"

She hesitated here. It certainly was not Joe, or K. Le Moyne of the gas office. It seem to her suddenly very sad that there was no one she loved. So many people went into hospitals because they had been disappointed in love.

"Dr. Wilson will see you now."

She followed Miss Harrison into the consulting room. Dr. Max--not the gloved and hatted Dr. Max of the Street, but a new person, one she had never known--stood in his white office, tall, dark-eyed, dark-haired, competent, holding out his long, immaculate surgeon's hand, and smiling down at her.

Men, like jewels, require a setting. A clerk on a high stool, poring over a ledger, is not unimpressive, or a cook over her stove. But place the cook on the stool, poring over the ledger! Dr. Max, who had lived all his life on the edge of Sidney's horizon, now, by the simple changing of her point of view, loomed large and magnificent. Perhaps he knew it. Certainly he stood very erect. Certainly, too, there was considerable manner in the way in which he asked Miss Harrison to go out and close the door behind her.

Sidney's heart, considering what was happening to it, behaved very well.

"For goodness' sake, Sidney," said Dr. Max, "here you are a young lady and I've never noticed it!"

This, of course, was not what he had intended to say, being staff and all that. But Sidney, visibly palpitant, was very pretty, much prettier than the Harrison girl, beating a tattoo with her heels in the next room.

Dr. Max, belonging to the class of man who settles his tie every time he sees an attractive woman, thrust his hands into the pockets of his long white coat and surveyed her quizzically.

"Did Dr. Ed tell you?"

"Sit down. He said something about the hospital. How's your mother and Aunt Harriet?"

"Very well--that is, mother's never quite well." She was sitting forward on her chair, her wide young eyes on him. "Is that--is your nurse from the hospital here?"

"Yes. But she's not my nurse. She's a substitute."

"The uniform is so pretty." Poor Sidney! with all the things she had meant to say about a life of service, and that, although she was young, she was terribly in earnest.

"It takes a lot of plugging before one gets the uniform. Look here, Sidney; if you are going to the hospital because of the uniform, and with any idea of soothing fevered brows and all that nonsense--"

She interrupted him, deeply flushed. Indeed, no. She wanted to work. She was young and strong, and surely a pair of willing hands--that was absurd about the uniform. She had no silly ideas. There was so much to do in the world, and she wanted to help. Some people could give money, but she couldn't. She could only offer service. And, partly through earnestness and partly through excitement, she ended in a sort of nervous sob, and, going to the window, stood with her back to him.

He followed her, and, because they were old neighbors, she did not resent it when he put his hand on her shoulder.

"I don't know--of course, if you feel like that about it," he said, "we'll see what can be done. It's hard work, and a good many times it seems futile. They die, you know, in spite of all we can do. And there are many things that are worse than death--"

His voice trailed off. When he had started out in his profession, he had had some such ideal of service as this girl beside him. For just a moment, as he stood there close to her, he saw things again with the eyes of his young faith: to relieve pain, to straighten the crooked, to hurt that he might heal,--not to show the other men what he could do,--that had been his early creed. He sighed a little as he turned away.

"I'll speak to the superintendent about you," he said. "Perhaps you'd like me to show you around a little."

"When? To-day?"

He had meant in a month, or a year. It was quite a minute before he replied:--

"Yes, to-day, if you say. I'm operating at four. How about three o'clock?"

She held out both hands, and he took them, smiling.

"You are the kindest person I ever met."

"And--perhaps you'd better not say you are applying until we find out if there is a vacancy."

"May I tell one person?"

"Mother?"

"No. We--we have a roomer now. He is very much interested. I should like to tell him."

He dropped her hands and looked at her in mock severity.

"Much interested! Is he in love with you?"

"Mercy, no!"

"I don't believe it. I'm jealous. You know, I've always been more than half in love with you myself!"

Play for him--the same victorious instinct that had made him touch Miss Harrison's fingers as she gave him the instrument. And Sidney knew how it was meant; she smiled into his eyes and drew down her veil briskly.

"Then we'll say at three," she said calmly, and took an orderly and unflurried departure.

But the little seed of tenderness had taken root. Sidney, passing in the last week or two from girlhood to womanhood,--outgrowing Joe, had she only known it, as she had outgrown the Street,--had come that day into her first contact with a man of the world. True, there was K. Le Moyne. But K. was now of the Street, of that small world of one dimension that she was leaving behind her.

She sent him a note at noon, with word to Tillie at Mrs. McKee's to put it under his plate:--

DEAR MR. LE MOYNE,--I am so excited I can hardly write. Dr. Wilson, the surgeon, is going to take me through the hospital this afternoon. Wish me luck.

SIDNEY PAGE.

K. read it, and, perhaps because the day was hot and his butter soft and the other "mealers" irritable with the heat, he ate little or no luncheon. Before he went out into the sun, he read the note again. To his jealous eyes came a vision of that excursion to the hospital. Sidney, all vibrant eagerness, luminous of eye, quick of bosom; and Wilson, sardonically smiling, amused and interested in spite of himself. He drew a long breath, and thrust the note in his pocket.

The little house across the way sat square in the sun. The shades of his windows had been lowered against the heat. K. Le Moyne made an impulsive movement toward it and checked himself.

As he went down the Street, Wilson's car came around the corner. Le Moyne moved quietly into the shadow of the church and watched the car go by.

CHAPTER V

SIDNEY and K. Le Moyne sat under a tree and talked. In Sidney's lap lay a small pasteboard box, punched with many holes. It was the day of releasing Reginald, but she had not yet been able to bring herself to the point of separation. Now and then a furry nose protruded from one of the apertures and sniffed the welcome scent of pine and buttonball, red and white clover, the thousand spicy odors of field and woodland.

"And so," said K. Le Moyne, "you liked it all? It didn't startle you?"

"Well, in one way, of course--you see, I didn't know it was quite like that: all order and peace and quiet, and white beds and whispers, on top,--you know what I mean,--and the misery there just the same. Have you ever gone through a hospital?"

K. Le Moyne was stretched out on the grass, his arms under his head. For this excursion to the end of the street-car line he had donned a pair of white flannel trousers and a belted Norfolk coat. Sidney had been divided between pride in his appearance and fear that the Street would deem him overdressed.

At her question he closed his eyes, shutting out the peaceful arch and the bit of blue heaven overhead. He did not reply at once.

"Good gracious, I believe he's asleep!" said Sidney to the pasteboard box.

But he opened his eyes and smiled at her.

"I've been around hospitals a little. I suppose now there is no question about your going?"

"The superintendent said I was young, but that any protegee of Dr. Wilson's would certainly be given a chance."

"It is hard work, night and day."

"Do you think I am afraid of work?"

"And--Joe?"

Sidney colored vigorously and sat erect.

"He is very silly. He's taken all sorts of idiotic notions in his head."

"Such as--"

"Well, he HATES the hospital, of course. As if, even if I meant to marry him, it wouldn't be years before he can be ready."

"Do you think you are quite fair to Joe?"

"I haven't promised to marry him."

"But he thinks you mean to. If you have quite made up your mind not to, better tell him, don't you think? What--what are these idiotic notions?"

Sidney considered, poking a slim finger into the little holes in the box.

"You can see how stupid he is, and--and young. For one thing, he's jealous of you!"

"I see. Of course that is silly, although your attitude toward his suspicion is hardly flattering to me."

He smiled up at her.

"I told him that I had asked you to bring me here to-day. He was furious. And that wasn't all."

"No?"

"He said I was flirting desperately with Dr. Wilson. You see, the day we went through the hospital, it was hot, and we went to Henderson's for soda-water. And, of course, Joe was there. It was really dramatic."

K. Le Moyne was daily gaining the ability to see things from the angle of the Street. A month ago he could have seen no situation in two people, a man and a girl, drinking soda-water together, even with a boy lover on the next stool. Now he could view things through Joe's tragic eyes. And there as more than that. All day he had noticed how inevitably the conversation turned to the young surgeon. Did they start with Reginald, with the condition of the morning-glory vines, with the proposition of taking up the quaint paving-stones and macadamizing the Street, they ended with the younger Wilson.

Sidney's active young brain, turned inward for the first time in her life, was still on herself.

"Mother is plaintively resigned--and Aunt Harriet has been a trump. She's going to keep her room. It's really up to you."

"To me?"

"To your staying on. Mother trusts you absolutely. I hope you noticed that you got one of the apostle spoons with the custard she sent up to you the other night. And she didn't object to this trip to-day. Of course, as she said herself, it isn't as if you were young, or at all wild."

In spite of himself, K. was rather startled. He felt old enough, God knew, but he had always thought of it as an age of the spirit. How old did this child think he was?

"I have promised to stay on, in the capacity of watch-dog, burglar-alarm, and occasional recipient of an apostle spoon in a dish of custard. Lightning-conductor, too--your mother says she isn't afraid of storms if there is a man in the house. I'll stay, of course."

The thought of his age weighed on him. He rose to his feet and threw back his fine shoulders.

"Aunt Harriet and your mother and Christine and her husband-to-be, whatever his name is--we'll be a happy family. But, I warn you, if I ever hear of Christine's husband getting an apostle spoon--"

She smiled up at him. "You are looking very grand to-day. But you have grass stains on your white trousers. Perhaps Katie can take them out."

Quite suddenly K. felt that she thought him too old for such frivolity of dress. It put him on his mettle.

"How old do you think I am, Miss Sidney?"

She considered, giving him, after her kindly way, the benefit of the doubt.

"Not over forty, I'm sure."

"I'm almost thirty. It is middle age, of course, but it is not senility."

She was genuinely surprised, almost disturbed.

"Perhaps we'd better not tell mother," she said. "You don't mind being thought older?"

"Not at all."

Clearly the subject of his years did not interest her vitally, for she harked back to the grass stains.

"I'm afraid you're not saving, as you promised. Those are new clothes, aren't they?"

"No, indeed. Bought years ago in England--the coat in London, the trousers in Bath, on a motor tour. Cost something like twelve shillings. Awfully cheap. They wear them for cricket."

That was a wrong move, of course. Sidney must hear about England; and she marveled politely, in view of his poverty, about his being there. Poor Le Moyne floundered in a sea of mendacity, rose to a truth here and there, clutched at luncheon, and achieved safety at last.

"To think," said Sidney, "that you have really been across the ocean! I never knew but one person who had been abroad. It is Dr. Max Wilson."

Back again to Dr. Max! Le Moyne, unpacking sandwiches from a basket, was aroused by a sheer resentment to an indiscretion.

"You like this Wilson chap pretty well, don't you?"

"What do you mean?"

"You talk about him rather a lot."

This was sheer recklessness, of course. He expected fury, annihilation. He did not look up, but busied himself with the luncheon. When the silence grew oppressive, he ventured to glance toward her. She was leaning forward, her chin cupped in her palms, staring out over the valley that stretched at their feet.

"Don't speak to me for a minute or two," she said. "I'm thinking over what you have just said."

Manlike, having raised the issue, K. would have given much to evade it. Not that he had owned himself in love with Sidney. Love was not for him. But into his loneliness and despair the girl had came like a ray of light. She typified that youth and hope that he had felt slipping away from him. Through her clear eyes he was beginning to see a new world. Lose her he must, and that he knew; but not this way.

Down through the valley ran a shallow river, making noisy pretensions to both depth and fury. He remembered just such a river in the Tyrol, with this same Wilson on a rock, holding the hand of a pretty Austrian girl, while he snapped the shutter of a camera. He had that picture somewhere now; but the girl was dead, and, of the three, Wilson was the only one who had met life and vanquished it.

"I've known him all my life," Sidney said at last. "You're perfectly right about one thing: I talk about him and I think about him. I'm being candid, because what's the use of being friends if we're not frank? I admire him--you'd have to see him in the hospital, with every one deferring to him and all that, to understand. And when you think of a manlike that, who holds life and death in his hands, of course you rather thrill. I--I honestly believe that's all there is to it."

"If that's the whole thing, that's hardly a mad passion." He tried to smile; succeeded faintly.

"Well, of course, there's this, too. I know he'll never look at me. I'll be one of forty nurses; indeed, for three months I'll be only a probationer. He'll probably never even remember I'm in the hospital at all."

"I see. Then, if you thought he was in love with you, things would be different?"

"If I thought Dr. Max Wilson was in love with me," said Sidney solemnly, "I'd go out of my head with joy."

One of the new qualities that K. Le Moyne was cultivating was of living each day for itself. Having no past and no future, each day was worth exactly what it brought. He was to look back to this day with mingled feelings: sheer gladness at being out in the open with Sidney; the memory of the shock with which he realized that she was, unknown to herself, already in the throes of a romantic attachment for Wilson; and, long, long after, when he had gone down to the depths with her and saved her by his steady hand, with something of mirth for the untoward happening that closed the day.

Sidney fell into the river.

They had released Reginald, released him with the tribute of a shamefaced tear on Sidney's part, and a handful of chestnuts from K. The little squirrel had squeaked his gladness, and, tail erect, had darted into the grass.

"Ungrateful little beast!" said Sidney, and dried her eyes. "Do you suppose he'll ever think of the nuts again, or find them?"

"He'll be all right," K. replied. "The little beggar can take care of himself, if only--"

"If only what?"

"If only he isn't too friendly. He's apt to crawl into the pockets of any one who happens around."

She was alarmed at that. To make up for his indiscretion, K. suggested a descent to the river. She accepted eagerly, and he helped her down. That was another memory that outlasted the day--her small warm hand in his; the time she slipped and he caught her; the pain in her eyes at one of his thoughtless remarks.

"I'm going to be pretty lonely," he said, when she had paused in the descent and was taking a stone out of her low shoe. "Reginald gone, and you going! I shall hate to come home at night." And then, seeing her wince: "I've been whining all day. For Heaven's sake, don't look like that. If there's one sort of man I detest more than another, it's a man who is sorry for himself. Do you suppose your mother would object if we stayed, out here at the hotel for supper? I've ordered a moon, orange-yellow and extra size."

"I should hate to have anything ordered and wasted."

"Then we'll stay."

"It's fearfully extravagant."

"I'll be thrifty as to moons while you are in the hospital."

So it was settled. And, as it happened, Sidney had to stay, anyhow. For, having perched herself out in the river on a sugar-loaf rock, she slid, slowly but with a dreadful inevitability, into the water. K. happened to be looking in another direction. So it occurred that at one moment, Sidney sat on a rock, fluffy white from head to feet, entrancingly pretty, and knowing it, and the next she was standing neck deep in water, much too startled to scream, and trying to be dignified under the rather trying circumstances. K. had not looked around. The splash had been a gentle one.

"If you will be good enough," said Sidney, with her chin well up, "to give me your hand or a pole or something--because if the river rises an inch I shall drown."

To his undying credit, K. Le Moyne did not laugh when he turned and saw her. He went out on the sugar-loaf rock, and lifted her bodily up its slippery sides. He had prodigious strength, in spite of his leanness.

"Well!" said Sidney, when they were both on the rock, carefully balanced.

"Are you cold?"

"Not a bit. But horribly unhappy. I must look a sight." Then, remembering her manners, as the Street had it, she said primly:--

"Thank you for saving me."

"There wasn't any danger, really, unless--unless the river had risen."

And then, suddenly, he burst into delighted laughter, the first, perhaps, for months. He shook with it, struggled at the sight of her injured face to restrain it, achieved finally a degree of sobriety by fixing his eyes on the river-bank.

"When you have quite finished," said Sidney severely, "perhaps you will take me to the hotel. I dare say I shall have to be washed and ironed."

He drew her cautiously to her feet. Her wet skirts clung to her; her shoes were sodden and heavy. She clung to him frantically, her eyes on the river below. With the touch of her hands the man's mirth died. He held her very carefully, very tenderly, as one holds something infinitely precious.

CHAPTER VI

THE same day Dr. Max operated at the hospital. It was a Wilson day, the young surgeon having six cases. One of the innovations Dr. Max had made was to change the hour for major operations from early morning to mid-afternoon. He could do as well later in the day,--his nerves were steady, and uncounted numbers of cigarettes did not make his hand shake,--and he hated to get up early.

The staff had fallen into the way of attending Wilson's operations. His technique was good; but technique alone never gets a surgeon anywhere. Wilson was getting results. Even the most jealous of that most jealous of professions, surgery, had to admit that he got results.

Operations were over for the afternoon. The last case had been wheeled out of the elevator. The pit of the operating-room was in disorder--towels everywhere, tables of instruments, steaming sterilizers. Orderlies were going about, carrying out linens, emptying pans. At a table two nurses were cleaning instruments and putting them away in their glass cases. Irrigators were being emptied, sponges recounted and checked off on written lists.

In the midst of the confusion, Wilson stood giving last orders to the interne at his elbow. As he talked he scoured his hands and arms with a small brush; bits of lather flew off on to the tiled floor. His speech was incisive, vigorous. At the hospital they said his nerves were iron; there was no let-down after the day's work. The internes worshiped and feared him. He was just, but without mercy. To be able to work like that, so certainly, with so sure a touch, and to look like a Greek god! Wilson's only rival, a gynecologist named O'Hara, got results, too; but he sweated and swore through his operations, was not too careful as to asepsis, and looked like a gorilla.

The day had been a hard one. The operating room nurses were fagged. Two or three probationers had been sent to help cleanup, and a senior nurse. Wilson's eyes caught the nurse's eyes as she passed him.

"Here, too, Miss Harrison!" he said gayly. "Have they set you on my trail?"

With the eyes of the room on her, the girl answered primly:--

"I'm to be in your office in the mornings, Dr. Wilson, and anywhere I am needed in the afternoons."

"And your vacation?"

"I shall take it when Miss Simpson comes back."

Although he went on at once with his conversation with the interne, he still heard the click of her heels about the room. He had not lost the fact that she had flushed when he spoke to her. The mischief that was latent in him came to the surface. When he had rinsed his hands, he followed her, carrying the towel to where she stood talking to the superintendent of the training school.

"Thanks very much, Miss Gregg," he said. "Everything went off nicely."

"I was sorry about that catgut. We have no trouble with what we prepare ourselves. But with so many operations--"

He was in a magnanimous mood. He smiled' at Miss Gregg, who was elderly and gray, but visibly his creature.

"That's all right. It's the first time, and of course it will be the last."

"The sponge list, doctor."

He glanced over it, noting accurately sponges prepared, used, turned in. But he missed no gesture of the girl who stood beside Miss Gregg.

"All right." He returned the list. "That was a mighty pretty probationer I brought you yesterday."

Two small frowning lines appeared between Miss Harrison's dark brows. He caught them, caught her somber eyes too, and was amused and rather stimulated.

"She is very young."

"Prefer 'em young," said Dr. Max. "Willing to learn at that age. You'll have to watch her, though. You'll have all the internes buzzing around, neglecting business."

Miss Gregg rather fluttered. She was divided between her disapproval of internes at all times and of young probationers generally, and her allegiance to the brilliant surgeon whose word was rapidly becoming law in the hospital. When an emergency of the cleaning up called her away, doubt still in her eyes, Wilson was left alone with Miss Harrison.

"Tired?" He adopted the gentle, almost tender tone that made most women his slaves.

"A little. It is warm."

"What are you going to do this evening? Any lectures?"

"Lectures are over for the summer. I shall go to prayers, and after that to the roof for air."

There was a note of bitterness in her voice. Under the eyes of the other nurses, she was carefully contained. They might have been outlining the morning's work at his office.

"The hand lotion, please."

She brought it obediently and poured it into his cupped hands. The solutions of the operating-room played havoc with the skin: the surgeons, and especially Wilson, soaked their hands plentifully with a healing lotion.

Over the bottle their eyes met again, and this time the girl smiled faintly.

"Can't you take a little ride to-night and cool off? I'll have the car wherever you say. A ride and some supper--how does it sound? You could get away at seven--"

"Miss Gregg is coming!"

With an impassive face, the girl took the bottle away. The workers of the operating-room surged between them. An interne presented an order-book; moppers had come in and waited to clean the tiled floor. There seemed no chance for Wilson to speak to Miss Harrison again.

But he was clever with the guile of the pursuing male. Eyes of all on him, he turned at the door of the wardrobe-room, where he would exchange his white garments for street clothing, and spoke to her over the heads of a dozen nurses.

"That patient's address that I had forgotten, Miss Harrison, is the corner of the Park and Ellington Avenue."

"Thank you."

She played the game well, was quite calm. He admired her coolness. Certainly she was pretty, and certainly, too, she was interested in him. The hurt to his pride of a few nights before was healed. He went whistling into the wardrobe-room. As he turned he caught the interne's eye, and there passed between them a glance of complete comprehension. The interne grinned.

The room was not empty. His brother was there, listening to the comments of O'Hara, his friendly rival.

"Good work, boy!" said O'Hara, and clapped a hairy hand on his shoulder. "That last case was a wonder. I'm proud of you, and your brother here is indecently exalted. It was the Edwardes method, wasn't it? I saw it done at his clinic in New York."

"Glad you liked it. Yes. Edwardes was a pal at mine in Berlin. A great surgeon, too, poor old chap!"

"There aren't three men in the country with the nerve and the hand for it."

O'Hara went out, glowing with his own magnanimity. Deep in his heart was a gnawing of envy--not for himself, but for his work. These young fellows with no family ties, who could run over to Europe and bring back anything new that was worth while, they had it all over the older men. Not that he would have changed things. God forbid!

Dr. Ed stood by and waited while his brother got into his street clothes. He was rather silent. There were many times when he wished that their mother could have lived to see how he had carried out his promise to "make a man of Max." This was one of them. Not that he took any credit for Max's brilliant career--but he would have liked her to know that things were going well. He had a picture of her over his office desk. Sometimes he wondered what she would think of his own untidy methods compared with Max's extravagant order--of the bag, for instance, with the dog's collar in it, and other things. On these occasions he always determined to clear out the bag.

"I guess I'll be getting along," he said. "Will you be home to dinner?"

"I think not. I'll--I'm going to run out of town, and eat where it's cool."

The Street was notoriously hot in summer. When Dr. Max was newly home from Europe, and Dr. Ed was selling a painfully acquired bond or two to furnish the new offices downtown, the brothers had occasionally gone together, by way of the trolley, to the White Springs Hotel for supper. Those had been gala days for the older man. To hear names that he had read with awe, and mispronounced, most of his life, roll off Max's tongue--"Old Steinmetz" and "that ass of a Heydenreich"; to hear the medical and surgical gossip of the Continent, new drugs, new technique, the small heart-burnings of the clinics, student scandal--had brought into his drab days a touch of color. But that was over now. Max had new friends, new social obligations; his time was taken up. And pride would not allow the older brother to show how he missed the early days.

Forty-two he was, and; what with sleepless nights and twenty years of hurried food, he looked fifty. Fifty, then, to Max's thirty.

"There's a roast of beef. It's a pity to cook a roast for one."

Wasteful, too, this cooking of food for two and only one to eat it. A roast of beef meant a visit, in Dr. Ed's modest-paying clientele. He still paid the expenses of the house on the Street.

"Sorry, old man; I've made another arrangement."

They left the hospital together. Everywhere the younger man received the homage of success. The elevator-man bowed and flung the doors open, with a smile; the pharmacy clerk, the doorkeeper, even the convalescent patient who was polishing the great brass doorplate, tendered their tribute. Dr. Ed looked neither to right nor left.

At the machine they separated. But Dr. Ed stood for a moment with his hand on the car.

"I was thinking, up there this afternoon," he said slowly, "that I'm not sure I want Sidney Page to become a nurse."

"Why?"

"There's a good deal in life that a girl need not know--not, at least, until her husband tells her. Sidney's been guarded, and it's bound to be a shock."

"It's her own choice."

"Exactly. A child reaches out for the fire."

The motor had started. For the moment, at least, the younger Wilson had no interest in Sidney Page.

"She'll manage all right. Plenty of other girls have taken the training and come through without spoiling their zest for life."

Already, as the car moved off, his mind was on his appointment for the evening.

Sidney, after her involuntary bath in the river, had gone into temporary eclipse at the White Springs Hotel. In the oven of the kitchen stove sat her two small white shoes, stuffed with paper so that they might dry in shape. Back in a detached laundry, a sympathetic maid was ironing various soft white garments, and singing as she worked.

Sidney sat in a rocking-chair in a hot bedroom. She was carefully swathed in a sheet from neck to toes, except for her arms, and she was being as philosophic as possible. After all, it was a good chance to think things over. She had very little time to think, generally.

She meant to give up Joe Drummond. She didn't want to hurt him. Well, there was that to think over and a matter of probation dresses to be talked over later with her Aunt Harriet. Also, there was a great deal of advice to K. Le Moyne, who was ridiculously extravagant, before trusting the house to him. She folded her white arms and prepared to think over all these things. As a matter of fact, she went mentally, like an arrow to its mark, to the younger Wilson--to his straight figure in its white coat, to his dark eyes and heavy hair, to the cleft in his chin when he smiled.

"You know, I have always been more than half in love with you myself..."

Some one tapped lightly at the door. She was back again in the stuffy hotel room, clutching the sheet about her.

"Yes?"

"It's Le Moyne. Are you all right?"

"Perfectly. How stupid it must be for you!"

"I'm doing very well. The maid will soon be ready. What shall I order for supper?"

"Anything. I'm starving."

Whatever visions K. Le Moyne may have had of a chill or of a feverish cold were dispelled by that.

"The moon has arrived, as per specifications. Shall we eat on the terrace?"

"I have never eaten on a terrace in my life. I'd love it."

"I think your shoes have shrunk."

"Flatterer!" She laughed. "Go away and order supper. And I can see fresh lettuce. Shall we have a salad?"

K. Le Moyne assured her through the door that he would order a salad, and prepared to descend.

But he stood for a moment in front of the closed door, for the mere sound of her moving, beyond it. Things had gone very far with the Pages' roomer that day in the country; not so far as they were to go, but far enough to let him see on the brink of what misery he stood.

He could not go away. He had promised her to stay: he was needed. He thought he could have endured seeing her marry Joe, had she cared for the boy. That way, at least, lay safety for her. The boy had fidelity and devotion written large over him. But this new complication--her romantic interest in Wilson, the surgeon's reciprocal interest in her, with what he knew of the man--made him quail.

From the top of the narrow staircase to the foot, and he had lived a year's torment! At the foot, however, he was startled out of his reverie. Joe Drummond stood there waiting for him, his blue eyes recklessly alight.

"You--you dog!" said Joe.

There were people in the hotel parlor. Le Moyne took the frenzied boy by the elbow and led him past the door to the empty porch.

"Now," he said, "if you will keep your voice down, I'll listen to what you have to say."

"You know what I've got to say."

This failing to draw from K. Le Moyne anything but his steady glance, Joe jerked his arm free, and clenched his fist.

"What did you bring her out here for?"

"I do not know that I owe you any explanation, but I am willing to give you one. I brought her out here for a trolley ride and a picnic luncheon. Incidentally we brought the ground squirrel out and set him free."

He was sorry for the boy. Life not having been all beer and skittles to him, he knew that Joe was suffering, and was marvelously patient with him.

"Where is she now?"

"She had the misfortune to fall in the river. She is upstairs." And, seeing the light of unbelief in Joe's eyes: "If you care to make a tour of investigation, you will find that I am entirely truthful. In the laundry a maid--"

"She is engaged to me"--doggedly. "Everybody in the neighborhood knows it; and yet you bring her out here for a picnic! It's--it's damned rotten treatment."

His fist had unclenched. Before K. Le Moyne's eyes his own fell. He felt suddenly young and futile; his just rage turned to blustering in his ears.

"Now, be honest with yourself. Is there really an engagement?"

"Yes," doggedly.

"Even in that case, isn't it rather arrogant to say that--that the young lady in question can accept no ordinary friendly attentions from another man?"

Utter astonishment left Joe almost speechless. The Street, of course, regarded an engagement as a setting aside of the affianced couple, an isolation of two, than which marriage itself was not more a solitude a deux. After a moment:--

"I don't know where you came from," he said, "but around here decent men cut out when a girl's engaged."

"I see!"

"What's more, what do we know about you? Who are you, anyhow? I've looked you up. Even at your office they don't know anything. You may be all right, but how do I know it? And, even if you are, renting a room in the Page house doesn't entitle you to interfere with the family. You get her into trouble and I'll kill you!"

It took courage, that speech, with K. Le Moyne towering five inches above him and growing a little white about the lips.

"Are you going to say all these things to Sidney?"

"Does she allow you to call her Sidney?"

"Are you?"

"I am. And I am going to find out why you were upstairs just now."

Perhaps never in his twenty-two years had young Drummond been so near a thrashing. Fury that he was ashamed of shook Le Moyne. For very fear of himself, he thrust his hands in the pockets of his Norfolk coat.

"Very well," he said. "You go to her with just one of these ugly insinuations, and I'll take mighty good care that you are sorry for it. I don't care to threaten. You're younger than I am, and lighter. But if you are going to behave like a bad child, you deserve a licking, and I'll give it to you."

An overflow from the parlor poured out on the porch. Le Moyne had got himself in hand somewhat. He was still angry, but the look in Joe's eyes startled him. He put a hand on the boy's shoulder.

"You're wrong, old man," he said. "You're insulting the girl you care for by the things you are thinking. And, if it's any comfort to you, I have no intention of interfering in any way. You can count me out. It's between you and her." Joe picked his straw hat from a chair and stood turning it in his hands.

"Even if you don't care for her, how do I know she isn't crazy about you?"

"My word of honor, she isn't."

"She sends you notes to McKees'."

"Just to clear the air, I'll show it to you. It's no breach of confidence. It's about the hospital."

Into the breast pocket of his coat he dived and brought up a wallet. The wallet had had a name on it in gilt letters that had been carefully scraped off. But Joe did not wait to see the note.

"Oh, damn the hospital!" he said--and went swiftly down the steps and into the gathering twilight of the June night.

It was only when he reached the street-car, and sat huddled in a corner, that he remembered something.

Only about the hospital--but Le Moyne had kept the note, treasured it! Joe was not subtle, not even clever; but he was a lover, and he knew the ways of love. The Pages' roomer was in love with Sidney whether he knew it or not.

CHAPTER VII

CARLOTTA Harrison pleaded a headache, and was excused from the operating-room and from prayers.

"I'm sorry about the vacation," Miss Gregg said kindly, "but in a day or two I can let you off. Go out now and get a little air."

The girl managed to dissemble the triumph in her eyes.

"Thank you," she said languidly, and turned away. Then: "About the vacation, I am not in a hurry. If Miss Simpson needs a few days to straighten things out, I can stay on with Dr. Wilson."

Young women on the eve of a vacation were not usually so reasonable. Miss Gregg was grateful.

"She will probably need a week. Thank you. I wish more of the girls were as thoughtful, with the house full and operations all day and every day."

Outside the door of the anaesthetizing-room Miss Harrison's languor vanished. She sped along corridors and up the stairs, not waiting for the deliberate elevator. Inside of her room, she closed and bolted the door, and, standing before her mirror, gazed long at her dark eyes and bright hair. Then she proceeded briskly with her dressing.

Carlotta Harrison was not a child. Though she was only three years older than Sidney, her experience of life was as of three to Sidney's one. The product of a curious marriage,--when Tommy Harrison of Harrison's Minstrels, touring Spain with his troupe, had met the pretty daughter of a Spanish shopkeeper and eloped with her,--she had certain qualities of both, a Yankee shrewdness and capacity that made her a capable nurse, complicated by occasional outcroppings of southern Europe, furious bursts of temper, slow and smouldering vindictiveness. A passionate creature, in reality, smothered under hereditary Massachusetts caution.

She was well aware of the risks of the evening's adventure. The only dread she had was of the discovery of her escapade by the hospital authorities. Lines were sharply drawn. Nurses were forbidden more than the exchange of professional conversation with the staff. In that world of her choosing, of hard work and little play, of service and self-denial and vigorous rules of conduct, discovery meant dismissal.

She put on a soft black dress, open at the throat, and with a wide white collar and cuffs of some sheer material. Her yellow hair was drawn high under her low black hat. From her Spanish mother she had learned to please the man, not herself. She guessed that Dr. Max would wish her to be inconspicuous, and she dressed accordingly. Then, being a cautious person, she disarranged her bed slightly and thumped a hollow into her pillow. The nurses' rooms were subject to inspection, and she had pleaded a headache.

She was exactly on time. Dr. Max, driving up to the corner five minutes late, found her there, quite matter-of-fact but exceedingly handsome, and acknowledged the evening's adventure much to his taste.

"A little air first, and then supper--how's that?"

"Air first, please. I'm very tired."

He turned the car toward the suburbs, and then, bending toward her, smiled into her eyes.

"Well, this is life!"

"I'm cool for the first time to-day."

After that they spoke very little. Even Wilson's superb nerves had felt the strain of the afternoon, and under the girl's dark eyes were purplish shadows. She leaned back, weary but luxuriously content.

"Not uneasy, are you?"

"Not particularly. I'm too comfortable. But I hope we're not seen."

"Even if we are, why not? You are going with me to a case. I've driven Miss Simpson about a lot."

It was almost eight when he turned the car into the drive of the White Springs Hotel. The six-to-eight supper was almost over. One or two motor parties were preparing for the moonlight drive back to the city. All around was virgin country, sweet with early summer odors of new-cut grass, of blossoming trees and warm earth. On the grass terrace over the valley, where ran Sidney's unlucky river, was a magnolia full of creamy blossoms among waxed leaves. Its silhouette against the sky was quaintly heart-shaped.

Under her mask of languor, Carlotta's heart was beating wildly. What an adventure! What a night! Let him lose his head a little; she could keep hers. If she were skillful and played things right, who could tell? To marry him, to leave behind the drudgery of the hospital, to feel safe as she had not felt for years, that was a stroke to play for!

The magnolia was just beside her. She reached up and, breaking off one of the heavy-scented flowers, placed it in the bosom of her black dress.

Sidney and K. Le Moyne were dining together. The novelty of the experience had made her eyes shine like stars. She saw only the magnolia tree shaped like a heart, the terrace edged with low shrubbery, and beyond the faint gleam that was the river. For her the dish-washing clatter of the kitchen was stilled, the noises from the bar were lost in the ripple of the river; the scent of the grass killed the odor of stale beer that wafted out through the open windows. The unshaded glare of the lights behind her in the house was eclipsed by the crescent edge of the rising moon. Dinner was over. Sidney was experiencing the rare treat of after-dinner coffee.

Le Moyne, grave and contained, sat across from her. To give so much pleasure, and so easily! How young she was, and radiant! No wonder the boy was mad about her. She fairly held out her arms to life.

Ah, that was too bad! Another table was being brought; they were not to be alone. But, what roused him in violent resentment only appealed to Sidney's curiosity. "Two places!" she commented. "Lovers, of course. Or perhaps honeymooners."

K. tried to fall into her mood.

"A box of candy against a good cigar, they are a stolid married couple."

"How shall we know?"

"That's easy. If they loll back and watch the kitchen door, I win. If they lean forward, elbows on the table, and talk, you get the candy."

Sidney, who had been leaning forward, talking eagerly over the table, suddenly straightened and flushed.

Carlotta Harrison came out alone. Although the tapping of her heels was dulled by the grass, although she had exchanged her cap for the black hat, Sidney knew her at once. A sort of thrill ran over her. It was the pretty nurse from Dr. Wilson's office. Was it possible--but of course not! The book of rules stated explicitly that such things were forbidden.

"Don't turn around," she said swiftly. "It is the Miss Harrison I told you about. She is looking at us."

Carlotta's eyes were blinded for a moment by the glare of the house lights. She dropped into her chair, with a flash of resentment at the proximity of the other table. She languidly surveyed its two occupants. Then she sat up, her eyes on Le Moyne's grave profile turned toward the valley.

Lucky for her that Wilson had stopped in the bar, that Sidney's instinctive good manners forbade her staring, that only the edge of the summer moon shone through the trees. She went white and clutched the edge of the table, with her eyes closed. That gave her quick brain a chance. It was madness, June madness. She was always seeing him even in her dreams. This man was older, much older. She looked again.

She had not been mistaken. Here, and after all these months! K. Le Moyne, quite unconscious of her presence, looked down into the valley.

Wilson appeared on the wooden porch above the terrace, and stood, his eyes searching the half light for her. If he came down to her, the man at the next table might turn, would see her--

She rose and went swiftly back toward the hotel. All the gayety was gone out of the evening for her, but she forced a lightness she did not feel:--

"It is so dark and depressing out there--it makes me sad."

"Surely you do not want to dine in the house?"

"Do you mind?"

"Just as you wish. This is your evening."

But he was not pleased. The prospect of the glaring lights and soiled linen of the dining-room jarred on his aesthetic sense. He wanted a setting for himself, for the girl. Environment was vital to him. But when, in the full light of the moon, he saw the purplish shadows under her eyes, he forgot his resentment. She had had a hard day. She was tired. His easy sympathies were roused. He leaned over and ran his and caressingly along her bare forearm.

"Your wish is my law--to-night," he said softly.

After all, the evening was a disappointment to him. The spontaneity had gone out of it, for some reason. The girl who had thrilled to his glance those two mornings in his office, whose somber eyes had met his fire for fire, across the operating-room, was not playing up. She sat back in her chair, eating little, starting at every step. Her eyes, which by every rule of the game should have been gazing into his, were fixed on the oilcloth-covered passage outside the door.

"I think, after all, you are frightened!"

"Terribly."

"A little danger adds to the zest of things. You know what Nietzsche says about that."

"I am not fond of Nietzsche." Then, with an effort: "What does he say?"

"Two things are wanted by the true man--danger and play. Therefore he seeketh woman as the most dangerous of toys."

"Women are dangerous only when you think of them as toys. When a man finds that a woman can reason,--do anything but feel,--he regards her as a menace. But the reasoning woman is really less dangerous than the other sort."

This was more like the real thing. To talk careful abstractions like this, with beneath each abstraction its concealed personal application, to talk of woman and look in her eyes, to discuss new philosophies with their freedoms, to discard old creeds and old moralities--that was his game. Wilson became content, interested again. The girl was nimble-minded. She challenged his philosophy and gave him a chance to defend it. With the conviction, as their meal went on, that Le Moyne and his companion must surely have gone, she gained ease.

It was only by wild driving that she got back to the hospital by ten o'clock.

Wilson left her at the corner, well content with himself. He had had the rest he needed in congenial company. The girl stimulated his interest. She was mental, but not too mental. And he approved of his own attitude. He had been discreet. Even if she talked, there was nothing to tell. But he felt confident that she would not talk.

As he drove up the Street, he glanced across at the Page house. Sidney was there on the doorstep, talking to a tall man who stood below and looked up at her. Wilson settled his tie, in the darkness. Sidney was a mighty pretty girl. The June night was in his blood. He was sorry he had not kissed Carlotta good-night. He rather thought, now he looked back, she had expected it.

As he got out of his car at the curb, a young man who had been standing in the shadow of the tree-box moved quickly away.

Wilson smiled after him in the darkness.

"That you, Joe?" he called.

But the boy went on.

CHAPTER VIII

SIDNEY entered the hospital as a probationer early in August. Christine was to be married in September to Palmer Howe, and, with Harriet and K. in the house, she felt that she could safely leave her mother.

The balcony outside the parlor was already under way. On the night before she went away, Sidney took chairs out there and sat with her mother until the dew drove Anna to the lamp in the sewing-room and her "Daily Thoughts" reading.

Sidney sat alone and viewed her world from this new and pleasant angle. She could see the garden and the whitewashed fence with its morning-glories, and at the same time, by turning her head, view the Wilson house across the Street. She looked mostly at the Wilson house.

K. Le Moyne was upstairs in his room. She could hear him tramping up and down, and catch, occasionally, the bitter-sweet odor of his old brier pipe.

All the small loose ends of her life were gathered up--except Joe. She would have liked to get that clear, too. She wanted him to know how she felt about it all: that she liked him as much as ever, that she did not want to hurt him. But she wanted to make it clear, too, that she knew now that she would never marry him. She thought she would never marry; but, if she did, it would be a man doing a man's work in the world. Her eyes turned wistfully to the house across the Street.

K.'s lamp still burned overhead, but his restless tramping about had ceased. He must be reading--he read a great deal. She really ought to go to bed. A neighborhood cat came stealthily across the Street, and stared up at the little balcony with green-glowing eyes.

"Come on, Bill Taft," she said. "Reginald is gone, so you are welcome. Come on."

Joe Drummond, passing the house for the fourth time that evening, heard her voice, and hesitated uncertainly on the pavement.

"That you, Sid?" he called softly.

"Joe! Come in."

"It's late; I'd better get home."

The misery in his voice hurt her.

"I'll not keep you long. I want to talk to you."

He came slowly toward her.

"Well?" he said hoarsely.

"You're not very kind to me, Joe."

"My God!" said poor Joe. "Kind to you! Isn't the kindest thing I can do to keep out of your way?"

"Not if you are hating me all the time."

"I don't hate you."

"Then why haven't you been to see me? If I have done anything--" Her voice was a-tingle with virtue and outraged friendship.

"You haven't done anything but--show me where I get off."

He sat down on the edge of the balcony and stared out blankly.

"If that's the way you feel about it--"

"I'm not blaming you. I was a fool to think you'd ever care about me. I don't know that I feel so bad--about the thing. I've been around seeing some other girls, and I notice they're glad to see me, and treat me right, too." There was boyish bravado in his voice. "But what makes me sick is to have everyone saying you've jilted me."

"Good gracious! Why, Joe, I never promised."

"Well, we look at it in different ways; that's all. I took it for a promise."

Then suddenly all his carefully conserved indifference fled. He bent forward quickly and, catching her hand, held it against his lips.

"I'm crazy about you, Sidney. That's the truth. I wish I could die!"

The cat, finding no active antagonism, sprang up on the balcony and rubbed against the boy's quivering shoulders; a breath of air stroked the morning-glory vine like the touch of a friendly hand. Sidney, facing for the first time the enigma of love and despair sat, rather frightened, in her chair.

"You don't mean that!"

"I mean it, all right. If it wasn't for the folks, I'd jump in the river. I lied when I said I'd been to see other girls. What do I want with other girls? I want you!"

"I'm not worth all that."

"No girl's worth what I've been going through," he retorted bitterly. "But that doesn't help any. I don't eat; I don't sleep--I'm afraid sometimes of the way I feel. When I saw you at the White Springs with that roomer chap--"

"Ah! You were there!"

"If I'd had a gun I'd have killed him. I thought--" So far, out of sheer pity, she had left her hand in his. Now she drew it away.

"This is wild, silly talk. You'll be sorry to-morrow."

"It's the truth," doggedly.

But he made a clutch at his self-respect. He was acting like a crazy boy, and he was a man, all of twenty-two!

"When are you going to the hospital?"

"To-morrow."

"Is that Wilson's hospital?"

"Yes."

Alas for his resolve! The red haze of jealousy came again. "You'll be seeing him every day, I suppose."

"I dare say. I shall also be seeing twenty or thirty other doctors, and a hundred or so men patients, not to mention visitors. Joe, you're not rational."

"No," he said heavily, "I'm not. If it's got to be someone, Sidney, I'd rather have it the roomer upstairs than Wilson. There's a lot of talk about Wilson."

"It isn't necessary to malign my friends." He rose.

"I thought perhaps, since you are going away, you would let me keep Reginald. He'd be something to remember you by."

"One would think I was about to die! I set Reginald free that day in the country. I'm sorry, Joe. You'll come to see me now and then, won't you?"

"If I do, do you think you may change your mind?"

"I'm afraid not."

"I've got to fight this out alone, and the less I see of you the better." But his next words belied his intention. "And Wilson had better lookout. I'll be watching. If I see him playing any of his tricks around you--well, he'd better look out!"

That, as it turned out, was Joe's farewell. He had reached the breaking-point. He gave her a long look, blinked, and walked rapidly out to the Street. Some of the dignity of his retreat was lost by the fact that the cat followed him, close at his heels.

Sidney was hurt, greatly troubled. If this was love, she did not want it--this strange compound of suspicion and despair, injured pride and threats. Lovers in fiction were of two classes--the accepted ones, who loved and trusted, and the rejected ones, who took themselves away in despair, but at least took themselves away. The thought of a future with Joe always around a corner, watching her, obsessed her. She felt aggrieved, insulted. She even shed a tear or two, very surreptitiously; and then, being human and much upset, and the cat startling her by its sudden return and selfish advances, she shooed it off the veranda and set an imaginary dog after it. Whereupon, feeling somewhat better, she went in and locked the balcony window and proceeded upstairs.

Le Moyne's light was still going. The rest of the household slept. She paused outside the door.

"Are you sleepy?"--very softly.

There was a movement inside, the sound of a book put down. Then: "No, indeed."

"I may not see you in the morning. I leave to-morrow."

"Just a minute."

From the sounds, she judged that he was putting on his shabby gray coat. The next moment he had opened the door and stepped out into the corridor.

"I believe you had forgotten!"

"I? Certainly not. I started downstairs a while ago, but you had a visitor."

"Only Joe Drummond."

He gazed down at her quizzically.

"And--is Joe more reasonable?"

"He will be. He knows now that I--that I shall not marry him."

"Poor chap! He'll buck up, of course. But it's a little hard just now."

"I believe you think I should have married him."

"I am only putting myself in his place and realizing--When do you leave?"

"Just after breakfast."

"I am going very early. Perhaps--"

He hesitated. Then, hurriedly:--

"I got a little present for you--nothing much, but your mother was quite willing. In fact, we bought it together."

He went back into his room, and returned with a small box.

"With all sorts of good luck," he said, and placed it in her hands.

"How dear of you! And may I look now?"

"I wish you would. Because, if you would rather have something else--"

She opened the box with excited fingers. Ticking away on its satin bed was a small gold watch.

"You'll need it, you see," he explained nervously, "It wasn't extravagant under the circumstances. Your mother's watch, which you had intended to take, had no second-hand. You'll need a second-hand to take pulses, you know."

"A watch," said Sidney, eyes on it. "A dear little watch, to pin on and not put in a pocket. Why, you're the best person!"

"I was afraid you might think it presumptuous," he said. "I haven't any right, of course. I thought of flowers--but they fade and what have you? You said that, you know, about Joe's roses. And then, your mother said you wouldn't be offended--"

"Don't apologize for making me so happy!" she cried. "It's wonderful, really. And the little hand is for pulses! How many queer things you know!"

After that she must pin it on, and slip in to stand before his mirror and inspect the result. It gave Le Moyne a queer thrill to see her there in the room among his books and his pipes. It make him a little sick, too, in view of to-morrow and the thousand-odd to-morrows when she would not be there.

"I've kept you up shamefully,'" she said at last, "and you get up so early. I shall write you a note from the hospital, delivering a little lecture on extravagance--because how can I now, with this joy shining on me? And about how to keep Katie in order about your socks, and all sorts of things. And--and now, good-night."

She had moved to the door, and he followed her, stooping a little to pass under the low chandelier.

"Good-night," said Sidney.

"Good-bye--and God bless you."

She went out, and he closed the door softly behind her.

CHAPTER IX

SIDNEY never forgot her early impressions of the hospital, although they were chaotic enough at first. There were uniformed young women coming and going, efficient, cool-eyed, low of voice. There were medicine-closets with orderly rows of labeled bottles, linen-rooms with great stacks of sheets and towels, long vistas of shining floors and lines of beds. There were brisk internes with duck clothes and brass buttons, who eyed her with friendly, patronizing glances. There were bandages and dressings, and great white screens behind which were played little or big dramas, baths or deaths, as the case might be. And over all brooded the mysterious authority of the superintendent of the training-school, dubbed the Head, for short.

Twelve hours a day, from seven to seven, with the off-duty intermission, Sidney labored at tasks which revolted her soul. She swept and dusted the wards, cleaned closets, folded sheets and towels, rolled bandages--did everything but nurse the sick, which was what she had come to do.

At night she did not go home. She sat on the edge of her narrow white bed and soaked her aching feet in hot water and witch hazel, and practiced taking pulses on her own slender wrist, with K.'s little watch.

Out of all the long, hot days, two periods stood out clearly, to be waited for and cherished. One was when, early in the afternoon, with the ward in spotless order, the shades drawn against the August sun, the tables covered with their red covers, and the only sound the drone of the bandage-machine as Sidney steadily turned it, Dr. Max passed the door on his way to the surgical ward beyond, and gave her a cheery greeting. At these times Sidney's heart beat almost in time with the ticking of the little watch.

The other hour was at twilight, when, work over for the day, the night nurse, with her rubber-soled shoes and tired eyes and jangling keys, having reported and received the night orders, the nurses gathered in their small parlor for prayers. It was months before Sidney got over the exaltation of that twilight hour, and never did it cease to bring her healing and peace. In a way, it crystallized for her what the day's work meant: charity and its sister, service, the promise of rest and peace. Into the little parlor filed the nurses, and knelt, folding their tired hands.

"The Lord is my shepherd," read the Head out of her worn Bible; "I shall not want."

And the nurses: "He maketh me to lie down in green pastures: he leadeth me beside the still waters."

And so on through the psalm to the assurance at the end, "And I will dwell in the house of the Lord forever." Now and then there was a death behind one of the white screens. It caused little change in the routine of the ward. A nurse stayed behind the screen, and her work was done by the others. When everything was over, the time was recorded exactly on the record, and the body was taken away.

At first it seemed to Sidney that she could not stand this nearness to death. She thought the nurses hard because they took it quietly. Then she found that it was only stoicism, resignation, that they had learned. These things must be, and the work must go on. Their philosophy made them no less tender. Some such patient detachment must be that of the angels who keep the Great Record.

On her first Sunday half-holiday she was free in the morning, and went to church with her mother, going back to the hospital after the service. So it was two weeks before she saw Le Moyne again. Even then, it was only for a short time. Christine and Palmer Howe came in to see her, and to inspect the balcony, now finished.

But Sidney and Le Moyne had a few words together first.

There was a change in Sidney. Le Moyne was quick to see it. She was a trifle subdued, with a puzzled look in her blue eyes. Her mouth was tender, as always, but he thought it drooped. There was a new atmosphere of wistfulness about the girl that made his heart ache.

They were alone in the little parlor with its brown lamp and blue silk shade, and its small nude Eve--which Anna kept because it had been a gift from her husband, but retired behind a photograph of the minister, so that only the head and a bare arm holding the apple appeared above the reverend gentleman.

K. never smoked in the parlor, but by sheer force of habit he held the pipe in his teeth.

"And how have things been going?" asked Sidney practically.

"Your steward has little to report. Aunt Harriet, who left you her love, has had the complete order for the Lorenz trousseau. She and I have picked out a stunning design for the wedding dress. I thought I'd ask you about the veil. We're rather in a quandary. Do you like this new fashion of draping the veil from behind the coiffure in the back--"

Sidney had been sitting on the edge of her chair, staring.

"There," she said--"I knew it! This house is fatal! They're making an old woman of you already." Her tone was tragic.

"Miss Lorenz likes the new method, but my personal preference is for the old way, with the bride's face covered."

He sucked calmly at his dead pipe.

"Katie has a new prescription--recipe--for bread. It has more bread and fewer air-holes. One cake of yeast--"

Sidney sprang to her feet.

"It's perfectly terrible!" she cried. "Because you rent a room in this house is no reason why you should give up your personality and your--intelligence. Not but that it's good for you. But Katie has made bread without masculine assistance for a good many years, and if Christine can't decide about her own veil she'd better not get married. Mother says you water the flowers every evening, and lock up the house before you go to bed. I--I never meant you to adopt the family!"

K. removed his pipe and gazed earnestly into the bowl.

"Bill Taft has had kittens under the porch," he said. "And the groceryman has been sending short weight. We've bought scales now, and weigh everything."

"You are evading the question."

"Dear child, I am doing these things because I like to do them. For--for some time I've been floating, and now I've got a home. Every time I lock up the windows at night, or cut a picture out of a magazine as a suggestion to your Aunt Harriet, it's an anchor to windward."

Sidney gazed helplessly at his imperturbable face. He seemed older than she had recalled him: the hair over his ears was almost white. And yet, he was just thirty. That was Palmer Howe's age, and Palmer seemed like a boy. But he held himself more erect than he had in the first days of his occupancy of the second-floor front.

"And now," he said cheerfully, "what about yourself? You've lost a lot of illusions, of course, but perhaps you've gained ideals. That's a step."

"Life," observed Sidney, with the wisdom of two weeks out in the world, "life is a terrible thing, K. We think we've got it, and--it's got us."

"Undoubtedly."

"When I think of how simple I used to think it all was! One grew up and got married, and--and perhaps had children. And when one got very old, one died. Lately, I've been seeing that life really consists of exceptions--children who don't grow up, and grown-ups who die before they are old. And"--this took an effort, but she looked at him squarely--"and people who have children, but are not married. It all rather hurts."

"All knowledge that is worth while hurts in the getting."

Sidney got up and wandered around the room, touching its little familiar objects with tender hands. K. watched her. There was this curious element in his love for her, that when he was with her it took on the guise of friendship and deceived even himself. It was only in the lonely hours that it took on truth, became a hopeless yearning for the touch of her hand or a glance from her clear eyes.

Sidney, having picked up the minister's picture, replaced it absently, so that Eve stood revealed in all her pre-apple innocence.

"There is something else," she said absently. "I cannot talk it over with mother. There is a girl in the ward--"

"A patient?"

"Yes. She is quite pretty. She has had typhoid, but she is a little better. She's--not a good person."

"I see."

"At first I couldn't bear to go near her. I shivered when I had to straighten her bed. I--I'm being very frank, but I've got to talk this out with someone. I worried a lot about it, because, although at first I hated her, now I don't. I rather like her."

She looked at K. defiantly, but there was no disapproval in his eyes.

"Yes."

"Well, this is the question. She's getting better. She'll be able to go out soon. Don't you think something ought to be done to keep her from--going back?"

There was a shadow in K.'s eyes now. She was so young to face all this; and yet, since face it she must, how much better to have her do it squarely.

"Does she want to change her mode of life?"

"I don't know, of course. There are some things one doesn't discuss. She cares a great deal for some man. The other day I propped her up in bed and gave her a newspaper, and after a while I found the paper on the floor, and she was crying. The other patients avoid her, and it was some time before I noticed it. The next day she told me that the man was going to marry some one else. 'He wouldn't marry me, of course,' she said; 'but he might have told me.'"

Le Moyne did his best, that afternoon in the little parlor, to provide Sidney with a philosophy to carry her through her training. He told her that certain responsibilities were hers, but that she could not reform the world. Broad charity, tenderness, and healing were her province.

"Help them all you can," he finished, feeling inadequate and hopelessly didactic. "Cure them; send them out with a smile; and--leave the rest to the Almighty."

Sidney was resigned, but not content. Newly facing the evil of the world, she was a rampant reformer at once. Only the arrival of Christine and her fiance saved his philosophy from complete rout. He had time for a question between the ring of the bell and Katie's deliberate progress from the kitchen to the front door.

"How about the surgeon, young Wilson? Do you ever see him?" His tone was carefully casual.

"Almost every day. He stops at the door of the ward and speaks to me. It makes me quite distinguished, for a probationer. Usually, you know, the staff never even see the probationers."

"And--the glamour persists?" He smiled down at her.

"I think he is very wonderful," said Sidney valiantly.

Christine Lorenz, while not large, seemed to fill the little room. Her voice, which was frequent and penetrating, her smile, which was wide and showed very white teeth that were a trifle large for beauty, her all-embracing good nature, dominated the entire lower floor. K., who had met her before, retired into silence and a corner. Young Howe smoked a cigarette in the hall.

"You poor thing!" said Christine, and put her cheek against Sidney's. "Why, you're positively thin! Palmer gives you a month to tire of it all; but I said--"

"I take that back," Palmer spoke indolently from the corridor. "There is the look of willing martyrdom in her face. Where is Reginald? I've brought some nuts for him."

"Reginald is back in the woods again."

"Now, look here," he said solemnly. "When we arranged about these rooms, there were certain properties that went with them--the lady next door who plays Paderewski's 'Minuet' six hours a day, and K. here, and Reginald. If you must take something to the woods, why not the minuet person?"

Howe was a good-looking man, thin, smooth-shaven, aggressively well dressed. This Sunday afternoon, in a cutaway coat and high hat, with an English malacca stick, he was just a little out of the picture. The Street said that he was "wild," and that to get into the Country Club set Christine was losing more than she was gaining.

Christine had stepped out on the balcony, and was speaking to K. just inside.

"It's rather a queer way to live, of course," she said. "But Palmer is a pauper, practically. We are going to take our meals at home for a while. You see, certain things that we want we can't have if we take a house--a car, for instance. We'll need one for running out to the Country Club to dinner. Of course, unless father gives me one for a wedding present, it will be a cheap one. And we're getting the Rosenfeld boy to drive it. He's crazy about machinery, and he'll come for practically nothing."

K. had never known a married couple to take two rooms and go to the bride's mother's for meals in order to keep a car. He looked faintly dazed. Also, certain sophistries of his former world about a cheap chauffeur being costly in the end rose in his mind and were carefully suppressed.

"You'll find a car a great comfort, I'm sure," he said politely.

Christine considered K. rather distinguished. She liked his graying hair and steady eyes, and insisted on considering his shabbiness a pose. She was conscious that she made a pretty picture in the French window, and preened herself like a bright bird.

"You'll come out with us now and then, I hope."

"Thank you."

"Isn't it odd to think that we are going to be practically one family!"

"Odd, but very pleasant."

He caught the flash of Christine's smile, and smiled back. Christine was glad she had decided to take the rooms, glad that K. lived there. This thing of marriage being the end of all things was absurd. A married woman should have men friends; they kept her up. She would take him to the Country Club. The women would be mad to know him. How clean-cut his profile was!

Across the Street, the Rosenfeld boy had stopped by Dr. Wilson's car, and was eyeing it with the cool, appraising glance of the street boy whose sole knowledge of machinery has been acquired from the clothes-washer at home. Joe Drummond, eyes carefully ahead, went up the Street. Tillie, at Mrs. McKee's, stood in the doorway and fanned herself with her apron. Max Wilson came out of the house and got into his car. For a minute, perhaps, all the actors, save Carlotta and Dr. Ed, were on the stage. It was that bete noir of the playwright, an ensemble; K. Le Moyne and Sidney, Palmer Howe, Christine, Tillie, the younger Wilson, Joe, even young Rosenfeld, all within speaking distance, almost touching distance, gathered within and about the little house on a side street which K. at first grimly and now tenderly called "home."

CHAPTER X

ON Monday morning, shortly after the McKee prolonged breakfast was over, a small man of perhaps fifty, with iron-gray hair and a sparse goatee, made his way along the Street. He moved with the air of one having a definite destination but a by no means definite reception.

As he walked along he eyed with a professional glance the ailanthus and maple trees which, with an occasional poplar, lined the Street. At the door of Mrs. McKee's boarding-house he stopped. Owing to a slight change in the grade of the street, the McKee house had no stoop, but one flat doorstep. Thus it was possible to ring the doorbell from the pavement, and this the stranger did. It gave him a curious appearance of being ready to cut and run if things were unfavorable.

For a moment things were indeed unfavorable. Mrs. McKee herself opened the door. She recognized him at once, but no smile met the nervous one that formed itself on the stranger's face.

"Oh, it's you, is it?"

"It's me, Mrs. McKee."

"Well?"

He made a conciliatory effort.

"I was thinking, as I came along," he said, "that you and the neighbors had better get after these here caterpillars. Look at them maples, now."

"If you want to see Tillie, she's busy."

"I only want to say how-d 'ye-do. I'm just on my way through town."

"I'll say it for you."

A certain doggedness took the place of his tentative smile.

"I'll say it to myself, I guess. I don't want any unpleasantness, but I've come a good ways to see her and I'll hang around until I do."

Mrs. McKee knew herself routed, and retreated to the kitchen.

"You're wanted out front," she said.

"Who is it?"

"Never mind. Only, my advice to you is, don't be a fool."

Tillie went suddenly pale. The hands with which she tied a white apron over her gingham one were shaking.

Her visitor had accepted the open door as permission to enter and was standing in the hall.

He went rather white himself when he saw Tillie coming toward him down the hall. He knew that for Tillie this visit would mean that he was free--and he was not free. Sheer terror of his errand filled him.

"Well, here I am, Tillie."

"All dressed up and highly perfumed!" said poor Tillie, with the question in her eyes. "You're quite a stranger, Mr. Schwitter."

"I was passing through, and I just thought I'd call around and tell you--My God, Tillie, I'm glad to see you!"

She made no reply, but opened the door into the cool and, shaded little parlor. He followed her in and closed the door behind him.

"I couldn't help it. I know I promised."

"Then she--?"

"She's still living. Playing with paper dolls--that's the latest."

Tillie sat down suddenly on one of the stiff chairs. Her lips were as white as her face.

"I thought, when I saw you--"

"I was afraid you'd think that."

Neither spoke for a moment. Tillie's hands twisted nervously in her lap. Mr. Schwitter's eyes were fixed on the window, which looked back on the McKee yard.

"That spiraea back there's not looking very good. If you'll save the cigar butts around here and put them in water, and spray it, you'll kill the lice."

Tillie found speech at last.

"I don't know why you come around bothering me," she said dully. "I've been getting along all right; now you come and upset everything."

Mr. Schwitter rose and took a step toward her.

"Well, I'll tell you why I came. Look at me. I ain't getting any younger, am I? Time's going on, and I'm wanting you all the time. And what am I getting? What've I got out of life, anyhow? I'm lonely, Tillie!"

"What's that got to do with me?"

"You're lonely, too, ain't you?"

"Me? I haven't got time to be. And, anyhow, there's always a crowd here."

"You can be lonely in a crowd, and I guess--is there any one around here you like better than me?"

"Oh, what's the use!" cried poor Tillie. "We can talk our heads off and not get anywhere. You've got a wife living, and, unless you intend to do away with her, I guess that's all there is to it."

"Is that all, Tillie? Haven't you got a right to be happy?"

She was quick of wit, and she read his tone as well as his words.

"You get out of here--and get out quick!"

She had jumped to her feet; but he only looked at her with understanding eyes.

"I know," he said. "That's the way I thought of it at first. Maybe I've just got used to the idea, but it doesn't seem so bad to me now. Here are you, drudging for other people when you ought to have a place all your own--and not gettin' younger any more than I am. Here's both of us lonely. I'd be a good husband to you, Till--because, whatever it'd be in law, I'd be your husband before God."

Tillie cowered against the door, her eyes on his. Here before her, embodied in this man, stood all that she had wanted and never had. He meant a home, tenderness, children, perhaps. He turned away from the look in her eyes and stared out of the front window.

"Them poplars out there ought to be taken away," he said heavily. "They're hell on sewers."

Tillie found her voice at last:--

"I couldn't do it, Mr. Schwitter. I guess I'm a coward. Maybe I'll be sorry."

"Perhaps, if you got used to the idea--"

"What's that to do with the right and wrong of it?"

"Maybe I'm queer. It don't seem like wrongdoing to me. It seems to me that the Lord would make an exception of us if He knew the circumstances. Perhaps, after you get used to the idea--What I thought was like this. I've got a little farm about seven miles from the city limits, and the tenant on it says that nearly every Sunday somebody motors out from town and wants a chicken-and-waffle supper. There ain't much in the nursery business anymore. These landscape fellows buy their stuff direct, and the middleman's out. I've got a good orchard, and there's a spring, so I could put running water in the house. I'd be good to you, Tillie,--I swear it. It'd be just the same as marriage. Nobody need know it."

"You'd know it. You wouldn't respect me."

"Don't a man respect a woman that's got courage enough to give up everything for him?"

Tillie was crying softly into her apron. He put a work-hardened hand on her head.

"It isn't as if I'd run around after women," he said. "You're the only one, since Maggie--" He drew a long breath. "I'll give you time to think it over. Suppose I stop in to-morrow morning. It doesn't commit you to anything to talk it over."

There had been no passion in the interview, and there was none in the touch of his hand. He was not young, and the tragic loneliness of approaching old age confronted him. He was trying to solve his problem and Tillie's, and what he had found was no solution, but a compromise.

"To-morrow morning, then," he said quietly, and went out the door.

All that hot August morning Tillie worked in a daze. Mrs. McKee watched her and said nothing. She interpreted the girl's white face and set lips as the result of having had to dismiss Schwitter again, and looked for time to bring peace, as it had done before.

Le Moyne came late to his midday meal. For once, the mental anaesthesia of endless figures had failed him. On his way home he had drawn his small savings from the bank, and mailed them, in cash and registered, to a back street in the slums of a distant city. He had done this before, and always with a feeling of exaltation, as if, for a time at least, the burden he carried was lightened. But to-day he experienced no compensatory relief. Life was dull and stale to him, effort ineffectual. At thirty a man should look back with tenderness, forward with hope. K. Le Moyne dared not look back, and had no desire to look ahead into empty years.

Although he ate little, the dining-room was empty when he finished. Usually he had some cheerful banter for Tillie, to which she responded in kind. But, what with the heat and with heaviness of spirit, he did not notice her depression until he rose.

"Why, you're not sick, are you, Tillie?"

"Me? Oh, no. Low in my mind, I guess."

"It's the heat. It's fearful. Look here. If I send you two tickets to a roof garden where there's a variety show, can't you take a friend and go to-night?"

"Thanks; I guess I'll not go out."

Then, unexpectedly, she bent her head against a chair-back and fell to silent crying. K. let her cry for a moment. Then:--

"Now--tell me about it."

"I'm just worried; that's all."

"Let's see if we can't fix up the worries. Come, now, out with them!"

"I'm a wicked woman, Mr. Le Moyne."

"Then I'm the person to tell it to. I--I'm pretty much a lost soul myself."

He put an arm over her shoulders and drew her up, facing him.

"Suppose we go into the parlor and talk it out. I'll bet things are not as bad as you imagine."

But when, in the parlor that had seen Mr. Schwitter's strange proposal of the morning, Tillie poured out her story, K.'s face grew grave.

"The wicked part is that I want to go with him," she finished. "I keep thinking about being out in the country, and him coming into supper, and everything nice for him and me cleaned up and waiting--O my God! I've always been a good woman until now."

"I--I understand a great deal better than you think I do. You're not wicked. The only thing is--"

"Go on. Hit me with it."

"You might go on and be very happy. And as for the--for his wife, it won't do her any harm. It's only--if there are children."

"I know. I've thought of that. But I'm so crazy for children!"

"Exactly. So you should be. But when they come, and you cannot give them a name--don't you see? I'm not preaching morality. God forbid that I--But no happiness is built on a foundation of wrong. It's been tried before, Tillie, and it doesn't pan out."

He was conscious of a feeling of failure when he left her at last. She had acquiesced in what he said, knew he was right, and even promised to talk to him again before making a decision one way or the other. But against his abstractions of conduct and morality there was pleading in Tillie the hungry mother-heart; law and creed and early training were fighting against the strongest instinct of the race. It was a losing battle.

CHAPTER XI

THE hot August days dragged on. Merciless sunlight beat in through the slatted shutters of ward windows. At night, from the roof to which the nurses retired after prayers for a breath of air, lower surrounding roofs were seen to be covered with sleepers. Children dozed precariously on the edge of eternity; men and women sprawled in the grotesque postures of sleep.

There was a sort of feverish irritability in the air. Even the nurses, stoically unmindful of bodily discomfort, spoke curtly or not at all. Miss Dana, in Sidney's ward, went down with a low fever, and for a day or so Sidney and Miss Grange got along as best they could. Sidney worked like two or more, performed marvels of bed-making, learned to give alcohol baths for fever with the maximum of result and the minimum of time, even made rounds with a member of the staff and came through creditably.

Dr. Ed Wilson had sent a woman patient into the ward, and his visits were the breath of life to the girl.

"How're they treating you?" he asked her, one day, abruptly.

"Very well."

"Look at me squarely. You're pretty and you're young. Some of them will try to take it out of you. That's human nature. Has anyone tried it yet?"

Sidney looked distressed.

"Positively, no. It's been hot, and of course it's troublesome to tell me everything. I--I think they're all very kind."

He reached out a square, competent hand, and put it over hers.

"We miss you in the Street," he said. "It's all sort of dead there since you left. Joe Drummond doesn't moon up and down any more, for one thing. What was wrong between you and Joe, Sidney?"

"I didn't want to marry him; that's all."

"That's considerable. The boy's taking it hard."

Then, seeing her face:--

"But you're right, of course. Don't marry anyone unless you can't live without him. That's been my motto, and here I am, still single."

He went out and down the corridor. He had known Sidney all his life. During the lonely times when Max was at college and in Europe, he had watched her grow from a child to a young girl. He did not suspect for a moment that in that secret heart of hers he sat newly enthroned, in a glow of white light, as Max's brother; that the mere thought that he lived in Max's house (it was, of course Max's house to her), sat at Max's breakfast table, could see him whenever he wished, made the touch of his hand on hers a benediction and a caress.

Sidney finished folding linen and went back to the ward. It was Friday and a visiting day. Almost every bed had its visitor beside it; but Sidney, running an eye over the ward, found the girl of whom she had spoken to Le Moyne quite alone. She was propped up in bed, reading; but at each new step in the corridor hope would spring into her eyes and die again.

"Want anything, Grace?"

"Me? I'm all right. If these people would only get out and let me read in peace--Say, sit down and talk to me, won't you? It beats the mischief the way your friends forget you when you're laid up in a place like this."

"People can't always come at visiting hours. Besides, it's hot."

"A girl I knew was sick here last year, and it wasn't too hot for me to trot in twice a week with a bunch of flowers for her. Do you think she's been here once? She hasn't."

Then, suddenly:--

"You know that man I told you about the other day?"

Sidney nodded. The girl's anxious eyes were on her.

"It was a shock to me, that's all. I didn't want you to think I'd break my heart over any fellow. All I meant was, I wished he'd let me know."

Her eyes searched Sidney's. They looked unnaturally large and somber in her face. Her hair had been cut short, and her nightgown, open at the neck, showed her thin throat and prominent clavicles.

"You're from the city, aren't you, Miss Page?"

"Yes."

"You told me the street, but I've forgotten it."

Sidney repeated the name of the Street, and slipped a fresh pillow under the girl's head.

"The evening paper says there's a girl going to be married on your street."

"Really! Oh, I think I know. A friend of mine is going to be married. Was the name Lorenz?"

"The girl's name was Lorenz. I--I don't remember the man's name."

"She is going to marry a Mr. Howe," said Sidney briskly. "Now, how do you feel? More comfy?"

"Fine! I suppose you'll be going to that wedding?"

"If I ever get time to have a dress made, I'll surely go."

Toward six o'clock the next morning, the night nurse was making out her reports. On one record, which said at the top, "Grace Irving, age 19," and an address which, to the initiated, told all her story, the night nurse wrote:--

"Did not sleep at all during night. Face set and eyes staring, but complains of no pain. Refused milk at eleven and three."

Carlotta Harrison, back from her vacation, reported for duty the next morning, and was assigned to E ward, which was Sidney's. She gave Sidney a curt little nod, and proceeded to change the entire routine with the thoroughness of a Central American revolutionary president. Sidney, who had yet to learn that with some people authority can only assert itself by change, found herself confused, at sea, half resentful.

Once she ventured a protest:--

"I've been taught to do it that way, Miss Harrison. If my method is wrong, show me what you want, and I'll do my best."

"I am not responsible for what you have been taught. And you will not speak back when you are spoken to."

Small as the incident was, it marked a change in Sidney's position in the ward. She got the worst off-duty of the day, or none. Small humiliations were hers: late meals, disagreeable duties, endless and often unnecessary tasks. Even Miss Grange, now reduced to second place, remonstrated with her senior.

"I think a certain amount of severity is good for a probationer," she said, "but you are brutal, Miss Harrison."

"She's stupid."

"She's not at all stupid. She's going to be one of the best nurses in the house."

"Report me, then. Tell the Head I'm abusing Dr. Wilson's pet probationer, that I don't always say 'please' when I ask her to change a bed or take a temperature."

Miss Grange was not lacking in keenness. She died not go to the Head, which is unethical under any circumstances; but gradually there spread through the training-school a story that Carlotta Harrison was jealous of the new Page girl, Dr. Wilson's protegee. Things were still highly unpleasant in the ward, but they grew much better when Sidney was off duty. She was asked to join a small class that was studying French at night. As ignorant of the cause of her popularity as of the reason of her persecution, she went steadily on her way.

And she was gaining every day. Her mind was forming. She was learning to think for herself. For the first time, she was facing problems and demanding an answer. Why must there be Grace Irvings in the world? Why must the healthy babies of the obstetric ward go out to the slums and come back, in months or years, crippled for the great fight by the handicap of their environment, rickety, tuberculous, twisted? Why need the huge mills feed the hospitals daily with injured men?

And there were other things that she thought of. Every night, on her knees in the nurses' parlor at prayers, she promised, if she were accepted as a nurse, to try never to become calloused, never to regard her patients as "cases," never to allow the cleanliness and routine of her ward to delay a cup of water to the thirsty, or her arms to a sick child.

On the whole, the world was good, she found. And, of all the good things in it, the best was service. True, there were hot days and restless nights, weary feet, and now and then a heartache. There was Miss Harrison, too. But to offset these there was the sound of Dr. Max's step in the corridor, and his smiling nod from the door; there was a "God bless you" now and then for the comfort she gave; there were wonderful nights on the roof under the stars, until K.'s little watch warned her to bed.

While Sidney watched the stars from her hospital roof, while all around her the slum children, on other roofs, fought for the very breath of life, others who knew and loved her watched the stars, too. K. was having his own troubles in those days. Late at night, when Anna and Harriet had retired, he sat on the balcony and thought of many things. Anna Page was not well. He had noticed that her lips were rather blue, and had called in Dr. Ed. It was valvular heart disease. Anna was not to be told, or Sidney. It was Harriet's ruling.

"Sidney can't help any," said Harriet, "and for Heaven's sake let her have her chance. Anna may live for years. You know her as well as I do. If you tell her anything at all, she'll have Sidney here, waiting on her hand and foot."

And Le Moyne, fearful of urging too much because his own heart was crying out to have the girl back, assented.

Then, K. was anxious about Joe. The boy did not seem to get over the thing the way he should. Now and then Le Moyne, resuming his old habit of wearying himself into sleep, would walk out into the country. On one such night he had overtaken Joe, tramping along with his head down.

Joe had not wanted his company, had plainly sulked. But Le Moyne had persisted.

"I'll not talk," he said; "but, since we're going the same way, we might as well walk together."

But after a time Joe had talked, after all. It was not much at first--a feverish complaint about the heat, and that if there was trouble in Mexico he thought he'd go.

"Wait until fall, if you're thinking of it," K. advised. "This is tepid compared with what you'll get down there."

"I've got to get away from here."

K. nodded understandingly. Since the scene at the White Springs Hotel, both knew that no explanation was necessary.

"It isn't so much that I mind her turning me down," Joe said, after a silence. "A girl can't marry all the men who want her. But I don't like this hospital idea. I don't understand it. She didn't have to go. Sometimes"--he turned bloodshot eyes on Le Moyne--"I think she went because she was crazy about somebody there."

"She went because she wanted to be useful."

"She could be useful at home."

For almost twenty minutes they tramped on without speech. They had made a circle, and the lights of the city were close again. K. stopped and put a kindly hand on Joe's shoulder.

"A man's got to stand up under a thing like this, you know. I mean, it mustn't be a knockout. Keeping busy is a darned good method."

Joe shook himself free, but without resentment. "I'll tell you what's eating me up," he exploded. "It's Max Wilson. Don't talk to me about her going to the hospital to be useful. She's crazy about him, and he's as crooked as a dog's hind leg."

"Perhaps. But it's always up to the girl. You know that."

He felt immeasurably old beside Joe's boyish blustering--old and rather helpless.

"I'm watching him. Some of these days I'll get something on him. Then she'll know what to think of her hero!"

"That's not quite square, is it?"

"He's not square."

Joe had left him then, wheeling abruptly off into the shadows. K. had gone home alone, rather uneasy. There seemed to be mischief in the very air.

CHAPTER XII

TILLIE was gone.

Oddly enough, the last person to see her before she left was Harriet Kennedy. On the third day after Mr. Schwitter's visit, Harriet's colored maid had announced a visitor.

Harriet's business instinct had been good. She had taken expensive rooms in a good location, and furnished them with the assistance of a decor store. Then she arranged with a New York house to sell her models on commission.

Her short excursion to New York had marked for Harriet the beginning of a new heaven and a new earth. Here, at last, she found people speaking her own language. She ventured a suggestion to a manufacturer, and found it greeted, not, after the manner of the Street, with scorn, but with approval and some surprise.

"About once in ten years," said Mr. Arthurs, "we have a woman from out of town bring us a suggestion that is both novel and practical. When we find people like that, we watch them. They climb, madame,--climb."

Harriet's climbing was not so rapid as to make her dizzy; but business was coming. The first time she made a price of seventy-five dollars for an evening gown, she went out immediately after and took a drink of water. Her throat was parched.

She began to learn little quips of the feminine mind: that a woman who can pay seventy-five will pay double that sum; that it is not considered good form to show surprise at a dressmaker's prices, no matter how high they may be; that long mirrors and artificial light help sales--no woman over thirty but was grateful for her pink-and-gray room with its soft lights. And Harriet herself conformed to the picture. She took a lesson from the New York modistes, and wore trailing black gowns. She strapped her thin figure into the best corset she could get, and had her black hair marcelled and dressed high. And, because she was a lady by birth and instinct, the result was not incongruous, but refined and rather impressive.

She took her business home with her at night, lay awake scheming, and wakened at dawn to find fresh color combinations in the early sky. She wakened early because she kept her head tied up in a towel, so that her hair need be done only three times a week. That and the corset were the penalties she paid. Her high-heeled shoes were a torment, too; but in the work-room she kicked them off.

To this new Harriet, then, came Tillie in her distress. Tillie was rather overwhelmed at first. The Street had always considered Harriet "proud." But Tillie's urgency was great, her methods direct.

"Why, Tillie!" said Harriet.

"Yes'm."

"Will you sit down?"

Tillie sat. She was not daunted now. While she worked at the fingers of her silk gloves, what Harriet took for nervousness was pure abstraction.

"It's very nice of you to come to see me. Do you like my rooms?"

Tillie surveyed the rooms, and Harriet caught her first full view of her face.

"Is there anything wrong? Have you left Mrs. McKee?"

"I think so. I came to talk to you about it."

It was Harriet's turn to be overwhelmed.

"She's very fond of you. If you have had any words--"

"It's not that. I'm just leaving. I'd like to talk to you, if you don't mind."

"Certainly."

Tillie hitched her chair closer.

"I'm up against something, and I can't seem to make up my mind. Last night I said to myself, 'I've got to talk to some woman who's not married, like me, and not as young as she used to be. There's no use going to Mrs. McKee: she's a widow, and wouldn't understand.'"

Harriet's voice was a trifle sharp as she replied. She never lied about her age, but she preferred to forget it.

"I wish you'd tell me what you're getting at."

"It ain't the sort of thing to come to too sudden. But it's like this. You and I can pretend all we like, Miss Harriet; but we're not getting all out of life that the Lord meant us to have. You've got them wax figures instead of children, and I have mealers."

A little spot of color came into Harriet's cheek. But she was interested. Regardless of the corset, she bent forward.

"Maybe that's true. Go on."

"I'm almost forty. Ten years more at the most, and I'm through. I'm slowing up. Can't get around the tables as I used to. Why, yesterday I put sugar into Mr. Le Moyne's coffee--well, never mind about that. Now I've got a chance to get a home, with a good man to look after me--I like him pretty well, and he thinks a lot of me."

"Mercy sake, Tillie! You are going to get married?"

"No'm," said Tillie; "that's it." And sat silent for a moment.

The gray curtains with their pink cording swung gently in the open windows. From the work-room came the distant hum of a sewing-machine and the sound of voices. Harriet sat with her hands in her lap and listened while Tillie poured out her story. The gates were down now. She told it all, consistently and with unconscious pathos: her little room under the roof at Mrs. McKee's, and the house in the country; her loneliness, and the loneliness of the man; even the faint stirrings of potential motherhood, her empty arms, her advancing age--all this she knit into the fabric of her story and laid at Harriet's feet, as the ancients put their questions to their gods.

Harriet was deeply moved. Too much that Tillie poured out to her found an echo in her own breast. What was this thing she was striving for but a substitute for the real things of life--love and tenderness, children, a home of her own? Quite suddenly she loathed the gray carpet on the floor, the pink chairs, the shaded lamps. Tillie was no longer the waitress at a cheap boarding-house. She loomed large, potential, courageous, a woman who held life in her hands.

"Why don't you go to Mrs. Rosenfeld? She's your aunt, isn't she?"

"She thinks any woman's a fool to take up with a man."

"You're giving me a terrible responsibility, Tillie, if you're asking my advice."

"No'm. I'm asking what you'd do if it happened to you. Suppose you had no people that cared anything about you, nobody to disgrace, and all your life nobody had really cared anything about you. And then a chance like this came along. What would you do?"

"I don't know," said poor Harriet. "It seems to me--I'm afraid I'd be tempted.

It does seem as if a woman had the right to be happy, even if--"

Her own words frightened her. It was as if some hidden self, and not she, had spoken. She hastened to point out the other side of the matter, the insecurity of it, the disgrace. Like K., she insisted that no right can be built out of a wrong. Tillie sat and smoothed her gloves. At last, when Harriet paused in sheer panic, the girl rose.

"I know how you feel, and I don't want you to take the responsibility of advising me," she said quietly. "I guess my mind was made up anyhow. But before I did it I just wanted to be sure that a decent woman would think the way I do about it."

And so, for a time, Tillie went out of the life of the Street as she went out of Harriet's handsome rooms, quietly, unobtrusively, with calm purpose in her eyes.

There were other changes in the Street. The Lorenz house was being painted for Christine's wedding. Johnny Rosenfeld, not perhaps of the Street itself, but certainly pertaining to it, was learning to drive Palmer Howe's new car, in mingled agony and bliss. He walked along the Street, not "right foot, left foot," but "brake foot, clutch foot," and took to calling off the vintage of passing cars. "So-and-So 1910," he would say, with contempt in his voice. He spent more than he could afford on a large streamer, meant to be fastened across the rear of the automobile, which said, "Excuse our dust," and was inconsolable when Palmer refused to let him use it.

K. had yielded to Anna's insistence, and was boarding as well as rooming at the Page house. The Street, rather snobbish to its occasional floating population, was accepting and liking him. It found him tender, infinitely human. And in return he found that this seemingly empty eddy into which he had drifted was teeming with life. He busied himself with small things, and found his outlook gradually less tinged with despair. When he found himself inclined to rail, he organized a baseball club, and sent down to everlasting defeat the Linburgs, consisting of cash-boys from Linden and Hofburg's department store.

The Rosenfelds adored him, with the single exception of the head of the family. The elder Rosenfeld having been "sent up," it was K. who discovered that by having him consigned to the workhouse his family would receive from the county some sixty-five cents a day for his labor. As this was exactly sixty-five cents a day more than he was worth to them free, Mrs. Rosenfeld voiced the pious hope that he be kept there forever.

K. made no further attempt to avoid Max Wilson. Some day they would meet face to face. He hoped, when it happened, they two might be alone; that was all. Even had he not been bound by his promise to Sidney, flight would have been foolish. The world was a small place, and, one way and another, he had known many people. Wherever he went, there would be the same chance.

And he did not deceive himself. Other things being equal,--the eddy and all that it meant--, he would not willingly take himself out of his small share of Sidney's life.

She was never to know what she meant to him, of course. He had scourged his heart until it no longer shone in his eyes when he looked at her. But he was very human--not at all meek. There were plenty of days when his philosophy lay in the dust and savage dogs of jealousy tore at it; more than one evening when he threw himself face downward on the bed and lay without moving for hours. And of these periods of despair he was always heartily ashamed the next day.

The meeting with Max Wilson took place early in September, and under better circumstances than he could have hoped for.

Sidney had come home for her weekly visit, and her mother's condition had alarmed her for the first time. When Le Moyne came home at six o'clock, he found her waiting for him in the hall.

"I am just a little frightened, K.," she said. "Do you think mother is looking quite well?"

"She has felt the heat, of course. The summer--I often think--"

"Her lips are blue!"

"It's probably nothing serious."

"She says you've had Dr. Ed over to see her."

She put her hands on his arm and looked up at him with appeal and something of terror in her face.

Thus cornered, he had to acknowledge that Anna had been out of sorts.

"I shall come home, of course. It's tragic and absurd that I should be caring for other people, when my own mother--"

She dropped her head on his arm, and he saw that she was crying. If he made a gesture to draw her to him, she never knew it. After a moment she looked up.

"I'm much braver than this in the hospital. But when it's one's own!"

K. was sorely tempted to tell her the truth and bring her back to the little house: to their old evenings together, to seeing the younger Wilson, not as the white god of the operating-room and the hospital, but as the dandy of the Street and the neighbor of her childhood--back even to Joe.

But, with Anna's precarious health and Harriet's increasing engrossment in her business, he felt it more and more necessary that Sidney go on with her training. A profession was a safeguard. And there was another point: it had been decided that Anna was not to know her condition. If she was not worried she might live for years. There was no surer way to make her suspect it than by bringing Sidney home.

Sidney sent Katie to ask Dr. Ed to come over after dinner. With the sunset Anna seemed better. She insisted on coming downstairs, and even sat with them on the balcony until the stars came out, talking of Christine's trousseau, and, rather fretfully, of what she would do without the parlors.

"You shall have your own boudoir upstairs," said Sidney valiantly. "Katie can carry your tray up there. We are going to make the sewing-room into your private sitting-room, and I shall nail the machine-top down."

This pleased her. When K. insisted on carrying her upstairs, she went in a flutter.

"He is so strong, Sidney!" she said, when he had placed her on her bed. "How can a clerk, bending over a ledger, be so muscular? When I have callers, will it be all right for Katie to show them upstairs?"

She dropped asleep before the doctor came; and when, at something after eight, the door of the Wilson house slammed and a figure crossed the street, it was not Ed at all, but the surgeon.

Sidney had been talking rather more frankly than usual. Lately there had been a reserve about her. K., listening intently that night, read between words a story of small persecutions and jealousies. But the girl minimized them, after her way.

"It's always hard for probationers," she said. "I often think Miss Harrison is trying my mettle."

"Harrison!"

"Carlotta Harrison. And now that Miss Gregg has said she will accept me, it's really all over. The other nurses are wonderful--so kind and so helpful. I hope I shall look well in my cap."

Carlotta Harrison was in Sidney's hospital! A thousand contingencies flashed through his mind. Sidney might grow to like her and bring her to the house. Sidney might insist on the thing she always spoke of--that he visit the hospital; and he would meet her, face to face. He could have depended on a man to keep his secret. This girl with her somber eyes and her threat to pay him out for what had happened to her--she meant danger of a sort that no man could fight.

"Soon," said Sidney, through the warm darkness, "I shall have a cap, and be always forgetting it and putting my hat on over it--the new ones always do. One of the girls slept in hers the other night! They are tulle, you know, and quite stiff, and it was the most erratic-looking thing the next day!"

It was then that the door across the street closed. Sidney did not hear it, but K. bent forward. There was a part of his brain always automatically on watch.

"I shall get my operating-room training, too," she went on. "That is the real romance of the hospital. A--a surgeon is a sort of hero in a hospital. You wouldn't think that, would you? There was a lot of excitement to-day. Even the probationers' table was talking about it. Dr. Max Wilson did the Edwardes operation."

The figure across the Street was lighting a cigarette. Perhaps, after all--

"Something tremendously difficult--I don't know what. It's going into the medical journals. A Dr. Edwardes invented it, or whatever they call it. They took a picture of the operating-room for the article. The photographer had to put on operating clothes and wrap the camera in sterilized towels. It was the most thrilling thing, they say--"

Her voice died away as her eyes followed K.'s. Max, cigarette in hand, was coming across, under the ailanthus tree. He hesitated on the pavement, his eyes searching the shadowy balcony.

"Sidney?"

"Here! Right back here!"

There was vibrant gladness in her tone. He came slowly toward them.

"My brother is not at home, so I came over. How select you are, with your balcony!"

"Can you see the step?"

"Coming, with bells on."

K. had risen and pushed back his chair. His mind was working quickly. Here in the darkness he could hold the situation for a moment. If he could get Sidney into the house, the rest would not matter. Luckily, the balcony was very dark.

"Is any one ill?"

"Mother is not well. This is Mr. Le Moyne, and he knows who you are very well, indeed."

The two men shook hands.

"I've heard a lot of Mr. Le Moyne. Didn't the Street beat the Linburgs the other day? And I believe the Rosenfelds are in receipt of sixty-five cents a day and considerable peace and quiet through you, Mr. Le Moyne. You're the most popular man on the Street."

"I've always heard that about YOU. Sidney, if Dr. Wilson is here to see your mother--"

"Going," said Sidney. "And Dr. Wilson is a very great person, K., so be polite to him."

Max had roused at the sound of Le Moyne's voice, not to suspicion, of course, but to memory. Without any apparent reason, he was back in Berlin, tramping the country roads, and beside him--

"Wonderful night!"

"Great," he replied. "The mind's a curious thing, isn't it. In the instant since Miss Page went through that window I've been to Berlin and back! Will you have a cigarette?"

"Thanks; I have my pipe here."

K. struck a match with his steady hands. Now that the thing had come, he was glad to face it. In the flare, his quiet profile glowed against the night. Then he flung the match over the rail.

"Perhaps my voice took you back to Berlin."

Max stared; then he rose. Blackness had descended on them again, except for the dull glow of K.'s old pipe.

"For God's sake!"

"Sh! The neighbors next door have a bad habit of sitting just inside the curtains."

"But--you!"

"Sit down. Sidney will be back in a moment. I'll talk to you, if you'll sit still. Can you hear me plainly?"

After a moment--"Yes."

"I've been here--in the city, I mean--for a year. Name's Le Moyne. Don't forget it--Le Moyne. I've got a position in the gas office, clerical. I get fifteen dollars a week. I have reason to think I'm going to be moved up. That will be twenty, maybe twenty-two."

Wilson stirred, but he found no adequate words. Only a part of what K. said got to him. For a moment he was back in a famous clinic, and this man across from him--it was not believable!

"It's not hard work, and it's safe. If I make a mistake there's no life hanging on it. Once I made a blunder, a month or two ago. It was a big one. It cost me three dollars out of my own pocket. But--that's all it cost."

Wilson's voice showed that he was more than incredulous; he was profoundly moved.

"We thought you were dead. There were all sorts of stories. When a year went by--the Titanic had gone down, and nobody knew but what you were on it--we gave up. I--in June we put up a tablet for you at the college. I went down for the--for the services."

"Let it stay," said K. quietly. "I'm dead as far as the college goes, anyhow. I'll never go back. I'm Le Moyne now. And, for Heaven's sake, don't be sorry for me. I'm more contented than I've been for a long time."

The wonder in Wilson's voice was giving way to irritation.

"But--when you had everything! Why, good Heavens, man, I did your operation to-day, and I've been blowing about it ever since."

"I had everything for a while. Then I lost the essential. When that happened I gave up. All a man in our profession has is a certain method, knowledge--call it what you like,--and faith in himself. I lost my self-confidence; that's all. Certain things happened; kept on happening. So I gave it up. That's all. It's not dramatic. For about a year I was damned sorry for myself. I've stopped whining now."

"If every surgeon gave up because he lost cases--I've just told you I did your operation to-day. There was just a chance for the man, and I took my courage in my hands and tried it. The poor devil's dead."

K. rose rather wearily and emptied his pipe over the balcony rail.

"That's not the same. That's the chance he and you took. What happened to me was--different."

Pipe in hand, he stood staring out at the ailanthus tree with its crown of stars. Instead of the Street with its quiet houses, he saw the men he had known and worked with and taught, his friends who spoke his language, who had loved him, many of them, gathered about a bronze tablet set in a wall of the old college; he saw their earnest faces and grave eyes. He heard--

He heard the soft rustle of Sidney's dress as she came into the little room behind them.

CHAPTER XIII

A few days after Wilson's recognition of K., two most exciting things happened to Sidney. One was that Christine asked her to be maid of honor at her wedding. The other was more wonderful. She was accepted, and given her cap.

Because she could not get home that night, and because the little house had no telephone, she wrote the news to her mother and sent a note to Le Moyne:

DEAR K.,--I am accepted, and IT is on my head at this minute. I am as conscious of it as if it were a halo, and as if I had done something to deserve it, instead of just hoping that someday I shall. I am writing this on the bureau, so that when I lift my eyes I may see It. I am afraid just now I am thinking more of the cap than of what it means. It IS becoming!

Very soon I shall slip down and show it to the ward. I have promised. I shall go to the door when the night nurse is busy somewhere, and turn all around and let them see it, without saying a word. They love a little excitement like that.

You have been very good to me, dear K. It is you who have made possible this happiness of mine to-night. I am promising myself to be very good, and not so vain, and to love my enemies--, although I have none now. Miss Harrison has just congratulated me most kindly, and I am sure poor Joe has both forgiven and forgotten.

Off to my first lecture!
SIDNEY.

K. found the note on the hall table when he got home that night, and carried it upstairs to read. Whatever faint hope he might have had that her youth would prevent her acceptance he knew now was over. With the letter in his hand, he sat by his table and looked ahead into the empty years. Not quite empty, of course. She would be coming home.

But more and more the life of the hospital would engross her. He surmised, too, very shrewdly, that, had he ever had a hope that she might come to care for him, his very presence in the little house militated against him. There was none of the illusion of separation; he was always there, like Katie. When she opened the door, she called "Mother" from the hall. If Anna did not answer, she called him, in much the same voice.

He had built a wall of philosophy that had withstood even Wilson's recognition and protest. But enduring philosophy comes only with time; and he was young. Now and then all his defenses crumbled before a passion that, when he dared to face it, shook him by its very strength. And that day all his stoicism went down before Sidney's letter. Its very frankness and affection hurt--not that he did not want her affection; but he craved so much more. He threw himself face down on the bed, with the paper crushed in his hand.

Sidney's letter was not the only one he received that day. When, in response to Katie's summons, he rose heavily and prepared for dinner, he found an unopened envelope on the table. It was from Max Wilson:--

DEAR LE MOYNE,--I have been going around in a sort of haze all day. The fact that I only heard your voice and scarcely saw you last night has made the whole thing even more unreal.

I have a feeling of delicacy about trying to see you again so soon. I'm bound to respect your seclusion. But there are some things that have got to be discussed.

You said last night that things were "different" with you. I know about that. You'd had one or two unlucky accidents. Do you know any man in our profession who has not? And, for fear you think I do not know what I am talking about, the thing was threshed out at the State Society when the question of the tablet came up. Old Barnes got up and said: "Gentlemen, all of us live more or less in glass houses. Let him who is without guilt among us throw the first stone!" By George! You should have heard them!

I didn't sleep last night. I took my little car and drove around the country roads, and the farther I went the more outrageous your position became. I'm not going to write any rot about the world needing men like you, although it's true enough. But our profession does. You working in a gas office, while old O'Hara bungles and hacks, and I struggle along on what I learned from you!

It takes courage to step down from the pinnacle you stood on. So it's not cowardice that has set you down here. It's wrong conception. And I've thought of two things. The first, and best, is for you to go back. No one has taken your place, because no one could do the work. But if that's out of the question,--and only you know that, for only you know the facts,--the next best thing is this, and in all humility I make the suggestion.

Take the State exams under your present name, and when you've got your certificate, come in with me. This isn't magnanimity. I'll be getting a damn sight more than I give.

Think it over, old man.

M.W.

It is a curious fact that a man who is absolutely untrustworthy about women is often the soul of honor to other men. The younger Wilson, taking his pleasures lightly and not too discriminatingly, was making an offer that meant his ultimate eclipse, and doing it cheerfully, with his eyes open.

K. was moved. It was like Max to make such an offer, like him to make it as if he were asking a favor and not conferring one. But the offer left him untempted. He had weighed himself in the balance, and found himself wanting. No tablet on the college wall could change that. And when, late that night, Wilson found him on the balcony and added appeal to argument, the situation remained unchanged. He realized its hopelessness when K. lapsed into whimsical humor.

"I'm not absolutely useless where I am, you know, Max," he said. "I've raised three tomato plants and a family of kittens this summer, helped to plan a trousseau, assisted in selecting wall-paper for the room just inside,--did you notice it?--and developed a boy pitcher with a ball that twists around the bat like a Colles fracture around a splint!"

"If you're going to be humorous--"

"My dear fellow," said K. quietly, "if I had no sense of humor, I should go upstairs to-night, turn on the gas, and make a stertorous entrance into eternity. By the way, that's something I forgot!"

"Eternity?" "No. Among my other activities, I wired the parlor for electric light. The bride-to-be expects some electroliers as wedding gifts, and--"

Wilson rose and flung his cigarette into the grass.

"I wish to God I understood you!" he said irritably.

K. rose with him, and all the suppressed feeling of the interview was crowded into his last few words.

"I'm not as ungrateful as you think, Max," he said. "I--you've helped a lot. Don't worry about me. I'm as well off as I deserve to be, and better. Good-night."

"Good-night."

Wilson's unexpected magnanimity put K. in a curious position--left him, as it were, with a divided allegiance. Sidney's frank infatuation for the young surgeon was growing. He was quick to see it. And where before he might have felt justified in going to the length of warning her, now his hands were tied.

Max was interested in her. K. could see that, too. More than once he had taken Sidney back to the hospital in his car. Le Moyne, handicapped at every turn, found himself facing two alternatives, one but little better than the other. The affair might run a legitimate course, ending in marriage--a year of happiness for her, and then what marriage with Max, as he knew him, would inevitably mean: wanderings away, remorseful returns to her, infidelities, misery. Or, it might be less serious but almost equally unhappy for her. Max might throw caution to the winds, pursue her for a time,--K. had seen him do this,--and then, growing tired, change to some new attraction. In either case, he could only wait and watch, eating his heart out during the long evenings when Anna read her "Daily Thoughts" upstairs and he sat alone with his pipe on the balcony.

Sidney went on night duty shortly after her acceptance. All of her orderly young life had been divided into two parts: day, when one played or worked, and night, when one slept. Now she was compelled to a readjustment: one worked in the night and slept in the day. Things seemed unnatural, chaotic. At the end of her first night report Sidney added what she could remember of a little verse of Stevenson's. She added it to the end of her general report, which was to the effect that everything had been quiet during the night except the neighborhood.

> "And does it not seem hard to you, When all the sky is clear and blue,
> And I should like so much to play, To have to go to bed by day?"

The day assistant happened on the report, and was quite scandalized.

"If the night nurses are to spend their time making up poetry," she said crossly, "we'd better change this hospital into a young ladies' seminary. If she wants to complain about the noise in the street, she should do so in proper form."

"I don't think she made it up," said the Head, trying not to smile. "I've heard something like it somewhere, and, what with the heat and the noise of traffic, I don't see how any of them get any sleep."

But, because discipline must be observed, she wrote on the slip the assistant carried around: "Please submit night reports in prose."

Sidney did not sleep much. She tumbled into her low bed at nine o'clock in the morning, those days, with her splendid hair neatly braided down her back and her prayers said, and immediately her active young mind filled with images--Christine's wedding, Dr. Max passing the door of her old ward and she not there, Joe--even Tillie, whose story was now the sensation of the Street. A few months before she would not have cared to think of Tillie. She would have retired her into the land of things-one-must-forget. But the Street's conventions were not holding Sidney's thoughts now. She puzzled over Tillie a great deal, and over Grace and her kind.

On her first night on duty, a girl had been brought in from the Avenue. She had taken a poison--nobody knew just what. When the internes had tried to find out, she had only said: "What's the use?"

And she had died.

Sidney kept asking herself, "Why?" those mornings when she could not get to sleep. People were kind--men were kind, really,--and yet, for some reason or other, those things had to be. Why?

After a time Sidney would doze fitfully. But by three o'clock she was always up and dressing. After a time the strain told on her. Lack of sleep wrote hollows around her eyes and killed some of her bright color. Between three and four o'clock in the morning she was overwhelmed on duty by a perfect madness of sleep. There was a penalty for sleeping on duty. The old night watchman had a way of slipping up on one nodding. The night nurses wished they might fasten a bell on him!

Luckily, at four came early-morning temperatures; that roused her. And after that came the clatter of early milk-wagons and the rose hues of dawn over the roofs. Twice in the night, once at supper and again toward dawn, she drank strong black coffee. But after a week or two her nerves were stretched taut as a string.

Her station was in a small room close to her three wards. But she sat very little, as a matter of fact. Her responsibility was heavy on her; she made frequent rounds.

The late summer nights were fitful, feverish; the darkened wards stretched away like caverns from the dim light near the door. And from out of these caverns came petulant voices, uneasy movements, the banging of a cup on a bedside, which was the signal of thirst.

The older nurses saved themselves when they could. To them, perhaps just a little weary with time and much service, the banging cup meant not so much thirst as annoyance. They visited Sidney sometimes and cautioned her.

"Don't jump like that, child; they're not parched, you know."

"But if you have a fever and are thirsty--"

"Thirsty nothing! They get lonely. All they want is to see somebody."

"Then," Sidney would say, rising resolutely, "they are going to see me."

Gradually the older girls saw that she would not save herself. They liked her very much, and they, too, had started in with willing feet and tender hands; but the thousand and one demands of their service had drained them dry. They were efficient, cool-headed, quick-thinking machines, doing their best, of course, but differing from Sidney in that their service was of the mind, while hers was of the heart. To them, pain was a thing to be recorded on a report; to Sidney, it was written on the tablets of her soul.

Carlotta Harrison went on night duty at the same time--her last night service, as it was Sidney's first. She accepted it stoically. She had charge of the three wards on the floor just below Sidney, and of the ward into which all emergency cases were taken. It was a difficult service, perhaps the most difficult in the house. Scarcely a night went by without its patrol or ambulance case. Ordinarily, the emergency ward had its own night nurse. But the house was full to overflowing. Belated vacations and illness had depleted the training-school. Carlotta, given double duty, merely shrugged her shoulders.

"I've always had things pretty hard here," she commented briefly. "When I go out, I'll either be competent enough to run a whole hospital singlehanded, or I'll be carried out feet first."

Sidney was glad to have her so near. She knew her better than she knew the other nurses. Small emergencies were constantly arising and finding her at a loss. Once at least every night, Miss Harrison would hear a soft hiss from the back staircase that connected the two floors, and, going out, would see Sidney's flushed face and slightly crooked cap bending over the stair-rail.

"I'm dreadfully sorry to bother you," she would say, "but So-and-So won't have a fever bath"; or, "I've a woman here who refuses her medicine." Then would follow rapid questions and equally rapid answers. Much as Carlotta disliked and feared the girl overhead, it never occurred to her to refuse her assistance. Perhaps the angels who keep the great record will put that to her credit.

Sidney saw her first death shortly after she went on night duty. It was the most terrible experience of all her life; and yet, as death goes, it was quiet enough. So gradual was it that Sidney, with K.'s little watch in hand, was not sure exactly when it happened. The light was very dim behind the little screen. One moment the sheet was quivering slightly under the struggle for breath, the next it was still. That was all. But to the girl it was catastrophe. That life, so potential, so tremendous a thing, could end so ignominiously, that the long battle should terminate always in this capitulation--it seemed to her that she could not stand it. Added to all her other new problems of living was this one of dying.

She made mistakes, of course, which the kindly nurses forgot to report--basins left about, errors on her records. She rinsed her thermometer in hot water one night, and startled an interne by sending him word that Mary McGuire's temperature was a hundred and ten degrees. She let a delirious patient escape from the ward another night and go airily down the fire-escape before she discovered what had happened! Then she distinguished herself by flying down the iron staircase and bringing the runaway back single-handed.

For Christine's wedding the Street threw off its drab attire and assumed a wedding garment. In the beginning it was incredulous about some of the details.

"An awning from the house door to the curbstone, and a policeman!" reported Mrs. Rosenfeld, who was finding steady employment at the Lorenz house. "And another awning at the church, with a red carpet!"

Mr. Rosenfeld had arrived home and was making up arrears of rest and recreation.

"Huh!" he said. "Suppose it don't rain. What then?" His Jewish father spoke in him.

"And another policeman at the church!" said Mrs. Rosenfeld triumphantly.

"Why do they ask 'em if they don't trust 'em?"

But the mention of the policemen had been unfortunate. It recalled to him many things that were better forgotten. He rose and scowled at his wife.

"You tell Johnny something for me," he snarled. "You tell him when he sees his father walking down street, and he sittin' up there alone on that automobile, I want him to stop and pick me up when I hail him. Me walking, while my son swells around in a car! And another thing." He turned savagely at the door. "You let me hear of him road-housin', and I'll kill him!"

The wedding was to be at five o'clock. This, in itself, defied all traditions of the Street, which was either married in the very early morning at the Catholic church or at eight o'clock in the evening at the Presbyterian. There was something reckless about five o'clock. The Street felt the dash of it. It had a queer feeling that perhaps such a marriage was not quite legal.

The question of what to wear became, for the men, an earnest one. Dr. Ed resurrected an old black frock-coat and had a "V" of black cambric set in the vest. Mr. Jenkins, the grocer, rented a cutaway, and bought a new Panama to wear with it. The deaf-and-dumb book agent who boarded at McKees', and who, by reason of his affliction, was calmly ignorant of the excitement around him, wore a borrowed dress-suit, and considered himself to the end of his days the only properly attired man in the church.

The younger Wilson was to be one of the ushers. When the newspapers came out with the published list and this was discovered, as well as that Sidney was the maid of honor, there was a distinct quiver through the hospital training-school. A probationer was authorized to find out particulars. It was the day of the wedding then, and Sidney, who had not been to bed at all, was sitting in a sunny window in the Dormitory Annex, drying her hair.

The probationer was distinctly uneasy.

"I--I just wonder," she said, "if you would let some of the girls come in to see you when you're dressed?"

"Why, of course I will."

"It's awfully thrilling, isn't it? And--isn't Dr. Wilson going to be an usher?"

Sidney colored. "I believe so."

"Are you going to walk down the aisle with him?"

"I don't know. They had a rehearsal last night, but of course I was not there.

I--I think I walk alone."

The probationer had been instructed to find out other things; so she set to work with a fan at Sidney's hair.

"You've known Dr. Wilson a long time, haven't you?"

"Ages."

"He's awfully good-looking, isn't he?"

Sidney considered. She was not ignorant of the methods of the school. If this girl was pumping her--

"I'll have to think that over," she said, with a glint of mischief in her eyes. "When you know a person terribly well, you hardly know whether he's good-looking or not."

"I suppose," said the probationer, running the long strands of Sidney's hair through her fingers, "that when you are at home you see him often."

Sidney got off the window-sill, and, taking the probationer smilingly by the shoulders, faced her toward the door.

"You go back to the girls," she said, "and tell them to come in and see me when I am dressed, and tell them this: I don't know whether I am to walk down the aisle with Dr. Wilson, but I hope I am. I see him very often. I like him very much. I hope he likes me. And I think he's handsome."

She shoved the probationer out into the hall and locked the door behind her.

That message in its entirety reached Carlotta Harrison. Her smouldering eyes flamed. The audacity of it startled her. Sidney must be very sure of herself.

She, too, had not slept during the day. When the probationer who had brought her the report had gone out, she lay in her long white night-gown, hands clasped under her head, and stared at the vault-like ceiling of her little room.

She saw there Sidney in her white dress going down the aisle of the church; she saw the group around the altar; and, as surely as she lay there, she knew that Max Wilson's eyes would be, not on the bride, but on the girl who stood beside her.

The curious thing was that Carlotta felt that she could stop the wedding if she wanted to. She'd happened on a bit of information--many a wedding had been stopped for less. It rather obsessed her to think of stopping the wedding, so that Sidney and Max would not walk down the aisle together.

There came, at last, an hour before the wedding, a lull in the feverish activities of the previous month. Everything was ready. In the Lorenz kitchen, piles of plates, negro waiters, ice-cream freezers, and Mrs. Rosenfeld stood in orderly array. In the attic, in the center of a sheet, before a toilet-table which had been carried upstairs for her benefit, sat, on this her day of days, the bride. All the second story had been prepared for guests and presents.

Florists were still busy in the room below. Bridesmaids were clustered on the little staircase, bending over at each new ring of the bell and calling reports to Christine through the closed door:--

"Another wooden box, Christine. It looks like more plates. What will you ever do with them all?"

"Good Heavens! Here's another of the neighbors who wants to see how you look. Do say you can't have any visitors now."

Christine sat alone in the center of her sheet. The bridesmaids had been sternly forbidden to come into her room.

"I haven't had a chance to think for a month," she said. "And I've got some things I've got to think out."

But, when Sidney came, she sent for her. Sidney found her sitting on a stiff chair, in her wedding gown, with her veil spread out on a small stand.

"Close the door," said Christine. And, after Sidney had kissed her:--

"I've a good mind not to do it."

"You're tired and nervous, that's all."

"I am, of course. But that isn't what's wrong with me. Throw that veil some place and sit down."

Christine was undoubtedly rouged, a very delicate touch. Sidney thought brides should be rather pale. But under her eyes were lines that Sidney had never seen there before.

"I'm not going to be foolish, Sidney. I'll go through with it, of course. It would put mamma in her grave if I made a scene now."

She suddenly turned on Sidney.

"Palmer gave his bachelor dinner at the Country Club last night. They all drank more than they should. Somebody called father up to-day and said that Palmer had emptied a bottle of wine into the piano. He hasn't been here to-day."

"He'll be along. And as for the other--perhaps it wasn't Palmer who did it."

"That's not it, Sidney. I'm frightened."

Three months before, perhaps, Sidney could not have comforted her; but three months had made a change in Sidney. The complacent sophistries of her girlhood no longer answered for truth. She put her arms around Christine's shoulders.

"A man who drinks is a broken reed," said Christine. "That's what I'm going to marry and lean on the rest of my life--a broken reed. And that isn't all!"

She got up quickly, and, trailing her long satin train across the floor, bolted the door. Then from inside her corsage she brought out and held to Sidney a letter. "Special delivery. Read it."

It was very short; Sidney read it at a glance:--

Ask your future husband if he knows a girl at 213 --- Avenue.

Three months before, the Avenue would have meant nothing to Sidney. Now she knew. Christine, more sophisticated, had always known.

"You see," she said. "That's what I'm up against."

Quite suddenly Sidney knew who the girl at 213 --- Avenue was. The paper she held in her hand was hospital paper with the heading torn off. The whole sordid story lay before her: Grace Irving, with her thin face and cropped hair, and the newspaper on the floor of the ward beside her!

One of the bridesmaids thumped violently on the door outside.

"Another electric lamp," she called excitedly through the door. "And Palmer is downstairs."

"You see," Christine said drearily. "I have received another electric lamp, and Palmer is downstairs! I've got to go through with it, I suppose. The only difference between me and other brides is that I know what I'm getting. Most of them do not."

"You're going on with it?"

"It's too late to do anything else. I am not going to give this neighborhood anything to talk about."

She picked up her veil and set the coronet on her head. Sidney stood with the letter in her hands. One of K.'s answers to her hot question had been this:--

"There is no sense in looking back unless it helps us to look ahead. What your little girl of the ward has been is not so important as what she is going to be."

"Even granting this to be true," she said to Christine slowly,--"and it may only be malicious after all, Christine,--it's surely over and done with. It's not Palmer's past that concerns you now; it's his future with you, isn't it?"

Christine had finally adjusted her veil. A band of duchesse lace rose like a coronet from her soft hair, and from it, sweeping to the end of her train, fell fold after fold of soft tulle. She arranged the coronet carefully with small pearl-topped pins. Then she rose and put her hands on Sidney's shoulders.

"The simple truth is," she said quietly, "that I might hold Palmer if I cared--terribly. I don't. And I'm afraid he knows it. It's my pride that's hurt, nothing else."

And thus did Christine Lorenz go down to her wedding.

Sidney stood for a moment, her eyes on the letter she held. Already, in her new philosophy, she had learned many strange things. One of them was this: that women like Grace Irving did not betray their lovers; that the code of the underworld was "death to the squealer"; that one played the game, and won or lost, and if he lost, took his medicine. If not Grace, then who? Somebody else in the hospital who knew her story, of course. But who? And again--why?

Before going downstairs, Sidney placed the letter in a saucer and set fire to it with a match. Some of the radiance had died out of her eyes.

The Street voted the wedding a great success. The alley, however, was rather confused by certain things. For instance, it regarded the awning as essentially for the carriage guests, and showed a tendency to duck in under the side when no one was looking. Mrs. Rosenfeld absolutely refused to take the usher's arm which was offered her, and said she guessed she was able to walk up alone.

Johnny Rosenfeld came, as befitted his position, in a complete chauffeur's outfit of leather cap and leggings, with the shield that was his State license pinned over his heart.

The Street came decorously, albeit with a degree of uncertainty as to supper. Should they put something on the stove before they left, in case only ice cream and cake were served at the house? Or was it just as well to trust to luck, and, if the Lorenz supper proved inadequate, to sit down to a cold snack when they got home?

To K., sitting in the back of the church between Harriet and Anna, the wedding was Sidney--Sidney only. He watched her first steps down the aisle, saw her chin go up as she gained poise and confidence, watched the swinging of her young figure in its gauzy white as she passed him and went forward past the long rows of craning necks. Afterward he could not remember the wedding party at all. The service for him was Sidney, rather awed and very serious, beside the altar. It was Sidney who came down the aisle to the triumphant strains of the wedding march, Sidney with Max beside her!

On his right sat Harriet, having reached the first pinnacle of her new career. The wedding gowns were successful. They were more than that--they were triumphant. Sitting there, she cast comprehensive eyes over the church, filled with potential brides.

To Harriet, then, that October afternoon was a future of endless lace and chiffon, the joy of creation, triumph eclipsing triumph. But to Anna, watching the ceremony with blurred eyes and ineffectual bluish lips, was coming her hour. Sitting back in the pew, with her hands folded over her prayer-book, she said a little prayer for her straight young daughter, facing out from the altar with clear, unafraid eyes.

As Sidney and Max drew near the door, Joe Drummond, who had been standing at the back of the church, turned quickly and went out. He stumbled, rather, as if he could not see.

CHAPTER XIV

THE supper at the White Springs Hotel had not been the last supper Carlotta Harrison and Max Wilson had taken together. Carlotta had selected for her vacation a small town within easy motoring distance of the city, and two or three times during her two weeks off duty Wilson had gone out to see her. He liked being with her. She stimulated him. For once that he could see Sidney, he saw Carlotta twice.

She had kept the affair well in hand. She was playing for high stakes. She knew quite well the kind of man with whom she was dealing--that he would pay as little as possible. But she knew, too, that, let him want a thing enough, he would pay any price for it, even marriage.

She was very skillful. The very ardor in her face was in her favor. Behind her hot eyes lurked cold calculation. She would put the thing through, and show those puling nurses, with their pious eyes and evening prayers, a thing or two.

During that entire vacation he never saw her in anything more elaborate than the simplest of white dresses modestly open at the throat, sleeves rolled up to show her satiny arms. There were no other boarders at the little farmhouse. She sat for hours in the summer evenings in the square yard filled with apple trees that bordered the highway, carefully posed over a book, but with her keen eyes always on the road. She read Browning, Emerson, Swinburne. Once he found her with a book that she hastily concealed. He insisted on seeing it, and secured it. It was a book on brain surgery. Confronted with it, she blushed and dropped her eyes.

His delighted vanity found in it the most insidious of compliments, as she had intended.

"I feel such an idiot when I am with you," she said. "I wanted to know a little more about the things you do."

That put their relationship on a new and advanced basis. Thereafter he occasionally talked surgery instead of sentiment. He found her responsive, intelligent. His work, a sealed book to his women before, lay open to her.

Now and then their professional discussions ended in something different. The two lines of their interest converged.

"Gad!" he said one day. "I look forward to these evenings. I can talk shop with you without either shocking or nauseating you. You are the most intelligent woman I know--and one of the prettiest."

He had stopped the machine on the crest of a hill for the ostensible purpose of admiring the view.

"As long as you talk shop," she said, "I feel that there is nothing wrong in our being together; but when you say the other thing--"

"Is it wrong to tell a pretty woman you admire her?"

"Under our circumstances, yes."

He twisted himself around in the seat and sat looking at her.

"The loveliest mouth in the world!" he said, and kissed her suddenly.

She had expected it for at least a week, but her surprise was well done. Well done also was her silence during the homeward ride.

No, she was not angry, she said. It was only that he had set her thinking. When she got out of the car, she bade him good-night and good-bye. He only laughed.

"Don't you trust me?" he said, leaning out to her.

She raised her dark eyes.

"It is not that. I do not trust myself."

After that nothing could have kept him away, and she knew it.

"Man demands both danger and play; therefore he selects woman as the most dangerous of toys." A spice of danger had entered into their relationship. It had become infinitely piquant.

He motored out to the farm the next day, to be told that Miss Harrison had gone for a long walk and had not said when she would be back. That pleased him. Evidently she was frightened. Every man likes to think that he is a bit of a devil. Dr. Max settled his tie, and, leaving his car outside the whitewashed fence, departed blithely on foot in the direction Carlotta had taken.

She knew her man, of course. He found her, face down, under a tree, looking pale and worn and bearing all the evidence of a severe mental struggle. She rose in confusion when she heard his step, and retreated a foot or two, with her hands out before her.

"How dare you?" she cried. "How dare you follow me! I--I have got to have a little time alone. I have got to think things out."

He knew it was play-acting, but rather liked it; and, because he was quite as skillful as she was, he struck a match on the trunk of the tree and lighted a cigarette before he answered.

"I was afraid of this," he said, playing up. "You take it entirely too hard. I am not really a villain, Carlotta."

It was the first time he had used her name.

"Sit down and let us talk things over."

She sat down at a safe distance, and looked across the little clearing to him with the somber eyes that were her great asset.

"You can afford to be very calm," she said, "because this is only play to you; I know it. I've known it all along. I'm a good listener and not--unattractive. But what is play for you is not necessarily play for me. I am going away from here."

For the first time, he found himself believing in her sincerity. Why, the girl was white. He didn't want to hurt her. If she cried--he was at the mercy of any woman who cried.

"Give up your training?"

"What else can I do? This sort of thing cannot go on, Dr. Max."

She did cry then--real tears; and he went over beside her and took her in his arms.

"Don't do that," he said. "Please don't do that. You make me feel like a scoundrel, and I've only been taking a little bit of happiness. That's all. I swear it."

She lifted her head from his shoulder.

"You mean you are happy with me?"

"Very, very happy," said Dr. Max, and kissed her again on the lips.

The one element Carlotta had left out of her calculations was herself. She had known the man, had taken the situation at its proper value. But she had left out this important factor in the equation,--that factor which in every relationship between man and woman determines the equation,--the woman.

Into her calculating ambition had come a new and destroying element. She who, like K. in his little room on the Street, had put aside love and the things thereof, found that it would not be put aside. By the end of her short vacation Carlotta Harrison was wildly in love with the younger Wilson.

They continued to meet, not as often as before, but once a week, perhaps. The meetings were full of danger now; and if for the girl they lost by this quality, they gained attraction for the man. She was shrewd enough to realize her own situation. The thing had gone wrong. She cared, and he did not. It was all a game now, not hers.

All women are intuitive; women in love are dangerously so. As well as she knew that his passion for her was not the real thing, so also she realized that there was growing up in his heart something akin to the real thing for Sidney Page. Suspicion became certainty after a talk they had over the supper table at a country road-house the day after Christine's wedding.

"How was the wedding--tiresome?" she asked.

"Thrilling! There's always something thrilling to me in a man tying himself up for life to one woman. It's--it's so reckless."

Her eyes narrowed. "That's not exactly the Law and the Prophets, is it?"

"It's the truth. To think of selecting out of all the world one woman, and electing to spend the rest of one's days with her! Although--"

His eyes looked past Carlotta into distance.

"Sidney Page was one of the bridesmaids," he said irrelevantly. "She was lovelier than the bride."

"Pretty, but stupid," said Carlotta. "I like her. I've really tried to teach her things, but--you know--" She shrugged her shoulders.

Dr. Max was learning wisdom. If there was a twinkle in his eye, he veiled it discreetly. But, once again in the machine, he bent over and put his cheek against hers.

"You little cat! You're jealous," he said exultantly.

Nevertheless, although he might smile, the image of Sidney lay very close to his heart those autumn days. And Carlotta knew it.

Sidney came off night duty the middle of November. The night duty had been a time of comparative peace to Carlotta. There were no evenings when Dr. Max could bring Sidney back to the hospital in his car.

Sidney's half-days at home were occasions for agonies of jealousy on Carlotta's part. On such an occasion, a month after the wedding, she could not contain herself. She pleaded her old excuse of headache, and took the trolley to a point near the end of the Street. After twilight fell, she slowly walked the length of the Street. Christine and Palmer had not returned from their wedding journey. The November evening was not cold, and on the little balcony sat Sidney and Dr. Max. K. was there, too, had she only known it, sitting back in the shadow and saying little, his steady eyes on Sidney's profile.

But this Carlotta did not know. She went on down the Street in a frenzy of jealous anger.

After that two ideas ran concurrent in Carlotta's mind: one was to get Sidney out of the way, the other was to make Wilson propose to her. In her heart she knew that on the first depended the second.

A week later she made the same frantic excursion, but with a different result. Sidney was not in sight, or Wilson. But standing on the wooden doorstep of the little house was Le Moyne. The ailanthus trees were bare at that time, throwing gaunt arms upward to the November sky. The street-lamp, which in the summer left the doorstep in the shadow, now shone through the branches and threw into strong relief Le Moyne's tall figure and set face. Carlotta saw him too late to retreat. But he did not see her. She went on, startled, her busy brain scheming anew. Another element had entered into her plotting. It was the first time she had known that K. lived in the Page house. It gave her a sense of uncertainty and deadly fear.

She made her first friendly overture of many days to Sidney the following day. They met in the locker-room in the basement where the street clothing for the ward patients was kept. Here, rolled in bundles and ticketed, side by side lay the heterogeneous garments in which the patients had met accident or illness. Rags and tidiness, filth and cleanliness, lay almost touching.

Far away on the other side of the white-washed basement, men were unloading gleaming cans of milk. Floods of sunlight came down the cellar-way, touching their white coats and turning the cans to silver. Everywhere was the religion of the hospital, which is order.

Sidney, harking back from recent slights to the staircase conversation of her night duty, smiled at Carlotta cheerfully.

"A miracle is happening," she said. "Grace Irving is going out to-day. When one remembers how ill she was and how we thought she could not live, it's rather a triumph, isn't it?"

"Are those her clothes?"

Sidney examined with some dismay the elaborate negligee garments in her hand.

"She can't go out in those; I shall have to lend her something." A little of the light died out of her face. "She's had a hard fight, and she has won," she said. "But when I think of what she's probably going back to--"

Carlotta shrugged her shoulders.

"It's all in the day's work," she observed indifferently. "You can take them up into the kitchen and give them steady work paring potatoes, or put them in the laundry ironing. In the end it's the same thing. They all go back."

She drew a package from the locker and looked at it ruefully.

"Well, what do you know about this? Here's a woman who came in in a night-gown and pair of slippers. And now she wants to go out in half an hour!"

She turned, on her way out of the locker-room, and shot a quick glance at Sidney.

"I happened to be on your street the other night," she said. "You live across the street from Wilsons', don't you?"

"Yes."

"I thought so; I had heard you speak of the house. Your--your brother was standing on the steps."

Sidney laughed.

"I have no brother. That's a roomer, a Mr. Le Moyne. It isn't really right to call him a roomer; he's one of the family now."

"Le Moyne!"

He had even taken another name. It had hit him hard, for sure.

K.'s name had struck an always responsive chord in Sidney. The two girls went toward the elevator together. With a very little encouragement, Sidney talked of K. She was pleased at Miss Harrison's friendly tone, glad that things were all right between them again. At her floor, she put a timid hand on the girl's arm.

"I was afraid I had offended you or displeased you," she said. "I'm so glad it isn't so."

Carlotta shivered under her hand.

Things were not going any too well with K. True, he had received his promotion at the office, and with this present affluence of twenty-two dollars a week he was able to do several things. Mrs. Rosenfeld now washed and ironed one day a week at the little house, so that Katie might have more time to look after Anna. He had increased also the amount of money that he periodically sent East.

So far, well enough. The thing that rankled and filled him with a sense of failure was Max Wilson's attitude. It was not unfriendly; it was, indeed, consistently respectful, almost reverential. But he clearly considered Le Moyne's position absurd.

There was no true comradeship between the two men; but there was beginning to be constant association, and lately a certain amount of friction. They thought differently about almost everything.

Wilson began to bring all his problems to Le Moyne. There were long consultations in that small upper room. Perhaps more than one man or woman who did not know of K.'s existence owed his life to him that fall.

Under K.'s direction, Max did marvels. Cases began to come in to him from the surrounding towns. To his own daring was added a new and remarkable technique. But Le Moyne, who had found resignation if not content, was once again in touch with the work he loved. There were times when, having thrashed a case out together and outlined the next day's work for Max, he would walk for hours into the night out over the hills, fighting his battle. The longing was on him to be in the thick of things again. The thought of the gas office and its deadly round sickened him.

It was on one of his long walks that K. found Tillie.

It was December then, gray and raw, with a wet snow that changed to rain as it fell. The country roads were ankle-deep with mud, the wayside paths thick with sodden leaves. The dreariness of the countryside that Saturday afternoon suited his mood. He had ridden to the end of the street-car line, and started his walk from there. As was his custom, he wore no overcoat, but a short sweater under his coat. Somewhere along the road he had picked up a mongrel dog, and, as if in sheer desire for human society, it trotted companionably at his heels.

Seven miles from the end of the car line he found a road-house, and stopped in for a glass of Scotch. He was chilled through. The dog went in with him, and stood looking up into his face. It was as if he submitted, but wondered why this indoors, with the scents of the road ahead and the trails of rabbits over the fields.

The house was set in a valley at the foot of two hills. Through the mist of the December afternoon, it had loomed pleasantly before him. The door was ajar, and he stepped into a little hall covered with ingrain carpet. To the right was the dining-room, the table covered with a white cloth, and in its exact center an uncompromising bunch of dried flowers. To the left, the typical parlor of such places. It might have been the parlor of the White Springs Hotel in duplicate, plush self-rocker and all. Over everything was silence and a pervading smell of fresh varnish. The house was aggressive with new paint--the sagging old floors shone with it, the doors gleamed.

"Hello!" called K.

There were slow footsteps upstairs, the closing of a bureau drawer, the rustle of a woman's dress coming down the stairs. K., standing uncertainly on a carpet oasis that was the center of the parlor varnish, stripped off his sweater.

"Not very busy here this afternoon!" he said to the unseen female on the staircase. Then he saw her. It was Tillie. She put a hand against the doorframe to steady herself. Tillie surely, but a new Tillie! With her hair loosened around her face, a fresh blue chintz dress open at the throat, a black velvet bow on her breast, here was a Tillie fuller, infinitely more attractive, than he had remembered her. But she did not smile at him. There was something about her eyes not unlike the dog's expression, submissive, but questioning.

"Well, you've found me, Mr. Le Moyne." And, when he held out his hand, smiling: "I just had to do it, Mr. K."

"And how's everything going? You look mighty fine and--happy, Tillie."

"I'm all right. Mr. Schwitter's gone to the postoffice. He'll be back at five. Will you have a cup of tea, or will you have something else?"

The instinct of the Street was still strong in Tillie. The Street did not approve of "something else."

"Scotch-and-soda," said Le Moyne. "And shall I buy a ticket for you to punch?"

But she only smiled faintly. He was sorry he had made the blunder. Evidently the Street and all that pertained was a sore subject.

So this was Tillie's new home! It was for this that she had exchanged the virginal integrity of her life at Mrs. McKee's--for this wind-swept little house, tidily ugly, infinitely lonely. There were two crayon enlargements over the mantel. One was Schwitter, evidently. The other was the paper-doll wife. K. wondered what curious instinct of self-abnegation had caused Tillie to leave the wife there undisturbed. Back of its position of honor he saw the girl's realization of her own situation. On a wooden shelf, exactly between the two pictures, was another vase of dried flowers.

Tillie brought the Scotch, already mixed, in a tall glass. K. would have preferred to mix it himself, but the Scotch was good. He felt a new respect for Mr. Schwitter.

"You gave me a turn at first," said Tillie. "But I am right glad to see you, Mr. Le Moyne. Now that the roads are bad, nobody comes very much. It's lonely."

Until now, K. and Tillie, when they met, had met conversationally on the common ground of food. They no longer had that, and between them both lay like a barrier their last conversation.

"Are you happy, Tillie?" said K. suddenly.

"I expected you'd ask me that. I've been thinking what to say."

Her reply set him watching her face. More attractive it certainly was, but happy? There was a wistfulness about Tillie's mouth that set him wondering.

"Is he good to you?"

"He's about the best man on earth. He's never said a cross word to me--even at first, when I was panicky and scared at every sound."

Le Moyne nodded understandingly.

"I burned a lot of victuals when I first came, running off and hiding when I heard people around the place. It used to seem to me that what I'd done was written on my face. But he never said a word."

"That's over now?"

"I don't run. I am still frightened."

"Then it has been worth while?"

Tillie glanced up at the two pictures over the mantel.

"Sometimes it is--when he comes in tired, and I've a chicken ready or some fried ham and eggs for his supper, and I see him begin to look rested. He lights his pipe, and many an evening he helps me with the dishes. He's happy; he's getting fat."

"But you?" Le Moyne persisted.

"I wouldn't go back to where I was, but I am not happy, Mr. Le Moyne. There's no use pretending. I want a baby. All along I've wanted a baby. He wants one. This place is his, and he'd like a boy to come into it when he's gone. But, my God! if I did have one; what would it be?"

K.'s eyes followed hers to the picture and the everlastings underneath.

"And she--there isn't any prospect of her--?"

"No."

There was no solution to Tillie's problem. Le Moyne, standing on the hearth and looking down at her, realized that, after all, Tillie must work out her own salvation. He could offer her no comfort.

They talked far into the growing twilight of the afternoon. Tillie was hungry for news of the Street: must know of Christine's wedding, of Harriet, of Sidney in her hospital. And when he had told her all, she sat silent, rolling her handkerchief in her fingers. Then:--

"Take the four of us," she said suddenly,--"Christine Lorenz and Sidney Page and Miss Harriet and me,--and which one would you have picked to go wrong like this? I guess, from the looks of things, most folks would have thought it would be the Lorenz girl. They'd have picked Harriet Kennedy for the hospital, and me for the dressmaking, and it would have been Sidney Page that got married and had an automobile. Well, that's life."

She looked up at K. shrewdly.

"There were some people out here lately. They didn't know me, and I heard them talking. They said Sidney Page was going to marry Dr. Max Wilson."

"Possibly. I believe there is no engagement yet."

He had finished with his glass. Tillie rose to take it away. As she stood before him she looked up into his face.

"If you like her as well as I think you do, Mr. Le Moyne, you won't let him get her."

"I am afraid that's not up to me, is it? What would I do with a wife, Tillie?"

"You'd be faithful to her. That's more than he would be. I guess, in the long run, that would count more than money."

That was what K. took home with him after his encounter with Tillie. He pondered it on his way back to the street-car, as he struggled against the wind. The weather had changed. Wagon-tracks along the road were filled with water and had begun to freeze. The rain had turned to a driving sleet that cut his face. Halfway to the trolley line, the dog turned off into a by-road. K. did not miss him. The dog stared after him, one foot raised. Once again his eyes were like Tillie's, as she had waved good-bye from the porch.

His head sunk on his breast, K. covered miles of road with his long, swinging pace, and fought his battle. Was Tillie right, after all, and had he been wrong? Why should he efface himself, if it meant Sidney's unhappiness? Why not accept Wilson's offer and start over again? Then if things went well--the temptation was strong that stormy afternoon. He put it from him at last, because of the conviction that whatever he did would make no change in Sidney's ultimate decision. If she cared enough for Wilson, she would marry him. He felt that she cared enough.

CHAPTER XV

PALMER and Christine returned from their wedding trip the day K. discovered Tillie. Anna Page made much of the arrival, insisted on dinner for them that night at the little house, must help Christine unpack her trunks and arrange her wedding gifts about the apartment. She was brighter than she had been for days, more interested. The wonders of the trousseau filled her with admiration and a sort of jealous envy for Sidney, who could have none of these things. In a pathetic sort of way, she mothered Christine in lieu of her own daughter.

And it was her quick eye that discerned something wrong. Christine was not quite happy. Under her excitement was an undercurrent of reserve. Anna, rich in maternity if in nothing else, felt it, and in reply to some speech of Christine's that struck her as hard, not quite fitting, she gave her a gentle admonishing.

"Married life takes a little adjusting, my dear," she said. "After we have lived to ourselves for a number of years, it is not easy to live for some one else."

Christine straightened from the tea-table she was arranging.

"That's true, of course. But why should the woman do all the adjusting?"

"Men are more set," said poor Anna, who had never been set in anything in her life. "It is harder for them to give in. And, of course, Palmer is older, and his habits--"

"The less said about Palmer's habits the better," flashed Christine. "I appear to have married a bunch of habits."

She gave over her unpacking, and sat down listlessly by the fire, while Anna moved about, busy with the small activities that delighted her.

Six weeks of Palmer's society in unlimited amounts had bored Christine to distraction. She sat with folded hands and looked into a future that seemed to include nothing but Palmer: Palmer asleep with his mouth open; Palmer shaving before breakfast, and irritable until he had had his coffee; Palmer yawning over the newspaper.

And there was a darker side to the picture than that. There was a vision of Palmer slipping quietly into his room and falling into the heavy sleep, not of drunkenness perhaps, but of drink. That had happened twice. She knew now that it would happen again and again, as long as he lived. Drinking leads to other things. The letter she had received on her wedding day was burned into her brain. There would be that in the future too, probably.

Christine was not without courage. She was making a brave clutch at happiness. But that afternoon of the first day at home she was terrified. She was glad when Anna went and left her alone by her fire.

But when she heard a step in the hall, she opened the door herself. She had determined to meet Palmer with a smile. Tears brought nothing; she had learned that already. Men liked smiling women and good cheer. "Daughters of joy," they called girls like the one on the Avenue. So she opened the door smiling.

But it was K. in the hall. She waited while, with his back to her, he shook himself like a great dog. When he turned, she was watching him.

"You!" said Le Moyne. "Why, welcome home."

He smiled down at her, his kindly eyes lighting.

"It's good to be home and to see you again. Won't you come in to my fire?"

"I'm wet."

"All the more reason why you should come," she cried gayly, and held the door wide.

The little parlor was cheerful with fire and soft lamps, bright with silver vases full of flowers. K. stepped inside and took a critical survey of the room.

"Well!" he said. "Between us we have made a pretty good job of this, I with the paper and the wiring, and you with your pretty furnishings and your pretty self."

He glanced at her appreciatively. Christine saw his approval, and was happier than she had been for weeks. She put on the thousand little airs and graces that were a part of her--held her chin high, looked up at him with the little appealing glances that she had found were wasted on Palmer. She lighted the spirit-lamp to make tea, drew out the best chair for him, and patted a cushion with her well-cared-for hands.

"A big chair for a big man!" she said. "And see, here's a footstool."

"I am ridiculously fond of being babied," said K., and quite basked in his new atmosphere of well-being. This was better than his empty room upstairs, than tramping along country roads, than his own thoughts.

"And now, how is everything?" asked Christine from across the fire. "Do tell me all the scandal of the Street."

"There has been no scandal since you went away," said K. And, because each was glad not to be left to his own thoughts, they laughed at this bit of unconscious humor.

"Seriously," said Le Moyne, "we have been very quiet. I have had my salary raised and am now rejoicing in twenty-two dollars a week. I am still not accustomed to it. Just when I had all my ideas fixed for fifteen, I get twenty-two and have to reassemble them. I am disgustingly rich."

"It is very disagreeable when one's income becomes a burden," said Christine gravely.

She was finding in Le Moyne something that she needed just then--a solidity, a sort of dependability, that had nothing to do with heaviness. She felt that here was a man she could trust, almost confide in. She liked his long hands, his shabby but well-cut clothes, his fine profile with its strong chin. She left off her little affectations,--a tribute to his own lack of them,--and sat back in her chair, watching the fire.

When K. chose, he could talk well. The Howes had been to Bermuda on their wedding trip. He knew Bermuda; that gave them a common ground. Christine relaxed under his steady voice. As for K., he frankly enjoyed the little visit--drew himself at last with regret out of his chair.

"You've been very nice to ask me in, Mrs. Howe," he said. "I hope you will allow me to come again. But, of course, you are going to be very gay."

It seemed to Christine she would never be gay again. She did not want him to go away. The sound of his deep voice gave her a sense of security. She liked the clasp of the hand he held out to her, when at last he made a move toward the door.

"Tell Mr. Howe I am sorry he missed our little party," said Le Moyne. "And-- thank you."

"Will you come again?" asked Christine rather wistfully.

"Just as often as you ask me."

As he closed the door behind him, there was a new light in Christine's eyes. Things were not right, but, after all, they were not hopeless. One might still have friends, big and strong, steady of eye and voice. When Palmer came home, the smile she gave him was not forced.

The day's exertion had been bad for Anna. Le Moyne found her on the couch in the transformed sewing-room, and gave her a quick glance of apprehension. She was propped up high with pillows, with a bottle of aromatic ammonia beside her.

"Just--short of breath," she panted. "I--I must get down. Sidney--is coming home--to supper; and--the others--Palmer and--"

That was as far as she got. K., watch in hand, found her pulse thin, stringy, irregular. He had been prepared for some such emergency, and he hurried into his room for amyl-nitrate. When he came back she was almost unconscious. There was no time even to call Katie. He broke the capsule in a towel, and held it over her face. After a time the spasm relaxed, but her condition remained alarming.

Harriet, who had come home by that time, sat by the couch and held her sister's hand. Only once in the next hour or so did she speak. They had sent for Dr. Ed, but he had not come yet. Harriet was too wretched to notice the professional manner in which K. set to work over Anna.

"I've been a very hard sister to her," she said. "If you can pull her through, I'll try to make up for it."

Christine sat on the stairs outside, frightened and helpless. They had sent for Sidney; but the little house had no telephone, and the message was slow in getting off.

At six o'clock Dr. Ed came panting up the stairs and into the room. K. stood back.

"Well, this is sad, Harriet," said Dr. Ed. "Why in the name of Heaven, when I wasn't around, didn't you get another doctor. If she had had some amyl-nitrate--"

"I gave her some nitrate of amyl," said K. quietly. "There was really no time to send for anybody. She almost went under at half-past five."

Max had kept his word, and even Dr. Ed did not suspect K.'s secret. He gave a quick glance at this tall young man who spoke so quietly of what he had done for the sick woman, and went on with his work.

Sidney arrived a little after six, and from that moment the confusion in the sick-room was at an end. She moved Christine from the stairs, where Katie on her numerous errands must crawl over her; set Harriet to warming her mother's bed and getting it ready; opened windows, brought order and quiet. And then, with death in her eyes, she took up her position beside her mother. This was no time for weeping; that would come later. Once she turned to K., standing watchfully beside her.

"I think you have known this for a long time," she said. And, when he did not answer: "Why did you let me stay away from her? It would have been such a little time!"

"We were trying to do our best for both of you," he replied.

Anna was unconscious and sinking fast. One thought obsessed Sidney. She repeated it over and over. It came as a cry from the depths of the girl's new experience.

"She has had so little of life," she said, over and over. "So little! Just this Street. She never knew anything else."

And finally K. took it up.

"After all, Sidney," he said, "the Street IS life: the world is only many streets. She had a great deal. She had love and content, and she had you."

Anna died a little after midnight, a quiet passing, so that only Sidney and the two men knew when she went away. It was Harriet who collapsed. During all that long evening she had sat looking back over years of small unkindnesses. The thorn of Anna's inefficiency had always rankled in her flesh. She had been hard, uncompromising, thwarted. And now it was forever too late.

K. had watched Sidney carefully. Once he thought she was fainting, and went to her. But she shook her head.

"I am all right. Do you think you could get them all out of the room and let me have her alone for just a few minutes?"

He cleared the room, and took up his vigil outside the door. And, as he stood there, he thought of what he had said to Sidney about the Street. It was a world of its own. Here in this very house were death and separation; Harriet's starved life; Christine and Palmer beginning a long and doubtful future together; himself, a failure, and an impostor.

When he opened the door again, Sidney was standing by her mother's bed. He went to her, and she turned and put her head against his shoulder like a tired child.

"Take me away, K.," she said pitifully.

And, with his arm around her, he led her out of the room.

Outside of her small immediate circle Anna's death was hardly felt. The little house went on much as before. Harriet carried back to her business a heaviness of spirit that made it difficult to bear with the small irritations of her day. Perhaps Anna's incapacity, which had always annoyed her, had been physical. She must have had her trouble a longtime. She remembered other women of the Street who had crept through inefficient days, and had at last laid down their burdens and closed their mild eyes, to the lasting astonishment of their families. What did they think about, these women, as they pottered about? Did they resent the impatience that met their lagging movements, the indifference that would not see how they were failing? Hot tears fell on Harriet's fashion-book as it lay on her knee. Not only for Anna--for Anna's prototypes everywhere.

On Sidney--and in less measure, of course, on K.--fell the real brunt of the disaster. Sidney kept up well until after the funeral, but went down the next day with a low fever.

"Overwork and grief," Dr. Ed said, and sternly forbade the hospital again until Christmas. Morning and evening K. stopped at her door and inquired for her, and morning and evening came Sidney's reply:--

"Much better. I'll surely be up to-morrow!"

But the days dragged on and she did not get about.

Downstairs, Christine and Palmer had entered on the round of midwinter gayeties. Palmer's "crowd" was a lively one. There were dinners and dances, week-end excursions to country-houses. The Street grew accustomed to seeing automobiles stop before the little house at all hours of the night. Johnny Rosenfeld, driving Palmer's car, took to falling asleep at the wheel in broad daylight, and voiced his discontent to his mother.

"You never know where you are with them guys," he said briefly. "We start out for half an hour's run in the evening, and get home with the milk-wagons. And the more some of them have had to drink, the more they want to drive the machine. If I get a chance, I'm going to beat it while the wind's my way."

But, talk as he might, in Johnny Rosenfeld's loyal heart there was no thought of desertion. Palmer had given him a man's job, and he would stick by it, no matter what came.

There were some things that Johnny Rosenfeld did not tell his mother. There were evenings when the Howe car was filled, not with Christine and her friends, but with women of a different world; evenings when the destination was not a country estate, but a road-house; evenings when Johnny Rosenfeld, ousted from the driver's seat by some drunken youth, would hold tight to the swinging car and say such fragments of prayers as he could remember. Johnny Rosenfeld, who had started life with few illusions, was in danger of losing such as he had.

One such night Christine put in, lying wakefully in her bed, while the clock on the mantel tolled hour after hour into the night. Palmer did not come home at all. He sent a note from the office in the morning:

"I hope you are not worried, darling. The car broke down near the Country Club last night, and there was nothing to do but to spend the night there. I would have sent you word, but I did not want to rouse you. What do you say to the theater to-night and supper afterward?"

Christine was learning. She telephoned the Country Club that morning, and found that Palmer had not been there. But, although she knew now that he was deceiving her, as he always had deceived her, as probably he always would, she hesitated to confront him with what she knew. She shrank, as many a woman has shrunk before, from confronting him with his lie.

But the second time it happened, she was roused. It was almost Christmas then, and Sidney was well on the way to recovery, thinner and very white, but going slowly up and down the staircase on K.'s arm, and sitting with Harriet and K. at the dinner table. She was begging to be back on duty for Christmas, and K. felt that he would have to give her up soon.

At three o'clock one morning Sidney roused from a light sleep to hear a rapping on her door.

"Is that you, Aunt Harriet?" she called.

"It's Christine. May I come in?"

Sidney unlocked her door. Christine slipped into the room. She carried a candle, and before she spoke she looked at Sidney's watch on the bedside table.

"I hoped my clock was wrong," she said. "I am sorry to waken you, Sidney, but I don't know what to do."

"Are you ill?"

"No. Palmer has not come home."

"What time is it?"

"After three o'clock."

Sidney had lighted the gas and was throwing on her dressing-gown.

"When he went out did he say--"

"He said nothing. We had been quarreling. Sidney, I am going home in the morning."

"You don't mean that, do you?"

"Don't I look as if I mean it? How much of this sort of thing is a woman supposed to endure?"

"Perhaps he has been delayed. These things always seem terrible in the middle of the night, but by morning--"

Christine whirled on her.

"This isn't the first time. You remember the letter I got on my wedding day?"

"Yes."

"He's gone back to her."

"Christine! Oh, I am sure you're wrong. He's devoted to you. I don't believe it!"

"Believe it or not," said Christine doggedly, "that's exactly what has happened. I got something out of that little rat of a Rosenfeld boy, and the rest I know because I know Palmer. He's out with her to-night."

The hospital had taught Sidney one thing: that it took many people to make a world, and that out of these some were inevitably vicious. But vice had remained for her a clear abstraction. There were such people, and because one was in the world for service one cared for them. Even the Saviour had been kind to the woman of the streets.

But here abruptly Sidney found the great injustice of the world--that because of this vice the good suffer more than the wicked. Her young spirit rose in hot rebellion.

"It isn't fair!" she cried. "It makes me hate all the men in the world. Palmer cares for you, and yet he can do a thing like this!"

Christine was pacing nervously up and down the room. Mere companionship had soothed her. She was now, on the surface at least, less excited than Sidney.

"They are not all like Palmer, thank Heaven," she said. "There are decent men. My father is one, and your K., here in the house, is another."

At four o'clock in the morning Palmer Howe came home. Christine met him in the lower hall. He was rather pale, but entirely sober. She confronted him in her straight white gown and waited for him to speak.

"I am sorry to be so late, Chris," he said. "The fact is, I am all in. I was driving the car out Seven Mile Run. We blew out a tire and the thing turned over."

Christine noticed then that his right arm was hanging inert by his side.

CHAPTER XVI

YOUNG Howe had been firmly resolved to give up all his bachelor habits with his wedding day. In his indolent, rather selfish way, he was much in love with his wife.

But with the inevitable misunderstandings of the first months of marriage had come a desire to be appreciated once again at his face value. Grace had taken him, not for what he was, but for what he seemed to be. With Christine the veil was rent. She knew him now--all his small indolences, his affectations, his weaknesses. Later on, like other women since the world began, she would learn to dissemble, to affect to believe him what he was not.

Grace had learned this lesson long ago. It was the ABC of her knowledge. And so, back to Grace six weeks after his wedding day came Palmer Howe, not with a suggestion to renew the old relationship, but for comradeship.

Christine sulked--he wanted good cheer; Christine was intolerant--he wanted tolerance; she disapproved of him and showed her disapproval--he wanted approval. He wanted life to be comfortable and cheerful, without recriminations, a little work and much play, a drink when one was thirsty. Distorted though it was, and founded on a wrong basis, perhaps, deep in his heart Palmer's only longing was for happiness; but this happiness must be of an active sort--not content, which is passive, but enjoyment.

"Come on out," he said. "I've got a car now. No taxi working its head off for us. Just a little run over the country roads, eh?"

It was the afternoon of the day before Christine's night visit to Sidney. The office had been closed, owing to a death, and Palmer was in possession of a holiday.

"Come on," he coaxed. "We'll go out to the Climbing Rose and have supper."

"I don't want to go."

"That's not true, Grace, and you know it."

"You and I are through."

"It's your doing, not mine. The roads are frozen hard; an hour's run into the country will bring your color back."

"Much you care about that. Go and ride with your wife," said the girl, and flung away from him.

The last few weeks had filled out her thin figure, but she still bore traces of her illness. Her short hair was curled over her head. She looked curiously boyish, almost sexless.

Because she saw him wince when she mentioned Christine, her ill temper increased. She showed her teeth.

"You get out of here," she said suddenly. "I didn't ask you to come back. I don't want you."

"Good Heavens, Grace! You always knew I would have to marry some day."

"I was sick; I nearly died. I didn't hear any reports of you hanging around the hospital to learn how I was getting along."

He laughed rather sheepishly.

"I had to be careful. You know that as well as I do. I know half the staff there. Besides, one of--" He hesitated over his wife's name. "A girl I know very well was in the training-school. There would have been the devil to pay if I'd as much as called up."

"You never told me you were going to get married."

Cornered, he slipped an arm around her. But she shook him off.

"I meant to tell you, honey; but you got sick. Anyhow, I--I hated to tell you, honey."

He had furnished the flat for her. There was a comfortable feeling of coming home about going there again. And, now that the worst minute of their meeting was over, he was visibly happier. But Grace continued to stand eyeing him somberly.

"I've got something to tell you," she said. "Don't have a fit, and don't laugh. If you do, I'll--I'll jump out of the window. I've got a place in a store. I'm going to be straight, Palmer."

"Good for you!"

He meant it. She was a nice girl and he was fond of her. The other was a dog's life. And he was not unselfish about it. She could not belong to him. He did not want her to belong to any one else.

"One of the nurses in the hospital, a Miss Page, has got me something to do at Lipton and Homburg's. I am going on for the January white sale. If I make good they will keep me."

He had put her aside without a qualm; and now he met her announcement with approval. He meant to let her alone. They would have a holiday together, and then they would say good-bye. And she had not fooled him. She still cared. He was getting off well, all things considered. She might have raised a row.

"Good work!" he said. "You'll be a lot happier. But that isn't any reason why we shouldn't be friends, is it? Just friends; I mean that. I would like to feel that I can stop in now and then and say how do you do."

"I promised Miss Page."

"Never mind Miss Page."

The mention of Sidney's name brought up in his mind Christine as he had left her that morning. He scowled. Things were not going well at home. There was something wrong with Christine. She used to be a good sport, but she had never been the same since the day of the wedding. He thought her attitude toward him was one of suspicion. It made him uncomfortable. But any attempt on his part to fathom it only met with cold silence. That had been her attitude that morning.

"I'll tell you what we'll do," he said. "We won't go to any of the old places. I've found a new roadhouse in the country that's respectable enough to suit anybody. We'll go out to Schwitter's and get some dinner. I'll promise to get you back early. How's that?"

In the end she gave in. And on the way out he lived up to the letter of their agreement. The situation exhilarated him: Grace with her new air of virtue, her new aloofness; his comfortable car; Johnny Rosenfeld's discreet back and alert ears.

The adventure had all the thrill of a new conquest in it. He treated the girl with deference, did not insist when she refused a cigarette, felt glowingly virtuous and exultant at the same time.

When the car drew up before the Schwitter place, he slipped a five-dollar bill into Johnny Rosenfeld's not over-clean hand.

"I don't mind the ears," he said. "Just watch your tongue, lad." And Johnny stalled his engine in sheer surprise.

"There's just enough of the Jew in me," said Johnny, "to know how to talk a lot and say nothing, Mr. Howe."

He crawled stiffly out of the car and prepared to crank it.

"I'll just give her the 'once over' now and then," he said. "She'll freeze solid if I let her stand."

Grace had gone up the narrow path to the house. She had the gift of looking well in her clothes, and her small hat with its long quill and her motor-coat were chic and becoming. She never overdressed, as Christine was inclined to do.

Fortunately for Palmer, Tillie did not see him. A heavy German maid waited at the table in the dining-room, while Tillie baked waffles in the kitchen.

Johnny Rosenfeld, going around the side path to the kitchen door with visions of hot coffee and a country supper for his frozen stomach, saw her through the window bending flushed over the stove, and hesitated. Then, without a word, he tiptoed back to the car again, and, crawling into the tonneau, covered himself with rugs. In his untutored mind were certain great qualities, and loyalty to his employer was one. The five dollars in his pocket had nothing whatever to do with it.

At eighteen he had developed a philosophy of four words. It took the place of the Golden Rule, the Ten Commandments, and the Catechism. It was: "Mind your own business."

The discovery of Tillie's hiding-place interested but did not thrill him. Tillie was his cousin. If she wanted to do the sort of thing she was doing, that was her affair. Tillie and her middle-aged lover, Palmer Howe and Grace--the alley was not unfamiliar with such relationships. It viewed them with tolerance until they were found out, when it raised its hands.

True to his promise, Palmer wakened the sleeping boy before nine o'clock. Grace had eaten little and drunk nothing; but Howe was slightly stimulated.

"Give her the 'once over,'" he told Johnny, "and then go back and crawl into the rugs again. I'll drive in."

Grace sat beside him. Their progress was slow and rough over the country roads, but when they reached the State road Howe threw open the throttle. He drove well. The liquor was in his blood. He took chances and got away with them, laughing at the girl's gasps of dismay.

"Wait until I get beyond Simkinsville," he said, "and I'll let her out. You're going to travel tonight, honey."

The girl sat beside him with her eyes fixed ahead. He had been drinking, and the warmth of the liquor was in his voice. She was determined on one thing. She was going to make him live up to the letter of his promise to go away at the house door; and more and more she realized that it would be difficult. His mood was reckless, masterful. Instead of laughing when she drew back from a proffered caress, he turned surly. Obstinate lines that she remembered appeared from his nostrils to the corners of his mouth. She was uneasy.

Finally she hit on a plan to make him stop somewhere in her neighborhood and let her get out of the car. She would not come back after that.

There was another car going toward the city. Now it passed them, and as often they passed it. It became a contest of wits. Palmer's car lost on the hills, but gained on the long level stretches, which gleamed with a coating of thin ice.

"I wish you'd let them get ahead, Palmer. It's silly and it's reckless."

"I told you we'd travel to-night."

He turned a little glance at her. What the deuce was the matter with women, anyhow? Were none of them cheerful any more? Here was Grace as sober as Christine. He felt outraged, defrauded.

His light car skidded and struck the big car heavily. On a smooth road perhaps nothing more serious than broken mudguards would have been the result. But on the ice the small car slewed around and slid over the edge of the bank. At the bottom of the declivity it turned over.

Grace was flung clear of the wreckage. Howe freed himself and stood erect, with one arm hanging at his side. There was no sound at all from the boy under the tonneau.

The big car had stopped. Down the bank plunged a heavy, gorilla-like figure, long arms pushing aside the frozen branches of trees. When he reached the car, O'Hara found Grace sitting unhurt on the ground. In the wreck of the car the lamps had not been extinguished, and by their light he made out Howe, swaying dizzily.

"Anybody underneath?"

"The chauffeur. He's dead, I think. He doesn't answer."

The other members of O'Hara's party had crawled down the bank by that time.

With the aid of a jack, they got the car up. Johnny Rosenfeld lay doubled on his face underneath. When he came to and opened his eyes, Grace almost shrieked with relief.

"I'm all right," said Johnny Rosenfeld. And, when they offered him whiskey: "Away with the fire-water. I am no drinker. I--I--" A spasm of pain twisted his face. "I guess I'll get up." With his arms he lifted himself to a sitting position, and fell back again.

"God!" he said. "I can't move my legs."

CHAPTER XVII

BY Christmas Day Sidney was back in the hospital, a little wan, but valiantly determined to keep her life to its mark of service. She had a talk with K. the night before she left.

Katie was out, and Sidney had put the dining-room in order. K. sat by the table and watched her as she moved about the room.

The past few weeks had been very wonderful to him: to help her up and down the stairs, to read to her in the evenings as she lay on the couch in the sewing-room; later, as she improved, to bring small dainties home for her tray, and, having stood over Katie while she cooked them, to bear them in triumph to that upper room--he had not been so happy in years.

And now it was over. He drew a long breath.

"I hope you don't feel as if you must stay on," she said anxiously. "Not that we don't want you--you know better than that."

"There is no place else in the whole world that I want to go to," he said simply.

"I seem to be always relying on somebody's kindness to--to keep things together. First, for years and years, it was Aunt Harriet; now it is you."

"Don't you realize that, instead of your being grateful to me, it is I who am undeniably grateful to you? This is home now. I have lived around--in different places and in different ways. I would rather be here than anywhere else in the world."

But he did not look at her. There was so much that was hopeless in his eyes that he did not want her to see. She would be quite capable, he told himself savagely, of marrying him out of sheer pity if she ever guessed. And he was afraid--afraid, since he wanted her so much--that he would be fool and weakling enough to take her even on those terms. So he looked away.

Everything was ready for her return to the hospital. She had been out that day to put flowers on the quiet grave where Anna lay with folded hands; she had made her round of little visits on the Street; and now her suit-case, packed, was in the hall.

"In one way, it will be a little better for you than if Christine and Palmer were not in the house. You like Christine, don't you?"

"Very much."

"She likes you, K. She depends on you, too, especially since that night when you took care of Palmer's arm before we got Dr. Max. I often think, K., what a good doctor you would have been. You knew so well what to do for mother."

She broke off. She still could not trust her voice about her mother.

"Palmer's arm is going to be quite straight. Dr. Ed is so proud of Max over it. It was a bad fracture."

He had been waiting for that. Once at least, whenever they were together, she brought Max into the conversation. She was quite unconscious of it.

"You and Max are great friends. I knew you would like him. He is interesting, don't you think?"

"Very," said K.

To save his life, he could not put any warmth into his voice. He would be fair. It was not in human nature to expect more of him.

"Those long talks you have, shut in your room--what in the world do you talk about? Politics?"

"Occasionally."

She was a little jealous of those evenings, when she sat alone, or when Harriet, sitting with her, made sketches under the lamp to the accompaniment of a steady hum of masculine voices from across the hall. Not that she was ignored, of course. Max came in always, before he went, and, leaning over the back of a chair, would inform her of the absolute blankness of life in the hospital without her.

"I go every day because I must," he would assure her gayly; "but, I tell you, the snap is gone out of it. When there was a chance that every cap was YOUR cap, the mere progress along a corridor became thrilling." He had a foreign trick of throwing out his hands, with a little shrug of the shoulders. "Cui bono?" he said--which, being translated, means: "What the devil's the use!"

And K. would stand in the doorway, quietly smoking, or go back to his room and lock away in his trunk the great German books on surgery with which he and Max had been working out a case.

So K. sat by the dining-room table and listened to her talk of Max that last evening together.

"I told Mrs. Rosenfeld to-day not to be too much discouraged about Johnny. I had seen Dr. Max do such wonderful things. Now that you are such friends,"--she eyed him wistfully,--"perhaps some day you will come to one of his operations. Even if you didn't understand exactly, I know it would thrill you. And--I'd like you to see me in my uniform, K. You never have."

She grew a little sad as the evening went on. She was going to miss K. very much. While she was ill she had watched the clock for the time to listen for him. She knew the way he slammed the front door. Palmer never slammed the door. She knew too that, just after a bang that threatened the very glass in the transom, K. would come to the foot of the stairs and call:--

"Ahoy, there!"

"Aye, aye," she would answer--which was, he assured her, the proper response.

Whether he came up the stairs at once or took his way back to Katie had depended on whether his tribute for the day was fruit or sweetbreads.

Now that was all over. They were such good friends. He would miss her, too; but he would have Harriet and Christine and--Max. Back in a circle to Max, of course.

She insisted, that last evening, on sitting up with him until midnight ushered in Christmas Day. Christine and Palmer were out; Harriet, having presented Sidney with a blouse that had been left over in the shop from the autumn's business, had yawned herself to bed.

When the bells announced midnight, Sidney roused with a start. She realized that neither of them had spoken, and that K.'s eyes were fixed on her. The little clock on the shelf took up the burden of the churches, and struck the hour in quick staccato notes.

Sidney rose and went over to K., her black dress in soft folds about her.

"He is born, K."

"He is born, dear."

She stooped and kissed his cheek lightly.

Christmas Day dawned thick and white. Sidney left the little house at six, with the street light still burning through a mist of falling snow.

The hospital wards and corridors were still lighted when she went on duty at seven o'clock. She had been assigned to the men's surgical ward, and went there at once. She had not seen Carlotta Harrison since her mother's death; but she found her on duty in the surgical ward. For the second time in four months, the two girls were working side by side.

Sidney's recollection of her previous service under Carlotta made her nervous. But the older girl greeted her pleasantly.

"We were all sorry to hear of your trouble," she said. "I hope we shall get on nicely."

Sidney surveyed the ward, full to overflowing. At the far end two cots had been placed.

"The ward is heavy, isn't it?"

"Very. I've been almost mad at dressing hour. There are three of us--you, myself, and a probationer."

The first light of the Christmas morning was coming through the windows. Carlotta put out the lights and turned in a business-like way to her records.

"The probationer's name is Wardwell," she said. "Perhaps you'd better help her with the breakfasts. If there's any way to make a mistake, she makes it."

It was after eight when Sidney found Johnny Rosenfeld.

"You here in the ward, Johnny!" she said.

Suffering had refined the boy's features. His dark, heavily fringed eyes looked at her from a pale face. But he smiled up at her cheerfully.

"I was in a private room; but it cost thirty plunks a week, so I moved. Why pay rent?"

Sidney had not seen him since his accident. She had wished to go, but K. had urged against it. She was not strong, and she had already suffered much. And now the work of the ward pressed hard. She had only a moment. She stood beside him and stroked his hand.

"I'm sorry, Johnny."

He pretended to think that her sympathy was for his fall from the estate of a private patient to the free ward.

"Oh, I'm all right, Miss Sidney," he said. "Mr. Howe is paying six dollars a week for me. The difference between me and the other fellows around here is that I get a napkin on my tray and they don't."

Before his determined cheerfulness Sidney choked.

"Six dollars a week for a napkin is going some. I wish you'd tell Mr. Howe to give ma the six dollars. She'll be needing it. I'm no bloated aristocrat; I don't have to have a napkin."

"Have they told you what the trouble is?"

"Back's broke. But don't let that worry you. Dr. Max Wilson is going to operate on me. I'll be doing the tango yet."

Sidney's eyes shone. Of course, Max could do it. What a thing it was to be able to take this life-in-death of Johnny Rosenfeld's and make it life again!

All sorts of men made up Sidney's world: the derelicts who wandered through the ward in flapping slippers, listlessly carrying trays; the unshaven men in the beds, looking forward to another day of boredom, if not of pain; Palmer Howe with his broken arm; K., tender and strong, but filling no especial place in the world. Towering over them all was the younger Wilson. He meant for her, that Christmas morning, all that the other men were not--to their weakness strength, courage, daring, power.

Johnny Rosenfeld lay back on the pillows and watched her face.

"When I was a kid," he said, "and ran along the Street, calling Dr. Max a dude, I never thought I'd lie here watching that door to see him come in. You have had trouble, too. Ain't it the hell of a world, anyhow? It ain't much of a Christmas to you, either."

Sidney fed him his morning beef tea, and, because her eyes filled up with tears now and then at his helplessness, she was not so skillful as she might have been. When one spoonful had gone down his neck, he smiled up at her whimsically.

"Run for your life. The dam's burst!" he said.

As much as was possible, the hospital rested on that Christmas Day. The internes went about in fresh white ducks with sprays of mistletoe in their buttonholes, doing few dressings. Over the upper floors, where the kitchens were located, spread toward noon the insidious odor of roasting turkeys. Every ward had its vase of holly. In the afternoon, services were held in the chapel downstairs.

Wheel-chairs made their slow progress along corridors and down elevators. Convalescents who were able to walk flapped along in carpet slippers.

Gradually the chapel filled up. Outside the wide doors of the corridor the wheel-chairs were arranged in a semicircle. Behind them, dressed for the occasion, were the elevator-men, the orderlies, and Big John, who drove the ambulance.

On one side of the aisle, near the front, sat the nurses in rows, in crisp caps and fresh uniforms. On the other side had been reserved a place for the staff. The internes stood back against the wall, ready to run out between rejoicings, as it were--for a cigarette or an ambulance call, as the case might be.

Over everything brooded the after-dinner peace of Christmas afternoon.

The nurses sang, and Sidney sang with them, her fresh young voice rising above the rest. Yellow winter sunlight came through the stained-glass windows and shone on her lovely flushed face, her smooth kerchief, her cap, always just a little awry.

Dr. Max, lounging against the wall, across the chapel, found his eyes straying toward her constantly. How she stood out from the others! What a zest for living and for happiness she had!

The Episcopal clergyman read the Epistle:

"Thou hast loved righteousness, and hated iniquity; therefore God, even thy God, hath anointed thee with the oil of gladness above thy fellows."

That was Sidney. She was good, and she had been anointed with the oil of gladness. And he--

His brother was singing. His deep bass voice, not always true, boomed out above the sound of the small organ. Ed had been a good brother to him; he had been a good son.

Max's vagrant mind wandered away from the service to the picture of his mother over his brother's littered desk, to the Street, to K., to the girl who had refused to marry him because she did not trust him, to Carlotta last of all. He turned a little and ran his eyes along the line of nurses.

Ah, there she was. As if she were conscious of his scrutiny, she lifted her head and glanced toward him. Swift color flooded her face.

The nurses sang:--

"O holy Child of Bethlehem!   Descend to us, we pray;   Cast out our sin, and enter in,   Be born in us to-day."

The wheel-chairs and convalescents quavered the familiar words. Dr. Ed's heavy throat shook with earnestness.

The Head, sitting a little apart with her hands folded in her lap and weary with the suffering of the world, closed her eyes and listened.

The Christmas morning had brought Sidney half a dozen gifts. K. sent her a silver thermometer case with her monogram, Christine a toilet mirror. But the gift of gifts, over which Sidney's eyes had glowed, was a great box of roses marked in Dr. Max's copper-plate writing, "From a neighbor."

Tucked in the soft folds of her kerchief was one of the roses that afternoon.

Services over, the nurses filed out. Max was waiting for Sidney in the corridor.

"Merry Christmas!" he said, and held out his hand.

"Merry Christmas!" she said. "You see!"--she glanced down to the rose she wore. "The others make the most splendid bit of color in the ward."

"But they were for you!"

"They are not any the less mine because I am letting other people have a chance to enjoy them."

Under all his gayety he was curiously diffident with her. All the pretty speeches he would have made to Carlotta under the circumstances died before her frank glance.

There were many things he wanted to say to her. He wanted to tell her that he was sorry her mother had died; that the Street was empty without her; that he looked forward to these daily meetings with her as a holy man to his hour before his saint. What he really said was to inquire politely whether she had had her Christmas dinner.

Sidney eyed him, half amused, half hurt.

"What have I done, Max? Is it bad for discipline for us to be good friends?"

"Damn discipline!" said the pride of the staff.

Carlotta was watching them from the chapel. Something in her eyes roused the devil of mischief that always slumbered in him.

"My car's been stalled in a snowdrift downtown since early this morning, and I have Ed's Peggy in a sleigh. Put on your things and come for a ride."

He hoped Carlotta could hear what he said; to be certain of it, he maliciously raised his voice a trifle.

"Just a little run," he urged. "Put on your warmest things."

Sidney protested. She was to be free that afternoon until six o'clock; but she had promised to go home.

"K. is alone."

"K. can sit with Christine. Ten to one, he's with her now."

The temptation was very strong. She had been working hard all day. The heavy odor of the hospital, mingled with the scent of pine and evergreen in the chapel; made her dizzy. The fresh outdoors called her. And, besides, if K. were with Christine--

"It's forbidden, isn't it?"

"I believe it is." He smiled at her.

"And yet, you continue to tempt me and expect me to yield!"

"One of the most delightful things about temptation is yielding now and then."

After all, the situation seemed absurd. Here was her old friend and neighbor asking to take her out for a daylight ride. The swift rebellion of youth against authority surged up in Sidney.

"Very well; I'll go."

Carlotta had gone by that time--gone with hate in her heart and black despair. She knew very well what the issue would be. Sidney would drive with him, and he would tell her how lovely she looked with the air on her face and the snow about her. The jerky motion of the little sleigh would throw them close together. How well she knew it all! He would touch Sidney's hand daringly and smile in her eyes. That was his method: to play at love-making like an audacious boy, until quite suddenly the cloak dropped and the danger was there.

The Christmas excitement had not died out in the ward when Carlotta went back to it. On each bedside table was an orange, and beside it a pair of woolen gloves and a folded white handkerchief. There were sprays of holly scattered about, too, and the after-dinner content of roast turkey and ice-cream.

The lame girl who played the violin limped down the corridor into the ward. She was greeted with silence, that truest tribute, and with the instant composing of the restless ward to peace.

She was pretty in a young, pathetic way, and because to her Christmas was a festival and meant hope and the promise of the young Lord, she played cheerful things.

The ward sat up, remembered that it was not the Sabbath, smiled across from bed to bed.

The probationer, whose name was Wardwell, was a tall, lean girl with a long, pointed nose. She kept up a running accompaniment of small talk to the music.

"Last Christmas," she said plaintively, "we went out into the country in a hay-wagon and had a real time. I don't know what I am here for, anyhow. I am a fool."

"Undoubtedly," said Carlotta.

"Turkey and goose, mince pie and pumpkin pie, four kinds of cake; that's the sort of spread we have up in our part of the world. When I think of what I sat down to to-day--!"

She had a profound respect for Carlotta, and her motto in the hospital differed from Sidney's in that it was to placate her superiors, while Sidney's had been to care for her patients.

Seeing Carlotta bored, she ventured a little gossip. She had idly glued the label of a medicine bottle on the back of her hand, and was scratching a skull and cross-bones on it.

"I wonder if you have noticed something," she said, eyes on the label.

"I have noticed that the three-o'clock medicines are not given," said Carlotta sharply; and Miss Wardwell, still labeled and adorned, made the rounds of the ward.

When she came back she was sulky.

"I'm no gossip," she said, putting the tray on the table. "If you won't see, you won't. That Rosenfeld boy is crying."

As it was not required that tears be recorded on the record, Carlotta paid no attention to this.

"What won't I see?"

It required a little urging now. Miss Wardwell swelled with importance and let her superior ask her twice. Then:--

"Dr. Wilson's crazy about Miss Page."

A hand seemed to catch Carlotta's heart and hold it.

"They're old friends."

"Piffle! Being an old friend doesn't make you look at a girl as if you wanted to take a bite out of her. Mark my word, Miss Harrison, she'll never finish her training; she'll marry him. I wish," concluded the probationer plaintively, "that some good-looking fellow like that would take a fancy to me. I'd do him credit. I am as ugly as a mud fence, but I've got style."

She was right, probably. She was long and sinuous, but she wore her lanky, ill-fitting clothes with a certain distinction. Harriet Kennedy would have dressed her in jade green to match her eyes, and with long jade earrings, and made her a fashion.

Carlotta's lips were dry. The violinist had seen the tears on Johnny Rosenfeld's white cheeks, and had rushed into rollicking, joyous music. The ward echoed with it. "I'm twenty-one and she's eighteen," hummed the ward under its breath. Miss Wardwell's thin body swayed.

"Lord, how I'd like to dance! If I ever get out of this charnel-house!"

The medicine-tray lay at Carlotta's elbow; beside it the box of labels. This crude girl was right--right. Carlotta knew it down to the depths of her tortured brain. As inevitably as the night followed the day, she was losing her game. She had lost already, unless--

If she could get Sidney out of the hospital, it would simplify things. She surmised shrewdly that on the Street their interests were wide apart. It was here that they met on common ground.

The lame violin-player limped out of the ward; the shadows of the early winter twilight settled down. At five o'clock Carlotta sent Miss Wardwell to first supper, to the surprise of that seldom surprised person. The ward lay still or shuffled about quietly. Christmas was over, and there were no evening papers to look forward to.

Carlotta gave the five-o'clock medicines. Then she sat down at the table near the door, with the tray in front of her. There are certain thoughts that are at first functions of the brain; after a long time the spinal cord takes them up and converts them into acts almost automatically. Perhaps because for the last month she had done the thing so often in her mind, its actual performance was almost without conscious thought.

Carlotta took a bottle from her medicine cupboard, and, writing a new label for it, pasted it over the old one. Then she exchanged it for one of the same size on the medicine tray.

In the dining-room, at the probationers' table, Miss Wardwell was talking.

"Believe me," she said, "me for the country and the simple life after this. They think I'm only a probationer and don't see anything, but I've got eyes in my head. Harrison is stark crazy over Dr. Wilson, and she thinks I don't see it. But never mind; I paid, her up to-day for a few of the jolts she has given me."

Throughout the dining-room busy and competent young women came and ate, hastily or leisurely as their opportunity was, and went on their way again. In their hands they held the keys, not always of life and death perhaps, but of ease from pain, of tenderness, of smooth pillows, and cups of water to thirsty lips. In their eyes, as in Sidney's, burned the light of service.

But here and there one found women, like Carlotta and Miss Wardwell, who had mistaken their vocation, who railed against the monotony of the life, its limitations, its endless sacrifices. They showed it in their eyes.

Fifty or so against two--fifty who looked out on the world with the fearless glance of those who have seen life to its depths, and, with the broad understanding of actual contact, still found it good. Fifty who were learning or had learned not to draw aside their clean starched skirts from the drab of the streets. And the fifty, who found the very scum of the gutters not too filthy for tenderness and care, let Carlotta and, in lesser measure, the new probationer alone. They could not have voiced their reasons.

The supper-room was filled with their soft voices, the rustle of their skirts, the gleam of their stiff white caps.

When Carlotta came in, she greeted none of them. They did not like her, and she knew it.

Before her, instead of the tidy supper-table, she was seeing the medicine-tray as she had left it.

"I guess I've fixed her," she said to herself.
Her very soul was sick with fear of what she had done.

CHAPTER XVIII

K. saw Sidney for only a moment on Christmas Day. This was when the gay little sleigh had stopped in front of the house.

Sidney had hurried radiantly in for a moment. Christine's parlor was gay with firelight and noisy with chatter and with the clatter of her teacups.

K., lounging indolently in front of the fire, had turned to see Sidney in the doorway, and leaped to his feet.

"I can't come in," she cried. "I am only here for a moment. I am out sleigh-riding with Dr. Wilson. It's perfectly delightful."

"Ask him in for a cup of tea," Christine called out. "Here's Aunt Harriet and mother and even Palmer!"

Christine had aged during the last weeks, but she was putting up a brave front.

"I'll ask him."

Sidney ran to the front door and called: "Will you come in for a cup of tea?"

"Tea! Good Heavens, no. Hurry."

As Sidney turned back into the house, she met Palmer. He had come out in the hall, and had closed the door into the parlor behind him. His arm was still in splints, and swung suspended in a gay silk sling.

The sound of laughter came through the door faintly.

"How is he to-day?" He meant Johnny, of course. The boy's face was always with him.

"Better in some ways, but of course--"

"When are they going to operate?"

"When he is a little stronger. Why don't you come into see him?"

"I can't. That's the truth. I can't face the poor youngster."

"He doesn't seem to blame you; he says it's all in the game."

"Sidney, does Christine know that I was not alone that night?"

"If she guesses, it is not because of anything the boy has said. He has told nothing."

Out of the firelight, away from the chatter and the laughter, Palmer's face showed worn and haggard. He put his free hand on Sidney's shoulder.

"I was thinking that perhaps if I went away--"

"That would be cowardly, wouldn't it?"

"If Christine would only say something and get it over with! She doesn't sulk; I think she's really trying to be kind. But she hates me, Sidney. She turns pale every time I touch her hand."

All the light had died out of Sidney's face. Life was terrible, after all--overwhelming. One did wrong things, and other people suffered; or one was good, as her mother had been, and was left lonely, a widow, or like Aunt Harriet. Life was a sham, too. Things were so different from what they seemed to be: Christine beyond the door, pouring tea and laughing with her heart in ashes; Palmer beside her, faultlessly dressed and wretched. The only one she thought really contented was K. He seemed to move so calmly in his little orbit. He was always so steady, so balanced. If life held no heights for him, at least it held no depths.

So Sidney thought, in her ignorance!

"There's only one thing, Palmer," she said gravely. "Johnny Rosenfeld is going to have his chance. If anybody in the world can save him, Max Wilson can."

The light of that speech was in her eyes when she went out to the sleigh again. K. followed her out and tucked the robes in carefully about her.

"Warm enough?"

"All right, thank you."

"Don't go too far. Is there any chance of having you home for supper?"

"I think not. I am to go on duty at six again."

If there was a shadow in K.'s eyes, she did not see it. He waved them off smilingly from the pavement, and went rather heavily back into the house.

"Just how many men are in love with you, Sidney?" asked Max, as Peggy started up the Street.

"No one that I know of, unless--"

"Exactly. Unless--"

"What I meant," she said with dignity, "is that unless one counts very young men, and that isn't really love."

"We'll leave out Joe Drummond and myself--for, of course, I am very young. Who is in love with you besides Le Moyne? Any of the internes at the hospital?"

"Me! Le Moyne is not in love with me."

There was such sincerity in her voice that Wilson was relieved.

K., older than himself and more grave, had always had an odd attraction for women. He had been frankly bored by them, but the fact had remained. And Max more than suspected that now, at last, he had been caught.

"Don't you really mean that you are in love with Le Moyne?"

"Please don't be absurd. I am not in love with anybody; I haven't time to be in love. I have my profession now."

"Bah! A woman's real profession is love."

Sidney differed from this hotly. So warm did the argument become that they passed without seeing a middle-aged gentleman, short and rather heavy set, struggling through a snowdrift on foot, and carrying in his hand a dilapidated leather bag.

Dr. Ed hailed them. But the cutter slipped by and left him knee-deep, looking ruefully after them.

"The young scamp!" he said. "So that's where Peggy is!"

Nevertheless, there was no anger in Dr. Ed's mind, only a vague and inarticulate regret. These things that came so easily to Max, the affection of women, gay little irresponsibilities like the stealing of Peggy and the sleigh, had never been his. If there was any faint resentment, it was at himself. He had raised the boy wrong-- he had taught him to be selfish. Holding the bag high out of the drifts, he made his slow progress up the Street.

At something after two o'clock that night, K. put down his pipe and listened. He had not been able to sleep since midnight. In his dressing-gown he had sat by the small fire, thinking. The content of his first few months on the Street was rapidly giving way to unrest. He who had meant to cut himself off from life found himself again in close touch with it; his eddy was deep with it.

For the first time, he had begun to question the wisdom of what he had done.

Had it been cowardice, after all? It had taken courage, God knew, to give up everything and come away. In a way, it would have taken more courage to have stayed. Had he been right or wrong?

And there was a new element. He had thought, at first, that he could fight down this love for Sidney. But it was increasingly hard. The innocent touch of her hand on his arm, the moment when he had held her in his arms after her mother's death, the thousand small contacts of her returns to the little house--all these set his blood on fire. And it was fighting blood.

Under his quiet exterior K. fought many conflicts those winter days--over his desk and ledger at the office, in his room alone, with Harriet planning fresh triumphs beyond the partition, even by Christine's fire, with Christine just across, sitting in silence and watching his grave profile and steady eyes.

He had a little picture of Sidney--a snap-shot that he had taken himself. It showed Sidney minus a hand, which had been out of range when the camera had been snapped, and standing on a steep declivity which would have been quite a level had he held the camera straight. Nevertheless it was Sidney, her hair blowing about her, eyes looking out, tender lips smiling. When she was not at home, it sat on K.'s dresser, propped against his collar-box. When she was in the house, it lay under the pin-cushion.

Two o'clock in the morning, then, and K. in his dressing-gown, with the picture propped, not against the collar-box, but against his lamp, where he could see it.

He sat forward in his chair, his hands folded around his knee, and looked at it. He was trying to picture the Sidney of the photograph in his old life--trying to find a place for her. But it was difficult. There had been few women in his old life. His mother had died many years before. There had been women who had cared for him, but he put them impatiently out of his mind.

Then the bell rang.

Christine was moving about below. He could hear her quick steps. Almost before he had heaved his long legs out of the chair, she was tapping at his door outside.

"It's Mrs. Rosenfeld. She says she wants to see you."

He went down the stairs. Mrs. Rosenfeld was standing in the lower hall, a shawl about her shoulders. Her face was white and drawn above it.

"I've had word to go to the hospital," she said. "I thought maybe you'd go with me. It seems as if I can't stand it alone. Oh, Johnny, Johnny!"

"Where's Palmer?" K. demanded of Christine.

"He's not in yet."

"Are you afraid to stay in the house alone?"

"No; please go."

He ran up the staircase to his room and flung on some clothing. In the lower hall, Mrs. Rosenfeld's sobs had become low moans; Christine stood helplessly over her.

"I am terribly sorry," she said--"terribly sorry! When I think whose fault all this is!"

Mrs. Rosenfeld put out a work-hardened hand and caught Christine's fingers.

"Never mind that," she said. "You didn't do it. I guess you and I understand each other. Only pray God you never have a child."

K. never forgot the scene in the small emergency ward to which Johnny had been taken. Under the white lights his boyish figure looked strangely long. There was a group around the bed--Max Wilson, two or three internes, the night nurse on duty, and the Head.

Sitting just inside the door on a straight chair was Sidney--such a Sidney as he never had seen before, her face colorless, her eyes wide and unseeing, her hands clenched in her lap. When he stood beside her, she did not move or look up. The group around the bed had parted to admit Mrs. Rosenfeld, and closed again. Only Sidney and K. remained by the door, isolated, alone.

"You must not take it like that, dear. It's sad, of course. But, after all, in that condition--"

It was her first knowledge that he was there. But she did not turn.

"They say I poisoned him." Her voice was dreary, inflectionless.

"You--what?"

"They say I gave him the wrong medicine; that he's dying; that I murdered him." She shivered.

K. touched her hands. They were ice-cold.

"Tell me about it."

"There is nothing to tell. I came on duty at six o'clock and gave the medicines. When the night nurse came on at seven, everything was all right. The medicine-tray was just as it should be. Johnny was asleep. I went to say good-night to him and he--he was asleep. I didn't give him anything but what was on the tray," she finished piteously. "I looked at the label; I always look."

By a shifting of the group around the bed, K.'s eyes looked for a moment directly into Carlotta's. Just for a moment; then the crowd closed up again. It was well for Carlotta that it did. She looked as if she had seen a ghost--closed her eyes, even reeled.

"Miss Harrison is worn out," Dr. Wilson said brusquely. "Get some one to take her place."

But Carlotta rallied. After all, the presence of this man in this room at such a time meant nothing. He was Sidney's friend, that was all.

But her nerve was shaken. The thing had gone beyond her. She had not meant to kill. It was the boy's weakened condition that was turning her revenge into tragedy.

"I am all right," she pleaded across the bed to the Head. "Let me stay, please. He's from my ward. I--I am responsible."

Wilson was at his wits' end. He had done everything he knew without result. The boy, rousing for an instant, would lapse again into stupor. With a healthy man they could have tried more vigorous measures--could have forced him to his feet and walked him about, could have beaten him with knotted towels dipped in ice-water. But the wrecked body on the bed could stand no such heroic treatment.

It was Le Moyne, after all, who saved Johnny Rosenfeld's life. For, when staff and nurses had exhausted all their resources, he stepped forward with a quiet word that brought the internes to their feet astonished.

There was a new treatment for such cases--it had been tried abroad. He looked at Max.

Max had never heard of it. He threw out his hands.

"Try it, for Heaven's sake," he said. "I'm all in."

The apparatus was not in the house--must be extemporized, indeed, at last, of odds and ends from the operating-room. K. did the work, his long fingers deft and skillful--while Mrs. Rosenfeld knelt by the bed with her face buried; while Sidney sat, dazed and bewildered, on her little chair inside the door; while night nurses tiptoed along the corridor, and the night watchman stared incredulous from outside the door.

When the two great rectangles that were the emergency ward windows had turned from mirrors reflecting the room to gray rectangles in the morning light; Johnny Rosenfeld opened his eyes and spoke the first words that marked his return from the dark valley.

"Gee, this is the life!" he said, and smiled into K.'s watchful face.

When it was clear that the boy would live, K. rose stiffly from the bedside and went over to Sidney's chair.

"He's all right now," he said--"as all right as he can be, poor lad!"

"You did it--you! How strange that you should know such a thing. How am I to thank you?"

The internes, talking among themselves, had wandered down to their dining-room for early coffee. Wilson was giving a few last instructions as to the boy's care. Quite unexpectedly, Sidney caught K.'s hand and held it to her lips. The iron repression of the night, of months indeed, fell away before her simple caress.

"My dear, my dear," he said huskily. "Anything that I can do--for you--at any time--"

It was after Sidney had crept like a broken thing to her room that Carlotta Harrison and K. came face to face. Johnny was quite conscious by that time, a little blue around the lips, but valiantly cheerful.

"More things can happen to a fellow than I ever knew there was!" he said to his mother, and submitted rather sheepishly to her tears and caresses.

"You were always a good boy, Johnny," she said. "Just you get well enough to come home. I'll take care of you the rest of my life. We will get you a wheelchair when you can be about, and I can take you out in the park when I come from work."

"I'll be passenger and you'll be chauffeur, ma."

"Mr. Le Moyne is going to get your father sent up again. With sixty-five cents a day and what I make, we'll get along."

"You bet we will!"

"Oh, Johnny, if I could see you coming in the door again and yelling 'mother' and 'supper' in one breath!"

The meeting between Carlotta and Le Moyne was very quiet. She had been making a sort of subconscious impression on the retina of his mind during all the night. It would be difficult to tell when he actually knew her.

When the preparations for moving Johnny back to the big ward had been made, the other nurses left the room, and Carlotta and the boy were together. K. stopped her on her way to the door.

"Miss Harrison!"

"Yes, Dr. Edwardes."

"I am not Dr. Edwardes here; my name is Le Moyne."

"Ah!"

"I have not seen you since you left St. John's."

"No; I--I rested for a few months."

"I suppose they do not know that you were--that you have had any previous hospital experience."

"No. Are you going to tell them?"

"I shall not tell them, of course."

And thus, by simple mutual consent, it was arranged that each should respect the other's confidence.

Carlotta staggered to her room. There had been a time, just before dawn, when she had had one of those swift revelations that sometimes come at the end of a long night. She had seen herself as she was. The boy was very low, hardly breathing. Her past stretched behind her, a series of small revenges and passionate outbursts, swift yieldings, slow remorse. She dared not look ahead. She would have given every hope she had in the world, just then, for Sidney's stainless past.

She hated herself with that deadliest loathing that comes of complete self-revelation.

And she carried to her room the knowledge that the night's struggle had been in vain--that, although Johnny Rosenfeld would live, she had gained nothing by what he had suffered. The whole night had shown her the hopelessness of any stratagem to win Wilson from his new allegiance. She had surprised him in the hallway, watching Sidney's slender figure as she made her way up the stairs to her room. Never, in all his past overtures to her, had she seen that look in his eyes.

CHAPTER XIX

TO Harriet Kennedy, Sidney's sentence of thirty days' suspension came as a blow. K. broke the news to her that evening before the time for Sidney's arrival.

The little household was sharing in Harriet's prosperity. Katie had a helper now, a little Austrian girl named Mimi. And Harriet had established on the Street the innovation of after-dinner coffee. It was over the after-dinner coffee that K. made his announcement.

"What do you mean by saying she is coming home for thirty days? Is the child ill?"

"Not ill, although she is not quite well. The fact is, Harriet,"--for it was "Harriet" and "K." by this time,--"there has been a sort of semi-accident up at the hospital. It hasn't resulted seriously, but--"

Harriet put down the apostle-spoon in her hand and stared across at him.

"Then she has been suspended? What did she do? I don't believe she did anything!"

"There was a mistake about the medicine, and she was blamed; that's all."

"She'd better come home and stay home," said Harriet shortly. "I hope it doesn't get in the papers. This dressmaking business is a funny sort of thing. One word against you or any of your family, and the crowd's off somewhere else."

"There's nothing against Sidney," K. reminded her. "Nothing in the world. I saw the superintendent myself this afternoon. It seems it's a mere matter of discipline. Somebody made a mistake, and they cannot let such a thing go by. But he believes, as I do, that it was not Sidney."

However Harriet had hardened herself against the girl's arrival, all she had meant to say fled when she saw Sidney's circled eyes and pathetic mouth.

"You child!" she said. "You poor little girl!" And took her corseted bosom.

For the time at least, Sidney's world had gone to pieces about her. All her brave vaunt of service faded before her disgrace.

When Christine would have seen her, she kept her door locked and asked for just that one evening alone. But after Harriet had retired, and Mimi, the Austrian, had crept out to the corner to mail a letter back to Gratz, Sidney unbolted her door and listened in the little upper hall. Harriet, her head in a towel, her face carefully cold-creamed, had gone to bed; but K.'s light, as usual, was shining over the transom. Sidney tiptoed to the door.

"K.!"

Almost immediately he opened the door.

"May I come in and talk to you?"

He turned and took a quick survey of the room. The picture was against the collar-box. But he took the risk and held the door wide.

Sidney came in and sat down by the fire. By being adroit he managed to slip the little picture over and under the box before she saw it. It is doubtful if she would have realized its significance, had she seen it.

"I've been thinking things over," she said. "It seems to me I'd better not go back."

He had left the door carefully open. Men are always more conventional than women.

"That would be foolish, wouldn't it, when you have done so well? And, besides, since you are not guilty, Sidney--"

"I didn't do it!" she cried passionately. "I know I didn't. But I've lost faith in myself. I can't keep on; that's all there is to it. All last night, in the emergency ward, I felt it going. I clutched at it. I kept saying to myself: 'You didn't do it, you didn't do it'; and all the time something inside of me was saying, 'Not now, perhaps; but sometime you may.'"

Poor K., who had reasoned all this out for himself and had come to the same impasse!

"To go on like this, feeling that one has life and death in one's hand, and then perhaps some day to make a mistake like that!" She looked up at him forlornly. "I am just not brave enough, K."

"Wouldn't it be braver to keep on? Aren't you giving up very easily?"

Her world was in pieces about her, and she felt alone in a wide and empty place. And, because her nerves were drawn taut until they were ready to snap, Sidney turned on him shrewishly.

"I think you are all afraid I will come back to stay. Nobody really wants me anywhere--in all the world! Not at the hospital, not here, not anyplace. I am no use."

"When you say that nobody wants you," said K., not very steadily, "I--I think you are making a mistake."

"Who?" she demanded. "Christine? Aunt Harriet? Katie? The only person who ever really wanted me was my mother, and I went away and left her!"

She scanned his face closely, and, reading there something she did not understand, she colored suddenly.

"I believe you mean Joe Drummond."

"No; I do not mean Joe Drummond."

If he had found any encouragement in her face, he would have gone on recklessly; but her blank eyes warned him.

"If you mean Max Wilson," said Sidney, "you are entirely wrong. He's not in love with me--not, that is, any more than he is in love with a dozen girls. He likes to be with me--oh, I know that; but that doesn't mean--anything else. Anyhow, after this disgrace--"

"There is no disgrace, child."

"He'll think me careless, at the least. And his ideals are so high, K."

"You say he likes to be with you. What about you?"

Sidney had been sitting in a low chair by the fire. She rose with a sudden passionate movement. In the informality of the household, she, had visited K. in her dressing-gown and slippers; and now she stood before him, a tragic young figure, clutching the folds of her gown across her breast.

"I worship him, K.," she said tragically. "When I see him coming, I want to get down and let him walk on me. I know his step in the hall. I know the very way he rings for the elevator. When I see him in the operating-room, cool and calm while every one else is flustered and excited, he--he looks like a god."

Then, half ashamed of her outburst, she turned her back to him and stood gazing at the small coal fire. It was as well for K. that she did not see his face. For that one moment the despair that was in him shone in his eyes. He glanced around the shabby little room, at the sagging bed, the collar-box, the pincushion, the old marble-topped bureau under which Reginald had formerly made his nest, at his untidy table, littered with pipes and books, at the image in the mirror of his own tall figure, stooped and weary.

"It's real, all this?" he asked after a pause. "You're sure it's not just--glamour, Sidney?"

"It's real--terribly real." Her voice was muffled, and he knew then that she was crying.

She was mightily ashamed of it. Tears, of course, except in the privacy of one's closet, were not ethical on the Street.

"Perhaps he cares very much, too."

"Give me a handkerchief," said Sidney in a muffled tone, and the little scene was broken into while K. searched through a bureau drawer. Then:

"It's all over, anyhow, since this. If he'd really cared he'd have come over tonight. When one is in trouble one needs friends."

Back in a circle she came inevitably to her suspension. She would never go back, she said passionately. She was innocent, had been falsely accused. If they could think such a thing about her, she didn't want to be in their old hospital.

K. questioned her, alternately soothing and probing.

"You are positive about it?"

"Absolutely. I have given him his medicines dozens of times."

"You looked at the label?"

"I swear I did, K."

"Who else had access to the medicine closet?"

"Carlotta Harrison carried the keys, of course. I was off duty from four to six. When Carlotta left the ward, the probationer would have them."

"Have you reason to think that either one of these girls would wish you harm?"

"None whatever," began Sidney vehemently; and then, checking herself,--"unless--but that's rather ridiculous."

"What is ridiculous?"

"I've sometimes thought that Carlotta--but I am sure she is perfectly fair with me. Even if she--if she--"

"Yes?"

"Even if she likes Dr. Wilson, I don't believe--Why, K., she wouldn't! It would be murder."

"Murder, of course," said K., "in intention, anyhow. Of course she didn't do it. I'm only trying to find out whose mistake it was."

Soon after that she said good-night and went out. She turned in the doorway and smiled tremulously back at him.

"You have done me a lot of good. You almost make me believe in myself."

"That's because I believe in you."

With a quick movement that was one of her charms, Sidney suddenly closed the door and slipped back into the room. K., hearing the door close, thought she had gone, and dropped heavily into a chair.

"My best friend in all the world!" said Sidney suddenly from behind him, and, bending over, she kissed him on the cheek.

The next instant the door had closed behind her, and K. was left alone to such wretchedness and bliss as the evening had brought him.

On toward morning, Harriet, who slept but restlessly in her towel, wakened to the glare of his light over the transom.

"K.!" she called pettishly from her door. "I wish you wouldn't go to sleep and let your light burn!"

K., surmising the towel and cold cream, had the tact not to open his door.

"I am not asleep, Harriet, and I am sorry about the light. It's going out now."

Before he extinguished the light, he walked over to the old dresser and surveyed himself in the glass. Two nights without sleep and much anxiety had told on him. He looked old, haggard; infinitely tired. Mentally he compared himself with Wilson, flushed with success, erect, triumphant, almost insolent. Nothing had more certainly told him the hopelessness of his love for Sidney than her good-night kiss. He was her brother, her friend. He would never be her lover. He drew a long breath and proceeded to undress in the dark.

Joe Drummond came to see Sidney the next day. She would have avoided him if she could, but Mimi had ushered him up to the sewing-room boudoir before she had time to escape. She had not seen the boy for two months, and the change in him startled her. He was thinner, rather hectic, scrupulously well dressed.

"Why, Joe!" she said, and then: "Won't you sit down?"

He was still rather theatrical. He dramatized himself, as he had that night the June before when he had asked Sidney to marry him. He stood just inside the doorway. He offered no conventional greeting whatever; but, after surveying her briefly, her black gown, the lines around her eyes:--

"You're not going back to that place, of course?"

"I--I haven't decided."

"Then somebody's got to decide for you. The thing for you to do is to stay right here, Sidney. People know you on the Street. Nobody here would ever accuse you of trying to murder anybody."

In spite of herself, Sidney smiled a little.

"Nobody thinks I tried to murder him. It was a mistake about the medicines. I didn't do it, Joe."

His love was purely selfish, for he brushed aside her protest as if she had not spoken.

"You give me the word and I'll go and get your things; I've got a car of my own now."

"But, Joe, they have only done what they thought was right. Whoever made it, there was a mistake."

He stared at her incredulously.

"You don't mean that you are going to stand for this sort of thing? Every time some fool makes a mistake, are they going to blame it on you?"

"Please don't be theatrical. Come in and sit down. I can't talk to you if you explode like a rocket all the time."

Her matter-of-fact tone had its effect. He advanced into the room, but he still scorned a chair.

"I guess you've been wondering why you haven't heard from me," he said. "I've seen you more than you've seen me."

Sidney looked uneasy. The idea of espionage is always repugnant, and to have a rejected lover always in the offing, as it were, was disconcerting.

"I wish you would be just a little bit sensible, Joe. It's so silly of you, really. It's not because you care for me; it's really because you care for yourself."

"You can't look at me and say that, Sid."

He ran his finger around his collar--an old gesture; but the collar was very loose. He was thin; his neck showed it.

"I'm just eating my heart out for you, and that's the truth. And it isn't only that. Everywhere I go, people say, 'There's the fellow Sidney Page turned down when she went to the hospital.' I've got so I keep off the Street as much as I can."

Sidney was half alarmed, half irritated. This wild, excited boy was not the doggedly faithful youth she had always known. It seemed to her that he was hardly sane--that underneath his quiet manner and carefully repressed voice there lurked something irrational, something she could not cope with. She looked up at him helplessly.

"But what do you want me to do? You--you almost frighten me. If you'd only sit down--"

"I want you to come home. I'm not asking anything else now. I just want you to come back, so that things will be the way they used to be. Now that they have turned you out--"

"They've done nothing of the sort. I've told you that."

"You're going back?"

"Absolutely."

"Because you love the hospital, or because you love somebody connected with the hospital?"

Sidney was thoroughly angry by this time, angry and reckless. She had come through so much that every nerve was crying in passionate protest.

"If it will make you understand things any better," she cried, "I am going back for both reasons!"

She was sorry the next moment. But her words seemed, surprisingly enough, to steady him. For the first time, he sat down.

"Then, as far as I am concerned, it's all over, is it?"

"Yes, Joe. I told you that long ago."

He seemed hardly to be listening. His thoughts had ranged far ahead. Suddenly:--

"You think Christine has her hands full with Palmer, don't you? Well, if you take Max Wilson, you're going to have more trouble than Christine ever dreamed of. I can tell you some things about him now that will make you think twice."

But Sidney had reached her limit. She went over and flung open the door.

"Every word that you say shows me how right I am in not marrying you, Joe," she said. "Real men do not say those things about each other under any circumstances. You're behaving like a bad boy. I don't want you to come back until you have grown up."

He was very white, but he picked up his hat and went to the door.

"I guess I AM crazy," he said. "I've been wanting to go away, but mother raises such a fuss--I'll not annoy you any more."

He reached in his pocket and, pulling out a small box, held it toward her. The lid was punched full of holes.

"Reginald," he said solemnly. "I've had him all winter. Some boys caught him in the park, and I brought him home."

He left her standing there speechless with surprise, with the box in her hand, and ran down the stairs and out into the Street. At the foot of the steps he almost collided with Dr. Ed.

"Back to see Sidney?" said Dr. Ed genially. "That's fine, Joe. I'm glad you've made it up."

The boy went blindly down the Street.

CHAPTER XX

WINTER relaxed its clutch slowly that year. March was bitterly cold; even April found the roads still frozen and the hedgerows clustered with ice. But at mid-day there was spring in the air. In the courtyard of the hospital, convalescents sat on the benches and watched for robins. The fountain, which had frozen out, was being repaired. Here and there on ward window-sills tulips opened their gaudy petals to the sun.

Harriet had gone abroad for a flying trip in March and came back laden with new ideas, model gowns, and fresh enthusiasm. She carried out and planted flowers on her sister's grave, and went back to her work with a feeling of duty done. A combination of crocuses and snow on the ground had given her an inspiration for a gown. She drew it in pencil on an envelope on her way back in the street car.

Grace Irving, having made good during the white sales, had been sent to the spring cottons. She began to walk with her head higher. The day she sold Sidney material for a simple white gown, she was very happy. Once a customer brought her a bunch of primroses. All day she kept them under the counter in a glass of water, and at evening she took them to Johnny Rosenfeld, still lying prone in the hospital.

On Sidney, on K., and on Christine the winter had left its mark heavily. Christine, readjusting her life to new conditions, was graver, more thoughtful. She was alone most of the time now. Under K.'s guidance, she had given up the "Duchess" and was reading real books. She was thinking real thoughts, too, for the first time in her life.

Sidney, as tender as ever, had lost a little of the radiance from her eyes; her voice had deepened. Where she had been a pretty girl, she was now lovely. She was back in the hospital again, this time in the children's ward. K., going in one day to take Johnny Rosenfeld a basket of fruit, saw her there with a child in her arms, and a light in her eyes that he had never seen before. It hurt him, rather--things being as they were with him. When he came out he looked straight ahead.

With the opening of spring the little house at Hillfoot took on fresh activities. Tillie was house-cleaning with great thoroughness. She scrubbed carpets, took down the clean curtains, and put them up again freshly starched. It was as if she found in sheer activity and fatigue a remedy for her uneasiness.

Business had not been very good. The impeccable character of the little house had been against it. True, Mr. Schwitter had a little bar and served the best liquors he could buy; but he discouraged rowdiness--had been known to refuse to sell to boys under twenty-one and to men who had already overindulged. The word went about that Schwitter's was no place for a good time. Even Tillie's chicken and waffles failed against this handicap.

By the middle of April the house-cleaning was done. One or two motor parties had come out, dined sedately and wined moderately, and had gone back to the city again. The next two weeks saw the weather clear. The roads dried up, robins filled the trees with their noisy spring songs, and still business continued dull.

By the first day of May, Tillie's uneasiness had become certainty. On that morning Mr. Schwitter, coming in from the early milking, found her sitting in the kitchen, her face buried in her apron. He put down the milk-pails and, going over to her, put a hand on her head.

"I guess there's no mistake, then?"

"There's no mistake," said poor Tillie into her apron.

He bent down and kissed the back of her neck. Then, when she failed to brighten, he tiptoed around the kitchen, poured the milk into pans, and rinsed the buckets, working methodically in his heavy way. The tea-kettle had boiled dry. He filled that, too. Then:--

"Do you want to see a doctor?"

"I'd better see somebody," she said, without looking up. "And--don't think I'm blaming you. I guess I don't really blame anybody. As far as that goes, I've wanted a child right along. It isn't the trouble I am thinking of either."

He nodded. Words were unnecessary between them. He made some tea clumsily and browned her a piece of toast. When he had put them on one end of the kitchen table, he went over to her again.

"I guess I'd ought to have thought of this before, but all I thought of was trying to get a little happiness out of life. And,"--he stroked her arm,--"as far as I am concerned, it's been worth while, Tillie. No matter what I've had to do, I've always looked forward to coming back here to you in the evening. Maybe I don't say it enough, but I guess you know I feel it all right."

Without looking up, she placed her hand over his.

"I guess we started wrong," he went on. "You can't build happiness on what isn't right. You and I can manage well enough; but now that there's going to be another, it looks different, somehow."

After that morning Tillie took up her burden stoically. The hope of motherhood alternated with black fits of depression. She sang at her work, to burst out into sudden tears.

Other things were not going well. Schwitter had given up his nursery business; but the motorists who came to Hillfoot did not come back. When, at last, he took the horse and buggy and drove about the country for orders, he was too late. Other nurserymen had been before him; shrubberies and orchards were already being set out. The second payment on his mortgage would be due in July. By the middle of May they were frankly up against it. Schwitter at last dared to put the situation into words.

"We're not making good, Til," he said. "And I guess you know the reason. We are too decent; that's what's the matter with us." There was no irony in his words.

With all her sophistication, Tillie was vastly ignorant of life. He had to explain.

"We'll have to keep a sort of hotel," he said lamely. "Sell to everybody that comes along, and--if parties want to stay over-night--"

Tillie's white face turned crimson.

He attempted a compromise. "If it's bad weather, and they're married--"

"How are we to know if they are married or not?"

He admired her very much for it. He had always respected her. But the situation was not less acute. There were two or three unfurnished rooms on the second floor. He began to make tentative suggestions as to their furnishing. Once he got a catalogue from an installment house, and tried to hide it from her. Tillie's eyes blazed. She burned it in the kitchen stove.

Schwitter himself was ashamed; but the idea obsessed him. Other people fattened on the frailties of human nature. Two miles away, on the other road, was a public house that had netted the owner ten thousand dollars profit the year before. They bought their beer from the same concern. He was not as young as he had been; there was the expense of keeping his wife--he had never allowed her to go into the charity ward at the asylum. Now that there was going to be a child, there would be three people dependent upon him. He was past fifty, and not robust.

One night, after Tillie was asleep, he slipped noiselessly into his clothes and out to the barn, where he hitched up the horse with nervous fingers.

Tillie never learned of that midnight excursion to the "Climbing Rose," two miles away. Lights blazed in every window; a dozen automobiles were parked before the barn. Somebody was playing a piano. From the bar came the jingle of glasses and loud, cheerful conversation.

When Schwitter turned the horse's head back toward Hillfoot, his mind was made up. He would furnish the upper rooms; he would bring a barkeeper from town--these people wanted mixed drinks; he could get a second-hand piano somewhere.

Tillie's rebellion was instant and complete. When she found him determined, she made the compromise that her condition necessitated. She could not leave him, but she would not stay in the rehabilitated little house. When, a week after Schwitter's visit to the "Climbing Rose," an installment van arrived from town with the new furniture, Tillie moved out to what had been the harness-room of the old barn and there established herself.

"I am not leaving you," she told him. "I don't even know that I am blaming you. But I am not going to have anything to do with it, and that's flat."

So it happened that K., making a spring pilgrimage to see Tillie, stopped astounded in the road. The weather was warm, and he carried his Norfolk coat over his arm. The little house was bustling; a dozen automobiles were parked in the barnyard. The bar was crowded, and a barkeeper in a white coat was mixing drinks with the casual indifference of his kind. There were tables under the trees on the lawn, and a new sign on the gate.

Even Schwitter bore a new look of prosperity. Over his schooner of beer K. gathered something of the story.

"I'm not proud of it, Mr. Le Moyne. I've come to do a good many things the last year or so that I never thought I would do. But one thing leads to another. First I took Tillie away from her good position, and after that nothing went right. Then there were things coming on"--he looked at K. anxiously--"that meant more expense. I would be glad if you wouldn't say anything about it at Mrs. McKee's."

"I'll not speak of it, of course."

It was then, when K. asked for Tillie, that Mr. Schwitter's unhappiness became more apparent.

"She wouldn't stand for it," he said. "She moved out the day I furnished the rooms upstairs and got the piano."

"Do you mean she has gone?"

"As far as the barn. She wouldn't stay in the house. I--I'll take you out there, if you would like to see her."

K. shrewdly surmised that Tillie would prefer to see him alone, under the circumstances.

"I guess I can find her," he said, and rose from the little table.

"If you--if you can say anything to help me out, sir, I'd appreciate it. Of course, she understands how I am driven. But--especially if you would tell her that the Street doesn't know--"

"I'll do all I can," K. promised, and followed the path to the barn.

Tillie received him with a certain dignity. The little harness-room was very comfortable. A white iron bed in a corner, a flat table with a mirror above it, a rocking-chair, and a sewing-machine furnished the room.

"I wouldn't stand for it," she said simply; "so here I am. Come in, Mr. Le Moyne."

There being but one chair, she sat on the bed. The room was littered with small garments in the making. She made no attempt to conceal them; rather, she pointed to them with pride.

"I am making them myself. I have a lot of time these days. He's got a hired girl at the house. It was hard enough to sew at first, with me making two right sleeves almost every time." Then, seeing his kindly eye on her: "Well, it's happened, Mr. Le Moyne. What am I going to do? What am I going to be?"

"You're going to be a very good mother, Tillie."

She was manifestly in need of cheering. K., who also needed cheering that spring day, found his consolation in seeing her brighten under the small gossip of the Street. The deaf-and-dumb book agent had taken on life insurance as a side issue, and was doing well; the grocery store at the corner was going to be torn down, and over the new store there were to be apartments; Reginald had been miraculously returned, and was building a new nest under his bureau; Harriet Kennedy had been to Paris, and had brought home six French words and a new figure.

Outside the open door the big barn loomed cool and shadowy, full of empty spaces where later the hay would be stored; anxious mother hens led their broods about; underneath in the horse stable the restless horses pawed in their stalls. From where he sat, Le Moyne could see only the round breasts of the two hills, the fresh green of the orchard the cows in a meadow beyond.

Tillie followed his eyes.

"I like it here," she confessed. "I've had more time to think since I moved out than I ever had in my life before. Them hills help. When the noise is worst down at the house, I look at the hills there and--"

There were great thoughts in her mind--that the hills meant God, and that in His good time perhaps it would all come right. But she was inarticulate. "The hills help a lot," she repeated.

K. rose. Tillie's work-basket lay near him. He picked up one of the little garments. In his big hands it looked small, absurd.

"I--I want to tell you something, Tillie. Don't count on it too much; but Mrs. Schwitter has been failing rapidly for the last month or two."

Tillie caught his arm.

"You've seen her?"

"I was interested. I wanted to see things work out right for you."

All the color had faded from Tillie's face.

"You're very good to me, Mr. Le Moyne," she said. "I don't wish the poor soul any harm, but--oh, my God! if she's going, let it be before the next four months are over."

K. had fallen into the habit, after his long walks, of dropping into Christine's little parlor for a chat before he went upstairs. Those early spring days found Harriet Kennedy busy late in the evenings, and, save for Christine and K., the house was practically deserted.

The breach between Palmer and Christine was steadily widening. She was too proud to ask him to spend more of his evenings with her. On those occasions when he voluntarily stayed at home with her, he was so discontented that he drove her almost to distraction. Although she was convinced that he was seeing nothing of the girl who had been with him the night of the accident, she did not trust him. Not that girl, perhaps, but there were others. There would always be others.

Into Christine's little parlor, then, K. turned, the evening after he had seen Tillie. She was reading by the lamp, and the door into the hall stood open.

"Come in," she said, as he hesitated in the doorway.

"I am frightfully dusty."

"There's a brush in the drawer of the hat-rack--although I don't really mind how you look."

The little room always cheered K. Its warmth and light appealed to his aesthetic sense; after the bareness of his bedroom, it spelled luxury. And perhaps, to be entirely frank, there was more than physical comfort and satisfaction in the evenings he spent in Christine's firelit parlor. He was entirely masculine, and her evident pleasure in his society gratified him. He had fallen into a way of thinking of himself as a sort of older brother to all the world because he was a sort of older brother to Sidney. The evenings with her did something to reinstate him in his own self-esteem. It was subtle, psychological, but also it was very human.

"Come and sit down," said Christine. "Here's a chair, and here are cigarettes and there are matches. Now!"

But, for once, K. declined the chair. He stood in front of the fireplace and looked down at her, his head bent slightly to one side.

"I wonder if you would like to do a very kind thing," he said unexpectedly.

"Make you coffee?"

"Something much more trouble and not so pleasant."

Christine glanced up at him. When she was with him, when his steady eyes looked down at her, small affectations fell away. She was more genuine with K. than with anyone else, even herself.

"Tell me what it is, or shall I promise first?"

"I want you to promise just one thing: to keep a secret."

"Yours?"

Christine was not over-intelligent, perhaps, but she was shrewd. That Le Moyne's past held a secret she had felt from the beginning. She sat up with eager curiosity.

"No, not mine. Is it a promise?"

"Of course."

"I've found Tillie, Christine. I want you to go out to see her."

Christine's red lips parted. The Street did not go out to see women in Tillie's situation.

"But, K.!" she protested.

"She needs another woman just now. She's going to have a child, Christine; and she has had no one to talk to but her hus--but Mr. Schwitter and myself. She is depressed and not very well."

"But what shall I say to her? I'd really rather not go, K. Not," she hastened to set herself right in his eyes--"not that I feel any unwillingness to see her. I know you understand that. But--what in the world shall I say to her?"

"Say what your own kind heart prompts."

It had been rather a long time since Christine had been accused of having a kind heart. Not that she was unkind, but in all her self-centered young life there had been little call on her sympathies. Her eyes clouded.

"I wish I were as good as you think I am."

There was a little silence between them. Then Le Moyne spoke briskly:--

"I'll tell you how to get there; perhaps I would better write it."

He moved over to Christine's small writing-table and, seating himself, proceeded to write out the directions for reaching Hillfoot.

Behind him, Christine had taken his place on the hearth-rug and stood watching his head in the light of the desk-lamp. "What a strong, quiet face it is," she thought. Why did she get the impression of such a tremendous reserve power in this man who was a clerk, and a clerk only? Behind him she made a quick, unconscious gesture of appeal, both hands out for an instant. She dropped them guiltily as K. rose with the paper in his hand.

"I've drawn a sort of map of the roads," he began. "You see, this--"

Christine was looking, not at the paper, but up at him.

"I wonder if you know, K.," she said, "what a lucky woman the woman will be who marries you?"

He laughed good-humoredly.

"I wonder how long I could hypnotize her into thinking that."

He was still holding out the paper.

"I've had time to do a little thinking lately," she said, without bitterness. "Palmer is away so much now. I've been looking back, wondering if I ever thought that about him. I don't believe I ever did. I wonder--"

She checked herself abruptly and took the paper from his hand.

"I'll go to see Tillie, of course," she consented. "It is like you to have found her."

She sat down. Although she picked up the book that she had been reading with the evident intention of discussing it, her thoughts were still on Tillie, on Palmer, on herself. After a moment:--

"Has it ever occurred to you how terribly mixed up things are? Take this Street, for instance. Can you think of anybody on it that--that things have gone entirely right with?"

"It's a little world of its own, of course," said K., "and it has plenty of contact points with life. But wherever one finds people, many or few, one finds all the elements that make up life--joy and sorrow, birth and death, and even tragedy. That's rather trite, isn't it?"

Christine was still pursuing her thoughts.

"Men are different," she said. "To a certain extent they make their own fates. But when you think of the women on the Street,--Tillie, Harriet Kennedy, Sidney Page, myself, even Mrs. Rosenfeld back in the alley,--somebody else moulds things for us, and all we can do is to sit back and suffer. I am beginning to think the world is a terrible place, K. Why do people so often marry the wrong people? Why can't a man care for one woman and only one all his life? Why--why is it all so complicated?"

"There are men who care for only one woman all their lives."

"You're that sort, aren't you?"

"I don't want to put myself on any pinnacle. If I cared enough for a woman to marry her, I'd hope to--But we are being very tragic, Christine."

"I feel tragic. There's going to be another mistake, K., unless you stop it."

He tried to leaven the conversation with a little fun.

"If you're going to ask me to interfere between Mrs. McKee and the deaf-and-dumb book and insurance agent, I shall do nothing of the sort. She can both speak and hear enough for both of them."

"I mean Sidney and Max Wilson. He's mad about her, K.; and, because she's the sort she is, he'll probably be mad about her all his life, even if he marries her. But he'll not be true to her; I know the type now."

K. leaned back with a flicker of pain in his eyes.

"What can I do about it?"

Astute as he was, he did not suspect that Christine was using this method to fathom his feeling for Sidney. Perhaps she hardly knew it herself.

"You might marry her yourself, K."

But he had himself in hand by this time, and she learned nothing from either his voice or his eyes.

"On twenty dollars a week? And without so much as asking her consent?" He dropped his light tone. "I'm not in a position to marry anybody. Even if Sidney cared for me, which she doesn't, of course--"

"Then you don't intend to interfere? You're going to let the Street see another failure?"

"I think you can understand," said K. rather wearily, "that if I cared less, Christine, it would be easier to interfere."

After all, Christine had known this, or surmised it, for weeks. But it hurt like a fresh stab in an old wound. It was K. who spoke again after a pause:--

"The deadly hard thing, of course, is to sit by and see things happening that one--that one would naturally try to prevent."

"I don't believe that you have always been of those who only stand and wait," said Christine. "Sometime, K., when you know me better and like me better, I want you to tell me about it, will you?"

"There's very little to tell. I held a trust. When I discovered that I was unfit to hold that trust any longer, I quit. That's all."

His tone of finality closed the discussion. But Christine's eyes were on him often that evening, puzzled, rather sad.

They talked of books, of music--Christine played well in a dashing way. K. had brought her soft, tender little things, and had stood over her until her noisy touch became gentle. She played for him a little, while he sat back in the big chair with his hand screening his eyes.

When, at last, he rose and picked up his cap; it was nine o'clock.

"I've taken your whole evening," he said remorsefully. "Why don't you tell me I am a nuisance and send me off?"

Christine was still at the piano, her hands on the keys. She spoke without looking at him:--

"You're never a nuisance, K., and--"

"You'll go out to see Tillie, won't you?"

"Yes. But I'll not go under false pretenses. I am going quite frankly because you want me to."

Something in her tone caught his attention.

"I forgot to tell you," she went on. "Father has given Palmer five thousand dollars. He's going to buy a share in a business."

"That's fine."

"Possibly. I don't believe much in Palmer's business ventures."

Her flat tone still held him. Underneath it he divined strain and repression.

"I hate to go and leave you alone," he said at last from the door. "Have you any idea when Palmer will be back?"

"Not the slightest. K., will you come here a moment? Stand behind me; I don't want to see you, and I want to tell you something."

He did as she bade him, rather puzzled.

"Here I am."

"I think I am a fool for saying this. Perhaps I am spoiling the only chance I have to get any happiness out of life. But I have got to say it. It's stronger than I am. I was terribly unhappy, K., and then you came into my life, and I--now I listen for your step in the hall. I can't be a hypocrite any longer, K."

When he stood behind her, silent and not moving, she turned slowly about and faced him. He towered there in the little room, grave eyes on hers.

"It's a long time since I have had a woman friend, Christine," he said soberly. "Your friendship has meant a good deal. In a good many ways, I'd not care to look ahead if it were not for you. I value our friendship so much that I--"

"That you don't want me to spoil it," she finished for him. "I know you don't care for me, K., not the way I--But I wanted you to know. It doesn't hurt a good man to know such a thing. And it--isn't going to stop your coming here, is it?"

"Of course not," said K. heartily. "But to-morrow, when we are both clear-headed, we will talk this over. You are mistaken about this thing, Christine; I am sure of that. Things have not been going well, and just because I am always around, and all that sort of thing, you think things that aren't really so. I'm only a reaction, Christine."

He tried to make her smile up at him. But just then she could not smile.

If she had cried, things might have been different for every one; for perhaps K. would have taken her in his arms. He was heart-hungry enough, those days, for anything. And perhaps, too, being intuitive, Christine felt this. But she had no mind to force him into a situation against his will.

"It is because you are good," she said, and held out her hand. "Good-night."

Le Moyne took it and bent over and kissed it lightly. There was in the kiss all that he could not say of respect, of affection and understanding.

"Good-night, Christine," he said, and went into the hall and upstairs.

The lamp was not lighted in his room, but the street light glowed through the windows. Once again the waving fronds of the ailanthus tree flung ghostly shadows on the walls. There was a faint sweet odor of blossoms, so soon to become rank and heavy.

Over the floor in a wild zigzag darted a strip of white paper which disappeared under the bureau. Reginald was building another nest.

CHAPTER XXI

SIDNEY went into the operating-room late in the spring as the result of a conversation between the younger Wilson and the Head.

"When are you going to put my protegee into the operating-room?" asked Wilson, meeting Miss Gregg in a corridor one bright, spring afternoon.

"That usually comes in the second year, Dr. Wilson."

He smiled down at her. "That isn't a rule, is it?"

"Not exactly. Miss Page is very young, and of course there are other girls who have not yet had the experience. But, if you make the request--"

"I am going to have some good cases soon. I'll not make a request, of course; but, if you see fit, it would be good training for Miss Page."

Miss Gregg went on, knowing perfectly that at his next operation Dr. Wilson would expect Sidney Page in the operating-room. The other doctors were not so exigent. She would have liked to have all the staff old and settled, like Dr. O'Hara or the older Wilson. These young men came in and tore things up.

She sighed as she went on. There were so many things to go wrong. The butter had been bad--she must speak to the matron. The sterilizer in the operating-room was out of order--that meant a quarrel with the chief engineer. Requisitions were too heavy--that meant going around to the wards and suggesting to the head nurses that lead pencils and bandages and adhesive plaster and safety-pins cost money.

It was particularly inconvenient to move Sidney just then. Carlotta Harrison was off duty, ill. She had been ailing for a month, and now she was down with a temperature. As the Head went toward Sidney's ward, her busy mind was playing her nurses in their wards like pieces on a checkerboard.

Sidney went into the operating-room that afternoon. For her blue uniform, kerchief, and cap she exchanged the hideous operating-room garb: long, straight white gown with short sleeves and mob-cap, gray-white from many sterilizations.

But the ugly costume seemed to emphasize her beauty, as the habit of a nun often brings out the placid saintliness of her face.

The relationship between Sidney and Max had reached that point that occurs in all relationships between men and women: when things must either go forward or go back, but cannot remain as they are. The condition had existed for the last three months. It exasperated the man.

As a matter of fact, Wilson could not go ahead. The situation with Carlotta had become tense, irritating. He felt that she stood ready to block any move he made. He would not go back, and he dared not go forward.

If Sidney was puzzled, she kept it bravely to herself. In her little room at night, with the door carefully locked, she tried to think things out. There were a few treasures that she looked over regularly: a dried flower from the Christmas roses; a label that he had pasted playfully on the back of her hand one day after the rush of surgical dressings was over and which said "Rx, Take once and forever."

There was another piece of paper over which Sidney spent much time. It was a page torn out of an order book, and it read: "Sigsbee may have light diet; Rosenfeld massage." Underneath was written, very small:

"You are the most beautiful person in the world."

Two reasons had prompted Wilson to request to have Sidney in the operating-room. He wanted her with him, and he wanted her to see him at work: the age-old instinct of the male to have his woman see him at his best.

He was in high spirits that first day of Sidney's operating-room experience. For the time at least, Carlotta was out of the way. Her somber eyes no longer watched him. Once he looked up from his work and glanced at Sidney where she stood at strained attention.

"Feeling faint?" he said.

She colored under the eyes that were turned on her.

"No, Dr. Wilson."

"A great many of them faint on the first day. We sometimes have them lying all over the floor."

He challenged Miss Gregg with his eyes, and she reproved him with a shake of her head, as she might a bad boy.

One way and another, he managed to turn the attention of the operating-room to Sidney several times. It suited his whim, and it did more than that: it gave him a chance to speak to her in his teasing way.

Sidney came through the operation as if she had been through fire--taut as a string, rather pale, but undaunted. But when the last case had been taken out, Max dropped his bantering manner. The internes were looking over instruments; the nurses were busy on the hundred and one tasks of clearing up; so he had a chance for a word with her alone.

"I am proud of you, Sidney; you came through it like a soldier."

"You made it very hard for me."

A nurse was coming toward him; he had only a moment.

"I shall leave a note in the mail-box," he said quickly, and proceeded with the scrubbing of his hands which signified the end of the day's work.

The operations had lasted until late in the afternoon. The night nurses had taken up their stations; prayers were over. The internes were gathered in the smoking-room, threshing over the day's work, as was their custom. When Sidney was free, she went to the office for the note. It was very brief:--

I have something I want to say to you, dear. I think you know what it is. I never see you alone at home any more. If you can get off for an hour, won't you take the trolley to the end of Division Street? I'll be there with the car at eight-thirty, and I promise to have you back by ten o'clock.

MAX.

The office was empty. No one saw her as she stood by the mail-box. The ticking of the office clock, the heavy rumble of a dray outside, the roll of the ambulance as it went out through the gateway, and in her hand the realization of what she had never confessed as a hope, even to herself! He, the great one, was going to stoop to her. It had been in his eyes that afternoon; it was there, in his letter, now.

It was eight by the office clock. To get out of her uniform and into street clothing, fifteen minutes; on the trolley, another fifteen. She would need to hurry.

But she did not meet him, after all. Miss Wardwell met her in the upper hall.

"Did you get my message?" she asked anxiously.

"What message?"

"Miss Harrison wants to see you. She has been moved to a private room."

Sidney glanced at K.'s little watch.

"Must she see me to-night?"

"She has been waiting for hours--ever since you went to the operating-room."

Sidney sighed, but she went to Carlotta at once. The girl's condition was puzzling the staff. There was talk of "T.R."--which is hospital for "typhoid restrictions." But T.R. has apathy, generally, and Carlotta was not apathetic. Sidney found her tossing restlessly on her high white bed, and put her cool hand over Carlotta's hot one.

"Did you send for me?"

"Hours ago." Then, seeing her operating-room uniform: "You've been THERE, have you?"

"Is there anything I can do, Carlotta?"

Excitement had dyed Sidney's cheeks with color and made her eyes luminous. The girl in the bed eyed her, and then abruptly drew her hand away.

"Were you going out?"

"Yes; but not right away."

"I'll not keep you if you have an engagement."

"The engagement will have to wait. I'm sorry you're ill. If you would like me to stay with you tonight--"

Carlotta shook her head on her pillow.

"Mercy, no!" she said irritably. "I'm only worn out. I need a rest. Are you going home to-night?"

"No," Sidney admitted, and flushed.

Nothing escaped Carlotta's eyes--the younger girl's radiance, her confusion, even her operating room uniform and what it signified. How she hated her, with her youth and freshness, her wide eyes, her soft red lips! And this engagement--she had the uncanny divination of fury.

"I was going to ask you to do something for me," she said shortly; "but I've changed my mind about it. Go on and keep your engagement."

To end the interview, she turned over and lay with her face to the wall. Sidney stood waiting uncertainly. All her training had been to ignore the irritability of the sick, and Carlotta was very ill; she could see that.

"Just remember that I am ready to do anything I can, Carlotta," she said. "Nothing will--will be a trouble."

She waited a moment, but, receiving no acknowledgement of her offer, she turned slowly and went toward the door.

"Sidney!"

She went back to the bed.

"Yes. Don't sit up, Carlotta. What is it?"

"I'm frightened!"

"You're feverish and nervous. There's nothing to be frightened about."

"If it's typhoid, I'm gone."

"That's childish. Of course you're not gone, or anything like it. Besides, it's probably not typhoid."

"I'm afraid to sleep. I doze for a little, and when I waken there are people in the room. They stand around the bed and talk about me."

Sidney's precious minutes were flying; but Carlotta had gone into a paroxysm of terror, holding to Sidney's hand and begging not to be left alone.

"I'm too young to die," she would whimper. And in the next breath: "I want to die--I don't want to live!"

The hands of the little watch pointed to eight-thirty when at last she lay quiet, with closed eyes. Sidney, tiptoeing to the door, was brought up short by her name again, this time in a more normal voice:--

"Sidney."

"Yes, dear."

"Perhaps you are right and I'm going to get over this."

"Certainly you are. Your nerves are playing tricks with you to-night."

"I'll tell you now why I sent for you."

"I'm listening."

"If--if I get very bad,--you know what I mean,--will you promise to do exactly what I tell you?"

"I promise, absolutely."

"My trunk key is in my pocket-book. There is a letter in the tray--just a name, no address on it. Promise to see that it is not delivered; that it is destroyed without being read."

Sidney promised promptly; and, because it was too late now for her meeting with Wilson, for the next hour she devoted herself to making Carlotta comfortable. So long as she was busy, a sort of exaltation of service upheld her. But when at last the night assistant came to sit with the sick girl, and Sidney was free, all the life faded from her face. He had waited for her and she had not come. Would he understand? Would he ask her to meet him again? Perhaps, after all, his question had not been what she had thought.

She went miserably to bed. K.'s little watch ticked under her pillow. Her stiff cap moved in the breeze as it swung from the corner of her mirror. Under her window passed and repassed the night life of the city--taxicabs, stealthy painted women, tired office-cleaners trudging home at midnight, a city patrol-wagon which rolled in through the gates to the hospital's always open door. When she could not sleep, she got up and padded to the window in bare feet. The light from a passing machine showed a youthful figure that looked like Joe Drummond.

Life, that had always seemed so simple, was growing very complicated for Sidney: Joe and K., Palmer and Christine, Johnny Rosenfeld, Carlotta--either lonely or tragic, all of them, or both. Life in the raw.

Toward morning Carlotta wakened. The night assistant was still there. It had been a quiet night and she was asleep in her chair. To save her cap she had taken it off, and early streaks of silver showed in her hair.

Carlotta roused her ruthlessly.

"I want something from my trunk," she said.

The assistant wakened reluctantly, and looked at her watch. Almost morning. She yawned and pinned on her cap.

"For Heaven's sake," she protested. "You don't want me to go to the trunk-room at this hour!"

"I can go myself," said Carlotta, and put her feet out of bed.

"What is it you want?"

"A letter on the top tray. If I wait my temperature will go up and I can't think."

"Shall I mail it for you?"

"Bring it here," said Carlotta shortly. "I want to destroy it."

The young woman went without haste, to show that a night assistant may do such things out of friendship, but not because she must. She stopped at the desk where the night nurse in charge of the rooms on that floor was filling out records.

"Give me twelve private patients to look after instead of one nurse like Carlotta Harrison!" she complained. "I've got to go to the trunk-room for her at this hour, and it next door to the mortuary!"

As the first rays of the summer sun came through the window, shadowing the fire-escape like a lattice on the wall of the little gray-walled room, Carlotta sat up in her bed and lighted the candle on the stand. The night assistant, who dreamed sometimes of fire, stood nervously by.

"Why don't you let me do it?" she asked irritably.

Carlotta did not reply at once. The candle was in her hand, and she was staring at the letter.

"Because I want to do it myself," she said at last, and thrust the envelope into the flame. It burned slowly, at first a thin blue flame tipped with yellow, then, eating its way with a small fine crackling, a widening, destroying blaze that left behind it black ash and destruction. The acrid odor of burning filled the room. Not until it was consumed, and the black ash fell into the saucer of the candlestick, did Carlotta speak again. Then:--

"If every fool of a woman who wrote a letter burnt it, there would be less trouble in the world," she said, and lay back among her pillows.

The assistant said nothing. She was sleepy and irritated, and she had crushed her best cap by letting the lid of Carlotta's trunk fall on her. She went out of the room with disapproval in every line of her back.

"She burned it," she informed the night nurse at her desk. "A letter to a man--one of her suitors, I suppose. The name was K. Le Moyne."

The deepening and broadening of Sidney's character had been very noticeable in the last few months. She had gained in decision without becoming hard; had learned to see things as they are, not through the rose mist of early girlhood; and, far from being daunted, had developed a philosophy that had for its basis God in His heaven and all well with the world.

But her new theory of acceptance did not comprehend everything. She was in a state of wild revolt, for instance, as to Johnny Rosenfeld, and more remotely but not less deeply concerned over Grace Irving. Soon she was to learn of Tillie's predicament, and to take up the cudgels valiantly for her.

But her revolt was to be for herself too. On the day after her failure to keep her appointment with Wilson she had her half-holiday. No word had come from him, and when, after a restless night, she went to her new station in the operating-room, it was to learn that he had been called out of the city in consultation and would not operate that day. O'Hara would take advantage of the free afternoon to run in some odds and ends of cases.

The operating-room made gauze that morning, and small packets of tampons: absorbent cotton covered with sterilized gauze, and fastened together--twelve, by careful count, in each bundle.

Miss Grange, who had been kind to Sidney in her probation months, taught her the method.

"Used instead of sponges," she explained. "If you noticed yesterday, they were counted before and after each operation. One of these missing is worse than a bank clerk out a dollar at the end of the day. There's no closing up until it's found!"

Sidney eyed the small packet before her anxiously.

"What a hideous responsibility!" she said.

From that time on she handled the small gauze sponges almost reverently.

The operating-room--all glass, white enamel, and shining nickel-plate--first frightened, then thrilled her. It was as if, having loved a great actor, she now trod the enchanted boards on which he achieved his triumphs. She was glad that it was her afternoon off, and that she would not see some lesser star--O'Hara, to wit--usurping his place.

But Max had not sent her any word. That hurt. He must have known that she had been delayed.

The operating-room was a hive of industry, and tongues kept pace with fingers. The hospital was a world, like the Street. The nurses had come from many places, and, like cloistered nuns, seemed to have left the other world behind. A new President of the country was less real than a new interne. The country might wash its soiled linen in public; what was that compared with enough sheets and towels for the wards? Big buildings were going up in the city. Ah! but the hospital took cognizance of that, gathering as it did a toll from each new story added. What news of the world came in through the great doors was translated at once into hospital terms. What the city forgot the hospital remembered. It took up life where the town left it at its gates, and carried it on or saw it ended, as the case might be. So these young women knew the ending of many stories, the beginning of some; but of none did they know both the first and last, the beginning and the end.

By many small kindnesses Sidney had made herself popular. And there was more to it than that. She never shirked. The other girls had the respect for her of one honest worker for another. The episode that had caused her suspension seemed entirely forgotten. They showed her carefully what she was to do; and, because she must know the "why" of everything, they explained as best they could.

It was while she was standing by the great sterilizer that she heard, through an open door, part of a conversation that sent her through the day with her world in revolt.

The talkers were putting the anaesthetizing-room in readiness for the afternoon. Sidney, waiting for the time to open the sterilizer, was busy, for the first time in her hurried morning, with her own thoughts. Because she was very human, there was a little exultation in her mind. What would these girls say when they learned of how things stood between her and their hero--that, out of all his world of society and clubs and beautiful women, he was going to choose her?

Not shameful, this: the honest pride of a woman in being chosen from many.

The voices were very clear.

"Typhoid! Of course not. She's eating her heart out."

"Do you think he has really broken with her?"

"Probably not. She knows it's coming; that's all."

"Sometimes I have wondered--"

"So have others. She oughtn't to be here, of course. But among so many there is bound to be one now and then who--who isn't quite--"

She hesitated, at a loss for a word.

"Did you--did you ever think over that trouble with Miss Page about the medicines? That would have been easy, and like her."

"She hates Miss Page, of course, but I hardly think--If that's true, it was nearly murder."

There were two voices, a young one, full of soft southern inflections, and an older voice, a trifle hard, as from disillusion.

They were working as they talked. Sidney could hear the clatter of bottles on the tray, the scraping of a moved table.

"He was crazy about her last fall."

"Miss Page?" (The younger voice, with a thrill in it.)

"Carlotta. Of course this is confidential."

"Surely."

"I saw her with him in his car one evening. And on her vacation last summer--"

The voices dropped to a whisper. Sidney, standing cold and white by the sterilizer, put out a hand to steady herself. So that was it! No wonder Carlotta had hated her. And those whispering voices! What were they saying? How hateful life was, and men and women. Must there always be something hideous in the background? Until now she had only seen life. Now she felt its hot breath on her cheek.

She was steady enough in a moment, cool and calm, moving about her work with ice-cold hands and slightly narrowed eyes. To a sort of physical nausea was succeeding anger, a blind fury of injured pride. He had been in love with Carlotta and had tired of her. He was bringing her his warmed-over emotions. She remembered the bitterness of her month's exile, and its probable cause. Max had stood by her then. Well he might, if he suspected the truth.

For just a moment she had an illuminating flash of Wilson as he really was, selfish and self-indulgent, just a trifle too carefully dressed, daring as to eye and speech, with a carefully calculated daring, frankly pleasure-loving. She put her hands over her eyes.

The voices in the next room had risen above their whisper.

"Genius has privileges, of course," said the older voice. "He is a very great surgeon. To-morrow he is to do the Edwardes operation again. I am glad I am to see him do it."

Sidney still held her hands over her eyes. He WAS a great surgeon: in his hands he held the keys of life and death. And perhaps he had never cared for Carlotta: she might have thrown herself at him. He was a man, at the mercy of any scheming woman.

She tried to summon his image to her aid. But a curious thing happened. She could not visualize him. Instead, there came, clear and distinct, a picture of K. Le Moyne in the hall of the little house, reaching one of his long arms to the chandelier over his head and looking up at her as she stood on the stairs.

CHAPTER XXII

"My God, Sidney, I'm asking you to marry me!"

"I--I know that. I am asking you something else, Max."

"I have never been in love with her."

His voice was sulky. He had drawn the car close to a bank, and they were sitting in the shade, on the grass. It was the Sunday afternoon after Sidney's experience in the operating-room.

"You took her out, Max, didn't you?"

"A few times, yes. She seemed to have no friends. I was sorry for her."

"That was all?"

"Absolutely. Good Heavens, you've put me through a catechism in the last ten minutes!"

"If my father were living, or even mother, I--one of them would have done this for me, Max. I'm sorry I had to. I've been very wretched for several days."

It was the first encouragement she had given him. There was no coquetry about her aloofness. It was only that her faith in him had had a shock and was slow of reviving.

"You are very, very lovely, Sidney. I wonder if you have any idea what you mean to me?"

"You meant a great deal to me, too," she said frankly, "until a few days ago. I thought you were the greatest man I had ever known, and the best. And then--I think I'd better tell you what I overheard. I didn't try to hear. It just happened that way."

He listened doggedly to her account of the hospital gossip, doggedly and with a sinking sense of fear, not of the talk, but of Carlotta herself. Usually one might count on the woman's silence, her instinct for self-protection. But Carlotta was different. Damn the girl, anyhow! She had known from the start that the affair was a temporary one; he had never pretended anything else.

There was silence for a moment after Sidney finished. Then:

"You are not a child any longer, Sidney. You have learned a great deal in this last year. One of the things you know is that almost every man has small affairs, many of them sometimes, before he finds the woman he wants to marry. When he finds her, the others are all off--there's nothing to them. It's the real thing then, instead of the sham."

"Palmer was very much in love with Christine, and yet--"

"Palmer is a cad."

"I don't want you to think I'm making terms. I'm not. But if this thing went on, and I found out afterward that you--that there was anyone else, it would kill me."

"Then you care, after all!"

There was something boyish in his triumph, in the very gesture with which he held out his arms, like a child who has escaped a whipping. He stood up and, catching her hands, drew her to her feet. "You love me, dear."

"I'm afraid I do, Max."

"Then I'm yours, and only yours, if you want me," he said, and took her in his arms.

He was riotously happy, must hold her off for the joy of drawing her to him again, must pull off her gloves and kiss her soft bare palms.

"I love you, love you!" he cried, and bent down to bury his face in the warm hollow of her neck.

Sidney glowed under his caresses--was rather startled at his passion, a little ashamed.

"Tell me you love me a little bit. Say it."

"I love you," said Sidney, and flushed scarlet.

But even in his arms, with the warm sunlight on his radiant face, with his lips to her ear, whispering the divine absurdities of passion, in the back of her obstinate little head was the thought that, while she had given him her first embrace, he had held other women in his arms. It made her passive, prevented her complete surrender.

And after a time he resented it. "You are only letting me love you," he complained. "I don't believe you care, after all."

He freed her, took a step back from her.

"I am afraid I am jealous," she said simply. "I keep thinking of--of Carlotta."

"Will it help any if I swear that that is off absolutely?"

"Don't be absurd. It is enough to have you say so."

But he insisted on swearing, standing with one hand upraised, his eyes on her. The Sunday landscape was very still, save for the hum of busy insect life. A mile or so away, at the foot of two hills, lay a white farmhouse with its barn and outbuildings. In a small room in the barn a woman sat; and because it was Sunday, and she could not sew, she read her Bible.

"--and that after this there will be only one woman for me," finished Max, and dropped his hand. He bent over and kissed Sidney on the lips.

At the white farmhouse, a little man stood in the doorway and surveyed the road with eyes shaded by a shirt-sleeved arm. Behind him, in a darkened room, a barkeeper was wiping the bar with a clean cloth.

"I guess I'll go and get my coat on, Bill," said the little man heavily. "They're starting to come now. I see a machine about a mile down the road."

Sidney broke the news of her engagement to K. herself, the evening of the same day. The little house was quiet when she got out of the car at the door. Harriet was asleep on the couch at the foot of her bed, and Christine's rooms were empty. She found Katie on the back porch, mountains of Sunday newspapers piled around her.

"I'd about give you up," said Katie. "I was thinking, rather than see your ice-cream that's left from dinner melt and go to waste, I'd take it around to the Rosenfelds."

"Please take it to them. I'd really rather they had it."

She stood in front of Katie, drawing off her gloves.

"Aunt Harriet's asleep. Is--is Mr. Le Moyne around?"

"You're gettin' prettier every day, Miss Sidney. Is that the blue suit Miss Harriet said she made for you? It's right stylish. I'd like to see the back."

Sidney obediently turned, and Katie admired.

"When I think how things have turned out!" she reflected. "You in a hospital, doing God knows what for all sorts of people, and Miss Harriet making a suit like that and asking a hundred dollars for it, and that tony that a person doesn't dare to speak to her when she's in the dining-room. And your poor ma...well, it's all in a lifetime! No; Mr. K.'s not here. He and Mrs. Howe are gallivanting around together."

"Katie!"

"Well, that's what I call it. I'm not blind. Don't I hear her dressing up about four o'clock every afternoon, and, when she's all ready, sittin' in the parlor with the door open, and a book on her knee, as if she'd been reading all afternoon? If he doesn't stop, she's at the foot of the stairs, calling up to him. 'K.,' she says, 'K., I'm waiting to ask you something!' or, 'K., wouldn't you like a cup of tea?' She's always feedin' him tea and cake, so that when he comes to table he won't eat honest victuals."

Sidney had paused with one glove half off. Katie's tone carried conviction. Was life making another of its queer errors, and were Christine and K. in love with each other? K. had always been HER friend, HER confidant. To give him up to Christine--she shook herself impatiently. What had come over her? Why not be glad that he had some sort of companionship?

She went upstairs to the room that had been her mother's, and took off her hat. She wanted to be alone, to realize what had happened to her. She did not belong to herself any more. It gave her an odd, lost feeling. She was going to be married--not very soon, but ultimately. A year ago her half promise to Joe had gratified her sense of romance. She was loved, and she had thrilled to it.

But this was different. Marriage, that had been but a vision then, loomed large, almost menacing. She had learned the law of compensation: that for every joy one pays in suffering. Women who married went down into the valley of death for their children. One must love and be loved very tenderly to pay for that. The scale must balance.

And there were other things. Women grew old, and age was not always lovely. This very maternity--was it not fatal to beauty? Visions of child-bearing women in the hospitals, with sagging breasts and relaxed bodies, came to her. That was a part of the price.

Harriet was stirring, across the hall. Sidney could hear her moving about with flat, inelastic steps.

That was the alternative. One married, happily or not as the case might be, and took the risk. Or one stayed single, like Harriet, growing a little hard, exchanging slimness for leanness and austerity of figure, flat-chested, thin-voiced. One blossomed and withered, then, or one shriveled up without having flowered. All at once it seemed very terrible to her. She felt as if she had been caught in an inexorable hand that had closed about her.

Harriet found her a little later, face down on her mother's bed, crying as if her heart would break. She scolded her roundly.

"You've been overworking," she said. "You've been getting thinner. Your measurements for that suit showed it. I have never approved of this hospital training, and after last January--"

She could hardly credit her senses when Sidney, still swollen with weeping, told her of her engagement.

"But I don't understand. If you care for him and he has asked you to marry him, why on earth are you crying your eyes out?"

"I do care. I don't know why I cried. It just came over me, all at once, that I--It was just foolishness. I am very happy, Aunt Harriet."

Harriet thought she understood. The girl needed her mother, and she, Harriet, was a hard, middle-aged woman and a poor substitute. She patted Sidney's moist hand.

"I guess I understand," she said. "I'll attend to your wedding things, Sidney. We'll show this street that even Christine Lorenz can be outdone." And, as an afterthought: "I hope Max Wilson will settle down now. He's been none too steady."

K. had taken Christine to see Tillie that Sunday afternoon. Palmer had the car out--had, indeed, not been home since the morning of the previous day. He played golf every Saturday afternoon and Sunday at the Country Club, and invariably spent the night there. So K. and Christine walked from the end of the trolley line, saying little, but under K.'s keen direction finding bright birds in the hedgerows, hidden field flowers, a dozen wonders of the country that Christine had never dreamed of.

The interview with Tillie had been a disappointment to K. Christine, with the best and kindliest intentions, struck a wrong note. In her endeavor to cover the fact that everything in Tillie's world was wrong, she fell into the error of pretending that everything was right.

Tillie, grotesque of figure and tragic-eyed, listened to her patiently, while K. stood, uneasy and uncomfortable, in the wide door of the hay-barn and watched automobiles turning in from the road. When Christine rose to leave, she confessed her failure frankly.

"I've meant well, Tillie," she said. "I'm afraid I've said exactly what I shouldn't. I can only think that, no matter what is wrong, two wonderful pieces of luck have come to you. Your husband--that is, Mr. Schwitter--cares for you,--you admit that,--and you are going to have a child."

Tillie's pale eyes filled.

"I used to be a good woman, Mrs. Howe," she said simply. "Now I'm not. When I look in that glass at myself, and call myself what I am, I'd give a good bit to be back on the Street again."

She found opportunity for a word with K. while Christine went ahead of him out of the barn.

"I've been wanting to speak to you, Mr. Le Moyne." She lowered her voice. "Joe Drummond's been coming out here pretty regular. Schwitter says he's drinking a little. He don't like him loafing around here: he sent him home last Sunday. What's come over the boy?"

"I'll talk to him."

"The barkeeper says he carries a revolver around, and talks wild. I thought maybe Sidney Page could do something with him."

"I think he'd not like her to know. I'll do what I can."

K.'s face was thoughtful as he followed Christine to the road.

Christine was very silent, on the way back to the city. More than once K. found her eyes fixed on him, and it puzzled him. Poor Christine was only trying to fit him into the world she knew--a world whose men were strong but seldom tender, who gave up their Sundays to golf, not to visiting unhappy outcasts in the country. How masculine he was, and yet how gentle! It gave her a choking feeling in her throat. She took advantage of a steep bit of road to stop and stand a moment, her fingers on his shabby gray sleeve.

It was late when they got home. Sidney was sitting on the low step, waiting for them.

Wilson had come across at seven, impatient because he must see a case that evening, and promising an early return. In the little hall he had drawn her to him and kissed her, this time not on the lips, but on the forehead and on each of her white eyelids.

"Little wife-to-be!" he had said, and was rather ashamed of his own emotion. From across the Street, as he got into his car, he had waved his hand to her.

Christine went to her room, and, with a long breath of content, K. folded up his long length on the step below Sidney.

"Well, dear ministering angel," he said, "how goes the world?"

"Things have been happening, K."

He sat erect and looked at her. Perhaps because she had a woman's instinct for making the most of a piece of news, perhaps--more likely, indeed--because she divined that the announcement would not be entirely agreeable, she delayed it, played with it.

"I have gone into the operating-room."

"Fine!"

"The costume is ugly. I look hideous in it."

"Doubtless."

He smiled up at her. There was relief in his eyes, and still a question.

"Is that all the news?"

"There is something else, K."

It was a moment before he spoke. He sat looking ahead, his face set. Apparently he did not wish to hear her say it; for when, after a moment, he spoke, it was to forestall her, after all.

"I think I know what it is, Sidney."

"You expected it, didn't you?"

"I--it's not an entire surprise."

"Aren't you going to wish me happiness?"

"If my wishing could bring anything good to you, you would have everything in the world."

His voice was not entirely steady, but his eyes smiled into hers.

"Am I--are we going to lose you soon?"

"I shall finish my training. I made that a condition."

Then, in a burst of confidence:--

"I know so little, K., and he knows so much! I am going to read and study, so that he can talk to me about his work. That's what marriage ought to be, a sort of partnership. Don't you think so?"

K. nodded. His mind refused to go forward to the unthinkable future. Instead, he was looking back--back to those days when he had hoped sometime to have a wife to talk to about his work, that beloved work that was no longer his. And, finding it agonizing, as indeed all thought was that summer night, he dwelt for a moment on that evening, a year before, when in the same June moonlight, he had come up the Street and had seen Sidney where she was now, with the tree shadows playing over her.

Even that first evening he had been jealous.

It had been Joe then. Now it was another and older man, daring, intelligent, unscrupulous. And this time he had lost her absolutely, lost her without a struggle to keep her. His only struggle had been with himself, to remember that he had nothing to offer but failure.

"Do you know," said Sidney suddenly, "that it is almost a year since that night you came up the Street, and I was here on the steps?"

"That's a fact, isn't it!" He managed to get some surprise into his voice.

"How Joe objected to your coming! Poor Joe!"

"Do you ever see him?"

"Hardly ever now. I think he hates me."

"Why?"

"Because--well, you know, K. Why do men always hate a woman who just happens not to love them?"

"I don't believe they do. It would be much better for them if they could. As a matter of fact, there are poor devils who go through life trying to do that very thing, and failing."

Sidney's eyes were on the tall house across. It was Dr. Ed's evening office hour, and through the open window she could see a line of people waiting their turn. They sat immobile, inert, doggedly patient, until the opening of the back office door promoted them all one chair toward the consulting-room.

"I shall be just across the Street," she said at last. "Nearer than I am at the hospital."

"You will be much farther away. You will be married."

"But we will still be friends, K.?"

Her voice was anxious, a little puzzled. She was often puzzled with him.

"Of course."

But, after another silence, he astounded her. She had fallen into the way of thinking of him as always belonging to the house, even, in a sense, belonging to her. And now--

"Shall you mind very much if I tell you that I am thinking of going away?"

"K.!"

"My dear child, you do not need a roomer here any more. I have always received infinitely more than I have paid for, even in the small services I have been able to render. Your Aunt Harriet is prosperous. You are away, and some day you are going to be married. Don't you see--I am not needed?"

"That does not mean you are not wanted."

"I shall not go far. I'll always be near enough, so that I can see you"--he changed this hastily--"so that we can still meet and talk things over. Old friends ought to be like that, not too near, but to be turned on when needed, like a tap."

"Where will you go?"

"The Rosenfelds are rather in straits. I thought of helping them to get a small house somewhere and of taking a room with them. It's largely a matter of furniture. If they could furnish it even plainly, it could be done. I--haven't saved anything."

"Do you ever think of yourself?" she cried. "Have you always gone through life helping people, K.? Save anything! I should think not! You spend it all on others." She bent over and put her hand on his shoulder. "It will not be home without you, K."

To save him, he could not have spoken just then. A riot of rebellion surged up in him, that he must let this best thing in his life go out of it. To go empty of heart through the rest of his days, while his very arms ached to hold her! And she was so near--just above, with her hand on his shoulder, her wistful face so close that, without moving, he could have brushed her hair.

"You have not wished me happiness, K. Do you remember, when I was going to the hospital and you gave me the little watch--do you remember what you said?"

"Yes"--huskily.

"Will you say it again?"

"But that was good-bye."

"Isn't this, in a way? You are going to leave us, and I--say it, K."

"Good-bye, dear, and--God bless you."

CHAPTER XXIII

THE announcement of Sidney's engagement was not to be made for a year. Wilson, chafing under the delay, was obliged to admit to himself that it was best. Many things could happen in a year. Carlotta would have finished her training, and by that time would probably be reconciled to the ending of their relationship.

He intended to end that. He had meant every word of what he had sworn to Sidney. He was genuinely in love, even unselfishly--as far as he could be unselfish. The secret was to be carefully kept also for Sidney's sake. The hospital did not approve of engagements between nurses and the staff. It was disorganizing, bad for discipline.

Sidney was very happy all that summer. She glowed with pride when her lover put through a difficult piece of work; flushed and palpitated when she heard his praises sung; grew to know, by a sort of intuition, when he was in the house. She wore his ring on a fine chain around her neck, and grew prettier every day.

Once or twice, however, when she was at home, away from the glamour, her early fears obsessed her. Would he always love her? He was so handsome and so gifted, and there were women who were mad about him. That was the gossip of the hospital. Suppose she married him and he tired of her? In her humility she thought that perhaps only her youth, and such charm as she had that belonged to youth, held him. And before her, always, she saw the tragic women of the wards.

K. had postponed his leaving until fall. Sidney had been insistent, and Harriet had topped the argument in her businesslike way. "If you insist on being an idiot and adopting the Rosenfeld family," she said, "wait until September. The season for boarders doesn't begin until fall."

So K. waited for "the season," and ate his heart out for Sidney in the interval.

Johnny Rosenfeld still lay in his ward, inert from the waist down. K. was his most frequent visitor. As a matter of fact, he was watching the boy closely, at Max Wilson's request.

"Tell me when I'm to do it," said Wilson, "and when the time comes, for God's sake, stand by me. Come to the operation. He's got so much confidence that I'll help him that I don't dare to fail."

So K. came on visiting days, and, by special dispensation, on Saturday afternoons. He was teaching the boy basket-making. Not that he knew anything about it himself; but, by means of a blind teacher, he kept just one lesson ahead. The ward was intensely interested. It found something absurd and rather touching in this tall, serious young man with the surprisingly deft fingers, tying raffia knots.

The first basket went, by Johnny's request, to Sidney Page.

"I want her to have it," he said. "She got corns on her fingers from rubbing me when I came in first; and, besides--"

"Yes?" said K. He was tying a most complicated knot, and could not look up.

"I know something," said Johnny. "I'm not going to get in wrong by talking, but I know something. You give her the basket."

K. looked up then, and surprised Johnny's secret in his face.

"Ah!" he said.

"If I'd squealed she'd have finished me for good. They've got me, you know. I'm not running in 2.40 these days."

"I'll not tell, or make it uncomfortable for you. What do you know?"

Johnny looked around. The ward was in the somnolence of mid-afternoon. The nearest patient, a man in a wheel-chair, was snoring heavily.

"It was the dark-eyed one that changed the medicine on me," he said. "The one with the heels that were always tapping around, waking me up. She did it; I saw her."

After all, it was only what K. had suspected before. But a sense of impending danger to Sidney obsessed him. If Carlotta would do that, what would she do when she learned of the engagement? And he had known her before. He believed she was totally unscrupulous. The odd coincidence of their paths crossing again troubled him.

Carlotta Harrison was well again, and back on duty. Luckily for Sidney, her three months' service in the operating-room kept them apart. For Carlotta was now not merely jealous. She found herself neglected, ignored. It ate her like a fever.

But she did not yet suspect an engagement. It had been her theory that Wilson would not marry easily--that, in a sense, he would have to be coerced into marriage. Some clever woman would marry him some day, and no one would be more astonished than himself. She thought merely that Sidney was playing a game like her own, with different weapons. So she planned her battle, ignorant that she had lost already.

Her method was simple enough. She stopped sulking, met Max with smiles, made no overtures toward a renewal of their relations. At first this annoyed him. Later it piqued him. To desert a woman was justifiable, under certain circumstances. But to desert a woman, and have her apparently not even know it, was against the rules of the game.

During a surgical dressing in a private room, one day, he allowed his fingers to touch hers, as on that day a year before when she had taken Miss Simpson's place in his office. He was rewarded by the same slow, smouldering glance that had caught his attention before. So she was only acting indifference!

Then Carlotta made her second move. A new interne had come into the house, and was going through the process of learning that from a senior at the medical school to a half-baked junior interne is a long step back. He had to endure the good-humored contempt of the older men, the patronizing instructions of nurses as to rules.

Carlotta alone treated him with deference. His uneasy rounds in Carlotta's precinct took on the state and form of staff visitations. She flattered, cajoled, looked up to him.

After a time it dawned on Wilson that this junior cub was getting more attention than himself: that, wherever he happened to be, somewhere in the offing would be Carlotta and the Lamb, the latter eyeing her with worship. Her indifference had only piqued him. The enthroning of a successor galled him. Between them, the Lamb suffered mightily--was subject to frequent "bawling out," as he termed it, in the operating-room as he assisted the anaesthetist. He took his troubles to Carlotta, who soothed him in the corridor--in plain sight of her quarry, of course--by putting a sympathetic hand on his sleeve.

Then, one day, Wilson was goaded to speech.

"For the love of Heaven, Carlotta," he said impatiently, "stop making love to that wretched boy. He wriggles like a worm if you look at him."

"I like him. He is thoroughly genuine. I respect him, and--he respects me."

"It's rather a silly game, you know."

"What game?"

"Do you think I don't understand?"

"Perhaps you do. I--I don't really care a lot about him, Max. But I've been down-hearted. He cheers me up."

Her attraction for him was almost gone--not quite. He felt rather sorry for her.

"I'm sorry. Then you are not angry with me?"

"Angry? No." She lifted her eyes to his, and for once she was not acting. "I knew it would end, of course. I have lost a--a lover. I expected that. But I wanted to keep a friend."

It was the right note. Why, after all, should he not be her friend? He had treated her cruelly, hideously. If she still desired his friendship, there was no disloyalty to Sidney in giving it. And Carlotta was very careful. Not once again did she allow him to see what lay in her eyes. She told him of her worries. Her training was almost over. She had a chance to take up institutional work. She abhorred the thought of private duty. What would he advise?

The Lamb was hovering near, hot eyes on them both. It was no place to talk.

"Come to the office and we'll talk it over."

"I don't like to go there; Miss Simpson is suspicious."

The institution she spoke of was in another city. It occurred to Wilson that if she took it the affair would have reached a graceful and legitimate end.

Also, the thought of another stolen evening alone with her was not unpleasant. It would be the last, he promised himself. After all, it was owing to her. He had treated her badly.

Sidney would be at a lecture that night. The evening loomed temptingly free.

"Suppose you meet me at the old corner," he said carelessly, eyes on the Lamb, who was forgetting that he was only a junior interne and was glaring ferociously. "We'll run out into the country and talk things over."

She demurred, with her heart beating triumphantly.

"What's the use of going back to that? It's over, isn't it?"

Her objection made him determined. When at last she had yielded, and he made his way down to the smoking-room, it was with the feeling that he had won a victory.

K. had been uneasy all that day; his ledgers irritated him. He had been sleeping badly since Sidney's announcement of her engagement. At five o'clock, when he left the office, he found Joe Drummond waiting outside on the pavement.

"Mother said you'd been up to see me a couple of times. I thought I'd come around."

K. looked at his watch.

"What do you say to a walk?"

"Not out in the country. I'm not as muscular as you are. I'll go about town for a half-hour or so."

Thus forestalled, K. found his subject hard to lead up to. But here again Joe met him more than halfway.

"Well, go on," he said, when they found themselves in the park; "I don't suppose you were paying a call."

"No."

"I guess I know what you are going to say."

"I'm not going to preach, if you're expecting that. Ordinarily, if a man insists on making a fool of himself, I let him alone."

"Why make an exception of me?"

"One reason is that I happen to like you. The other reason is that, whether you admit it or not, you are acting like a young idiot, and are putting the responsibility on the shoulders of some one else."

"She is responsible, isn't she?"

"Not in the least. How old are you, Joe?"

"Twenty-three, almost."

"Exactly. You are a man, and you are acting like a bad boy. It's a disappointment to me. It's more than that to Sidney."

"Much she cares! She's going to marry Wilson, isn't she?"

"There is no announcement of any engagement."

"She is, and you know it. Well, she'll be happy--not! If I'd go to her to-night and tell her what I know, she'd never see him again." The idea, thus born in his overwrought brain, obsessed him. He returned to it again and again. Le Moyne was uneasy. He was not certain that the boy's statement had any basis in fact. His single determination was to save Sidney from any pain.

When Joe suddenly announced his inclination to go out into the country after all, he suspected a ruse to get rid of him, and insisted on going along. Joe consented grudgingly.

"Car's at Bailey's garage," he said sullenly. "I don't know when I'll get back."

"That won't matter." K.'s tone was cheerful. "I'm not sleeping, anyhow."

That passed unnoticed until they were on the highroad, with the car running smoothly between yellowing fields of wheat. Then:--

"So you've got it too!" he said. "We're a fine pair of fools. We'd both be better off if I sent the car over a bank."

He gave the wheel a reckless twist, and Le Moyne called him to time sternly.

They had supper at the White Springs Hotel--not on the terrace, but in the little room where Carlotta and Wilson had taken their first meal together. K. ordered beer for them both, and Joe submitted with bad grace.

But the meal cheered and steadied him. K. found him more amenable to reason, and, gaining his confidence, learned of his desire to leave the city.

"I'm stuck here," he said. "I'm the only one, and mother yells blue murder when I talk about it. I want to go to Cuba. My uncle owns a farm down there."

"Perhaps I can talk your mother over. I've been there."

Joe was all interest. His dilated pupils became more normal, his restless hands grew quiet. K.'s even voice, the picture he drew of life on the island, the stillness of the little hotel in its mid-week dullness, seemed to quiet the boy's tortured nerves. He was nearer to peace than he had been for many days. But he smoked incessantly, lighting one cigarette from another.

At ten o'clock he left K. and went for the car. He paused for a moment, rather sheepishly, by K.'s chair.

"I'm feeling a lot better," he said. "I haven't got the band around my head. You talk to mother."

That was the last K. saw of Joe Drummond until the next day.

CHAPTER XXIV

CARLOTTA dressed herself with unusual care--not in black this time, but in white. She coiled her yellow hair in a soft knot at the back of her head, and she resorted to the faintest shading of rouge. She intended to be gay, cheerful. The ride was to be a bright spot in Wilson's memory. He expected recriminations; she meant to make him happy. That was the secret of the charm some women had for men. They went to such women to forget their troubles. She set the hour of their meeting at nine, when the late dusk of summer had fallen; and she met him then, smiling, a faintly perfumed white figure, slim and young, with a thrill in her voice that was only half assumed.

"It's very late," he complained. "Surely you are not going to be back at ten."

"I have special permission to be out late."

"Good!" And then, recollecting their new situation: "We have a lot to talk over. It will take time."

At the White Springs Hotel they stopped to fill the gasolene tank of the car. Joe Drummond saw Wilson there, in the sheet-iron garage alongside of the road. The Wilson car was in the shadow. It did not occur to Joe that the white figure in the car was not Sidney. He went rather white, and stepped out of the zone of light. The influence of Le Moyne was still on him, however, and he went on quietly with what he was doing. But his hands shook as he filled the radiator.

When Wilson's car had gone on, he went automatically about his preparations for the return trip--lifted a seat cushion to investigate his own store of gasolene, replacing carefully the revolver he always carried under the seat and packed in waste to prevent its accidental discharge, lighted his lamps, examined a loose brake-band.

His coolness gratified him. He had been an ass: Le Moyne was right. He'd get away--to Cuba if he could--and start over again. He would forget the Street and let it forget him.

The men in the garage were talking.

"To Schwitter's, of course," one of them grumbled. "We might as well go out of business."

"There's no money in running a straight place. Schwitter and half a dozen others are getting rich."

"That was Wilson, the surgeon in town. He cut off my brother-in-law's leg--charged him as much as if he had grown a new one for him. He used to come here. Now he goes to Schwitter's, like the rest. Pretty girl he had with him. You can bet on Wilson."

So Max Wilson was taking Sidney to Schwitter's, making her the butt of garage talk! The smiles of the men were evil. Joe's hands grew cold, his head hot. A red mist spread between him and the line of electric lights. He knew Schwitter's, and he knew Wilson.

He flung himself into his car and threw the throttle open. The car jerked, stalled.

"You can't start like that, son," one of the men remonstrated. "You let 'er in too fast."

"You go to hell!" Joe snarled, and made a second ineffectual effort.

Thus adjured, the men offered neither further advice nor assistance. The minutes went by in useless cranking--fifteen. The red mist grew heavier. Every lamp was a danger signal. But when K., growing uneasy, came out into the yard, the engine had started at last. He was in time to see Joe run his car into the road and turn it viciously toward Schwitter's.

Carlotta's nearness was having its calculated effect on Max Wilson. His spirits rose as the engine, marking perfect time, carried them along the quiet roads.

Partly it was reaction--relief that she should be so reasonable, so complaisant--and a sort of holiday spirit after the day's hard work. Oddly enough, and not so irrational as may appear, Sidney formed a part of the evening's happiness--that she loved him; that, back in the lecture-room, eyes and even mind on the lecturer, her heart was with him.

So, with Sidney the basis of his happiness, he made the most of his evening's freedom. He sang a little in his clear tenor--even, once when they had slowed down at a crossing, bent over audaciously and kissed Carlotta's hand in the full glare of a passing train.

"How reckless of you!"

"I like to be reckless," he replied.

His boyishness annoyed Carlotta. She did not want the situation to get out of hand. Moreover, what was so real for her was only too plainly a lark for him. She began to doubt her power.

The hopelessness of her situation was dawning on her. Even when the touch of her beside him and the solitude of the country roads got in his blood, and he bent toward her, she found no encouragement in his words:--"I am mad about you to-night."

She took her courage in her hands:--"Then why give me up for some one else?"

"That's--different."

"Why is it different? I am a woman. I--I love you, Max. No one else will ever care as I do."

"You are in love with the Lamb!"

"That was a trick. I'm sorry, Max. I don't care for anyone else in the world. If you let me go I'll want to die."

Then, as he was silent:--

"If you'll marry me, I'll be true to you all my life. I swear it. There will be nobody else, ever."

The sense, if not the words, of what he had sworn to Sidney that Sunday afternoon under the trees, on this very road! Swift shame overtook him, that he should be here, that he had allowed Carlotta to remain in ignorance of how things really stood between them.

"I'm sorry, Carlotta. It's impossible. I'm engaged to marry some one else."

"Sidney Page?"--almost a whisper.

"Yes."

He was ashamed at the way she took the news. If she had stormed or wept, he would have known what to do. But she sat still, not speaking.

"You must have expected it, sooner or later."

Still she made no reply. He thought she might faint, and looked at her anxiously. Her profile, indistinct beside him, looked white and drawn. But Carlotta was not fainting. She was making a desperate plan. If their escapade became known, it would end things between Sidney and him. She was sure of that. She needed time to think it out. It must become known without any apparent move on her part. If, for instance, she became ill, and was away from the hospital all night, that might answer. The thing would be investigated, and who knew--

The car turned in at Schwitter's road and drew up before the house. The narrow porch was filled with small tables, above which hung rows of electric lights enclosed in Japanese paper lanterns. Midweek, which had found the White Springs Hotel almost deserted, saw Schwitter's crowded tables set out under the trees. Seeing the crowd, Wilson drove directly to the yard and parked his machine.

"No need of running any risk," he explained to the still figure beside him. "We can walk back and take a table under the trees, away from those infernal lanterns."

She reeled a little as he helped her out.

"Not sick, are you?"

"I'm dizzy. I'm all right."

She looked white. He felt a stab of pity for her. She leaned rather heavily on him as they walked toward the house. The faint perfume that had almost intoxicated him, earlier, vaguely irritated him now.

At the rear of the house she shook off his arm and preceded him around the building. She chose the end of the porch as the place in which to drop, and went down like a stone, falling back.

There was a moderate excitement. The visitors at Schwitter's were too much engrossed with themselves to be much interested. She opened her eyes almost as soon as she fell--to forestall any tests; she was shrewd enough to know that Wilson would detect her malingering very quickly--and begged to be taken into the house. "I feel very ill," she said, and her white face bore her out.

Schwitter and Bill carried her in and up the stairs to one of the newly furnished rooms. The little man was twittering with anxiety. He had a horror of knockout drops and the police. They laid her on the bed, her hat beside her; and Wilson, stripping down the long sleeve of her glove, felt her pulse.

"There's a doctor in the next town," said Schwitter. "I was going to send for him, anyhow--my wife's not very well."

"I'm a doctor."

"Is it anything serious?"

"Nothing serious."

He closed the door behind the relieved figure of the landlord, and, going back to Carlotta, stood looking down at her.

"What did you mean by doing that?"

"Doing what?"

"You were no more faint than I am."

She closed her eyes.

"I don't remember. Everything went black. The lanterns--"

He crossed the room deliberately and went out, closing the door behind him. He saw at once where he stood--in what danger. If she insisted that she was ill and unable to go back, there would be a fuss. The story would come out. Everything would be gone. Schwitter's, of all places!

At the foot of the stairs, Schwitter pulled himself together. After all, the girl was only ill. There was nothing for the police. He looked at his watch. The doctor ought to be here by this time. It was sooner than they had expected. Even the nurse had not come. Tillie was alone, out in the harness-room. He looked through the crowded rooms, at the overflowing porch with its travesty of pleasure, and he hated the whole thing with a desperate hatred.

Another car. Would they never stop coming! But perhaps it was the doctor. A young man edged his way into the hall and confronted him.

"Two people just arrived here. A man and a woman--in white. Where are they?"

It was trouble then, after all!

"Upstairs--first bedroom to the right." His teeth chattered. Surely, as a man sowed he reaped.

Joe went up the staircase. At the top, on the landing, he confronted Wilson. He fired at him without a word--saw him fling up his arms and fall back, striking first the wall, then the floor.

The buzz of conversation on the porch suddenly ceased. Joe put his revolver in his pocket and went quietly down the stairs. The crowd parted to let him through.

Carlotta, crouched in her room, listening, not daring to open the door, heard the sound of a car as it swung out into the road.

CHAPTER XXV

ON the evening of the shooting at Schwitter's, there had been a late operation at the hospital. Sidney, having duly transcribed her lecture notes and said her prayers, was already asleep when she received the insistent summons to the operating-room. She dressed again with flying fingers. These night battles with death roused all her fighting blood. There were times when she felt as if, by sheer will, she could force strength, life itself, into failing bodies. Her sensitive nostrils dilated, her brain worked like a machine.

That night she received well-deserved praise. When the Lamb, telephoning hysterically, had failed to locate the younger Wilson, another staff surgeon was called. His keen eyes watched Sidney--felt her capacity, her fiber, so to speak; and, when everything was over, he told her what was in his mind.

"Don't wear yourself out, girl," he said gravely. "We need people like you. It was good work to-night--fine work. I wish we had more like you."

By midnight the work was done, and the nurse in charge sent Sidney to bed.

It was the Lamb who received the message about Wilson; and because he was not very keen at the best, and because the news was so startling, he refused to credit his ears.

"Who is this at the 'phone?"

"That doesn't matter. Le Moyne's my name. Get the message to Dr. Ed Wilson at once. We are starting to the city."

"Tell me again. I mustn't make a mess of this."

"Dr. Wilson, the surgeon, has been shot," came slowly and distinctly. "Get the staff there and have a room ready. Get the operating-room ready, too."

The Lamb wakened then, and roused the house. He was incoherent, rather, so that Dr. Ed got the impression that it was Le Moyne who had been shot, and only learned the truth when he got to the hospital.

"Where is he?" he demanded. He liked K., and his heart was sore within him.

"Not in yet, sir. A Mr. Le Moyne is bringing him. Staff's in the executive committee room, sir."

"But--who has been shot? I thought you said--"

The Lamb turned pale at that, and braced himself.

"I'm sorry--I thought you understood. I believe it's not--not serious. It's Dr. Max, sir."

Dr. Ed, who was heavy and not very young, sat down on an office chair. Out of sheer habit he had brought the bag. He put it down on the floor beside him, and moistened his lips.

"Is he living?"

"Oh, yes, sir. I gathered that Mr. Le Moyne did not think it serious."

He lied, and Dr. Ed knew he lied.

The Lamb stood by the door, and Dr. Ed sat and waited. The office clock said half after three. Outside the windows, the night world went by--taxi-cabs full of roisterers, women who walked stealthily close to the buildings, a truck carrying steel, so heavy that it shook the hospital as it rumbled by.

Dr. Ed sat and waited. The bag with the dog-collar in it was on the floor. He thought of many things, but mostly of the promise he had made his mother. And, having forgotten the injured man's shortcomings, he was remembering his good qualities--his cheerfulness, his courage, his achievements. He remembered the day Max had done the Edwardes operation, and how proud he had been of him. He figured out how old he was--not thirty-one yet, and already, perhaps--There he stopped thinking. Cold beads of sweat stood out on his forehead.

"I think I hear them now, sir," said the Lamb, and stood back respectfully to let him pass out of the door.

Carlotta stayed in the room during the consultation. No one seemed to wonder why she was there, or to pay any attention to her. The staff was stricken. They moved back to make room for Dr. Ed beside the bed, and then closed in again.

Carlotta waited, her hand over her mouth to keep herself from screaming. Surely they would operate; they wouldn't let him die like that!

When she saw the phalanx break up, and realized that they would not operate, she went mad. She stood against the door, and accused them of cowardice--taunted them.

"Do you think he would let any of you die like that?" she cried. "Die like a hurt dog, and none of you to lift a hand?"

It was Pfeiffer who drew her out of the room and tried to talk reason and sanity to her.

"It's hopeless," he said. "If there was a chance, we'd operate, and you know it."

The staff went hopelessly down the stairs to the smoking-room, and smoked. It was all they could do. The night assistant sent coffee down to them, and they drank it. Dr. Ed stayed in his brother's room, and said to his mother, under his breath, that he'd tried to do his best by Max, and that from now on it would be up to her.

K. had brought the injured man in. The country doctor had come, too, finding Tillie's trial not imminent. On the way in he had taken it for granted that K. was a medical man like himself, and had placed his hypodermic case at his disposal.

When he missed him,--in the smoking-room, that was,--he asked for him.

"I don't see the chap who came in with us," he said. "Clever fellow. Like to know his name."

The staff did not know.

K. sat alone on a bench in the hall. He wondered who would tell Sidney; he hoped they would be very gentle with her. He sat in the shadow, waiting. He did not want to go home and leave her to what she might have to face. There was a chance she would ask for him. He wanted to be near, in that case.

He sat in the shadow, on the bench. The night watchman went by twice and stared at him. At last he asked K. to mind the door until he got some coffee.

"One of the staff's been hurt," he explained. "If I don't get some coffee now, I won't get any."

K. promised to watch the door.

A desperate thing had occurred to Carlotta. Somehow, she had not thought of it before. Now she wondered how she could have failed to think of it. If only she could find him and he would do it! She would go down on her knees--would tell him everything, if only he would consent.

When she found him on his bench, however, she passed him by. She had a terrible fear that he might go away if she put the thing to him first. He clung hard to his new identity.

So first she went to the staff and confronted them. They were men of courage, only declining to undertake what they considered hopeless work. The one man among them who might have done the thing with any chance of success lay stricken. Not one among them but would have given of his best--only his best was not good enough.

"It would be the Edwardes operation, wouldn't it?" demanded Carlotta.

The staff was bewildered. There were no rules to cover such conduct on the part of a nurse. One of them--Pfeiffer again, by chance--replied rather heavily:--

"If any, it would be the Edwardes operation."

"Would Dr. Edwardes himself be able to do anything?"

This was going a little far.

"Possibly. One chance in a thousand, perhaps. But Edwardes is dead. How did this thing happen, Miss Harrison?"

She ignored his question. Her face was ghastly, save for the trace of rouge; her eyes were red-rimmed.

"Dr. Edwardes is sitting on a bench in the hall outside!" she announced.

Her voice rang out. K. heard her and raised his head. His attitude was weary, resigned. The thing had come, then! He was to take up the old burden. The girl had told.

Dr. Ed had sent for Sidney. Max was still unconscious. Ed remembered about her when, tracing his brother's career from his babyhood to man's estate and to what seemed now to be its ending, he had remembered that Max was very fond of Sidney. He had hoped that Sidney would take him and do for him what he, Ed, had failed to do.

So Sidney was summoned.

She thought it was another operation, and her spirit was just a little weary. But her courage was indomitable. She forced her shoes on her tired feet, and bathed her face in cold water to rouse herself.

The night watchman was in the hall. He was fond of Sidney; she always smiled at him; and, on his morning rounds at six o'clock to waken the nurses, her voice was always amiable. So she found him in the hall, holding a cup of tepid coffee. He was old and bleary, unmistakably dirty too--but he had divined Sidney's romance.

"Coffee! For me?" She was astonished.

"Drink it. You haven't had much sleep."

She took it obediently, but over the cup her eyes searched his.

"There is something wrong, daddy."

That was his name, among the nurses. He had had another name, but it was lost in the mists of years.

"Get it down."

So she finished it, not without anxiety that she might be needed. But daddy's attentions were for few, and not to be lightly received.

"Can you stand a piece of bad news?"

Strangely, her first thought was of K.

"There has been an accident. Dr. Wilson--"

"Which one?"

"Dr. Max--has been hurt. It ain't much, but I guess you'd like to know it."

"Where is he?"

"Downstairs, in Seventeen."

So she went down alone to the room where Dr. Ed sat in a chair, with his untidy bag beside him on the floor, and his eyes fixed on a straight figure on the bed. When he saw Sidney, he got up and put his arms around her. His eyes told her the truth before he told her anything. She hardly listened to what he said. The fact was all that concerned her--that her lover was dying there, so near that she could touch him with her hand, so far away that no voice, no caress of hers, could reach him.

The why would come later. Now she could only stand, with Dr. Ed's arms about her, and wait.

"If they would only do something!" Sidney's voice sounded strange to her ears.

"There is nothing to do."

But that, it seemed, was wrong. For suddenly Sidney's small world, which had always sedately revolved in one direction, began to move the other way.

The door opened, and the staff came in. But where before they had moved heavily, with drooped heads, now they came quickly, as men with a purpose. There was a tall man in a white coat with them. He ordered them about like children, and they hastened to do his will. At first Sidney only knew that now, at last, they were going to do something--the tall man was going to do something. He stood with his back to Sidney, and gave orders.

The heaviness of inactivity lifted. The room buzzed. The nurses stood by, while the staff did nurses' work. The senior surgical interne, essaying assistance, was shoved aside by the senior surgical consultant, and stood by, aggrieved.

It was the Lamb, after all, who brought the news to Sidney. The new activity had caught Dr. Ed, and she was alone now, her face buried against the back of a chair.

"There'll be something doing now, Miss Page," he offered.

"What are they going to do?"

"Going after the bullet. Do you know who's going to do it?"

His voice echoed the subdued excitement of the room--excitement and new hope.

"Did you ever hear of Edwardes, the surgeon?--the Edwardes operation, you know. Well, he's here. It sounds like a miracle. They found him sitting on a bench in the hall downstairs."

Sidney raised her head, but she could not see the miraculously found Edwardes. She could see the familiar faces of the staff, and that other face on the pillow, and--she gave a little cry. There was K.! How like him to be there, to be wherever anyone was in trouble! Tears came to her eyes--the first tears she had shed.

As if her eyes had called him, he looked up and saw her. He came toward her at once. The staff stood back to let him pass, and gazed after him. The wonder of what had happened was growing on them.

K. stood beside Sidney, and looked down at her. Just at first it seemed as if he found nothing to say. Then:

"There's just a chance, Sidney dear. Don't count too much on it."

"I have got to count on it. If I don't, I shall die."

If a shadow passed over his face, no one saw it.

"I'll not ask you to go back to your room. If you will wait somewhere near, I'll see that you have immediate word."

"I am going to the operating-room."

"Not to the operating-room. Somewhere near."

His steady voice controlled her hysteria. But she resented it. She was not herself, of course, what with strain and weariness.

"I shall ask Dr. Edwardes."

He was puzzled for a moment. Then he understood. After all, it was as well. Whether she knew him as Le Moyne or as Edwardes mattered very little, after all. The thing that really mattered was that he must try to save Wilson for her. If he failed--It ran through his mind that if he failed she might hate him the rest of her life--not for himself, but for his failure; that, whichever way things went, he must lose.

"Dr. Edwardes says you are to stay away from the operation, but to remain near. He--he promises to call you if--things go wrong."

She had to be content with that.

Nothing about that night was real to Sidney. She sat in the anaesthetizing-room, and after a time she knew that she was not alone. There was somebody else. She realized dully that Carlotta was there, too, pacing up and down the little room. She was never sure, for instance, whether she imagined it, or whether Carlotta really stopped before her and surveyed her with burning eyes.

"So you thought he was going to marry you!" said Carlotta--or the dream. "Well, you see he isn't."

Sidney tried to answer, and failed--or that was the way the dream went.

"If you had enough character, I'd think you did it. How do I know you didn't follow us, and shoot him as he left the room?"

It must have been reality, after all; for Sidney's numbed mind grasped the essential fact here, and held on to it. He had been out with Carlotta. He had promised--sworn that this should not happen. It had happened. It surprised her. It seemed as if nothing more could hurt her.

In the movement to and from the operating room, the door stood open for a moment. A tall figure--how much it looked like K.!--straightened and held out something in its hand.

"The bullet!" said Carlotta in a whisper.

Then more waiting, a stir of movement in the room beyond the closed door. Carlotta was standing, her face buried in her hands, against the door. Sidney suddenly felt sorry for her. She cared a great deal. It must be tragic to care like that! She herself was not caring much; she was too numb.

Beyond, across the courtyard, was the stable. Before the day of the motor ambulances, horses had waited there for their summons, eager as fire horses, heads lifted to the gong. When Sidney saw the outline of the stable roof, she knew that it was dawn. The city still slept, but the torturing night was over. And in the gray dawn the staff, looking gray too, and elderly and weary, came out through the closed door and took their hushed way toward the elevator. They were talking among themselves. Sidney, straining her ears, gathered that they had seen a miracle, and that the wonder was still on them.

Carlotta followed them out.

Almost on their heels came K. He was in the white coat, and more and more he looked like the man who had raised up from his work and held out something in his hand. Sidney's head was aching and confused.

She sat there in her chair, looking small and childish. The dawn was morning now--horizontal rays of sunlight on the stable roof and across the windowsill of the anaesthetizing-room, where a row of bottles sat on a clean towel.

The tall man--or was it K.?--looked at her, and then reached up and turned off the electric light. Why, it was K., of course; and he was putting out the hall light before he went upstairs. When the light was out everything was gray. She could not see. She slid very quietly out of her chair, and lay at his feet in a dead faint.

K. carried her to the elevator. He held her as he had held her that day at the park when she fell in the river, very carefully, tenderly, as one holds something infinitely precious. Not until he had placed her on her bed did she open her eyes. But she was conscious before that. She was so tired, and to be carried like that, in strong arms, not knowing where one was going, or caring--

The nurse he had summoned hustled out for aromatic ammonia. Sidney, lying among her pillows, looked up at K.

"How is he?"

"A little better. There's a chance, dear."

"I have been so mixed up. All the time I was sitting waiting, I kept thinking that it was you who were operating! Will he really get well?"

"It looks promising."

"I should like to thank Dr. Edwardes."

The nurse was a long time getting the ammonia. There was so much to talk about: that Dr. Max had been out with Carlotta Harrison, and had been shot by a jealous woman; the inexplicable return to life of the great Edwardes; and--a fact the nurse herself was willing to vouch for, and that thrilled the training-school to the core--that this very Edwardes, newly risen, as it were, and being a miracle himself as well as performing one, this very Edwardes, carrying Sidney to her bed and putting her down, had kissed her on her white forehead.

The training-school doubted this. How could he know Sidney Page? And, after all, the nurse had only seen it in the mirror, being occupied at the time in seeing if her cap was straight. The school, therefore, accepted the miracle, but refused the kiss.

The miracle was no miracle, of course. But something had happened to K. that savored of the marvelous. His faith in himself was coming back--not strongly, with a rush, but with all humility. He had been loath to take up the burden; but, now that he had it, he breathed a sort of inarticulate prayer to be able to carry it.

And, since men have looked for signs since the beginning of time, he too asked for a sign. Not, of course, that he put it that way, or that he was making terms with Providence. It was like this: if Wilson got well, he'd keep on working. He'd feel that, perhaps, after all, this was meant. If Wilson died--Sidney held out her hand to him.

"What should I do without you, K.?" she asked wistfully.

"All you have to do is to want me."

His voice was not too steady, and he took her pulse in a most businesslike way to distract her attention from it.

"How very many things you know! You are quite professional about pulses."

Even then he did not tell her. He was not sure, to be frank, that she'd be interested. Now, with Wilson as he was, was no time to obtrude his own story. There was time enough for that.

"Will you drink some beef tea if I send it to you?"

"I'm not hungry. I will, of course."

"And--will you try to sleep?"

"Sleep, while he--"

"I promise to tell you if there is any change. I shall stay with him."

"I'll try to sleep."

But, as he rose from the chair beside her low bed, she put out her hand to him.

"K."

"Yes, dear."

"He was out with Carlotta. He promised, and he broke his promise."

"There may have been reasons. Suppose we wait until he can explain."

"How can he explain?" And, when he hesitated: "I bring all my troubles to you, as if you had none. Somehow, I can't go to Aunt Harriet, and of course mother--Carlotta cares a great deal for him. She said that I shot him. Does anyone really think that?"

"Of course not. Please stop thinking."

"But who did, K.? He had so many friends, and no enemies that I knew of."

Her mind seemed to stagger about in a circle, making little excursions, but always coming back to the one thing.

"Some drunken visitor to the road-house."

He could have killed himself for the words the moment they were spoken.

"They were at a road-house?"

"It is not just to judge anyone before you hear the story."

She stirred restlessly.

"What time is it?"

"Half-past six."

"I must get up and go on duty."

He was glad to be stern with her. He forbade her rising. When the nurse came in with the belated ammonia, she found K. making an arbitrary ruling, and Sidney looking up at him mutinously.

"Miss Page is not to go on duty to-day. She is to stay in bed until further orders."

"Very well, Dr. Edwardes."

The confusion in Sidney's mind cleared away suddenly. K. was Dr. Edwardes! It was K. who had performed the miracle operation--K. who had dared and perhaps won! Dear K., with his steady eyes and his long surgeon's fingers! Then, because she seemed to see ahead as well as back into the past in that flash that comes to the drowning and to those recovering from shock, and because she knew that now the little house would no longer be home to K., she turned her face into her pillow and cried. Her world had fallen indeed. Her lover was not true and might be dying; her friend would go away to his own world, which was not the Street.

K. left her at last and went back to Seventeen, where Dr. Ed still sat by the bed. Inaction was telling on him. If Max would only open his eyes, so he could tell him what had been in his mind all these years--his pride in him and all that.

With a sort of belated desire to make up for where he had failed, he put the bag that had been Max's bete noir on the bedside table, and began to clear it of rubbish--odd bits of dirty cotton, the tubing from a long defunct stethoscope, glass from a broken bottle, a scrap of paper on which was a memorandum, in his illegible writing, to send Max a check for his graduating suit. When K. came in, he had the old dog-collar in his hand.

"Belonged to an old collie of ours," he said heavily. "Milkman ran over him and killed him. Max chased the wagon and licked the driver with his own whip."

His face worked.

"Poor old Bobby Burns!" he said. "We'd raised him from a pup. Got him in a grape-basket."

The sick man opened his eyes.

CHAPTER XXVI

MAX had rallied well, and things looked bright for him. His patient did not need him, but K. was anxious to find Joe; so he telephoned the gas office and got a day off. The sordid little tragedy was easy to reconstruct, except that, like Joe, K. did not believe in the innocence of the excursion to Schwitter's. His spirit was heavy with the conviction that he had saved Wilson to make Sidney ultimately wretched.

For the present, at least, K.'s revealed identity was safe. Hospitals keep their secrets well. And it is doubtful if the Street would have been greatly concerned even had it known. It had never heard of Edwardes, of the Edwardes clinic or the Edwardes operation. Its medical knowledge comprised the two Wilsons and the osteopath around the corner. When, as would happen soon, it learned of Max Wilson's injury, it would be more concerned with his chances of recovery than with the manner of it. That was as it should be.

But Joe's affair with Sidney had been the talk of the neighborhood. If the boy disappeared, a scandal would be inevitable. Twenty people had seen him at Schwitter's and would know him again.

To save Joe, then, was K.'s first care.

At first it seemed as if the boy had frustrated him. He had not been home all night. Christine, waylaying K. in the little hall, told him that. "Mrs. Drummond was here," she said. "She is almost frantic. She says Joe has not been home all night. She says he looks up to you, and she thought if you could find him and would talk to him--"

"Joe was with me last night. We had supper at the White Springs Hotel. Tell Mrs. Drummond he was in good spirits, and that she's not to worry. I feel sure she will hear from him to-day. Something went wrong with his car, perhaps, after he left me."

He bathed and shaved hurriedly. Katie brought his coffee to his room, and he drank it standing. He was working out a theory about the boy. Beyond Schwitter's the highroad stretched, broad and inviting, across the State. Either he would have gone that way, his little car eating up the miles all that night, or--K. would not formulate his fear of what might have happened, even to himself.

As he went down the Street, he saw Mrs. McKee in her doorway, with a little knot of people around her. The Street was getting the night's news.

He rented a car at a local garage, and drove himself out into the country. He was not minded to have any eyes on him that day. He went to Schwitter's first. Schwitter himself was not in sight. Bill was scrubbing the porch, and a farmhand was gathering bottles from the grass into a box. The dead lanterns swung in the morning air, and from back on the hill came the staccato sounds of a reaping-machine.

"Where's Schwitter?"

"At the barn with the missus. Got a boy back there."

Bill grinned. He recognized K., and, mopping dry a part of the porch, shoved a chair on it.

"Sit down. Well, how's the man who got his last night? Dead?"

"No."

"County detectives were here bright and early. After the lady's husband. I guess we lose our license over this."

"What does Schwitter say?"

"Oh, him!" Bill's tone was full of disgust. "He hopes we do. He hates the place. Only man I ever knew that hated money. That's what this house is--money."

"Bill, did you see the man who fired that shot last night?"

A sort of haze came over Bill's face, as if he had dropped a curtain before his eyes. But his reply came promptly:

"Surest thing in the world. Close to him as you are to me. Dark man, about thirty, small mustache--"

"Bill, you're lying, and I know it. Where is he?"

The barkeeper kept his head, but his color changed.

"I don't know anything about him." He thrust his mop into the pail. K. rose. "Does Schwitter know?"

"He doesn't know nothing. He's been out at the barn all night."

The farmhand had filled his box and disappeared around the corner of the house. K. put his hand on Bill's shirt-sleeved arm.

"We've got to get him away from here, Bill."

"Get who away?"

"You know. The county men may come back to search the premises."

"How do I know you aren't one of them?"

"I guess you know I'm not. He's a friend of mine. As a matter of fact, I followed him here; but I was too late. Did he take the revolver away with him?"

"I took it from him. It's under the bar."

"Get it for me."

In sheer relief, K.'s spirits rose. After all, it was a good world: Tillie with her baby in her arms; Wilson conscious and rallying; Joe safe, and, without the revolver, secure from his own remorse. Other things there were, too--the feel of Sidney's inert body in his arms, the way she had turned to him in trouble. It was not what he wanted, this last, but it was worth while. The reaping-machine was in sight now; it had stopped on the hillside. The men were drinking out of a bucket that flashed in the sun.

There was one thing wrong. What had come over Wilson, to do so reckless a thing? K., who was a one-woman man, could not explain it.

From inside the bar Bill took a careful survey of Le Moyne. He noted his tall figure and shabby suit, the slight stoop, the hair graying over his ears. Barkeepers know men: that's a part of the job. After his survey he went behind the bar and got the revolver from under an overturned pail.

K. thrust it into his pocket.

"Now," he said quietly, "where is he?"

"In my room--top of the house."

K. followed Bill up the stairs. He remembered the day when he had sat waiting in the parlor, and had heard Tillie's slow step coming down. And last night he himself had carried down Wilson's unconscious figure. Surely the wages of sin were wretchedness and misery. None of it paid. No one got away with it.

The room under the eaves was stifling. An unmade bed stood in a corner. From nails in the rafters hung Bill's holiday wardrobe. A tin cup and a cracked pitcher of spring water stood on the window-sill.

Joe was sitting in the corner farthest from the window. When the door swung open, he looked up. He showed no interest on seeing K., who had to stoop to enter the low room.

"Hello, Joe."

"I thought you were the police."

"Not much. Open that window, Bill. This place is stifling."

"Is he dead?"

"No, indeed."

"I wish I'd killed him!"

"Oh, no, you don't. You're damned glad you didn't, and so am I."

"What will they do with me?"

"Nothing until they find you. I came to talk about that. They'd better not find you."

"Huh!"

"It's easier than it sounds."

K. sat down on the bed.

"If I only had some money!" he said. "But never mind about that, Joe; I'll get some."

Loud calls from below took Bill out of the room. As he closed the door behind him, K.'s voice took on a new tone: "Joe, why did you do it?"

"You know."

"You saw him with somebody at the White Springs, and followed them?"

"Yes."

"Do you know who was with him?"

"Yes, and so do you. Don't go into that. I did it, and I'll stand by it."

"Has it occurred to you that you made a mistake?"

"Go and tell that to somebody who'll believe you!" he sneered. "They came here and took a room. I met him coming out of it. I'd do it again if I had a chance, and do it better."

"It was not Sidney."

"Aw, chuck it!"

"It's a fact. I got here not two minutes after you left. The girl was still there. It was some one else. Sidney was not out of the hospital last night. She attended a lecture, and then an operation."

Joe listened. It was undoubtedly a relief to him to know that it had not been Sidney; but if K. expected any remorse, he did not get it.

"If he is that sort, he deserves what he got," said the boy grimly.

And K. had no reply. But Joe was glad to talk. The hours he had spent alone in the little room had been very bitter, and preceded by a time that he shuddered to remember. K. got it by degrees--his descent of the staircase, leaving Wilson lying on the landing above; his resolve to walk back and surrender himself at Schwitter's, so that there could be no mistake as to who had committed the crime.

"I intended to write a confession and then shoot myself," he told K. "But the barkeeper got my gun out of my pocket. And--"

After a pause: "Does she know who did it?"

"Sidney? No."

"Then, if he gets better, she'll marry him anyhow."

"Possibly. That's not up to us, Joe. The thing we've got to do is to hush the thing up, and get you away."

"I'd go to Cuba, but I haven't the money."

K. rose. "I think I can get it."

He turned in the doorway.

"Sidney need never know who did it."

"I'm not ashamed of it." But his face showed relief.

There are times when some cataclysm tears down the walls of reserve between men. That time had come for Joe, and to a lesser extent for K. The boy rose and followed him to the door.

"Why don't you tell her the whole thing?--the whole filthy story?" he asked. "She'd never look at him again. You're crazy about her. I haven't got a chance. It would give you one."

"I want her, God knows!" said K. "But not that way, boy."

Schwitter had taken in five hundred dollars the previous day.

"Five hundred gross," the little man hastened to explain. "But you're right, Mr. Le Moyne. And I guess it would please HER. It's going hard with her, just now, that she hasn't any women friends about. It's in the safe, in cash; I haven't had time to take it to the bank." He seemed to apologize to himself for the unbusinesslike proceeding of lending an entire day's gross receipts on no security. "It's better to get him away, of course. It's good business. I have tried to have an orderly place. If they arrest him here--"

His voice trailed off. He had come a far way from the day he had walked down the Street, and eyed Its poplars with appraising eyes--a far way. Now he had a son, and the child's mother looked at him with tragic eyes. It was arranged that K. should go back to town, returning late that night to pick up Joe at a lonely point on the road, and to drive him to a railroad station. But, as it happened, he went back that afternoon.

He had told Schwitter he would be at the hospital, and the message found him there. Wilson was holding his own, conscious now and making a hard fight. The message from Schwitter was very brief:--

"Something has happened, and Tillie wants you. I don't like to trouble you again, but she--wants you."

K. was rather gray of face by that time, having had no sleep and little food since the day before. But he got into the rented machine again--its rental was running up; he tried to forget it--and turned it toward Hillfoot. But first of all he drove back to the Street, and walked without ringing into Mrs. McKee's.

Neither a year's time nor Mrs. McKee's approaching change of state had altered the "mealing" house. The ticket-punch still lay on the hat-rack in the hall. Through the rusty screen of the back parlor window one viewed the spiraea, still in need of spraying. Mrs. McKee herself was in the pantry, placing one slice of tomato and three small lettuce leaves on each of an interminable succession of plates.

K., who was privileged, walked back.

"I've got a car at the door," he announced, "and there's nothing so extravagant as an empty seat in an automobile. Will you take a ride?"

Mrs. McKee agreed. Being of the class who believe a boudoir cap the ideal headdress for a motor-car, she apologized for having none.

"If I'd known you were coming I would have borrowed a cap," she said. "Miss Tripp, third floor front, has a nice one. If you'll take me in my toque--"

K. said he'd take her in her toque, and waited with some anxiety, having not the faintest idea what a toque was. He was not without other anxieties. What if the sight of Tillie's baby did not do all that he expected? Good women could be most cruel. And Schwitter had been very vague. But here K. was more sure of himself: the little man's voice had expressed as exactly as words the sense of a bereavement that was not a grief.

He was counting on Mrs. McKee's old fondness for the girl to bring them together. But, as they neared the house with its lanterns and tables, its whitewashed stones outlining the drive, its small upper window behind which Joe was waiting for night, his heart failed him, rather. He had a masculine dislike for meddling, and yet--Mrs. McKee had suddenly seen the name in the wooden arch over the gate: "Schwitter's."

"I'm not going in there, Mr. Le Moyne."

"Tillie's not in the house. She's back in the barn."

"In the barn!"

"She didn't approve of all that went on there, so she moved out. It's very comfortable and clean; it smells of hay. You'd be surprised how nice it is."

"The like of her!" snorted Mrs. McKee. "She's late with her conscience, I'm thinking."

"Last night," K. remarked, hands on the wheel, but car stopped, "she had a child there. It--it's rather like very old times, isn't it? A man-child, Mrs. McKee, not in a manger, of course."

"What do you want me to do?" Mrs. McKee's tone, which had been fierce at the beginning, ended feebly.

"I want you to go in and visit her, as you would any woman who'd had a new baby and needed a friend. Lie a little--" Mrs. McKee gasped. "Tell her the baby's pretty. Tell her you've been wanting to see her." His tone was suddenly stern. "Lie a little, for your soul's sake."

She wavered, and while she wavered he drove her in under the arch with the shameful name, and back to the barn. But there he had the tact to remain in the car, and Mrs. McKee's peace with Tillie was made alone. When, five minutes later, she beckoned him from the door of the barn, her eyes were red.

"Come in, Mr. K.," she said. "The wife's dead, poor thing. They're going to be married right away."

The clergyman was coming along the path with Schwitter at his heels. K. entered the barn. At the door to Tillie's room he uncovered his head. The child was asleep at her breast.

The five thousand dollar check from Mr. Lorenz had saved Palmer Howe's credit. On the strength of the deposit, he borrowed a thousand at the bank with which he meant to pay his bills, arrears at the University and Country Clubs, a hundred dollars lost throwing aces with poker dice, and various small obligations of Christine's.

The immediate result of the money was good. He drank nothing for a week, went into the details of the new venture with Christine's father, sat at home with Christine on her balcony in the evenings. With the knowledge that he could pay his debts, he postponed the day. He liked the feeling of a bank account in four figures.

The first evening or two Christine's pleasure in having him there gratified him. He felt kind, magnanimous, almost virtuous. On the third evening he was restless. It occurred to him that his wife was beginning to take his presence as a matter of course. He wanted cold bottled beer. When he found that the ice was out and the beer warm and flat, he was furious.

Christine had been making a fight, although her heart was only half in it. She was resolutely good-humored, ignored the past, dressed for Palmer in the things he liked. They still took their dinners at the Lorenz house up the street. When she saw that the haphazard table service there irritated him, she coaxed her mother into getting a butler.

The Street sniffed at the butler behind his stately back. Secretly and in its heart, it was proud of him. With a half-dozen automobiles, and Christine Howe putting on low neck in the evenings, and now a butler, not to mention Harriet Kennedy's Mimi, it ceased to pride itself on its commonplaceness, ignorant of the fact that in its very lack of affectation had lain its charm.

On the night that Joe shot Max Wilson, Palmer was noticeably restless. He had seen Grace Irving that day for the first time but once since the motor accident. To do him justice, his dissipation of the past few months had not included women.

The girl had a strange fascination for him. Perhaps she typified the care-free days before his marriage; perhaps the attraction was deeper, fundamental. He met her in the street the day before Max Wilson was shot. The sight of her walking sedately along in her shop-girl's black dress had been enough to set his pulses racing.

When he saw that she meant to pass him, he fell into step beside her.

"I believe you were going to cut me!"

"I was in a hurry."

"Still in the store?"

"Yes." And, after a second's hesitation: "I'm keeping straight, too."

"How are you getting along?"

"Pretty well. I've had my salary raised."

"Do you have to walk as fast as this?"

"I said I was in a hurry. Once a week I get off a little early. I--"

He eyed her suspiciously.

"Early! What for?"

"I go to the hospital. The Rosenfeld boy is still there, you know."

"Oh!"

But a moment later he burst out irritably:--

"That was an accident, Grace. The boy took the chance when he engaged to drive the car. I'm sorry, of course. I dream of the little devil sometimes, lying there. I'll tell you what I'll do," he added magnanimously. "I'll stop in and talk to Wilson. He ought to have done something before this."

"The boy's not strong enough yet. I don't think you can do anything for him, unless--"

The monstrous injustice of the thing overcame her. Palmer and she walking about, and the boy lying on his hot bed! She choked.

"Well?"

"He worries about his mother. If you could give her some money, it would help."

"Money! Good Heavens--I owe everybody."

"You owe him too, don't you? He'll never walk again."

"I can't give them ten dollars. I don't see that I'm under any obligation, anyhow. I paid his board for two months in the hospital."

When she did not acknowledge this generosity,--amounting to forty-eight dollars,--his irritation grew. Her silence was an accusation. Her manner galled him, into the bargain. She was too calm in his presence, too cold. Where she had once palpitated visibly under his warm gaze, she was now self-possessed and quiet.

Where it had pleased his pride to think that he had given her up, he found that the shoe was on the other foot.

At the entrance to a side street she stopped.

"I turn off here."

"May I come and see you sometime?"

"No, please."

"That's flat, is it?"

"It is, Palmer."

He swung around savagely and left her.

The next day he drew the thousand dollars from the bank. A good many of his debts he wanted to pay in cash; there was no use putting checks through, with incriminating indorsements. Also, he liked the idea of carrying a roll of money around. The big fellows at the clubs always had a wad and peeled off bills like skin off an onion. He took a couple of drinks to celebrate his approaching immunity from debt.

He played auction bridge that afternoon in a private room at one of the hotels with the three men he had lunched with. Luck seemed to be with him. He won eighty dollars, and thrust it loose in his trousers pocket. Money seemed to bring money! If he could carry the thousand around for a day or so, something pretty good might come of it.

He had been drinking a little all afternoon. When the game was over, he bought drinks to celebrate his victory. The losers treated, too, to show they were no pikers. Palmer was in high spirits. He offered to put up the eighty and throw for it. The losers mentioned dinner and various engagements.

Palmer did not want to go home. Christine would greet him with raised eyebrows. They would eat a stuffy Lorenz dinner, and in the evening Christine would sit in the lamplight and drive him mad with soft music. He wanted lights, noise, the smiles of women. Luck was with him, and he wanted to be happy.

At nine o'clock that night he found Grace. She had moved to a cheap apartment which she shared with two other girls from the store. The others were out. It was his lucky day, surely.

His drunkenness was of the mind, mostly. His muscles were well controlled. The lines from his nose to the corners of his mouth were slightly accentuated, his eyes open a trifle wider than usual. That and a slight paleness of the nostrils were the only evidences of his condition. But Grace knew the signs.

"You can't come in."

"Of course I'm coming in."

She retreated before him, her eyes watchful. Men in his condition were apt to be as quick with a blow as with a caress. But, having gained his point, he was amiable.

"Get your things on and come out. We can take in a roof-garden."

"I've told you I'm not doing that sort of thing."

He was ugly in a flash.

"You've got somebody else on the string."

"Honestly, no. There--there has never been anybody else, Palmer."

He caught her suddenly and jerked her toward him.

"You let me hear of anybody else, and I'll cut the guts out of him!"

He held her for a second, his face black and fierce. Then, slowly and inevitably, he drew her into his arms. He was drunk, and she knew it. But, in the queer loyalty of her class, he was the only man she had cared for. She cared now. She took him for that moment, felt his hot kisses on her mouth, her throat, submitted while his rather brutal hands bruised her arms in fierce caresses. Then she put him from her resolutely.

"Now you're going."

"The hell I'm going!"

But he was less steady than he had been. The heat of the little flat brought more blood to his head. He wavered as he stood just inside the door.

"You must go back to your wife."

"She doesn't want me. She's in love with a fellow at the house."

"Palmer, hush!"

"Lemme come in and sit down, won't you?"

She let him pass her into the sitting-room. He dropped into a chair.

"You've turned me down, and now Christine--she thinks I don't know. I'm no fool; I see a lot of things. I'm no good. I know that I've made her miserable. But I made a merry little hell for you too, and you don't kick about it."

"You know that."

She was watching him gravely. She had never seen him just like this. Nothing else, perhaps, could have shown her so well what a broken reed he was.

"I got you in wrong. You were a good girl before I knew you. You're a good girl now. I'm not going to do you any harm, I swear it. I only wanted to take you out for a good time. I've got money. Look here!" He drew out the roll of bills and showed it to her. Her eyes opened wide. She had never known him to have much money.

"Lots more where that comes from."

A new look flashed into her eyes, not cupidity, but purpose.

She was instantly cunning.

"Aren't you going to give me some of that?"

"What for?"

"I--I want some clothes."

The very drunk have the intuition sometimes of savages or brute beasts.

"You lie."

"I want it for Johnny Rosenfeld."

He thrust it back into his pocket, but his hand retained its grasp of it.

"That's it," he complained. "Don't lemme be happy for a minute! Throw it all up to me!"

"You give me that for the Rosenfeld boy, and I'll go out with you."

"If I give you all that, I won't have any money to go out with!"

But his eyes were wavering. She could see victory.

"Take off enough for the evening."

But he drew himself up.

"I'm no piker," he said largely. "Whole hog or nothing. Take it."

He held it out to her, and from another pocket produced the eighty dollars, in crushed and wrinkled notes.

"It's my lucky day," he said thickly. "Plenty more where this came from. Do anything for you. Give it to the little devil. I--" He yawned. "God, this place is hot!"

His head dropped back on his chair; he propped his sagging legs on a stool. She knew him--knew that he would sleep almost all night. She would have to make up something to tell the other girls; but no matter--she could attend to that later.

She had never had a thousand dollars in her hands before. It seemed smaller than that amount. Perhaps he had lied to her. She paused, in pinning on her hat, to count the bills. It was all there.

CHAPTER XXVII

K. spent all of the evening of that day with Wilson. He was not to go for Joe until eleven o'clock. The injured man's vitality was standing him in good stead. He had asked for Sidney and she was at his bedside. Dr. Ed had gone.

"I'm going, Max. The office is full, they tell me," he said, bending over the bed. "I'll come in later, and if they'll make me a shakedown, I'll stay with you to-night."

The answer was faint, broken but distinct. "Get some sleep...I've been a poor stick...try to do better--" His roving eyes fell on the dog collar on the stand. He smiled, "Good old Bob!" he said, and put his hand over Dr. Ed's, as it lay on the bed.

K. found Sidney in the room, not sitting, but standing by the window. The sick man was dozing. One shaded light burned in a far corner. She turned slowly and met his eyes. It seemed to K. that she looked at him as if she had never really seen him before, and he was right. Readjustments are always difficult.

Sidney was trying to reconcile the K. she had known so well with this new K., no longer obscure, although still shabby, whose height had suddenly become presence, whose quiet was the quiet of infinite power.

She was suddenly shy of him, as he stood looking down at her. He saw the gleam of her engagement ring on her finger. It seemed almost defiant. As though she had meant by wearing it to emphasize her belief in her lover.

They did not speak beyond their greeting, until he had gone over the record. Then:--

"We can't talk here. I want to talk to you, K."

He led the way into the corridor. It was very dim. Far away was the night nurse's desk, with its lamp, its annunciator, its pile of records. The passage floor reflected the light on glistening boards.

"I have been thinking until I am almost crazy, K. And now I know how it happened. It was Joe."

"The principal thing is, not how it happened, but that he is going to get well, Sidney."

She stood looking down, twisting her ring around her finger.

"Is Joe in any danger?"

"We are going to get him away to-night. He wants to go to Cuba. He'll get off safely, I think."

"WE are going to get him away! YOU are, you mean. You shoulder all our troubles, K., as if they were your own."

"I?" He was genuinely surprised. "Oh, I see. You mean--but my part in getting Joe off is practically nothing. As a matter of fact, Schwitter has put up the money. My total capital in the world, after paying the taxicab to-day, is seven dollars."

"The taxicab?"

"By Jove, I was forgetting! Best news you ever heard of! Tillie married and has a baby--all in twenty-four hours! Boy--they named it Le Moyne. Squalled like a maniac when the water went on its head. I--I took Mrs. McKee out in a hired machine. That's what happened to my capital." He grinned sheepishly. "She said she would have to go in her toque. I had awful qualms. I thought it was a wrapper."

"You, of course," she said. "You find Max and save him--don't look like that! You did, didn't you? And you get Joe away, borrowing money to send him. And as if that isn't enough, when you ought to have been getting some sleep, you are out taking a friend to Tillie, and being godfather to the baby."

He looked uncomfortable, almost guilty.

"I had a day off. I--"

"When I look back and remember how all these months I've been talking about service, and you said nothing at all, and all the time you were living what I preached--I'm so ashamed, K."

He would not allow that. It distressed him. She saw that, and tried to smile.

"When does Joe go?"

"To-night. I'm to take him across the country to the railroad. I was wondering--"

"Yes?"

"I'd better explain first what happened, and why it happened. Then if you are willing to send him a line, I think it would help. He saw a girl in white in the car and followed in his own machine. He thought it was you, of course. He didn't like the idea of your going to Schwitter's. Carlotta was taken ill. And Schwitter and--and Wilson took her upstairs to a room."

"Do you believe that, K.?"

"I do. He saw Max coming out and misunderstood. He fired at him then."

"He did it for me. I feel very guilty, K., as if it all comes back to me. I'll write to him, of course. Poor Joe!"

He watched her go down the hall toward the night nurse's desk. He would have given everything just then for the right to call her back, to take her in his arms and comfort her. She seemed so alone. He himself had gone through loneliness and heartache, and the shadow was still on him. He waited until he saw her sit down at the desk and take up a pen. Then he went back into the quiet room.

He stood by the bedside, looking down. Wilson was breathing quietly: his color was coming up, as he rallied from the shock. In K.'s mind now was just one thought--to bring him through for Sidney, and then to go away. He might follow Joe to Cuba. There were chances there. He could do sanitation work, or he might try the Canal.

The Street would go on working out its own salvation. He would have to think of something for the Rosenfelds. And he was worried about Christine. But there again, perhaps it would be better if he went away. Christine's story would have to work itself out. His hands were tied.

He was glad in a way that Sidney had asked no questions about him, had accepted his new identity so calmly. It had been overshadowed by the night tragedy. It would have pleased him if she had shown more interest, of course. But he understood. It was enough, he told himself, that he had helped her, that she counted on him. But more and more he knew in his heart that it was not enough. "I'd better get away from here," he told himself savagely.

And having taken the first step toward flight, as happens in such cases, he was suddenly panicky with fear, fear that he would get out of hand, and take her in his arms, whether or no; a temptation to run from temptation, to cut everything and go with Joe that night. But there his sense of humor saved him. That would be a sight for the gods, two defeated lovers flying together under the soft September moon.

Some one entered the room. He thought it was Sidney and turned with the light in his eyes that was only for her. It was Carlotta.

She was not in uniform. She wore a dark skirt and white waist and her high heels tapped as she crossed the room. She came directly to him.

"He is better, isn't he?"

"He is rallying. Of course it will be a day or two before we are quite sure."

She stood looking down at Wilson's quiet figure.

"I guess you know I've been crazy about him," she said quietly. "Well, that's all over. He never really cared for me. I played his game and I--lost. I've been expelled from the school."

Quite suddenly she dropped on her knees beside the bed, and put her cheek close to the sleeping man's hand. When after a moment she rose, she was controlled again, calm, very white.

"Will you tell him, Dr. Edwardes, when he is conscious, that I came in and said good-bye?"

"I will, of course. Do you want to leave any other message?"

She hesitated, as if the thought tempted her. Then she shrugged her shoulders.

"What would be the use? He doesn't want any message from me."

She turned toward the door. But K. could not let her go like that. Her face frightened him. It was too calm, too controlled. He followed her across the room.

"What are your plans?"

"I haven't any. I'm about through with my training, but I've lost my diploma."

"I don't like to see you going away like this."

She avoided his eyes, but his kindly tone did what neither the Head nor the Executive Committee had done that day. It shook her control.

"What does it matter to you? You don't owe me anything."

"Perhaps not. One way and another I've known you a long time."

"You never knew anything very good."

"I'll tell you where I live, and--"

"I know where you live."

"Will you come to see me there? We may be able to think of something."

"What is there to think of? This story will follow me wherever I go! I've tried twice for a diploma and failed. What's the use?"

But in the end he prevailed on her to promise not to leave the city until she had seen him again. It was not until she had gone, a straight figure with haunted eyes, that he reflected whimsically that once again he had defeated his own plans for flight.

In the corridor outside the door Carlotta hesitated. Why not go back? Why not tell him? He was kind; he was going to do something for her. But the old instinct of self-preservation prevailed. She went on to her room.

Sidney brought her letter to Joe back to K. She was flushed with the effort and with a new excitement.

"This is the letter, K., and--I haven't been able to say what I wanted, exactly. You'll let him know, won't you, how I feel, and how I blame myself?"

K. promised gravely.

"And the most remarkable thing has happened. What a day this has been! Somebody has sent Johnny Rosenfeld a lot of money. The ward nurse wants you to come back."

The ward had settled for the night. The well-ordered beds of the daytime were chaotic now, torn apart by tossing figures. The night was hot and an electric fan hummed in a far corner. Under its sporadic breezes, as it turned, the ward was trying to sleep.

Johnny Rosenfeld was not asleep. An incredible thing had happened to him. A fortune lay under his pillow. He was sure it was there, for ever since it came his hot hand had clutched it.

He was quite sure that somehow or other K. had had a hand in it. When he disclaimed it, the boy was bewildered.

"It'll buy the old lady what she wants for the house, anyhow," he said. "But I hope nobody's took up a collection for me. I don't want no charity."

"Maybe Mr. Howe sent it."

"You can bet your last match he didn't."

In some unknown way the news had reached the ward that Johnny's friend,

Mr. Le Moyne, was a great surgeon. Johnny had rejected it scornfully.

"He works in the gas office," he said, "I've seen him there. If he's a surgeon, what's he doing in the gas office. If he's a surgeon, what's he doing teaching me raffia-work? Why isn't he on his job?"

But the story had seized on his imagination.

"Say, Mr. Le Moyne."

"Yes, Jack."

He called him "Jack." The boy liked it. It savored of man to man. After all, he was a man, or almost. Hadn't he driven a car? Didn't he have a state license?

"They've got a queer story about you here in the ward."

"Not scandal, I trust, Jack!"

"They say that you're a surgeon; that you operated on Dr. Wilson and saved his life. They say that you're the king pin where you came from." He eyed K. wistfully. "I know it's a damn lie, but if it's true--"

"I used to be a surgeon. As a matter of fact I operated on Dr. Wilson to-day. I--I am rather apologetic, Jack, because I didn't explain to you sooner. For--various reasons--I gave up that--that line of business. To-day they rather forced my hand."

"Don't you think you could do something for me, sir?"

When K. did not reply at once, he launched into an explanation.

"I've been lying here a good while. I didn't say much because I knew I'd have to take a chance. Either I'd pull through or I wouldn't, and the odds were--well, I didn't say much. The old lady's had a lot of trouble. But now, with THIS under my pillow for her, I've got a right to ask. I'll take a chance, if you will."

"It's only a chance, Jack."

"I know that. But lie here and watch these soaks off the street. Old, a lot of them, and gettin' well to go out and starve, and--My God! Mr. Le Moyne, they can walk, and I can't."

K. drew a long breath. He had started, and now he must go on. Faith in himself or no faith, he must go on. Life, that had loosed its hold on him for a time, had found him again.

"I'll go over you carefully to-morrow, Jack. I'll tell you your chances honestly."

"I have a thousand dollars. Whatever you charge--"

"I'll take it out of my board bill in the new house!"

At four o'clock that morning K. got back from seeing Joe off. The trip had been without accident.

Over Sidney's letter Joe had shed a shamefaced tear or two. And during the night ride, with K. pushing the car to the utmost, he had felt that the boy, in keeping his hand in his pocket, had kept it on the letter. When the road was smooth and stretched ahead, a gray-white line into the night, he tried to talk a little courage into the boy's sick heart.

"You'll see new people, new life," he said. "In a month from now you'll wonder why you ever hung around the Street. I have a feeling that you're going to make good down there."

And once, when the time for parting was very near,--"No matter what happens, keep on believing in yourself. I lost my faith in myself once. It was pretty close to hell."

Joe's response showed his entire self-engrossment.

"If he dies, I'm a murderer."

"He's not going to die," said K. stoutly.

At four o'clock in the morning he left the car at the garage and walked around to the little house. He had had no sleep for forty-five hours; his eyes were sunken in his head; the skin over his temples looked drawn and white. His clothes were wrinkled; the soft hat he habitually wore was white with the dust of the road.

As he opened the hall door, Christine stirred in the room beyond. She came out fully dressed.

"K., are you sick?"

"Rather tired. Why in the world aren't you in bed?"

"Palmer has just come home in a terrible rage. He says he's been robbed of a thousand dollars."

"Where?"

Christine shrugged her shoulders.

"He doesn't know, or says he doesn't. I'm glad of it. He seems thoroughly frightened. It may be a lesson."

In the dim hall light he realized that her face was strained and set. She looked on the verge of hysteria.

"Poor little woman," he said. "I'm sorry, Christine."

The tender words broke down the last barrier of her self-control.

"Oh, K.! Take me away. Take me away! I can't stand it any longer."

She held her arms out to him, and because he was very tired and lonely, and because more than anything else in the world just then he needed a woman's arms, he drew her to him and held her close, his cheek to her hair.

"Poor girl!" he said. "Poor Christine! Surely there must be some happiness for us somewhere."

But the next moment he let her go and stepped back.

"I'm sorry." Characteristically he took the blame. "I shouldn't have done that--You know how it is with me."

"Will it always be Sidney?"

"I'm afraid it will always be Sidney."

CHAPTER XXVIII

JOHNNY Rosenfeld was dead. All of K.'s skill had not sufficed to save him. The operation had been a marvel, but the boy's long-sapped strength failed at the last.

K., set of face, stayed with him to the end. The boy did not know he was going. He roused from the coma and smiled up at Le Moyne.

"I've got a hunch that I can move my right foot," he said. "Look and see."

K. lifted the light covering.

"You're right, old man. It's moving."

"Brake foot, clutch foot," said Johnny, and closed his eyes again.

K. had forbidden the white screens, that outward symbol of death. Time enough for them later. So the ward had no suspicion, nor had the boy.

The ward passed in review. It was Sunday, and from the chapel far below came the faint singing of a hymn. When Johnny spoke again he did not open his eyes.

"You're some operator, Mr. Le Moyne. I'll put in a word for you whenever I get a chance."

"Yes, put in a word for me," said K. huskily.

He felt that Johnny would be a good mediator--that whatever he, K., had done of omission or commission, Johnny's voice before the Tribunal would count.

The lame young violin-player came into the ward. She had cherished a secret and romantic affection for Max Wilson, and now he was in the hospital and ill. So she wore the sacrificial air of a young nun and played "The Holy City."

Johnny was close on the edge of his long sleep by that time, and very comfortable.

"Tell her nix on the sob stuff," he complained. "Ask her to play 'I'm twenty-one and she's eighteen.'"

She was rather outraged, but on K.'s quick explanation she changed to the staccato air.

"Ask her if she'll come a little nearer; I can't hear her."

So she moved to the foot of the bed, and to the gay little tune Johnny began his long sleep. But first he asked K. a question: "Are you sure I'm going to walk, Mr. Le Moyne?"

"I give you my solemn word," said K. huskily, "that you are going to be better than you have ever been in your life."

It was K. who, seeing he would no longer notice, ordered the screens to be set around the bed, K. who drew the coverings smooth and folded the boy's hands over his breast.

The violin-player stood by uncertainly.

"How very young he is! Was it an accident?"

"It was the result of a man's damnable folly," said K. grimly. "Somebody always pays."

And so Johnny Rosenfeld paid.

The immediate result of his death was that K., who had gained some of his faith in himself on seeing Wilson on the way to recovery, was beset by his old doubts. What right had he to arrogate to himself again powers of life and death? Over and over he told himself that there had been no carelessness here, that the boy would have died ultimately, that he had taken the only chance, that the boy himself had known the risk and begged for it.

The old doubts came back.

And now came a question that demanded immediate answer. Wilson would be out of commission for several months, probably. He was gaining, but slowly. And he wanted K. to take over his work.

"Why not?" he demanded, half irritably. "The secret is out. Everybody knows who you are. You're not thinking about going back to that ridiculous gas office, are you?"

"I had some thought of going to Cuba."

"I'm damned if I understand you. You've done a marvelous thing; I lie here and listen to the staff singing your praises until I'm sick of your name! And now, because a boy who wouldn't have lived anyhow--"

"That's not it," K. put in hastily. "I know all that. I guess I could do it and get away with it as well as the average. All that deters me--I've never told you, have I, why I gave up before?"

Wilson was propped up in his bed. K. was walking restlessly about the room, as was his habit when troubled.

"I've heard the gossip; that's all."

"When you recognized me that night on the balcony, I told you I'd lost my faith in myself, and you said the whole affair had been gone over at the State Society. As a matter of fact, the Society knew of only two cases. There had been three."

"Even at that--"

"You know what I always felt about the profession, Max. We went into that more than once in Berlin. Either one's best or nothing. I had done pretty well. When I left Lorch and built my own hospital, I hadn't a doubt of myself. And because I was getting results I got a lot of advertising. Men began coming to the clinics. I found I was making enough out of the patients who could pay to add a few free wards. I want to tell you now, Wilson, that the opening of those free wards was the greatest self-indulgence I ever permitted myself. I'd seen so much careless attention given the poor--well, never mind that. It was almost three years ago that things began to go wrong. I lost a big case."

"I know. All this doesn't influence me, Edwardes."

"Wait a moment. We had a system in the operating-room as perfect as I could devise it. I never finished an operation without having my first assistant verify the clip and sponge count. But that first case died because a sponge had been left in the operating field. You know how those things go; you can't always see them, and one goes by the count, after reasonable caution. Then I lost another case in the same way--a free case.

"As well as I could tell, the precautions had not been relaxed. I was doing from four to six cases a day. After the second one I almost went crazy. I made up my mind, if there was ever another, I'd give up and go away."

"There was another?"

"Not for several months. When the last case died, a free case again, I performed my own autopsy. I allowed only my first assistant in the room. He was almost as frenzied as I was. It was the same thing again. When I told him I was going away, he offered to take the blame himself, to say he had closed the incision. He tried to make me think he was responsible. I knew--better."

"It's incredible."

"Exactly; but it's true. The last patient was a laborer. He left a family. I've sent them money from time to time. I used to sit and think about the children he left, and what would become of them. The ironic part of it was that, for all that had happened, I was busier all the time. Men were sending me cases from all over the country. It was either stay and keep on working, with that chance, or--quit. I quit." "But if you had stayed, and taken extra precautions--"

"We'd taken every precaution we knew."

Neither of the men spoke for a time. K. stood, his tall figure outlined against the window. Far off, in the children's ward, children were laughing; from near by a very young baby wailed a thin cry of protest against life; a bell rang constantly. K.'s mind was busy with the past--with the day he decided to give up and go away, with the months of wandering and homelessness, with the night he had come upon the Street and had seen Sidney on the doorstep of the little house.

"That's the worst, is it?" Max Wilson demanded at last.

"That's enough."

"It's extremely significant. You had an enemy somewhere--on your staff, probably. This profession of ours is a big one, but you know its jealousies. Let a man get his shoulders above the crowd, and the pack is after him." He laughed a little. "Mixed figure, but you know what I mean."

K. shook his head. He had had that gift of the big man everywhere, in every profession, of securing the loyalty of his followers. He would have trusted every one of them with his life.

"You're going to do it, of course."

"Take up your work?"

"Yes."

He stirred restlessly. To stay on, to be near Sidney, perhaps to stand by as Wilson's best man when he was married--it turned him cold. But he did not give a decided negative. The sick man was flushed and growing fretful; it would not do to irritate him.

"Give me another day on it," he said at last. And so the matter stood.

Max's injury had been productive of good, in one way. It had brought the two brothers closer together. In the mornings Max was restless until Dr. Ed arrived. When he came, he brought books in the shabby bag--his beloved Burns, although he needed no book for that, the "Pickwick Papers," Renan's "Lives of the Disciples." Very often Max world doze off; at the cessation of Dr. Ed's sonorous voice the sick man would stir fretfully and demand more. But because he listened to everything without discrimination, the older man came to the conclusion that it was the companionship that counted. It pleased him vastly. It reminded him of Max's boyhood, when he had read to Max at night. For once in the last dozen years, he needed him.

"Go on, Ed. What in blazes makes you stop every five minutes?" Max protested, one day.

Dr. Ed, who had only stopped to bite off the end of a stogie to hold in his cheek, picked up his book in a hurry, and eyed the invalid over it.

"Stop bullying. I'll read when I'm ready. Have you any idea what I'm reading?"

"Of course."

"Well, I haven't. For ten minutes I've been reading across both pages!"

Max laughed, and suddenly put out his hand. Demonstrations of affection were so rare with him that for a moment Dr. Ed was puzzled. Then, rather sheepishly, he took it.

"When I get out," Max said, "we'll have to go out to the White Springs again and have supper."

That was all; but Ed understood.

Morning and evening, Sidney went to Max's room. In the morning she only smiled at him from the doorway. In the evening she went to him after prayers. She was allowed an hour with him then.

The shooting had been a closed book between them. At first, when he began to recover, he tried to talk to her about it. But she refused to listen. She was very gentle with him, but very firm.

"I know how it happened, Max," she said--"about Joe's mistake and all that. The rest can wait until you are much better."

If there had been any change in her manner to him, he would not have submitted so easily, probably. But she was as tender as ever, unfailingly patient, prompt to come to him and slow to leave. After a time he began to dread reopening the subject. She seemed so effectually to have closed it. Carlotta was gone. And, after all, what good could he do his cause by pleading it? The fact was there, and Sidney knew it.

On the day when K. had told Max his reason for giving up his work, Max was allowed out of bed for the first time. It was a great day. A box of red roses came that day from the girl who had refused him a year or more ago. He viewed them with a carelessness that was half assumed.

The news had traveled to the Street that he was to get up that day. Early that morning the doorkeeper had opened the door to a gentleman who did not speak, but who handed in a bunch of early chrysanthemums and proceeded to write, on a pad he drew from his pocket:--

"From Mrs. McKee's family and guests, with their congratulations on your recovery, and their hope that they will see you again soon. If their ends are clipped every day and they are placed in ammonia water, they will last indefinitely." Sidney spent her hour with Max that evening as usual. His big chair had been drawn close to a window, and she found him there, looking out. She kissed him. But this time, instead of letting her draw away, he put out his arms and caught her to him.

"Are you glad?"

"Very glad, indeed," she said soberly.

"Then smile at me. You don't smile any more. You ought to smile; your mouth--"

"I am almost always tired; that's all, Max."

She eyed him bravely.

"Aren't you going to let me make love to you at all? You get away beyond my reach."

"I was looking for the paper to read to you."

A sudden suspicion flamed in his eyes.

"Sidney."

"Yes, dear."

"You don't like me to touch you any more. Come here where I can see you."

The fear of agitating him brought her quickly. For a moment he was appeased.

"That's more like it. How lovely you are, Sidney!" He lifted first one hand and then the other to his lips. "Are you ever going to forgive me?"

"If you mean about Carlotta, I forgave that long ago."

He was almost boyishly relieved. What a wonder she was! So lovely, and so sane. Many a woman would have held that over him for years--not that he had done anything really wrong on that nightmare excursion. But so many women are exigent about promises.

"When are you going to marry me?"

"We needn't discuss that to-night, Max."

"I want you so very much. I don't want to wait, dear. Let me tell Ed that you will marry me soon. Then, when I go away, I'll take you with me."

"Can't we talk things over when you are stronger?"

Her tone caught his attention, and turned him a little white. He faced her to the window, so that the light fell full on her.

"What things? What do you mean?"

He had forced her hand. She had meant to wait; but, with his keen eyes on her, she could not dissemble.

"I am going to make you very unhappy for a little while."

"Well?"

"I've had a lot of time to think. If you had really wanted me, Max--"

"My God, of course I want you!"

"It isn't that I am angry. I am not even jealous. I was at first. It isn't that. It's hard to make you understand. I think you care for me--"

"I love you! I swear I never loved any other woman as I love you."

Suddenly he remembered that he had also sworn to put Carlotta out of his life. He knew that Sidney remembered, too; but she gave no sign.

"Perhaps that's true. You might go on caring for me. Sometimes I think you would. But there would always be other women, Max. You're like that. Perhaps you can't help it."

"If you loved me you could do anything with me." He was half sullen.

By the way her color leaped, he knew he had struck fire. All his conjectures as to how Sidney would take the knowledge of his entanglement with Carlotta had been founded on one major premise--that she loved him. The mere suspicion made him gasp.

"But, good Heavens, Sidney, you do care for me, don't you?"

"I'm afraid I don't, Max; not enough."

She tried to explain, rather pitifully. After one look at his face, she spoke to the window.

"I'm so wretched about it. I thought I cared. To me you were the best and greatest man that ever lived. I--when I said my prayers, I--But that doesn't matter. You were a sort of god to me. When the Lamb--that's one of the internes, you know--nicknamed you the 'Little Tin God,' I was angry. You could never be anything little to me, or do anything that wasn't big. Do you see?"

He groaned under his breath.

"No man could live up to that, Sidney."

"No. I see that now. But that's the way I cared. Now I know that I didn't care for you, really, at all. I built up an idol and worshiped it. I always saw you through a sort of haze. You were operating, with everybody standing by, saying how wonderful it was. Or you were coming to the wards, and everything was excitement, getting ready for you. I blame myself terribly. But you see, don't you? It isn't that I think you are wicked. It's just that I never loved the real you, because I never knew you."

When he remained silent, she made an attempt to justify herself.

"I'd known very few men," she said. "I came into the hospital, and for a time life seemed very terrible. There were wickednesses I had never heard of, and somebody always paying for them. I was always asking, Why? Why? Then you would come in, and a lot of them you cured and sent out. You gave them their chance, don't you see? Until I knew about Carlotta, you always meant that to me. You were like K.--always helping."

The room was very silent. In the nurses' parlor, a few feet down the corridor, the nurses were at prayers.

"The Lord is my shepherd; I shall not want," read the Head, her voice calm with the quiet of twilight and the end of the day.

"He maketh me to lie down in green pastures: he leadeth me beside the still waters."

The nurses read the response a little slowly, as if they, too, were weary.

"Yea, though I walk through the valley of the shadow of death--"

The man in the chair stirred. He had come through the valley of the shadow, and for what? He was very bitter. He said to himself savagely that they would better have let him die. "You say you never loved me because you never knew me. I'm not a rotter, Sidney. Isn't it possible that the man you, cared about, who--who did his best by people and all that--is the real me?"

She gazed at him thoughtfully. He missed something out of her eyes, the sort of luminous, wistful look with which she had been wont to survey his greatness. Measured by this new glance, so clear, so appraising, he sank back into his chair.

"The man who did his best is quite real. You have always done the best in your work; you always will. But the other is a part of you too, Max. Even if I cared, I would not dare to run the risk."

Under the window rang the sharp gong of a city patrol-wagon. It rumbled through the gates back to the courtyard, where its continued clamor summoned white-coated orderlies.

An operating-room case, probably. Sidney, chin lifted, listened carefully. If it was a case for her, the elevator would go up to the operating-room. With a renewed sense of loss, Max saw that already she had put him out of her mind. The call to service was to her a call to battle. Her sensitive nostrils quivered; her young figure stood erect, alert.

"It has gone up!"

She took a step toward the door, hesitated, came back, and put a light hand on his shoulder.

"I'm sorry, dear Max."

She had kissed him lightly on the cheek before he knew what she intended to do. So passionless was the little caress that, perhaps more than anything else, it typified the change in their relation.

When the door closed behind her, he saw that she had left her ring on the arm of his chair. He picked it up. It was still warm from her finger. He held it to his lips with a quick gesture. In all his successful young life he had never before felt the bitterness of failure. The very warmth of the little ring hurt.

Why hadn't they let him die? He didn't want to live--he wouldn't live. Nobody cared for him! He would--

His eyes, lifted from the ring, fell on the red glow of the roses that had come that morning. Even in the half light, they glowed with fiery color.

The ring was in his right hand. With the left he settled his collar and soft silk tie.

K. saw Carlotta that evening for the last time. Katie brought word to him, where he was helping Harriet close her trunk,--she was on her way to Europe for the fall styles,--that he was wanted in the lower hall.

"A lady!" she said, closing the door behind her by way of caution. "And a good thing for her she's not from the alley. The way those people beg off you is a sin and a shame, and it's not at home you're going to be to them from now on."

So K. had put on his coat and, without so much as a glance in Harriet's mirror, had gone down the stairs. Carlotta was in the lower hall. She stood under the chandelier, and he saw at once the ravages that trouble had made in her. She was a dead white, and she looked ten years older than her age.

"I came, you see, Dr. Edwardes."

Now and then, when some one came to him for help, which was generally money, he used Christine's parlor, if she happened to be out. So now, finding the door ajar, and the room dark, he went in and turned on the light.

"Come in here; we can talk better."

She did not sit down at first; but, observing that her standing kept him on his feet, she sat finally. Evidently she found it hard to speak.

"You were to come," K. encouraged her, "to see if we couldn't plan something for you. Now, I think I've got it."

"If it's another hospital--and I don't want to stay here, in the city."

"You like surgical work, don't you?"

"I don't care for anything else."

"Before we settle this, I'd better tell you what I'm thinking of. You know, of course, that I closed my hospital. I--a series of things happened, and I decided I was in the wrong business. That wouldn't be important, except for what it leads to. They are trying to persuade me to go back, and--I'm trying to persuade myself that I'm fit to go back. You see,"--his tone was determinedly cheerful, "my faith in myself has been pretty nearly gone. When one loses that, there isn't much left."

"You had been very successful." She did not look up.

"Well, I had and I hadn't. I'm not going to worry you about that. My offer is this: We'll just try to forget about--about Schwitter's and all the rest, and if I go back I'll take you on in the operating-room."

"You sent me away once!"

"Well, I can ask you to come back, can't I?" He smiled at her encouragingly.

"Are you sure you understand about Max Wilson and myself?"

"I understand."

"Don't you think you are taking a risk?"

"Every one makes mistakes now and then, and loving women have made mistakes since the world began. Most people live in glass houses, Miss Harrison. And don't make any mistake about this: people can always come back. No depth is too low. All they need is the willpower."

He smiled down at her. She had come armed with confession. But the offer he made was too alluring. It meant reinstatement, another chance, when she had thought everything was over. After all, why should she damn herself? She would go back. She would work her finger-ends off for him. She would make it up to him in other ways. But she could not tell him and lose everything.

"Come," he said. "Shall we go back and start over again?"

He held out his hand.

CHAPTER XXIX

LATE September had come, with the Street, after its summer indolence taking up the burden of the year. At eight-thirty and at one the school bell called the children. Little girls in pig-tails, carrying freshly sharpened pencils, went primly toward the school, gathering, comet fashion, a tail of unwilling brothers as they went.

An occasional football hurtled through the air. Le Moyne had promised the baseball club a football outfit, rumor said, but would not coach them himself this year. A story was going about that Mr. Le Moyne intended to go away.

The Street had been furiously busy for a month. The cobblestones had gone, and from curb to curb stretched smooth asphalt. The fascination of writing on it with chalk still obsessed the children. Every few yards was a hop-scotch diagram. Generally speaking, too, the Street had put up new curtains, and even, here and there, had added a coat of paint.

To this general excitement the strange case of Mr. Le Moyne had added its quota. One day he was in the gas office, making out statements that were absolutely ridiculous. (What with no baking all last month, and every Sunday spent in the country, nobody could have used that amount of gas. They could come and take their old meter out!) And the next there was the news that Mr. Le Moyne had been only taking a holiday in the gas office,--paying off old scores, the barytone at Mrs. McKee's hazarded!--and that he was really a very great surgeon and had saved Dr. Max Wilson.

The Street, which was busy at the time deciding whether to leave the old sidewalks or to put down cement ones, had one evening of mad excitement over the matter,--of K., not the sidewalks,--and then had accepted the new situation.

But over the news of K.'s approaching departure it mourned. What was the matter with things, anyhow? Here was Christine's marriage, which had promised so well,--awnings and palms and everything,--turning out badly. True, Palmer Howe was doing better, but he would break out again. And Johnny Rosenfeld was dead, so that his mother came on washing-days, and brought no cheery gossip; but bent over her tubs dry-eyed and silent--even the approaching move to a larger house failed to thrill her. There was Tillie, too. But one did not speak of her. She was married now, of course; but the Street did not tolerate such a reversal of the usual processes as Tillie had indulged in. It censured Mrs. McKee severely for having been, so to speak, and accessory after the fact.

The Street made a resolve to keep K., if possible. If he had shown any "high and mightiness," as they called it, since the change in his estate, it would have let him go without protest. But when a man is the real thing,--so that the newspapers give a column to his having been in the city almost two years,--and still goes about in the same shabby clothes, with the same friendly greeting for every one, it demonstrates clearly, as the barytone put it, that "he's got no swelled head on him; that's sure."

"Anybody can see by the way he drives that machine of Wilson's that he's been used to a car--likely a foreign one. All the swells have foreign cars." Still the barytone, who was almost as fond of conversation as of what he termed "vocal." "And another thing. Do you notice the way he takes Dr. Ed around? Has him at every consultation. The old boy's tickled to death."

A little later, K., coming up the Street as he had that first day, heard the barytone singing:--

"Home is the hunter, home from the hill,
And the sailor, home from sea."

Home! Why, this WAS home. The Street seemed to stretch out its arms to him. The ailanthus tree waved in the sunlight before the little house. Tree and house were old; September had touched them. Christine sat sewing on the balcony. A boy with a piece of chalk was writing something on the new cement under the tree. He stood back, head on one side, when he had finished, and inspected his work. K. caught him up from behind, and, swinging him around--

"Hey!" he said severely. "Don't you know better than to write all over the street? What'll I do to you? Give you to a policeman?"

"Aw, lemme down, Mr. K."

"You tell the boys that if I find this street scrawled over any more, the picnic's off."

"Aw, Mr. K.!"

"I mean it. Go and spend some of that chalk energy of yours in school."

He put the boy down. There was a certain tenderness in his hands, as in his voice, when he dealt with children. All his severity did not conceal it. "Get along with you, Bill. Last bell's rung."

As the boy ran off, K.'s eye fell on what he had written on the cement. At a certain part of his career, the child of such a neighborhood as the Street "cancels" names. It is a part of his birthright. He does it as he whittles his school desk or tries to smoke the long dried fruit of the Indian cigar tree. So K. read in chalk an the smooth street:--

Max Wilson Marriage.   Sidney Page Love.

[Note: the a, l, s, and n of "Max Wilson" are crossed through, as are the S, d, n, and a of "Sidney Page"]

The childish scrawl stared up at him impudently, a sacred thing profaned by the day. K. stood and looked at it. The barytone was still singing; but now it was "I'm twenty-one, and she's eighteen." It was a cheerful air, as should be the air that had accompanied Johnny Rosenfeld to his long sleep. The light was gone from K.'s face again. After all, the Street meant for him not so much home as it meant Sidney. And now, before very long, that book of his life, like others, would have to be closed.

He turned and went heavily into the little house.

Christine called to him from her little balcony:--

"I thought I heard your step outside. Have you time to come out?"

K. went through the parlor and stood in the long window. His steady eyes looked down at her.

"I see very little of you now," she complained. And, when he did not reply immediately: "Have you made any definite plans, K.?"

"I shall do Max's work until he is able to take hold again. After that--"

"You will go away?"

"I think so. I am getting a good many letters, one way and another. I suppose, now I'm back in harness, I'll stay. My old place is closed. I'd go back there--they want me. But it seems so futile, Christine, to leave as I did, because I felt that I had no right to go on as things were; and now to crawl back on the strength of having had my hand forced, and to take up things again, not knowing that I've a bit more right to do it than when I left!"

"I went to see Max yesterday. You know what he thinks about all that."

He took an uneasy turn up and down the balcony.

"But who?" he demanded. "Who would do such a thing? I tell you, Christine, it isn't possible."

She did not pursue the subject. Her thoughts had flown ahead to the little house without K., to days without his steps on the stairs or the heavy creak of his big chair overhead as he dropped into it.

But perhaps it would be better if he went. She had her own life to live. She had no expectation of happiness, but, somehow or other, she must build on the shaky foundation of her marriage a house of life, with resignation serving for content, perhaps with fear lurking always. That she knew. But with no active misery. Misery implied affection, and her love for Palmer was quite dead.

"Sidney will be here this afternoon."

"Good." His tone was non-committal.

"Has it occurred to you, K., that Sidney is not very happy?"

He stopped in front of her.

"She's had a great anxiety."

"She has no anxiety now. Max is doing well."

"Then what is it?"

"I'm not quite sure, but I think I know. She's lost faith in Max, and she's not like me. I--I knew about Palmer before I married him. I got a letter. It's all rather hideous--I needn't go into it. I was afraid to back out; it was just before my wedding. But Sidney has more character than I have. Max isn't what she thought he was, and I doubt whether she'll marry him."

K. glanced toward the street where Sidney's name and Max's lay open to the sun and to the smiles of the Street. Christine might be right, but that did not alter things for him.

Christine's thoughts went back inevitably to herself; to Palmer, who was doing better just now; to K., who was going away--went back with an ache to the night K. had taken her in his arms and then put her away. How wrong things were! What a mess life was!

"When you go away," she said at last, "I want you to remember this. I'm going to do my best, K. You have taught me all I know. All my life I'll have to overlook things; I know that. But, in his way, Palmer cares for me. He will always come back, and perhaps sometime--"

Her voice trailed off. Far ahead of her she saw the years stretching out, marked, not by days and months, but by Palmer's wanderings away, his remorseful returns.

"Do a little more than forgetting," K. said. "Try to care for him, Christine. You did once. And that's your strongest weapon. It's always a woman's strongest weapon. And it wins in the end."

"I shall try, K.," she answered obediently.

But he turned away from the look in her eyes.

Harriet was abroad. She had sent cards from Paris to her "trade." It was an innovation. The two or three people on the Street who received her engraved announcement that she was there, "buying new chic models for the autumn and winter--afternoon frocks, evening gowns, reception dresses, and wraps, from Poiret, Martial et Armand, and others," left the envelopes casually on the parlor table, as if communications from Paris were quite to be expected.

So K. lunched alone, and ate little. After luncheon he fixed a broken ironing-stand for Katie, and in return she pressed a pair of trousers for him. He had it in mind to ask Sidney to go out with him in Max's car, and his most presentable suit was very shabby.

"I'm thinking," said Katie, when she brought the pressed garments up over her arm and passed them in through a discreet crack in the door, "that these pants will stand more walking than sitting, Mr. K. They're getting mighty thin."

"I'll take a duster along in case of accident," he promised her; "and to-morrow I'll order a suit, Katie."

"I'll believe it when I see it," said Katie from the stairs. "Some fool of a woman from the alley will come in to-night and tell you she can't pay her rent, and she'll take your suit away in her pocket-book--as like as not to pay an installment on a piano. There's two new pianos in the alley since you came here."

"I promise it, Katie."

"Show it to me," said Katie laconically. "And don't go to picking up anything you drop!"

Sidney came home at half-past two--came delicately flushed, as if she had hurried, and with a tremulous smile that caught Katie's eye at once.

"Bless the child!" she said. "There's no need to ask how he is to-day. You're all one smile."

The smile set just a trifle.

"Katie, some one has written my name out on the street, in chalk. It's with Dr. Wilson's, and it looks so silly. Please go out and sweep it off."

"I'm about crazy with their old chalk. I'll do it after a while."

"Please do it now. I don't want anyone to see it. Is--is Mr. K. upstairs?"

But when she learned that K. was upstairs, oddly enough, she did not go up at once. She stood in the lower hall and listened. Yes, he was there. She could hear him moving about. Her lips parted slightly as she listened.

Christine, looking in from her balcony, saw her there, and, seeing something in her face that she had never suspected, put her hand to her throat.

"Sidney!"

"Oh--hello, Chris."

"Won't you come and sit with me?"

"I haven't much time--that is, I want to speak to K."

"You can see him when he comes down."

Sidney came slowly through the parlor. It occurred to her, all at once, that Christine must see a lot of K., especially now. No doubt he was in and out of the house often. And how pretty Christine was! She was unhappy, too. All that seemed to be necessary to win K.'s attention was to be unhappy enough. Well, surely, in that case--

"How is Max?"

"Still better."

Sidney sat down on the edge of the railing; but she was careful, Christine saw, to face the staircase. There was silence on the balcony. Christine sewed; Sidney sat and swung her feet idly.

"Dr. Ed says Max wants you to give up your training and marry him now."

"I'm not going to marry him at all, Chris."

Upstairs, K.'s door slammed. It was one of his failings that he always slammed doors. Harriet used to be quite disagreeable about it.

Sidney slid from the railing.

"There he is now."

Perhaps, in all her frivolous, selfish life, Christine had never had a bigger moment than the one that followed. She could have said nothing, and, in the queer way that life goes, K. might have gone away from the Street as empty of heart as he had come to it.

"Be very good to him, Sidney," she said unsteadily. "He cares so much."

CHAPTER XXX

K. was being very dense. For so long had he considered Sidney as unattainable that now his masculine mind, a little weary with much wretchedness, refused to move from its old attitude.

"It was glamour, that was all, K.," said Sidney bravely.

"But, perhaps," said K., "it's just because of that miserable incident with Carlotta. That wasn't the right thing, of course, but Max has told me the story. It was really quite innocent. She fainted in the yard, and--"

Sidney was exasperated.

"Do you want me to marry him, K.?"

K. looked straight ahead.

"I want you to be happy, dear."

They were on the terrace of the White Springs Hotel again. K. had ordered dinner, making a great to-do about getting the dishes they both liked. But now that it was there, they were not eating. K. had placed his chair so that his profile was turned toward her. He had worn the duster religiously until nightfall, and then had discarded it. It hung limp and dejected on the back of his chair. Past K.'s profile Sidney could see the magnolia tree shaped like a heart.

"It seems to me," said Sidney suddenly, "that you are kind to every one but me, K."

He fairly stammered his astonishment:--

"Why, what on earth have I done?"

"You are trying to make me marry Max, aren't you?"

She was very properly ashamed of that, and, when he failed of reply out of sheer inability to think of one that would not say too much, she went hastily to something else:

"It is hard for me to realize that you--that you lived a life of your own, a busy life, doing useful things, before you came to us. I wish you would tell me something about yourself. If we're to be friends when you go away,"--she had to stop there, for the lump in her throat--"I'll want to know how to think of you,--who your friends are,--all that."

He made an effort. He was thinking, of course, that he would be visualizing her, in the hospital, in the little house on its side street, as she looked just then, her eyes like stars, her lips just parted, her hands folded before her on the table.

"I shall be working," he said at last. "So will you."

"Does that mean you won't have time to think of me?"

"I'm afraid I'm stupider than usual to-night. You can think of me as never forgetting you or the Street, working or playing."

Playing! Of course he would not work all the time. And he was going back to his old friends, to people who had always known him, to girls--

He did his best then. He told her of the old family house, built by one of his forebears who had been a king's man until Washington had put the case for the colonies, and who had given himself and his oldest son then to the cause that he made his own. He told of old servants who had wept when he decided to close the house and go away. When she fell silent, he thought he was interesting her. He told her the family traditions that had been the fairy tales of his childhood. He described the library, the choice room of the house, full of family paintings in old gilt frames, and of his father's collection of books. Because it was home, he waxed warm over it at last, although it had rather hurt him at first to remember. It brought back the other things that he wanted to forget.

But a terrible thing was happening to Sidney. Side by side with the wonders he described so casually, she was placing the little house. What an exile it must have been for him! How hopelessly middle-class they must have seemed! How idiotic of her to think, for one moment, that she could ever belong in this new-old life of his!

What traditions had she? None, of course, save to be honest and good and to do her best for the people around her. Her mother's people, the Kennedys went back a long way, but they had always been poor. A library full of paintings and books! She remembered the lamp with the blue-silk shade, the figure of Eve that used to stand behind the minister's portrait, and the cherry bookcase with the Encyclopaedia in it and "Beacon Lights of History." When K., trying his best to interest her and to conceal his own heaviness of spirit, told her of his grandfather's old carriage, she sat back in the shadow.

"Fearful old thing," said K.,--"regular cabriolet. I can remember yet the family rows over it. But the old gentleman liked it--used to have it repainted every year. Strangers in the city used to turn around and stare at it--thought it was advertising something!"

"When I was a child," said Sidney quietly, "and a carriage drove up and stopped on the Street, I always knew some one had died!"

There was a strained note in her voice. K., whose ear was attuned to every note in her voice, looked at her quickly. "My great-grandfather," said Sidney in the same tone, "sold chickens at market. He didn't do it himself; but the fact's there, isn't it?"

K. was puzzled.

"What about it?" he said.

But Sidney's agile mind had already traveled on. This K. she had never known, who had lived in a wonderful house, and all the rest of it--he must have known numbers of lovely women, his own sort of women, who had traveled and knew all kinds of things: girls like the daughters of the Executive Committee who came in from their country places in summer with great armfuls of flowers, and hurried off, after consulting their jeweled watches, to luncheon or tea or tennis.

"Go on," said Sidney dully. "Tell me about the women you have known, your friends, the ones you liked and the ones who liked you."

K. was rather apologetic.

"I've always been so busy," he confessed. "I know a lot, but I don't think they would interest you. They don't do anything, you know--they travel around and have a good time. They're rather nice to look at, some of them. But when you've said that you've said it all."

Nice to look at! Of course they would be, with nothing else to think of in all the world but of how they looked.

Suddenly Sidney felt very tired. She wanted to go back to the hospital, and turn the key in the door of her little room, and lie with her face down on the bed.

"Would you mind very much if I asked you to take me back?"

He did mind. He had a depressed feeling that the evening had failed. And his depression grew as he brought the car around. He understood, he thought. She was grieving about Max. After all, a girl couldn't care as she had for a year and a half, and then give a man up because of another woman, without a wrench.

"Do you really want to go home, Sidney, or were you tired of sitting there? In that case, we could drive around for an hour or two. I'll not talk if you'd like to be quiet." Being with K. had become an agony, now that she realized how wrong Christine had been, and that their worlds, hers and K.'s, had only touched for a time. Soon they would be separated by as wide a gulf as that which lay between the cherry bookcase--for instance,--and a book-lined library hung with family portraits. But she was not disposed to skimp as to agony. She would go through with it, every word a stab, if only she might sit beside K. a little longer, might feel the touch of his old gray coat against her arm. "I'd like to ride, if you don't mind."

K. turned the automobile toward the country roads. He was remembering acutely that other ride after Joe in his small car, the trouble he had had to get a machine, the fear of he knew not what ahead, and his arrival at last at the road-house, to find Max lying at the head of the stairs and Carlotta on her knees beside him.

"K." "Yes?"

"Was there anybody you cared about,--any girl,--when you left home?"

"I was not in love with anyone, if that's what you mean."

"You knew Max before, didn't you?"

"Yes. You know that."

"If you knew things about him that I should have known, why didn't you tell me?"

"I couldn't do that, could I? Anyhow--"

"Yes?"

"I thought everything would be all right. It seemed to me that the mere fact of your caring for him--" That was shaky ground; he got off it quickly. "Schwitter has closed up. Do you want to stop there?"

"Not to-night, please."

They were near the white house now. Schwitter's had closed up, indeed. The sign over the entrance was gone. The lanterns had been taken down, and in the dusk they could see Tillie rocking her baby on the porch. As if to cover the last traces of his late infamy, Schwitter himself was watering the worn places on the lawn with the garden can.

The car went by. Above the low hum of the engine they could hear Tillie's voice, flat and unmusical, but filled with the harmonies of love as she sang to the child.

When they had left the house far behind, K. was suddenly aware that Sidney was crying. She sat with her head turned away, using her handkerchief stealthily. He drew the car up beside the road, and in a masterful fashion turned her shoulders about until she faced him.

"Now, tell me about it," he said.

"It's just silliness. I'm--I'm a little bit lonely."

"Lonely!"

"Aunt Harriet's in Paris, and with Joe gone and everybody--"

"Aunt Harriet!"

He was properly dazed, for sure. If she had said she was lonely because the cherry bookcase was in Paris, he could not have been more bewildered. And Joe! "And with you going away and never coming back--"

"I'll come back, of course. How's this? I'll promise to come back when you graduate, and send you flowers."

"I think," said Sidney, "that I'll become an army nurse."

"I hope you won't do that."

"You won't know, K. You'll be back with your old friends. You'll have forgotten the Street and all of us."

"Do you really think that?"

"Girls who have been everywhere, and have lovely clothes, and who won't know a T bandage from a figure eight!"

"There will never be anybody in the world like you to me, dear."

His voice was husky.

"You are saying that to comfort me."

"To comfort you! I--who have wanted you so long that it hurts even to think about it! Ever since the night I came up the Street, and you were sitting there on the steps--oh, my dear, my dear, if you only cared a little!"

Because he was afraid that he would get out of hand and take her in his arms,-

-which would be idiotic, since, of course, she did not care for him that way,--he gripped the steering-wheel. It gave him a curious appearance of making a pathetic appeal to the wind-shield.

"I have been trying to make you say that all evening!" said Sidney. "I love you so much that--K., won't you take me in your arms?"

Take her in his arms! He almost crushed her. He held her to him and muttered incoherencies until she gasped. It was as if he must make up for long arrears of hopelessness. He held her off a bit to look at her, as if to be sure it was she and no changeling, and as if he wanted her eyes to corroborate her lips. There was no lack of confession in her eyes; they showed him a new heaven and a new earth.

"It was you always, K.," she confessed. "I just didn't realize it. But now, when you look back, don't you see it was?"

He looked back over the months when she had seemed as unattainable as the stars, and he did not see it. He shook his head.

"I never had even a hope."

"Not when I came to you with everything? I brought you all my troubles, and you always helped."

Her eyes filled. She bent down and kissed one of his hands. He was so happy that the foolish little caress made his heart hammer in his ears.

"I think, K., that is how one can always tell when it is the right one, and will be the right one forever and ever. It is the person--one goes to in trouble."

He had no words for that, only little caressing touches of her arm, her hand. Perhaps, without knowing it, he was formulating a sort of prayer that, since there must be troubles, she would, always come to him and he would always be able to help her.

And Sidney, too, fell silent. She was recalling the day she became engaged to Max, and the lost feeling she had had. She did not feel the same at all now. She felt as if she had been wandering, and had come home to the arms that were about her. She would be married, and take the risk that all women took, with her eyes open. She would go through the valley of the shadow, as other women did; but K. would be with her. Nothing else mattered. Looking into his steady eyes, she knew that she was safe. She would never wither for him.

Where before she had felt the clutch of inexorable destiny, the woman's fate, now she felt only his arms about her, her cheek on his shabby coat.

"I shall love you all my life," she said shakily.

His arms tightened about her.

The little house was dark when they got back to it. The Street, which had heard that Mr. Le Moyne approved of night air, was raising its windows for the night and pinning cheesecloth bags over its curtains to keep them clean.

In the second-story front room at Mrs. McKee's, the barytone slept heavily, and made divers unvocal sounds. He was hardening his throat, and so slept with a wet towel about it.

Down on the doorstep, Mrs. McKee and Mr. Wagner sat and made love with the aid of a lighted match and the pencil-pad.

The car drew up at the little house, and Sidney got out. Then it drove away, for K. must take it to the garage and walk back.

Sidney sat on the doorstep and waited. How lovely it all was! How beautiful life was! If one did one's best by life, it did its best too. How steady K.'s eyes were! She saw the flicker of the match across the street, and knew what it meant. Once she would have thought that that was funny; now it seemed very touching to her.

Katie had heard the car, and now she came heavily along the hall. "A woman left this for Mr. K.," she said. "If you think it's a begging letter, you'd better keep it until he's bought his new suit to-morrow. Almost any moment he's likely to bust out."

But it was not a begging letter. K. read it in the hall, with Sidney's shining eyes on him. It began abruptly:--

"I'm going to Africa with one of my cousins. She is a medical missionary. Perhaps I can work things out there. It is a bad station on the West Coast. I am not going because I feel any call to the work, but because I do not know what else to do.

"You were kind to me the other day. I believe, if I had told you then, you would still have been kind. I tried to tell you, but I was so terribly afraid.

"If I caused death, I did not mean to. You will think that no excuse, but it is true. In the hospital, when I changed the bottles on Miss Page's medicine-tray, I did not care much what happened. But it was different with you.

"You dismissed me, you remember. I had been careless about a sponge count. I made up my mind to get back at you. It seemed hopeless--you were so secure. For two or three days I tried to think of some way to hurt you. I almost gave up. Then I found the way.

"You remember the packets of gauze sponges we made and used in the operating-room? There were twelve to each package. When we counted them as we got them out, we counted by packages. On the night before I left, I went to the operating-room and added one sponge every here and there. Out of every dozen packets, perhaps, I fixed one that had thirteen. The next day I went away.

"Then I was terrified. What if somebody died? I had meant to give you trouble, so you would have to do certain cases a second time. I swear that was all. I was so frightened that I went down sick over it. When I got better, I heard you had lost a case and the cause was being whispered about. I almost died of terror.

"I tried to get back into the hospital one night. I went up the fire-escape, but the windows were locked. Then I left the city. I couldn't stand it. I was afraid to read a newspaper.

"I am not going to sign this letter. You know who it is from. And I am not going to ask your forgiveness, or anything of that sort. I don't expect it. But one thing hurt me more than anything else, the other night. You said you'd lost your faith in yourself. This is to tell you that you need not. And you said something else--that any one can 'come back.' I wonder!"

K. stood in the hall of the little house with the letter in his hand. Just beyond on the doorstep was Sidney, waiting for him. His arms were still warm from the touch of her. Beyond lay the Street, and beyond that lay the world and a man's work to do. Work, and faith to do it, a good woman's hand in the dark, a Providence that made things right in the end.

"Are you coming, K.?"

"Coming," he said. And, when he was beside her, his long figure folded to the short measure of the step, he stooped humbly and kissed the hem of her soft white dress.

Across the Street, Mr. Wagner wrote something in the dark and then lighted a match.

"So K. is in love with Sidney Page, after all!" he had written. "She is a sweet girl, and he is every inch a man. But, to my mind, a certain lady--"

Mrs. McKee flushed and blew out the match.

Late September now on the Street, with Joe gone and his mother eyeing the postman with pitiful eagerness; with Mrs. Rosenfeld moving heavily about the setting-up of the new furniture; and with Johnny driving heavenly cars, brake and clutch legs well and Strong. Late September, with Max recovering and settling his tie for any pretty nurse who happened along, but listening eagerly for Dr. Ed's square tread in the hall; with Tillie rocking her baby on the porch at Schwitter's, and Carlotta staring westward over rolling seas; with Christine taking up her burden and Grace laying hers down; with Joe's tragic young eyes growing quiet with the peace of the tropics.

"The Lord is my shepherd," she reads. "I shall not want."..."Yea, though I walk through the valley of the shadow of death, I will fear no evil."

Sidney, on her knees in the little parlor, repeats the words with the others. K. has gone from the Street, and before long she will join him. With the vision of his steady eyes before her, she adds her own prayer to the others--that the touch of his arms about her may not make her forget the vow she has taken, of charity and its sister, service, of a cup of water to the thirsty, of open arms to a tired child.